GREENHORNS AND
KILLER MOUNTAINS

Other Books by Jim Conover

LYNCH LAW

JIM CONOVER

Jim Conover

Feb. 5, 2000

GREENHORNS AND KILLER MOUNTAINS

LYNCH LAW

PRODUCTIONS

Published by
Lynch Law Productions
3 Reuling Court, Pekin, Illinois 61554
June - 1999

First Edition

ISBN: 0-9669472-1-5

Library of Congress Catalog Card Number: 99-90242

Cover and book design by Jim Conover

Illustrations by Jim Conover

Printed in the United States of America

Dedicated to all the Treasure Hunters and Adventurers in the world

and

To all the Writers who chronicle the escapades of these Treasure Hunters and Adventurers, be it non-fiction or fiction.

ACKNOWLEDGEMENTS

For any writer, good editors, proofreaders and *supporters* are a must. My case is no exception. In order to nourish and develop my manuscript from conception to birth of a book, I was lucky enough to have several wonderful people at my side. Personally thanking these exceptional people doesn't seem enough; therefore, I want to acknowledge them here so that my gratitude will be known for as long as there are copies of the book - perhaps even forever.

First the supporters. There's the wonderful support of my family. The love of my life - my beautiful wife, **Judie**, who gave up her own reading pleasures to proofread copies of the same scenes over and over for years.

My daughters and sons-in-law, **Kimberly** and **Todd Moore** and **Tammie** and **Jim Fletcher**, who have been wonderfully supportive and helped me to establish a publishing company and who I have neglected for way too many years.

And thanks to my grandchildren, **Brittany Moore, Justin Fletcher** and **Jace Fletcher**, who always had a hundred questions to ask while I was writing.

And there's the great support and advice of my sisters, **Barbara Conover Watkins, Carmelita Conover Nash, Linda Conover Jones,** and **Sherry Conover**, who passed away before she got to see the finished product. They read, re-read and read again chapters, bits and pieces, and finally the whole story, all the while urging me onward over the years it took to bring this book to publication. Thanks, girls!

Thanks to my brothers and sisters-in-law, **Dennis** and **Tammie Conover** and **Rob** and **Alesia Conover**, who kept me going with their support when things looked a little dark. Thanks for the coffee and lunch breaks, boys.

And how can I leave out all my nieces who read my manuscripts and kept telling me how they were progressing. Thank you, **Lita Sanchez, Lorretta Fernandez, Becky Katz, Sheila Ringenberger, Sara Schlegel, Lori Merritt, Courtney Conover,** and **Kaleigh Conover**

Nephews always seem to come last, but at least they're not left out. Thanks to **Perry Watkins, Dallas Jones, Larry Jones, Brian Jones, Jeffrey Jones, Jason Conover, Brad Conover,** and **Colton Conover,** who urged me to continue.

Another thanks goes to my wonderful mother-in-law, **Mary VanNattan,** who kept telling me I could do it.

And thanks to all my friends who have lent their support and praises, especially my good friend, **James Frye**.

With all that support, how can a person lose? I thank you *all* for putting up with all my book talk over the years.

Next the editors and proofreaders. I would like to thank a great editor, **Craig Shurtleff,** who teaches courses in creative writing at Illinois Central College, for taking the time out of his busy schedule to do an in-depth edit of the manuscript. His no-holds barred critique and suggestions helped develop not only the story, but my writing as well.

Thanks to **Heather Burdick,** who did the final edit and proofing, the book is at least readable. Her suggestions put the icing on the cake.

Way down there in Daniel Boone country, I want to thank **Russ Bauer,** an old friend and fellow law enforcement officer, who read my manuscripts and gave honest critiques of them. Thanks, Rushin' Bear.

GREENHORNS AND
KILLER MOUNTAINS

1

Don Miguel Peralta, his musket held firmly in his grip, wiped sweat from the dark, wrinkled, leather-like skin of his forehead as he strained to see any sign of Apache Indians through the heat waves that rose from the stifling desert mountain terrain of Northern Mexico.

It was hard to make out anything against the ever brown, near barren background of sand and rock that had a sprinkling of chollo bushes, sage bushes, and stubby palo verde trees. A few tall saguaro cacti scattered here and there cast long shadows in the late afternoon sun. The strain on Don Miguel's eyes caused every shadow to seem to move.

Off in the distance, almost like a different world, he could see the tall cottonwoods along a now dry creek bed. Scattered among them were the stark white trunks of the sycamores, like stone sentries watching over the valley. Great trees like these grew only where there was an underground water supply and there were only a few such places. It was from here that he expected the Indians to come - or perhaps from the deep shadow of the strange spear of sheer rock that rose straight up from the desert floor for hundreds of feet. Don Miguel had seen rocks like this only once in his lifetime. He and his brothers had ventured far to the north in search of gold and traveled through the Navaho Indian lands. There had been many such huge buttes that rose straight to the heavens above. He remembered seeing the many eagles that soared high above the rims of the buttes.

Pulling his wide brimmed straw hat down over his eyes, he glanced down from his perch on a outcropping of rock to where several Mexicans labored in the 120 degree summer sun, hauling yokes of ore-filled buckets from the mine to a nearby crusher. They dumped the buckets into the crusher and hurried back into the mine for more. Huge hammers wielded by muscular, bare chested men slammed down crushing the ore as other workers picked gold baring pieces from the debris and carried them to a nearby crudely made smelter where they would be melted down and poured into bars.

Don Miguel knew the Indians were out there somewhere, no doubt preparing for another attack on his camp, but this time he would be ready for them.

It had been the year before, in the summer of 1847 when he and two of his brothers had discovered a rich deposit of pure gold in the high reaches of the Mazatzal Mountains, some two hundred miles north of Nogales, Mexico.

The Peralto brothers knew that area of the mountains was known to be sacred grounds to the fierce Apache Indians; but they had come looking for gold and when they found it, they were determined to get it.

The gold was plentiful, and they had worked the mine for two months without any sign of Indians. They were wealthy beyond their dreams and would soon make a trip home to enjoy some of the pleasures gold afforded.

The glaring sun, losing some of its heat, had just settled on the western mountain peaks and the Peraltos were relaxing around their cook fire after a hard day in the mine, when the first arrow struck Don Miguel in the leg just above the knee.

Even as he screamed out in pain, he, like his brothers, was grabbing for his musket. The Peraltos found themselves engulfed in a swarm of Apache Indians.

Don Miguel and his brothers fought hard, but the arrow in his leg made it difficult for him to maneuver. He felt a searing pain in his lower back as another arrow found its mark. He fell to ground and rolled into some heavy sage bushes, where he managed to conceal himself from the attackers.

From there he had watched the Indians brutally slay both his brothers with lances and arrows.

It was long after darkness fell upon the arid desert land that Don Miguel, hearing no sound from the Indians, crawled from his hiding place and staggered for home hundreds of miles away, with two arrows in his body and only a few gold nuggets in his pocket.

* * *

A year later, fully recovered from his wounds, Don Miguel had recruited a force of one hundred hard-working, hard-fighting men, and returned to the Mazatzal Mountains for his gold. He would be ready for the Indians this time.

Don Miguel could see several of his armed guards watching the countryside with great intent. He had just settled back on his heels to rest when one of his men caught his eye.

Standing on a ledge above the mine, the man was pointing. "Don Peralta! Something moves!"

The man stiffened and dropped his musket as an arrow plunged into his back. He fell headlong from his perch, screaming.

Peralta raised his musket trying to find a target. "Indians! Indians! Every man out! We must fight!"

Peralta spied an Indian, aimed, and fired his musket. The Indian fell from sight, but several more took his place. With no time to reload his musket, Don Miguel grabbed his pistol from his waistband and fired at another Apache.

Below, yelling men ran from the mine carrying everything from muskets to clubs. They charged the Indians.

If Don Miguel had thought that his one hundred men could handle the Indians, he had underestimated the Indians. They outnumbered the Mexicans, three to one.

With bows and arrows, spears and knives, the Indians met the yelling men. It was the Mexicans who fell.

Don Miguel ran from his perch to help his men. Unable to reload his pistol, he was forced to draw his machete and slash out at the charging Indians.

Don Miguel fought hard, swinging his huge blade left and right, and Indians fell before it, but they were too many. He knew their only hope was to get back inside of the mine. "Back to the mine! We have to get back to the mine!"

If they heard the call, they did not respond, for most of his men were already dead. The ground was littered with dead men, and Indians were busy mutilating the bodies.

Don Miguel was still fifty feet from the mine when an Indian launched his long spear and it found its mark, plunging all the way through Don Miguel. He grabbed the spear's shaft with one hand and tried to pull it from his body, while still slashing away with the machete.

An Indian screamed and fell as he made contact, but the strength slowly ebbed from Don Miguel's body and he sank to his knees beside the crusher. He swung his blade again, but made no contact as he pitched forward, face down into the hot dust.

Sweat rolled from his face. His eyes were wide. Blood ran freely from his mouth as it pressed against the ground. He drew a deep breath and exhaled. Gold dust sparkled before his eyes. Like all one hundred of his men, Don Miguel Peralto was dead.

* * *

Young Don Miguel Peralto II sat at a table in the corner of a dark saloon a few miles north of the town of Florence in Arizona Territory, playing cards with three nasty-looking men. His large sombrero was pushed back on his head and sweat beaded on his forehead as his eyes went from the hand of cards he held to the stacks of money in front of the other men, and then the empty space before him. Glancing up, he stared into the cold eyes of the man sitting across the table.

"Well, you gonna bet that damned map or not? I told you it was only worth five dollars," the man said, spitting tobacco juice onto the floor beside him.

"I would not bet the map, Señor, even though it is worth much more than you say. It is a true gold map," Don Miguel nervously replied. "My father drew it himself thirty years ago." He shook his head. "No, Señor, I would not part with it for any amount."

"I want that map, Mexican!" The man yelled, springing to his feet and reaching for a pistol in his waistband. A much larger hand grabbed his, hard. He spun around to look into the barrel of a revolver.

A tall bearded man stared at him with ice blue eyes. His other hand held the long-barreled revolver steady. "You can see the Mexican is unarmed," the man said in a calm, deadly voice. "Now, I suggest you and your friends gather your gear and git, before me and my friend over there decide to have a little fun of our own."

All three men swung their attention to a shorter, rather skinny man pointing a rifle at them.

Muttering something under his breath, the man gathered his hat and motioned for his friends to follow him.

Don Miguel watched them leave. When the door had swung closed, he turned to the man. "Thank you, Señor. I believe that man would have killed me. I owe you my life. Please sit and have a drink with me."

The man offered his hand. "Jacob Waltz, but they call me The Dutchman. That there's Jacob Miser."

Both men sat down as Don Miguel Peralto poured tequila into glasses.

"They wanted my father's map to his gold mine to the north, but I would not let them have it." He stopped pouring and looked at the men. "You have saved my life and now I am indebted to you both, Señors. I must repay you, somehow." He pause in thought for a moment, then added, "Perhaps you would be interested in becoming partners with me in the gold mine. No?"

Jacob Waltz looked at his friend, Jacob Wiser, who shrugged. "Sí," Waltz replied. He raised his glass in a toast. "To the partnership."

2

T he deafening blast of a whistle interrupted lunch and the conversation between Clay Morgan and his long time friend, Virgil Patton, who were seated at a table in the crowded, immaculate cafeteria of the Chevrolet manufacturing plant in Los Angeles.

Virgil, a slim, middle-aged, mild-mannered man was a pilot for the corporation and Clay's best friend. He swiped his last French fry through a mound of catsup on his plate. "Now what the hell do they want? "

Clay, an executive officer in the engineering department, shook his head of black hair to clear his ears of the ringing. "Who knows? But that whistle means listen up, so we'd better do just that."

A man's voice came over the PA system. "Your attention, please. The parent company has decided that this Los Angeles plant will close down permanently this coming Friday, at the end of the first shift. Consider this your official notice. All personnel are to see their supervisors for further details." A click signaled the end of the message.

"For a minute there I thought it was something serious," Clay said

Virgil gave him a curious look as the French fry disappeared into his mouth. "Of course, it's serious. What the hell's wrong with you, Clay? We're out of work come Friday."

Clay looked down at the half-eaten meatloaf and French fries on his plate. It had been a long time since he had been out of work. He wondered what it would be like. Might even be enjoyable. "Could be fun, you know."

He had been expecting a major lay off sometime in 1998, but not this soon, and nothing like the whole plant shutting down. He looked around the room at workers who sat staring at the speaker on the wall. Everyone was out of a job. He wasn't worried about himself. Engineering jobs were always available with other companies. He worried about the line workers who earned hourly wages. From the looks on their faces, it was obvious that the same thoughts were also racing through their minds. "All these people out of work. Most of 'em live from paycheck to paycheck and without work, things are going to be mighty tight for 'em."

"Does that include you?"

Clay shook his head. "No, I'll be fine." He looked across at Virgil. "What the hell, I need some time off anyway."

"Well, looks like we're going to get it whether we want it or not," Virgil replied, running his fingers through his close cropped, blonde hair. He stared down at the table, letting his thoughts wander. He had worked at this plant for fifteen years, flying top executive officers from city to city or flying auto parts all over the country. He knew the company would not transfer him to another plant, so the closing meant he, too, was out of work. Even at forty-five years of age though, a good pilot could always find work. Besides, it would be nice to spend more time with his family. Maybe they would do a little traveling or just relax at the beach. He looked across at his friend. "Life in the big city, huh, Clay?"

Clay didn't answer right away. He was absorbed in his own thoughts again. He suddenly found himself actually looking forward to time off from the hectic, day to day rat race of computer screens and numbers. He was forty, married with two children, and felt like he was over the hill - old and worn out. Maybe this break would help him pull himself back together. "You know, Virge, this might be just what the doctor ordered. I've worked since high school without any time off. I'm tired. I need a break."

"What do you call the vacation we take every year? That's time off. "

"Yeah, but that's with the family. What I mean is time away from even that. Time to ourselves. Just the men. No kids, no wives, no dogs and no house work. You know - head for the mountains or the desert. Do some treasure hunting. Have an adventure."

Virgil gave him a skeptical look. "Adventure...? Treasure hunting...?"

Clay looked around secretively and leaned in close. "Virge, I've got this wild idea that I've been working on for a long time. Now's the time for us to do it."

"And what might that wild idea be, my friend?"

Clay looked around again to make sure no one was listening. "Search for the Lost Dutchman's gold mine!"

Virgil raised his eyebrows in surprise. "The Lost what...?"

"Shhhhhh," Clay warned, looking around again. "No need to tell the world." He turned back and studied Virgil for a few seconds. "The Lost Dutchman's gold mine, Virge. I've been researching it for years and I think I've figured out just about where it is."

Virgil started to laugh, but was cut short by Clay. "Don't laugh, Virgil Patton. It's a real treasure and it's there. Pure gold. Ours for the taking. All we have to do is go get it. Think of it, Virge. People have searched for the Dutchman's gold mine for more'n a hundred years and we'd be the ones to find it! Now *that* would be an adventure!"

Before Virgil could reply, Clay pointed at three men headed their way. "Here comes trouble." He grinned as he watched them cross the floor. All three wore basically the same clothing as Clay - dress pants, white shirts, ties, and no jackets - the difference being that he paid a hell of a lot less for his suits than they did. The closing of the plant sure wouldn't hurt them. They were young yuppie types, engineers in their twenties who had never worked a day until they had landed a job in his department. Didn't have to. Their families had loads of money. They could probably pool their holdings and buy the company if they wanted to, but their personal worth didn't figure into the way they worked. They were good at their jobs, and the longer he was around them, the more he had grown to like them.

Clay looked at each one as they worked their way through the maze of tables and people. There was the robust Rob Clark, a dark, handsome, giant of a man who always had a smile, but was quick with a barbed tongue if riled. Then there was the shorter, stocky, bearded Brian Speller. He was an out-going, out-spoken young man who was always game for anything. Clay's eyes went to the third man, a slim, quiet, shy, naive little worrywart named Kenneth Smith, who always questioned everything. Even with those faults, however, he was Clay's friend.

The three men flopped down in chairs around the table.

Clay grinned and motioned his arm around. "Have a seat, gentlemen."

Rob was the first to speak. "What the hell you boys make of this shit?"

Virgil started to answer. "Well, I...."

Clay cut him short. "I think it's great!"

Rob couldn't believe what he heard. He cocked his brow at Clay, then looked at Virgil. "He nuts or what?"

Virgil nodded and laughed. "Yep. Nuttier'n a fruit cake."

Brian reached over and helped himself to Clay's now cold French fries. "What does that mean, Virgil?"

"Let him tell you, Brian. I don't think I could do it justice."

All eyes fell upon Clay, waiting for his response.

Virgil waved his arm in a sweeping motion over the table. "Well, tell 'em, Clay. You have center stage!"

Looking at Virgil, Clay feigned anger. "Don't make fun of it, Virge. Millions in gold is nothing to laugh at."

"What's this 'millions in gold shit,' Clay?" Rob asked.

Clay looked at Rob. *Why the hell not. We're all good friends here. Maybe they'll want in on it. It would be much safer and easier if there were five of us, instead of two.* He motioned for them to lean closer as he looked around the room, making sure he could not be heard. "The Lost Dutchman's Gold Mine. I'm going after it."

Shaking his head, Ken gave a thumbs down motion. "You can forget that crap, Clay. The Dutchman is supposed to be way down in the Superstition Mountains in Arizona. And it's haunted at that."

Brian cast Ken a disbeliever's look. "Bullshit, Ken. There's no such things as ghosts!"

"Well, maybe not, but everything I ever read on the Dutchman indicates it's just an old wives' tale. It's not really there."

"Wrongo, Bucko!" Clay corrected Ken. "It's there and we can find it!"

"We? Who's *we*?" Rob asked.

"Look guys, we've never had time to do things that real men do. You know, adventurous things, maybe even dangerous. I think this shutdown hit just right. We'll all be off at the same time. We can all take an adventurous trip together. Who knows, we might just get lucky and get rich."

"These guys are already rich, Clay," Virgil laughed. "Why should they want to take all those risks just to get richer?"

"Don't let that bother you, Virgil," Rob said, jerking his eyebrows up and down like Groucho Marks. "We may have money, but I don't think any of us have a gold mine yet." He chuckled. "Something I always wanted."

Already supporting a worried look on his face, Ken knew his mother would raise hell with him if she had the faintest idea he was even thinking of going on such a dangerous mission. He shook his head. "Don't you guys remember that old movie, Treasure of The Sierra Madre? Look what happened to all those guys."

"You're being a pessimist again, Ken," Clay said. "You gotta think positive."

"Maybe so, but you know most of us have never been outside Los Angeles, except on an Interstate Highway. I've never even gone fishing."

"Well, don't you think it's about time you did?" Clay asked.

"I've been camping many times," Brian countered.

"Yeah," Ken replied. "But with thirty other boy scouts in the local park. Never like what Clay's talking about."

Brian tried to hide the excitement in his voice. He was always game for anything. He enjoyed a challenge. He had been raised in Beverly Hills. His father had invested wisely in real estate in downtown Los Angeles. When Brian had finished his last year at the University of California, he had joined his father's firm for a while, but like many offspring, soon found working with old dad not to his liking. That was when he had landed a position in the engineering department of the Chevrolet Camaro Plant. This little adventure was right down his alley. "So where exactly are we going on this trip, Clay?"

"Well, Ken's right about it being in the Superstition Mountains and that exactly where we're going." Clay sat back to watch the expressions on the faces of the four men - expressions that ranged from total disbelief to Brian's why not.

Minutes passed before anyone said a word.

Finally, Virgil broke the silence. "I suppose you have a plan all ready to go?"

Clay was quick to reply, "As a matter of fact, I do. Like I said, I've been researching this for years. Just recently I bought a new type of metal detector that will pick up gold or silver a quarter of a mile away."

"Bullshit." Virgil said. "They don't make such a detector. I've seen the ones you use. They work but, not good enough for locating a lost mine in the middle of a huge desert mountain range."

"You're wrong, Virge. There is one and I have it."

Brian already had visions of gold floating through his mind as he rolled his eyes and replied, "Gold! Gold! "I love it! I love it! One time I held a whole handful of gold coins. There's no feeling like it." He reached over and grabbed Clay's hand, shaking it violently. "Great idea, Clay! I believe you can find it! Now let's put this thing together and head for the mountains!"

Virgil shrugged. "Well, hell. We might just as well do something. We aren't going to be hanging around here after Friday."

Brian was excited. He jumped to his feet and announced, "We'll leave tonight!"

Clay grabbed his arm. "Settle down, Brian. Settle down. We still have to finish out the week here. But that'll give us time to get prepared. There's a lot of work to be done before we can leave. Besides, if you keep shouting, everybody will be there ahead of us."

Rob laughed and turned to Virgil, "And what about you two old married men's wives? What are they going to say about this big trip?"

Virgil shrugged his shoulders. "Pat will be glad to get me from under foot for a while."

"Judie and I haven't been away from each other for years. It'll do us both good," said Clay

As Clay, Virgil, Rob, and Brian put their hands together to form a pact, Ken held back. He had never done anything like this. His mind shot to his mother. *What would she say? The same as she had said all his life. No! She'd be angry. She'd cry. She'd beg him not to go. He might get hurt, or even killed out there.* Ken looked at his friends. *No, they aren't going to talk me into going this time.*

The others were waiting for him.

Ken shook his head. "I don't think I'll be going with you guys. Sounds too wild for me."

Clay nodded. "That'll be up to you, Ken. It could very well get dangerous out there."

Everyone stared at Ken. He walked away without another word.

Rob chuckled. "Don't worry. He'll be back. He just has to go off alone and convince himself he can do it."

Clay turned his attention to the others. "Now let me tell you all about the Dutchman."

"Don Miguel Peralto the Second, Jacob Waltz, and Jacob Wiser found the Peralto mine and worked it for several weeks. In a short time they had more than $60,000.00 in gold. Don Miguel Peralta II perhaps afraid that he would suffer the same fate as his father, wanted out of the mountains and sold his mine to Waltz and Wiser for their share of the $60,000.00."

Clay saw eyes widen when he mentioned the $60,000 in gold. He continued. "At least, that is what Waltz would later claim. It has been written that he and Wiser murdered Peralto for his map."

"When did the mountains get the name Superstition Mountains?" Virgil asked.

"No ones really knows when that section of mountain range was named The Superstitions. It's believed by many that the name comes from the Indians." Clay answered.

He was interrupted when Ken returned to the table carrying a tray with several cups of hot coffee. Clay stopped talking until the coffee had been passed around. He was glad Ken had changed his mind.

Pulling up a chair, Ken sat down without uttering a word.

With a wink to Ken, Clay continued with his story. "For months Waltz continued to mine the gold, making several trips down to the small towns in the area to drink and buy things for his camp. He paid for them with pure gold nuggets. Though he was questioned many times, he never told anyone the location of the mine.

"You say Waltz mined the gold. What happened to his partner?" Ken asked.

"One day Waltz took a trip into town for supplies while Wiser stayed behind to work the mine. When Waltz returned a few days later, he found Wiser's body roasted over a fire by the Indians." Clay stole a quick glance at Ken.

Ken's face went pale. He looked like he was about to be sick.

"But then again that was what Waltz told everybody," Clay continued. "He may very well have roasted Wiser over the fire himself. Anyway, to get on with the story, a few years later as he lay dying in a nearby town, Waltz told the lady caring for him about his mine and drew her a crude map to it. After his death, the lady made many trips into the mountains, but failed to locate the mine. To this day, it has never been found." Clay stopped.

Each man sat weighing Clay's words.

"So where in the mountains is it located?" Rob asked.

"All the research I've done indicates the mine is somewhere in the area of Weaver's Needle - a butte of sheer rock walls, sticking up like those in Monument Valley. It was named after the man who discovered it. That's where we'll look."

Ken cleared his throat. "Just how dangerous is this trip going to be, Clay?"

"I'll level with you, Ken. It won't be a picnic and it'll be dangerous. Many of those who hunted for the Dutchman failed to return from the mountains. Some simply disappeared. Others were found dead. Some killed in accidental falls or cave-ins. Some had been shot and some even had their heads cut off." Clay stopped talking long enough for it all to sink in.

No one spoke. They sipped their coffee and pondered the situation.

Ken whitened. He couldn't believe there really were killings. Not in this day and age. "You mean the people were really killed? You mean real people? Modern day people?"

"As recent as last year," Clay replied. "A man was found with a bullet between his eyes - that is, his skeleton was found."

Brian chuckled. "What's the matter, Ken? Is the tough young man getting scared already?"

"Hell no! I ain't scared! I was just asking."

Virgil got serious. "But what if it *is* just a legend? We would be taking big chances for nothing."

Clay looked around the table at each of his friends. "I personally think it is there, but even if it isn't, look what an adventure it would be for us. Just to spend a little time out of the noisy ass city would help me."

Clay already had Brian, Rob and maybe Ken, but he wanted his best friend along. "I've got copies of documents of Waltz's crudely drawn map and county records that showed Jacob Waltz was actually in the area." He grabbed a napkin and quickly drew a rough sketch of the mountain range and stabbed a finger at a point on it. "There! Right there near Weaver's Needle!"

Clay waited while the others looked over the sketch. He needed this trip. He had never done anything like it before. He had never been out of the city except maybe driving along the interstate highways going from one city to another. Never off the beaten trail. He had slaved over those Dutchman plans for years and now it was time he made a stab at it. He didn't really think that they would find the gold mine, but maybe just trying would satisfy his hunger.

Virgil looked over at Clay. He had taken a liking to Clay from their first meeting. He was different from most men. Not afraid to take a chance. Not afraid to speak out when he didn't like something. He had a way with people. He was the kind of man you could trust with your life, but like Clay, he had his own doubts about finding the Dutchman. "This metal detector, is it going to work?"

"Of course it's going to work, Virge. Hell, man, I'm an engineer. I don't just assume something will work. I test it. I've already conducted several tests with the detector and it works. And don't forget I also have two conventional metal detectors. They'll work well for finding nuggets or veins hidden in rocks."

"Okay," Virgil sighed, "we might just as well get it over with or you'll never let us rest."

"Great!" Brian exclaimed, excitedly. "What now? Where do we start?"

Clay mentally patted himself on the back for a job well done. The trip to Superstition Mountains was in the bag. He started laying out his plans. "Rob, you'll be in charge of the mining equipment. You know, shovels, picks and the like." He paused to think. "Dynamite? Who can get some dynamite?"

Rob spoke up. "That's my department. I have an engineer friend who will supply us with enough to blow up the whole mountain if we want." He stopped. "Question. What mode of transportation are we taking? A car, truck, van or what?"

"None of the above," Virgil said. "If we're going to do this thing, we're going to do it right. We'll take a helicopter. I've moonlighted for years as a helicopter instructor out at Van Nuys Airport. I have a friend there who will grant us the use of one."

"A helicopter? Why do we have to fly, Virge?"

"Do you have any idea how far into those mountains Weaver's Needle is? Where it would take days on horseback or walking, we can fly a helicopter in a matter of minutes."

Clay remembered that it was against the law to drive a motor vehicle into a wilderness area except on designated roads. They wouldn't be able to get to the area he wanted in a land vehicle. Virgil was right about using a helicopter. It would sure save time and energy.

Brian said. "Why carry all this stuff up a mountain when you can just drop it right in with a helicopter?"

"I second the motion," Rob agreed. "How 'bout you, Ken?"

Ken nodded his head. "I agree, but I think the equipment's going to be awfully heavy for a helicopter."

"No problem," Virgil said. "The chopper I have in mind is not one of those little bubble jobs you see buzzing the city all the time. It's an old UH-1 - Huey - gunship, designed to carry two pilots and eight men, with room left for a payload."

Clay nodded his approval. "A Huey will certainly be big enough for us and the equipment. I like the idea."

Now that the trip was in place and he knew they were really going, Ken was worried. He thought about his mother. She was a real worrywart. He was an only child and she had hovered over him like a mother hen over a chick, even after he was grown. His father, owner of a large publishing company, never had time for Ken. He was too busy making money. Raised under his mother's skirts, Ken had never been allowed to go anywhere on his own. No fishing, no hunting, no camping. He didn't want to admit it, but he was already scared.

"What's on your mind, Ken," Clay asked.

"How long a trip we talking about here?

"Oh, I don't know. Maybe three-four weeks. That too long?"

Ken shook his head. "No. It's just that I've never been away from home for any length of time and now talking about taking a dangerous trip into the wilderness. . . I just don't know."

"You'll do just fine, Ken," said Virgil. "Beside, you're in good company. The rest of us haven't been in anything wilder than the City Park."

"Well, that's almost true," Clay said. "Except for old Virgil here. He was in Vietnam during the war." Clay looked at Virgil and chuckled. "We'll have us an experienced pathfinder to turn to in case of trouble."

"Pathfinder, my ass. I was never out of the helicopter in those jungles," Virgil remarked. " But then on the other hand, I never got so lost I couldn't find the air strip on my return flight."

Clay turned his attention to Ken and Brian. "Brian, you and Ken round up the tents and camping gear we'll need. What we don't already have, we'll buy." He handed Brian a piece of paper. "Here's a list of things we'll need for this trip."

"When do we depart on this adventure, Clay?" Brian asked.

"If we have everything ready, how about next Sunday?"

The men nodded in agreement.

"Now let's get back to drawing lines in the office. Lunch hour is over."

* * *

On Sunday morning, the newly proclaimed gold prospectors were at Van Nuys Airport. The plant had closed on schedule and the five friends had scurried to finish gathering equipment they would need for the trip. Virgil had made arrangements for the helicopter, the equipment had been purchased and loaded, and now they were ready to go.

Bags in hand, Clay stood staring at the helicopter. It looked like an old dilapidated piece of junk badly in need of a paint job. The original olive green paint was chipped and faded. A darker shade of green that had been used to cover the military markings gave the Huey a dark and light green polka dot look. He felt his stomach roll. He swallowed hard. It rolled again. Suddenly, he knew he was in trouble. He dropped his bags, grabbed his mouth, and raced for a small shed at the edge of the tarmac. He managed to grab hold of the wires of a security fence behind the shed to steady himself as hot fluid erupted forth.

When he was finished, he wiped his mouth with a handkerchief and peeped around the corner of the shed to see if anyone had seen him. He was safe. They were busy with the helicopter. He reached into his pocket and pulled out the bottle of pills his doctor had prescribed for him earlier. He looked at the label. Doctor N. Johnson - Larazepam - take one an hour before flight.

Well, he had taken one and it hadn't eased his anxiety enough to prevent him from vomiting. He twisted the lid off and shook a pill into his hand. As he started to pop it into his mouth, he took another look at the helicopter.

Virgil was inspecting everything in and around the aircraft. Rob, Brian and Ken were stowing their gear inside the helicopter, excitedly talking about their trip.

"Let 'er go and come on, Clay," Virgil yelled. "You're holding up the ship!"

Gazing upon the ragged looking old gunship he swallowed hard. He knew the directions said take just one, but then Doctor Johnson hadn't seen this helicopter. He quickly shook another pill into the palm of his hand. He looked the ship over again. Debating for only a second longer, he popped it into his mouth.

Clay, struggling to get the dry pills down as he hurried to his bags and headed for the helicopter, replied, "You sure this thing will fly?"

"It may not look like much, but it's a flying machine. It's in better flying condition than most airliners." Virgil said.

"If you say so," Clay whispered to no one in particular as he slowly approached the door of the huge green machine. He had seen enough war movies to know the helicopter. It was a Huey all right. Built by the Bell Helicopter Company as a transport, it had been the Cadillac of all choppers during Vietnam. But this one looked like a wrecked Chevy.

Rob leaned out. "Come on, you two. Let's get going."

Tossing him his bag, Clay gave one last look around, made the sign of a cross over his chest, and jumped aboard the Huey.

Virgil was excited. He hadn't flown a Huey since Vietnam and was anxious to get started. He cranked the engine. It sputtered, then caught. He grinned. Same old sound. He was going to enjoy this trip.

Clay climbed into the co-pilot's seat and looked back into the cargo area. Rob, Brian, and Ken had already buckled up in the seat that ran along the left wall. Like the cockpit seats, they were small but afforded a lot of legroom. Further back, duffel bags, rolled up tents, boxes, and suitcases had been strapped in place. "You sure my detectors are on board, Rob?"

"Sure are! We couldn't go without those little jewels!"

"Okay Virge, let's go - I guess," Clay said, trying to act brave as the helicopter motor gained power and the rotors whirled.

Virgil took one last look back at the guys and equipment. Nodding his approval, he gripped the cyclic pitch control that rose between his legs and held it firmly in place with his right hand, while he lifted up on the collective pitch control with his left. At the same time, he slowly up twisted the throttle at the end of the collective control.

Virgil grinned as the old Huey shuttered and shook, then slowly lifted upward. "Awaaaay we go!"

Clay clutched the sides of his seat, his eyes clamped shut and teeth clinched together. Sweat bobbed out on his face. His stomach, at first high in his throat, plunged to his feet as the Huey climbed faster. He was scared out of his wits. He thought he was going to be sick again. He fought the urge, hoping no one would notice.

Once the Huey gained a comfortable cruising altitude of about 7,000 feet, it smoothed out and sailed through the sky like an eagle toward Apache Junction, Arizona, the jumping off spot for the Superstition Mountains.

Clay opened his eyes. It was quieter now. He could actually hear the others talking without having to yell. He felt better.

Virgil leaned toward Clay and chuckled. "It'll be over before you know it, Clay."

Clay got the feeling that Virgil had somehow guessed that he was afraid to fly. He sat pondering the situation, not daring to look out the window, and preferring instead to stare down at his knees. Fixing his eyes on something stable gave him a feeling of security. Before long, he noticed the chatter of the others was fading into the distance. Finally, his chin fell to his chest as the last three tranquilizers took effect. He was out like a light.

At a cruising speed of 95 miles per hour, the Huey would be able to cover the distance to Apache Junction in good time. It was a beautiful day, and the mountains of southern California were a sight to behold. The men stared down in silence at the awesome beauty of it, all knowing full well that those same beautiful mountains, not unlike the Superstitions, could turn deadly without warning.

Thoughts of the dangers seeped into Rob's mind as he studied the view below. Clay had told them that many men had been murdered in the Superstition Mountains. If that wasn't enough to worry about, he had gone on to tell them about the wild animals, rattlesnakes, scorpions and those great big hairy spiders. *Damn, how he hated spiders.* He shuttered and turned away to clear the thoughts from his mind. The son of an investment broker, Rob Clark had been raised in Los Angeles. He had attended high school and later graduated from UCLA. After college he landed the job at the Chevy plant. Rob glanced over at Ken, remembering what he had said earlier about them never having been out in the wild. He sat wondering how he would endure this adventure. Leaning forward he asked, "How fast we going, Virgil?"

"Oh, about 95 miles an hour. No need to press it faster."

"How fast will it fly?"

"Well, when it was new, it was loaded with armory. You know guns, rockets, and things like that. It was heavier and only had a maximum speed of about 148 miles an hour. Stripped down like it is, it should fly much faster, but given its age, I'd say no more than 150 tops."

"How many times you flown a Huey since the war, Virge?".

"First time!"

Rob wished he had never asked. He leaned back and let the subject drop.

Their short conversation had caused Ken to look around at the others. They were preoccupied with their thoughts. He nudged Rob's leg and whispered, "Rob, what do you think about all those killings on the mountain? Think there's really anything to 'em?"

Rob shrugged. "They say it's true. Never have caught the killer either." He could see Ken was worried. Reaching over, he patted him on the leg. "Nothing to worry about, Ken. Just keep in mind that there are five of us to watch after each other. Together we could lick an army if we had to."

Ken nodded. "Yes, but maybe those Indian legends are right. Maybe it is some kind of ghost or spirit doing it."

Rob chuckled. "Hell, Kenneth boy, there's no such thing as a ghost. At least I've never heard of anyone getting killed by one. It's probably just some crazy old coot who thinks he owns the mountains."

Ken wasn't going to be put off. "What about Indians? Maybe it's the Apaches doing it."

Rob studied the desert terrain below. "Well, there are still Indians around, but they aren't savages like they used to be. They're civilized now. Besides, I doubt there are any living right in the Superstition Mountains. It's a federal wilderness area now."

Ken hoped Rob was right. He reached up and rubbed his hair, then felt around his neck. He would sure hate to lose his head on this trip. He settled back and listened to the sound of the noisy engine, already wishing he had stayed back in L.A. But like always, he had let his friends shame him into doing something he really didn't want to do. Some friends they were.

Brian had been listening and picked up the conversation. "I hear you're part Indian, Clay. Is that right?"

Clay didn't answer. He was asleep.

"Yeah, he's part Indian," Virgil yelled over his shoulder. "One-eighth Apache, I think. But that's not enough to count where we're going!"

"You know, I'm part Indian myself," Rob said. "Don't know how much or what kind. Probably like Clay, not enough to talk about."

The conversation dried up.

Virgil was enjoying himself. Being in a cockpit was second nature to him and that loud old, chop - chop - chop was music to his ears. But this time, he didn't have that hard knot in his stomach or the accompanying lump in his throat that was ever present during the war, caused by the fear of not coming back from the mission, losing a door gunner, or not being able to help the ground troops. Thank God those were just memories now. This time he was enjoying the flight.

As he had done so many times during the war, he reached down and thumped a couple instruments to make sure they weren't sticking.

Satisfied, he glanced at Clay. He knew Clay was afraid to fly and had an idea he had taken something before the flight. Listening to Clay snore, Virgil recalled the many cases of fear he had seen in the past. Yeah, Clay was afraid of flying. Showed all the classic signs, but it would remain his secret. No need to give the others something to rib Clay about. Virgil grinned and turned his attention back to his flying.

3

The four hundred miles to Apache Junction took just over four hours, and by early afternoon, Virgil started descending on the town.

Set in the middle of a desert of cholla bushes, palo verde trees, and saguaro cactus, Apache Junction had started out as just a crossroads used by prospectors searching for gold in the Superstition Mountains. Slowly, more and more people had settled in the area until now it was a thriving little city of 18,000. Of course, this included all the retirees from the north who came to escape the bitter cold winters. It also included the hundreds of people up on the mountain who maintained post office boxes where their monthly checks were deposited. Once a month or so, they came down off the mountain, cashed the welfare or social security checks, bought supplies, and headed right back up.

Built at the intersection of busy Highway 60 and the lesser Highway 88, the town is located near a huge section of land set aside by the Federal Government as a National Wilderness Area in 1940. The Wilderness Act, voted in some time later, made it off limits to all mining unless you obtained a permit. When the bill was hustled through Congress, it certainly caused a commotion among treasure hunters and prospectors everywhere. But it was too late. It was now law - a law largely ignored over the years. Especially in the Superstitions. The mountains were still full of people searching for the Lost Dutchman. And soon there would be at least five more lawbreakers invading that territory.

Dropping low as they approached town, all eyes were searching for the Crossroads Motel where they would be staying for a day or so to obtain supplies and learn what they could about the local terrain.

Brian spotted a long log building at the edge of town. "That must be it, Virge. Just ahead!"

Virgil watched for a good place near the motel to set the craft down. He spotted an open field right out back of the motel and headed for it. Slowly and smoothly, he eased the big bird to the ground, kicking weeds and dust around like a giant whirlwind.

A terrified jackrabbit, frightened from its shallow bed under a cholla bush, darted away through the stubble. When Virgil shut the engine off, the silence was startling. It woke the sleeping prince.

Clay rubbed his eyes and looked around. "Must have drifted off for a minute. Where are we?" he asked.

Everyone laughed.

"We're there, buddy!" Rob said. "You slept all the way and missed some of the greatest scenery in the world!"

"You mean we're already there?"

"Want to tell us what you did last night to make you so tired, my friend?" Virgil asked.

Clay suddenly realized that he had, in fact, slept through the whole trip. Those pills really worked, but he would have to watch that he didn't take as many next time. "Let's get hopping," he said. "We have to register at the motel and check out the town." He opened the door and jumped out.

The others followed and walked around to the front of the motel. They were stunned by the first glance at the Crossroads Motel. It was as old and dilapidated as the Huey. Maybe worse.

Clay looked at his friends. He knew how it must look to them. They had never had to stay in such run down places. Shrugging his shoulders, he headed for the office to register. "At least we won't have far to walk to eat," he said, nodding his head toward a restaurant across the street.

A few minutes later, having rented one large room with three beds that would accommodate Rob, Brian, and Ken, and one smaller room with two beds that Virgil and Clay would share, they found the rooms to be just as bad as the outside. The carpets were old, worn and dirty looking. The walls needed a lot of soap and water and a paint job. The beds looked like they had already been slept in. Old, ragged bedspreads of different colors haphazardly covered the beds that sagged in the middle. The bathroom plumbing was old, rusty, and in need of a good scrubbing.

They stood staring in disbelief.

"I think it's unsafe to stay in here," Ken said, easing toward the door.

Clay attempted to ease the situation. "I guess you just have to remember that we're not in Los Angeles now. We're roughing it." He dumped his gear on one of the beds and headed for the bathroom. The non-stop flight had caused reason to hurry.

After washing up a bit, the men headed for the restaurant across the street. It looked to be in somewhat better shape than the motel. It was a stucco building, fashioned after the old Mexican cantinas, only with a few more windows. A sign across the front announced that it was Will's Family Restaurant.

When they entered the restaurant, all heads turned their way. Feeling like fish in a bowl, they stood near the door waiting for their eyes to get accustomed to the dimmer light.

The inside looked presentable and clean. As it was mid-afternoon, there were only two or three patrons at some of the ten or twelve tables scattered about the room. Each table bore a bright red checked tablecloth. It was the typical working man's restaurant.

Clay headed for a table and made an issue of sitting in a chair with his back to the wall. "Strange town. Saw this in a John Wayne movie once," he said, looking around the room as the others drew up chairs.

"At least it's cool and it looks clean," Virgil said, shoving his cap back on his head and glancing at the counter. He saw no waitresses, just a man wiping the counter with a wet towel.

Will Barnett, a pleasant looking, pounchy, gray haired man in his middle fifties, was owner and operator of the restaurant. He had lived in Apache Junction for years, watching people come and go. He made a hobby of studying people. He would guess who they were, where they came from, what they were doing there, and where they were going next.

He watched these five men enter as he wiped the counter top. The very clothes they wore and their pale skin told him they were city folk. City folk always spent too much time indoors. Didn't tan well. Pale skin always gave 'em a kinda sickly look. He hoped they were just passing through, but deep down he knew better. These men were going up on the mountain and, having no experience in that wilderness, they were men known as *greenhorns*.

When they were settled in and waiting for service, he walked to their table, wiping his hands on the white apron tied around his middle. Leaning between Clay and Virgil, he gave it a good wiping with his towel, straightened, and presented them with a pleasant smile. "Hard to keep clean of dust out here in the desert," he said. "Now, you fellas ready to order or you want to see a menu?"

"What's your special?" Brian piped up.

"Sorry, boys, we're all out of the special. But you wouldn't have liked it anyway - tuna casserole and cottage cheese."

"You got that right, Mister. Just throw me on a good steak," Rob said.

That sparked the hunger of the others and it was steaks all around. When the man had written down the order, he paused, "You boys are new in town, aren't you?"

Clay answered. "That's right. Just got here a little while ago."

"Just passing through or prospecting?"

Clay looked the waiter over. He felt the man was sincere but didn't want to divulge too much. After all, it was against the law to prospect on the mountain. "Thought we'd hike up into the mountains and do a little camping. We're from the city and need to get some of that good country air people are always talking about."

The man nodded. "I figured as much." He walked away. His voice could be heard all over the room as he shouted their order to the cook. "Steaks all around, five times! Medium well, all!"

He walked back to the table and looked each man over carefully. "Fellas, my name is Will Barnett. Now I know you don't want to hear this, but I feel it my duty to say it anyway," he said, matter of factly. "That way I know I've done everything I could." He paused to look the men over. "You fellas shouldn't go into those mountains at all, but if you must go, at least take someone along who knows their way around up there. Boys, I'm telling you those mountains are killers."

"How's that?" Virgil asked.

"I've owned this place for many a year and have seen men from the city, much like you fellas, come here thinking they're wild and tough and can handle anything. They head up into the mountains and either get killed out right or come up among the missing." He stopped to shake his head slowly. "Just last week they found a man who had been missing for months, shot twice through the head. Doubt it was suicide."

"Who's doing the killing? Have they been arrested?" asked Ken.

"That's just it. There are people up on that mountain who've lived there for years and they have a code of sorts - they don't tell anybody anything, especially the law. Any one of 'em will shoot you on sight if you get near their claim. Most likely, one of them shot the man they found last week."

Rob's interest was peaked. "The shootings I understand, but I hear some people have had their heads cut off. Any idea who's doing that?"

Will looked at Rob for a minute, then answered. "Now that's a real mystery. Some say it's the ghost of the old Dutchman himself that's doing it. Others believe it's the spirits of the Apache Indians guarding their sacred grounds. So far the law has found nothing around the killings to indicate either way."

Clay spoke up, "How about you? What do you personally think, Mr. Barnett?"

"Just call me Will," Barnett said, scratching his head, as he gave the matter some thought. "Well, first off, I don't believe in ghosts, though there's sure a lot of talk of 'em hereabouts. I personally think there's some crazy man doing it. Someone who's been there so long he's lost touch with reality."

Virgil shook his head and looked at Clay. "See what you got us into this time, old boy?"

"There's nothing up there we can't handle, Virge. You did bring that old gun of yours, didn't you?"

Will shook his head. "I told you, you wouldn't want to hear what I had to say. You just be very careful up there, you hear?" He walked away.

"Sure thing, Will. We'll be careful." Rob called after him. He leaned over to Clay. "Now, how the hell you reckon he knew we was after the Dutchman?"

Clay grinned. "Who do you know in their right mind that would go camping up there among all those killers and in all that heat just for the fun of it?"

Ken leaned inward and motioned the others closer, "You guys think we should give it up and head back to Los Angeles?"

"Give it up?" Clay whispered loudly, "No way! We just got here. I'm not going to chicken out now."

"No one's chickening out, Clay. I was merely asking." Ken leaned back in his chair. *Damn, I've had done it again. Why was it always me who asks the dumb questions?*

Virgil sipped his coffee. "Well, I think we should go on, seeing as how we've come this far. And I did bring the 'old peacemaker' just in case."

"Look, there's five of us," Rob said. "If we watch out for each other on that mountain, nobody's going to fool with us."

"Out here if we stay alert...we stay alive," Clay said.

Will brought the steaks and placed them on the table. The aroma that suddenly invaded their nostrils stopped all talk of the Superstition Mountains. The boys fell to devouring the huge chunks of beef.

4

The sun had just dropped below the horizon when they stepped out of the restaurant. They stood looking around the street, enjoying the feel of the dry hot desert air against their skin. The town looked exactly like what it represented - a supply town on the edge of a gold field. The streets were wide, the buildings old, but there were signs of new construction all around, indicating what Clay had read was right. The little desert city had growing pains.

One place in their view stood out. A universally recognized sign swaying in the breeze. A sign indicating a bar, pub, tavern, or in this case, a saloon - GUS' SALOON.

"I don't know about you guys," Brian said, rubbing his hands together and licking his lips, "but that saloon sure looks interesting. What say we go have us a little nightcap?" He sauntered off toward the beckoning sign without waiting for an answer. Four eager partners quickly joined him.

A jukebox hammered out a western swing, but through the blue haze of cigarette smoke they saw nobody on the dance floor. A bartender cleaned glasses at one end of the bar. Several rugged looking men, their skin blackened by all the years spent in the desert sun, sat at the bar. One or two sat at tables. At one table a pretty blonde woman sat alone patting her feet to the music.

The boys took a table and noticed that like the restaurant, there wasn't a barmaid to serve them. Only the bartender.

Rob bounced out of his chair. "Roughing it, remember? What'll you gents have?"

It was beer all around and Rob hurried to the bar to fetch the order.

While they waited, they checked out the locals, who, engrossed in their own business, seemed to be paying no attention to the newcomers. Even the young blonde woman paid no attention to them. She was singing softly with the music.

The door burst open and a tall man wearing a western cut suit and white Stetson strutted in. Paul Rockford, a very wealthy rancher, was followed closely by his two body guards, Danny Wiscoff, a slender man in his late twenties, and Tom Davis, stocky built and thirty. Both men were dressed in suits. They strolled to the bar and ordered drinks.

Rockford looked around. His gaze fell upon Clay's group. He stared at them.

They stared back.

He pulled his gaze around to the young blonde. He grinned and headed for her table. He flopped down in a chair and pushed back his Stetson. "Why Miss Laura Pratt! Fancy meeting you here. Bet you've been waiting for me."

"Not hardly, Rockford! Now please leave my table." Laura looked off toward the dance floor. She had encountered Rockford before. Every time he saw her, he pestered her to go with him. She disliked the man very much. He was evil and she wanted nothing to do with him.

"Still little Miss Goodie Two Shoes, huh?"

Laura Pratt ignored him.

He reached across the table and took her hand. "Look Honey, I don't have all night. Let's go to my place and make love."

Pratt jerked her hand back. "Rockford, I don't know who you think you are, but I've already told you I want nothing to do with you. Now, please leave me alone."

Rockford was persistent. "Aw, you don't mean that. I'm not that hard to look at, am I?"

She looked toward the bar. Gus McAdams, the owner, was her uncle. If she could get his attention he would put a stop to this and fast. But Gus was busy at the other end of the bar.

"You get away from my table," Laura said. "I want nothing to do with you."

Rockford glared at the woman. How can she possibly deny herself what she really wants? Losing his patience with her, he grabbed her arm and jerked her toward him. "Look, bitch! I know women like you. I know why you hang out in this bar. You're looking for a man. Right now you want me, so let's get out of here and go party."

All eyes at Clay's table were watching the two. They didn't like what they saw.

Laura slapped him across the face and jerked free. "I said NO!" she screamed at him.

Clay Morgan was on his feet and at her table before Rockford could react.

Wiscoff and Davis hurried from the bar.

Clay watched them approach, but promptly forgot them when he felt Brian, Virgil, Rob, and Ken step up behind him.

"Having trouble, lady?" Clay asked, his eyes fixed on Rockford.

"Yes, I am! Rockford here thinks he owns everything and everyone in the valley, including me."

Rockford glared at the five intruders. "I think you city boys ought to go sit down. This is between me and the lady."

Clay's eyes never left Rockford. He grinned. "You don't have to be a country boy to spot an asshole like you, Mister.

Wiscoff and Davis stuck their hands under their coats.

Rockford waved them away and got to his feet. He glared at Clay, then turned to look at Laura. "Miss Goody Two Shoes, you should be honored to go with someone like me. You being nothing but a worn out old whore and all."

Clay lunged forward, his right fist already in full swing. It landed hard on Rockford's left jaw. He slammed to the floor.

Wiscoff and Davis' hands jerked at something under their coats, but a loud thumping sound coming from the bar caught their attention.

They froze and looked back. It was apparent they had heard this sound before.

Gus held a double-barreled shotgun and was thumping its stock on the bar. It was pointed at Rockford. "She's not a whore, Rockford, you bastard! Now get the hell out of my saloon before I unload both barrels in your ass! And take your two henchmen with you."

Rockford got to his feet. He took a step toward Clay.

Gus cocked the shotgun. "I said git! Now!"

Rockford glared at Clay, rubbing his jaw. He pointed his finger like a gun at the boys, then Laura. "Okay, old man, we'll leave. But I won't forget this."

He glared at Laura. "I don't need you, bitch! You're nothing but a little whore anyway." He quickly turned and stalked toward the door, his men close behind. When he reached the door, Rockford turned with an evil smirk. He pointed his finger again. This time at Laura as he walked out the door backwards.

Everyone watched them go.

Laura turned to Clay. "Thanks, Mister."

"No thanks necessary, Miss. That man was rude and I don't like rude people."

She offered her hand. "I'm Laura Pratt and I come here to see my Uncle Gus, the owner."

"Clay Morgan. This is Virgil Patton. The big one is Rob Clark, the fuzzy one is Brian Speller, and that skinny thing there is Kenneth Smith."

The boys nodded to her.

Gus walked over and shook their hands. "Thanks for stepping in to help my niece, fellas. But I oughta warn you. You'll have to watch out for him. He's a mean one. Never seen anyone hit him before. No telling what he'll do.""

"We'll keep that in mind," Clay said.

Gus and Laura walked to the bar.

Clay and his friends returned to their table.

Virgil took a long swallow of beer. "First damn day here and already we're finding trouble."

Ken glanced nervously at the door. "I told you this was dangerous country. We got no business here."

He got glares from every one at the table.

Gus walked over with two large pitchers of beer. "On the house, boys. Thanks again."

As Gus walked away, the door opened and a man in buckskin clothes shuffled in, looking very much like a real mountainman. He had a wild look about him. Scrawny, ragged, and looking like he hadn't bathed or changed his buckskins in months.

Clay watched him walk past their table to one in a corner and sit down, his eyes fixed in a steady gaze at them. Clay eyed the man's long, white, stringy hair and matching beard. His dark, weather-beaten face looked like it had seen the better part of fifty years.

Ken returned with the beer and diverted Clay's attention back to his friends. Most of their conversation was idle talk, laughing and joking, as beer after beer was drained.

Brian had to relieve himself and headed for the men's room.

Brian was at the urinal staring at the wall when the door opened and the mountain man walked in. He leaned against a wall and stood watching Brian until he had finished. "I hear you might be looking for a guide to take you into the mountains."

Brian looked him over suspiciously. They had not been asking around for a guide. The only one who had said anything about a guide was Will Barnett. "Where'd you hear that?"

"Over at Will's cafe. I was in there right after you fellas left."

Brian nodded and started to walk out. The man grabbed the door and held it shut.

"Look Mister, I gotta talk to you," he whispered.

Brian took a combat stance, his fists ready.

Seeing this, the man quickly threw up both hands. "No! No! No trouble. I just want to talk."

Brian relaxed a little and stood watching as the man walked over to the commode stall and looked in. He then walked to the door and opened it slowly about an inch and peeped out. Seemingly satisfied with what he had seen, he walked back to Brian. "I know these mountains, front and back. I've been prospecting in them for years."

Brian was getting impatient. "Look fella, we're not looking for a guide. Besides, the shit house is not the proper place to be discussing business, if in fact you are a guide, which I doubt."

"I'm a guide alright." He looked about nervously. "Looky here, lad, you look like someone I can trust. Someone who knows how to keep a secret."

"That's true."

"Well, son, I've found the Lost Dutchman's mine!"

Brian chuckled and again started to open the door. "If that was true, you wouldn't be standing here in this smelly shithouse talking about it. You'd be up there hauling out all that gold."

Again the man stopped him. "Can't haul it out. Not yet. I need help and there's no one around I can trust. People 'round here'd cut my throat in a second if I showed 'em the gold." He shook his head. "No, I need someone who is not of these parts. Someone who ain't been exposed to all the greed hereabouts."

Brian studied the old man for a full minute. "Tell me more."

"If you guys will help me haul it out, I'll give you half of it. There's more'n enough for all of us."

"Aren't you afraid someone will steal it while you're down here messing around?"

"No. It's so well hidden, nobody's going to find it but me."

Brian was getting very interested now. "You say there's really gold up there?"

"Sho'nuf and lots of it!" The old man smiled.

"Well, we can't talk here." Brian started out the door. He stopped. "You got a name?"

"Name's Norman Calhoun. C. Norman Calhoun."

"Okay, C. Norman Calhoun, let's go meet the boys."

Hurrying to the table, Brian waved his hand for silence. "Come on, guys," he whispered. "Let's head for the motel. I got great news." He walked off, but stopped when no one moved.

Clay looked at the old man. "Brian, what the hell's the matter with you and who the hell's Davy Crockett here?"

Brian stepped back to the table and whispered, "Can't tell you here, someone might hear. Come on." This time he headed out the door with Calhoun close behind.

Clay looked at Virgil and then at the others. He hurriedly downed his beer. "Bastard's flipped out already."

"Yeah, I think so," Virgil said and stood up. "Might just as well go get him to bed, before he gets hurt."

In the now crowded motel room, six men found places to land as Brian quickly pulled the shades and locked the door. He turned and a big grin crossed his face as he announced, "Gentlemen, meet C. Norman Calhoun!"

Everyone nodded to Calhoun, and then Clay looked at Brian. "What the hell's all this secret shit about, Brian?"

"You took us from our beer, you know," Virgil added, feigning anger.

"This is far more important than your beer. Listen up." Brian pointed at Calhoun. "This man has already found the Dutchman's gold mine."

Everyone stared suspiciously at Calhoun.

Brian saw their skepticism. "I know. I didn't believe it either at first, but he seems to know a lot about what you told us, Clay - about the cave and the Spanish and all." Brian motioned to Calhoun. "Norman, you tell 'em. Tell 'em what you just told me. Go on, tell 'em."

Calhoun cast a suspicious glance at each of the boys. Finally, he nodded. "I hunted for years up there and just a while ago, I found it. Yes sir, there it was, right in front of me. I never saw anything like it. The sparkle of it almost blinded me." He stopped as though deep in thought. "Yes sir, I crawled into this here cave way up on the face of the mountain, up there near the old needle. First, I saw some bones, then some Spanish breastplates - old and tarnished. Then there it was. Gold! Piles of it! Just lying there."

The room was quiet as everyone absorbed what he was saying.

Virgil broke the silence. "If that's true, why didn't you bring it down with you?"

"I had no way to bring it. I lost my horse in a fall over a cliff and had to walk out. I knew there was a chance someone was watching me and would try to rob me. If they did and found any gold on me, they would have tortured me until I told them where the rest of it was. I had to find someone I could trust to help me."

"How do you know you can trust us?" Ken asked.

"Well, I really don't know that I can, but you ain't from these parts and you ain't like all the rest. Greedy bastards, all!"

"Okay, let's go over it one more time," Rob said. "What's in the cave?"

The old man told the story over and over until finally everyone was satisfied that he was telling the truth.

Clay paced in front of the man. "Okay, Calhoun, we believe you. So what do we do now?"

Calhoun was eager to explain. "First light, we get horses from the outfitter down the road a ways."

"We have a helicopter that will take us there, why horses?" Virgil asked.

"That big thing you landed in will draw the attention of everyone in this town as well as up on that mountain. No Sir! We have to be sneaky about this. No one will suspect anything about six men on horseback heading out on a trail ride. They do it all the time 'round these parts."

Virgil nodded. "That makes sense."

"We'll need two pack mules and some camping gear," Calhoun continued. "Not too much, it's only a day and a half's ride from here. We'll need to travel light."

Everyone nodded their approval and they all shook hands.

"Thanks, fellas." Calhoun grinned big and headed out the door.

After he left, Virgil turned to Clay. "You sure about this? He looks crazy to me."

"He does look that alright, but everything he said makes sense, including why he didn't bring it down."

Brian smacked a fist into a palm. "Man! How lucky can you get! The very first day here and already we got a gold mine!"

Clay was still somewhat skeptical. "I don't know if he's telling the truth or not, Brian. Seems kind of strange, he didn't bring even one nugget out."

The room was silent.

"Well, the torture bit sounded right, didn't it?" Brian asked.

"I guess so. And it's obvious by the smell of him that he hasn't had a bath in weeks. Maybe there *is* something to his story." Clay stood up to leave. "I'm going to bed...'first light' you know!"

Sleep did not come easily for the men, as they lay in anticipation of the upcoming trip. Thoughts of all that gold raced though their minds. What would they do with their share? Was it really as dangerous as they had been told? Would they all come out of it okay? So many things they had to think about...until sleep finally took each one.

5

Laura Pratt picked up her purse, finished the rest of her drink and placed the empty glass on the bar in front of Gus. "Thanks again, Uncle Gus," Laura said. "I think I'll scoot out of here before Rockford comes back."

"Maybe you should wait until I close and I'll see you home."

"I'll be careful. See you later." Laura headed for the door.

Opening the door, she looked all around for any sign of the man. Seeing nothing, she left.

Gus went to the door and stood watching her walk to her car across the street. Laura was his only living relative. Her parents had been killed in a car accident when she was just thirteen. Gus had taken her in and raised her as his own. Now 24 years old, she had matured into a beautiful woman and worked as a secretary for an insurance firm in Mesa. He worried about her still being single and not even having a steady boy friend. She kept telling him she was waiting for the right man to come along. As far as he knew, her entire life consisted of working and coming to the saloon in the evenings to listen to music. As Laura drove away, he made a mental note to talk to her about getting some more excitement in her life. He strolled back to the bar and started getting ready to close.

Laura had driven only a few blocks when, suddenly, a large black car cut her off at the intersection and forced her to stop. Already frightened by the near miss, sheer terror set in when she saw Rockford get out of the back seat.

Rockford stood watching her for a minute, then motioned to the man driving. He got out and approached her car. She recognized Danny Wiscoff

Laura slammed the car in reverse and tried to back away, but slammed into a pickup truck that had pulled up behind her. She was trapped. She jerked around to hit the door locks, but it was too late. She screamed as Wiscoff yanked the door open and grabbed her. Struggling hard, striking him with her fists and kicking him with her feet, she was pulled from her car.

Tom Davis ran from the pickup to help Wiscoff with her. He clamped a hand over her mouth and helped force her into the back seat of the black car.

Laura struggled hard to get out, but Davis held her back. Rockford slid in beside her and helped hold her down. "Davis, you get her car and drive it to the ranch. We'll have to dispose of it later."

"Yes, sir, Boss. We'll come back later for my truck."

Rockford slapped Laura hard across the face. "Nobody treats Paul Rockford the way you did and gets away with it, young lady. Now you will pay, and pay dearly." He laughed loudly. "Danny! Get us to the ranch! Hurry!"

The car roared off, with Laura a prisoner.

The two cars made a sharp turn onto the Rockford Ranch road. The white wooden fence on either side of the road stood out in the moonlight as they raced up the driveway to a large two-story, Mexican style hacienda built in the late 1800s.

Davis ran from Laura's car to help Wiscoff drag Laura from Rockford's car.

She kicked and struggled for all she was worth. She couldn't scream past the hand clamped over her mouth. She fought hard, struggling and kicking her legs.

Rockford grew impatient and slugged her hard on the chin.

Everything went dark for Laura. She hung limply in the arms of her attackers. Unconscious, she was carried up the steps into the ranch house and dumped onto the huge, hand-carved, four poster bed in Rockford's bedroom.

Davis and Wiscoff stood like two Doberman pinchers lusting for food, but afraid to move for fear their master would punish them.

Rockford stood looking down at Laura sprawled across the green satin bedspread. An evil grin broke across his face. "Get out." His eyes never left Laura's body, nor did he lose the evil grin from his face. "Go get rid of her car somewhere." His eyes locked on Laura's long legs.

"Sure thing, Boss," Wiscoff replied. He and Davis grinned wickedly, made little knowing gestures to each other, and hurried out, closing the door behind them.

Rockford stood for a minute staring down at Laura. My god, he thought. How different it feels when you force someone to do it. How good!

He slowly began to undress himself, his eyes never leaving her body. When he was completely naked, he eased down next to her and ran his hand over her body. She stirred slightly. He hurriedly ripped her dress off, throwing it across the room. His hand caressed her breasts through the black lace bra that encased them. With a single jerk, he ripped the bra from her body. He was aroused.

Laura was slowly coming to. She moaned softly.

Quickly, Rockford ripped the black lace panties from her, just as she became aware of what was happening.

Laura screamed.

Rockford reacted by backhanding her across the mouth. She stopped struggling and lay still, blood oozing from her lip.

Rockford wiped it away with a finger and held it up to watch the blood trickle down it. His face still held the wicked grin. He kissed her hard on the mouth. She struggled desperately. He forced her legs apart and fell between them.

Sobbing hysterically, Laura tried with all her might to throw him off. It was of no use. Through her wracking sobs, she tried begging. "Please don't. Please. Just let me go. I won't tell anyone. I promise. Just let me go."

This only served to excite Rockford more. "That's it, bitch. Beg! I love to hear you beg." He grabbed her by the hair, forcing her head back. "I said beg, bitch!" He slapped her across the face again.

Laura screamed out from the pain.

Rockford clamped one hand over her mouth and reached for his pants on the floor next to the bed with the other. Fumbling through the pockets he came up with a large switch blade knife. He hit the button and the long slender blade shot out. He moved it back and forth in front of her eyes. "I said beg, not scream. Scream one more time, and I'll cut that delicious little throat of yours from ear to ear." He released her mouth.

Terror seized Laura. She knew she had no hope of escaping this madman. There was no doubt that Rockford would kill her. The only thing left for her now was to try to stay alive. She laid motionless, resigned to the fact that he was going to have his way with her, no matter what. She tried to will herself to another place. Some place peaceful and beautiful. She would not give this man cause to kill her, yet she would not do his bidding, either. Her hands at her sides, she relaxed, closed her eyes and laid perfectly still.

When she wouldn't beg anymore, he forcefully plunged into her. The searing pain caused her to cry out. It was enough to satisfy his lustful need to hurt her, and he increased his tempo. Her moans of pain were lost under his loud, laborious breathing.

Rockford collapsed on top of her. He lay still, sweating profusely and gasping for breath. After what seemed like hours to Laura, he rolled off her.

Laura turned her back to him and drew herself up in a fetal position. She lay sobbing softly.

After a few minutes, Rockford rose from the bed and started dressing.

Laura lay hoping he would just leave - go away and leave her there. But that was not to be.

"Get up and get dressed," he ordered.

When she didn't move fast enough to suit him, he grabbed her by a leg and dragged her off the bed.

She struck the floor hard, yelling out in pain.

"God dammit, move when I tell you to!"

Still in pain, Laura rose from the floor and gathered her torn clothes. The bra and panties were ruined and her dress was so tattered she had to hold it together to hide her nakedness. Shaking with fear and pain, she huddled in a corner of the room, waiting for more orders. She did not look at him.

He stood - his legs apart - hands on his hips and that same evil grin on his face, glaring at her. "Like I told you, bitch, you're nothing but a whore. Now you'll see what it's like to live like a whore. You're going with me. I know just the place for the likes of you!"

She started crying again. "Please let me go! You got what you wanted. I just want to go home. Please!"

He laughed. The loud roaring laugh of a crazy man. "You should have thought of that when we were in the tavern. You would be free to go by now. But, no! You were too good for me. Well, now you'll pay for that."

He turned his back on her pitiful sobbing and walked to the bedroom door. Jerking it open he had to jump back to keep from being knocked down by Wiscoff and Davis who had been leaning against the door listening.

They muttered something of an apology to him as they struggled to regain their footing. "Sorry, Boss. Real sorry." It was evident they feared this man. "We ditched the car. It'll never be found."

"Well, seeing as how you two are so interested in what I was doing, make yourselves useful. Take her to the helicopter!"

Eagerly, they grabbed Laura and dragged her out of the room.

Outside, Davis and Wiscoff carried Laura through the night's hot desert air to the helicopter in the yard. Rockford was close behind. Designed to carry a pilot and four passengers, the helicopter had been used extensively during the Vietnam War as a "LOH" - Light Observation Helicopter. Commonly referred to as the flying egg, it was now a popular mode of travel by the wealthy and served as a status symbol for men like Rockford.

Dumping Laura in the rear seat, Wiscoff jumped in and cranked the engine while Davis took the front passenger seat and Rockford slid in beside Laura.

Her body jerked with heavy sobbing. She opened her mouth to say something, but before she could, Rockford flashed the knife and growled, "Stop that damn whimpering!"

The rotors on the helicopter slowly gained momentum and it lifted off the ground.

Rockford took out a large bandanna and tied it over Laura's eyes.

Blinded, tasting blood from her cut, swollen lip, she clutched her torn dress together as she sat trembling in her seat, fearful of the unknown. She didn't know where they were taking her or what they were going to do to her. She couldn't help but fear that this man might even throw her out of the helicopter while in flight over the mountains. She fought to stifle her sobs.

Wiscoff glanced over his shoulder at Rockford. "Where to, Boss?"

"Head up on the mountain. We'll take her to Big Alice."

Wiscoff grinned and turned the helicopter to the east.

6

$\mathbb{B}$ig Alice Hatfield was a huge black woman whose heart was as black as her skin. She ran a saloon at the base of the Superstition Mountains with several rooms in the back where her girls entertained men who came to search for gold.

The saloon was a large log cabin, with a porch that wrapped around on three sides. One could always find Big Alice sitting on the porch staring through her binoculars at the mountains that loomed high above her. She had been after the Dutchman's gold ever since she had been run out of Denver, Colorado by the law years earlier for running a whorehouse. It had been during those times that she had traded sex to a man for $5 and a map to the Lost Dutchman's gold mine.

So with map in hand, she had bid the law and Denver good-bye and headed for Apache Junction, Arizona. After establishing her saloon and procuring some girls to work for her, she set about searching for the Dutchman's gold.

Even though she was unable to traipse off into the mountains herself, she had, over the years, hired several men to do the searching for her. She selected her hired men carefully from those who visited the saloon and her girls.

When she hired a man and he could not find the mine as she felt he should, she would hire another to follow him to see what he was doing. If he hadn't made a good effort to search for it, she would get him back to the saloon and have him beaten or killed. In one instance, she had hired two men to make the search. When she became suspicious of one, she paid the other to kill him by pushing him off a four hundred-foot cliff near Weaver's Needle. Like many others involved with Big Alice, his death had been marked up as an accident.

Big Alice's girls were strays, brought there by their men who went wandering off through the mountains in search of gold and wandered in broke, hungry, and needing a place to sleep. Alice, not one to help anyone just out of the goodness of her heart, turned the girls out as whores and reaped the money. They got only a few dollars a week, room and board, and clothes for their work.

If a girl ran off, she sent Sanchaz and Gonzales after them and they were punished in whatever way Big Alice deemed necessary. However, if a girl wanted to leave and she would seek Big Alice's permission first, it was usually granted.

Big Alice had at her beck and call two huge Mexican men - Padro Sanchez and Manuel Gonzales. They enforced the rules she set down for her girls, handled unruly customers, served as her bodyguards, and in general did her bidding. That included going into the mountains after one of her hired men searching for the Dutchman and making sure he did not return.

Big Alice was also Rockford's eyes and ears on the mountain. Anytime she spotted strangers on the mountains, she would send a runner to tell Rockford. He would send out his henchmen to handle the matter. He paid her well for that service.

The saloon was dark when Wiscoff eased the helicopter to the ground just outside the front door.

Rockford patted Laura on the rump. "You're going love Big Alice, Laura Pratt!" He laughed.

Laura felt the helicopter settle to a stop. She tried to peep under the blindfold, but it was on too tight. She shivered violently. She had no idea where she was or what they were going to do to her.

Roughly, she was jerked from the helicopter and pushed along. She could barely keep her footing. She was still blindfolded, and to make matters worse, she was barefoot. She stumbled.

Rockford caught her. He yanked off the blindfold. "Take a good look at your new home, whore!"

Laura stared at the dark, sinister looking log saloon. She saw nobody around. She shuddered with fear.

"Scared, aren't you, bitch?" Rockford snarled. "Don't you wish you had been nicer to me back there in dear old Uncle Gus' Saloon?" He pushed her toward the saloon without waiting for an answer. "Move it!"

Wiscoff and Davis tried the door and found it locked.

"She's closed up, Boss," Davis said. "Late as it is she must be asleep."

"Well, wake her up, Dummy!" Rockford ordered.

Davis hesitated. His eyes showed fear. "What about that old shotgun she carries, Boss?"

"You cowardly bastard! Beat on that door like I told you!"

Davis pounded on the door.

A huge Mexican man, barefoot and naked to the waist, opened it a crack. "What you want, gringo?"

"Open the god damned door, Padro. It's me, Rockford!"

The door quickly swung open. Padro Sanchez stepped out. "Sorry, Señor Rockford. I did not know it was you."

Rockford hurried Laura through the door yelling, "Alice! Big Alice! Get your ass out here. You have company!"

At the rear of the dark saloon a Coleman lantern flared up. In its light stood Big Alice in her huge rumpled nightgown. She glared at Rockford. She hated this man, but tolerated him because he was a good source of money. Money she needed to hire the men to make her searches. "What the hell you want, Rockford? Don't you know it's night time?"

"Don't be so damn grouchy."

She didn't have to tolerate him that much. "Don't you come in here cussing me like that, you damn gringo. I'll have Padro and Manuel cut your nasty tongue plumb out of your head. You hear me, Paul Rockford?"

Rockford laughed nervously. "Now, now. Let's don't get testy, Alice." He looked at Padro who made a long machete appear from nowhere and made slashing motions with it. Rockford was truly afraid of this woman and he wasn't ready to die just yet. He knew he had just came on too strong. "You know I was just joking."

"If that's the case, just tell me why you woke me up in the middle of the night, and go on and leave so I can get back to bed."

Rockford breathed a sigh of relief and pushed Laura out in front of him. This should perk her up a little and put him back in her good graces, he thought. A pretty little girl like Laura would bring her in a lot of money. He grinned. "Look what I brought you, Big Alice. This little lady wants to be a whore for you."

"I ain't got no 'hoes here and I don't want none. My girls are all working girls."

Rockford chuckled. "Well then, this little lady wants to be one of your *working* girls. You just take her and turn her out proper. She's a little hellcat and needs some of your tender loving help."

Big Alice cocked her head to one side and looked at him suspiciously. "Where'd you get this one?"

"Over in Apache Junction. But don't worry, no one will miss her. She was hanging out in a bar as bad as this one."

Laura knew she had to do something. She had to tell this woman she had been kidnapped. Maybe she would help her. "Please help me, Ma'am," Laura begged. "He kidnapped me. I just want to go home." She started crying.

"You son-of-a-bitch, Rockford! What in the hell's wrong with you? Kidnapping someone and bringing her here?"

"It's too late to worry about that now. What's done is done and she has to stay or we all go to jail."

Big Alice glared at him. "We?"

Rockford walked over and put his arm around the big lady and whispered loud enough for everyone to hear. "Yes, Big Alice -- we. I made her a gift to you. She's all yours now. You have to keep her."

"Get the hell out of here, Rockford. You ain't never gave anything away. Besides if I don't take her, I'm not involved."

"I'm afraid you're already in up to your pretty black eyes, Big Alice." Rockford turned to his two flunkies. "Right boys?"

"Right, Boss!" Wiscoff said.

"That's the way I see it, Boss," Davis answered.

"What the hell you mean, I'm already involved?"

"Remember those men your two animals beheaded in the mountains a while back?"

"You got no proof it was my boys that did that thing."

"Davis and Wiscoff were up there in the helicopter the day it happened. They saw everything. I'm afraid they'd have to tell Sheriff Wilkins all about what they saw and then, of course, he'd know who told them to do it."

Big Alice glared at the man, wondering if he was telling the truth or just bluffing. She couldn't afford to take a chance. "You're a real son-of-a-bitch, Rockford. You know that?"

"Yeah, I know," Rockford replied. "It's an affliction I was born with. Anyway, she's yours now. Just you make sure you turn her out and keep her at it 'til hell freezes over."

Big Alice stared at him. "You bastard!" She turned to Laura. She looked her over then reached out to touch Laura's face.

Laura knew now she would get no help from this woman. She drew back in fright.

Big Alice grinned. "Now don't be like that, girl. You going to like it around here once you get used to it." She turned to Padro. "Padro, see that she is made comfortable in the far bedroom. The one with the lock on the outside of the door."

Padro took Laura by the arm and half led, half dragged her toward the back of the saloon.

Big Alice turned to Rockford. Her dark eyes narrowed in the lamplight. "You going to get us both caught one of these days, Rockford," she snapped. "You know Apache Junction is too close to snatch someone."

"Big Alice, that's thirty miles from here! Who in hell would ever think to look way up here for some girl missing in Apache Junction? Stop worrying and go back to bed. I'm leaving." He motioned to his men and headed out the door.

Big Alice watched the door close behind him, wondering why she put up with his crap.

In a dark, bare room at the back of the saloon, Laura sat huddled on a corner of the tiny bed that was the only piece of furniture in the room. Why was this happening to her? She had never hurt anyone. Tears filled her eyes. She drew her knees up and wrapped her arms around them. With her head resting on her knees she sat rocking back and forth, sobbing. The only other sound was the whirling, chop - chop - chop of the helicopter as it gained power and lifted off the ground. Soon there was nothing but silence. Laura had never felt so alone.

7

C lay sat straight up in bed, his heart pounding. The alarm clock was going off. He looked at it. Four o'clock. He fell back onto his pillow, then remembered that Calhoun had said first light. He jumped from bed and headed for the shower. It was Monday morning and the mountains were waiting.

First light broke over the Superstition Mountains to find Clay and his four friends standing in front of the Mountain View Outfitter's Store. They were decked out in their western best, complete with boots and hats, looking every bit like the city dudes they were.

The building had all the appearances of an old time general store, complete with a wooden Indian on the porch. Out back, several horses and mules milled about in a split rail corral.

Yawning and rubbing the sleep from their eyes, they waited for Calhoun.

The door swung open and Calhoun stepped out with a tall heavy-set man. Calhoun looked the five dudes over. "Fellas, this here is Liege Blackhorse, owner of the store. He needs money for the animals and supplies."

"How much does he need?" Clay asked.

Liege Blackhorse was quick to answer. "Five Hundred Dollars will take you all the way for the week."

Clay frowned and looked at the rest of the boys.

They shrugged their shoulders and waited.

"I thought we were going fifty-fifty on this trip, Calhoun," Clay said.

"Only on the return cargo."

Clay turned to Blackhorse. "You take credit cards?"

"Sure! They're good as gold." Blackhorse laughed a deep belly-rolling laugh.

Soberly, Clay watched. He didn't appreciate being the butt of a joke.

Seeing his stare Blackhorse stopped laughing. "Sorry, just a play on words, you know."

"What if we aren't gone for a whole week - say only two or three days?" Clay asked.

"Then I'll prorate the fee and give you a refund."

Clay handed him a credit card and watched him hurry back into the store. He turned on Calhoun. "You didn't tell us about this, Calhoun. What if we hadn't had that much money?"

"I knew you had it. You're from the city." Calhoun jumped off the porch and headed for the corral.

Clay looked at Brian. "I wonder how many more surprises he has in store for us?"

Six horses were already saddled and waiting. Two mules, complete with loaded packs, stood tied to the fence. Calhoun had indeed been busy this morning.

Clay walked into the corral and picked out the horse he felt best suited him. He secretly hoped he had chosen a good-natured one, for like the rest of the city born and raised boys, he had only ridden once or twice in his life and was uncertain how he would manage.

Everyone had picked a horse by the time Liege returned. He walked around to the corral with an armload of leather goods and the receipt for the credit card for Clay to sign. "You boys better put on these chaps if you're going into those mountains." Blackhorse passed out the equipment. "Out there, even the plants have teeth. Here's some spurs, too. Might need them to control your horse better."

"And how much extra for those?" asked Clay.

"Just to show I'm not really an ass like you might think, there's no extra charge. I trust you'll bring 'em back."

Clay gave the man another look. Maybe he wasn't so bad after all. He joined the others as they set about trying to get the chaps and spurs on properly. This was a first for them.

Blackhorse chuckled as he watched. He had been in the outfitting business for many years and had seen hundreds of city people just like these guys come through wanting to be cowboys, but knew little about being one. It amazed him, how many different ways they could try on the equipment. "Like an apron, boys. They go on like an apron with buckle in back. Take a look at the way Norman wears his."

He watched Clay putting on his spurs. "Outside, boys. The strap buckle goes on the outside." Liege leaned against the fence shaking his head as he watched the five men trying to get mounted. "Now, you boys take good care of my horses. I want them all back in the same shape they're in now."

Virgil reined up beside him. "I can assure you, mister, they'll probably fair much better than we will." He guided his horse through the gate to follow Calhoun.

Blackhorse saw that Ken was having trouble with his horse. It was not doing what he wanted it to. Blackhorse walked over and took hold of the reins. He could see Ken was afraid of the horse. "He smells the fear in you, son," he said softly so the others couldn't hear. "Just let the reins hang freely and he'll follow the others like a little lamb. You just hold onto the saddle horn."

Ken lowered the reins and the horse settled right down. He glanced at Blackhorse and nodded his thanks.

Blackhorse winked. "Now you got 'im."

Clay had been watching. He nodded his approval. "We'll bring 'em back in good shape, Mr. Blackhorse."

"Just call me Liege. Everyone else does."

Rob and Brian grabbed the lead ropes for the two mules and followed. They were like two kids at a carnival. They had never been so excited.

"Brian, you look like Tom Mix with that ten gallon hat on," Rob laughed and tugged on the rope to get the ornery mule moving faster.

"If you remember, my friend, I borrowed it from you. I wonder what you looked like in it - Hoss Cartwright?"

They both laughed as they followed the others into the rugged desert and mountain range, five city boys following their trusted guide, C. Norman Calhoun, the mountain man.

8

Dawn light cascaded through the window, falling upon Laura who lay staring at the ceiling. Even as tired as she had been, she had been too afraid to sleep. She had cried all night, jumping at every sound, not knowing what was coming next. She still had on the tattered dress she wore when she was kidnapped.

Drained of tears after hours of crying Laura sat up and looked around the room. She knew that if she didn't get away, Big Alice would force her to prostitute herself or kill her. She glanced around the bare room, looking for a way out. The wall had no paint or wallpaper, just roughly sawed boards. There was nothing in the room but the bed, and it didn't have any covers. Just the mattress.

She rose to her feet, holding the dress together with one hand to hide her nakedness. Easing around the bed, she checked the only window. Through it she could see only desert outside. There were no other buildings or people. She gripped the window and pushed upward. To her surprise, it slid up an inch or two with ease. She looked around and listened for any sounds. It was quiet. She didn't think anyone was awake yet. Her heart pounded. Maybe she could slip out without anyone noticing. Excitedly, she eased the window open more, and then her heart sank. There were steel bars on the outside.

Though defeated in her purpose, she left the window open for air and checked the rest of the room. The floor squeaked loudly as she eased over to the door. She was sure someone heard it. She stopped to listen. Hearing nothing, she tried the knob and found it locked. Putting her shoulder against it, she pushed as hard as she could. It would not budge. She walked back to the bed and sat down.

She knew there would be no one looking for her yet. She had only Uncle Gus. She lived alone in Apache Junction and would often spend the night with girlfriends. No one would know she was missing for several days. By then she might be dead - or worse - having to give herself to filthy prospectors. She shuddered. Then and there she made up her mind that she would rather be dead.

Moving again from the bed to the door, she listened for movement outside. Hearing none, she checked around the edges of the door. She had no idea what she was looking for, but she had to do something.

She spotted the door's hinges. They were on the inside. She tried to pull the hinge pin out, but years of being in the musky log building had frozen it in place. Laura began searching the room for something to remove the pin with. There was nothing.

She gave up and lay down. In doing so, she heard the slight rattle of wood against metal under the bed. Her eyes widened. She had heard that noise before. She knew it was bed slats. The bed had wooden slats under the mattress.

She grabbed the edge of the bed and lifted. The heavy mattress came up, exposing three wooden slats. Straining with all her power, she held the mattress in one hand and grabbed one of the slats. It came free in her hand and she dropped the mattress back in place. It made a loud noise. She froze.

Outside the door, Padro had stepped from his room and was walking down the hallway when he heard the noise. He paused to listen. When he heard nothing more, he yelled through the door. "You would do well to settle down in there, little one. There is no way out. Besides, there is nothing but desert for twenty miles or more. No one can hear you, little one "

Laura quickly laid down on the bed hugging the wooden slat to her chest. There was total silence for a minute or two, then she heard Padro's heavy footsteps heading into the saloon. Minutes passed before she moved. Then she slipped from the bed and, ignoring her open dress, gripped the slat like a club. She swung it at an imaginary person. She was pleased. "At least now I have a weapon to fight the bastards with," she said under her breath.

She eased over to the door. She tried to pry the pins upward by slipping the end of the slat under the round head of the pin and pushing, but each time the slat slipped off. After each slip of the slat, she would listen closely to see if anyone had heard. Several tries later the pin slipped a fraction of an inch. She grinned. Maybe she could escape this hellhole after all. She made several more attempts at the pin, but it would budge no more. Giving up again, she went back to the bed, slipping the slat under the mattress where it would be easy to grab. With at least a shadow of hope in sight, she lay down, closed her weary eyes and drifted off into a troubled sleep.

9

For what seemed like hours, Clay, Virgil, Rob, Brian, and Ken trailed blindly behind Calhoun through the dry, hot desert with the blazing sun beating down on them. They were thankful for the long sleeved shirts and wide brimmed hats they had brought along.

They clutched the saddle horns and their horses jumped and shied to one side as the sudden fluttering from the wings of an occasional covey of quail sprang into flight beneath their feet. Roadrunners darted from bush to bush almost as if they were playing hide-and-seek.

A black-tailed jackrabbit burst from beneath a sage bush and scampered away, its long strides quickly carrying it out of sight.

"Jeezus, would you look at the size of that thing?" Clay shouted to the others. He was enjoying himself. This was what he had meant about having an adventure. He eagerly watched for the next bird or animal to appear.

He had already discovered what Liege was talking about when he said everything in the desert had teeth. He was thankful for the chaps Liege had given them as the sharp cholla needles raked across the leather. Even sharper were the cat's paw plants' needles. There were many different types of cactus that had spines that dug into the leather - from the tall, thin, stringy ones to the huge saguaro with the holes pecked in them from birds seeking a place to raise their young. And there was sand. Lots of sand. And rocks. Like gravel, the smaller, loose ones covered the terrain with larger rocks scattered about for the horses to stumble over.

As far as Clay could see, the terrain was the same and had the same color - a dull brown with only a hint here and there of the green branches of a stubby palo verde tree that looked very much like a willow tree from a distance. Through the heat waves rising from the hot sand, he could see that the saguaro cactus was the tallest plant life around, and off in the distance he could see the outline of the mountains breaking the sky line.

So far the animal sightings and scenery were great, but he was having some difficulty, too. He was getting saddle-sore and sunburned.

"Hey, Virge!" He called. "Bring any sun screen with you? I'm starting to look like a lobster!"

"Looks like we're both out of luck."

"We're roughing it! Remember?" Rob called out from behind them.

Clay didn't answer. He pushed up in the stirrups and rubbed his backside. He had forgotten about the pain associated with riding horses. He could feel the saddle sores already forming from the constant rubbing and bouncing against the hard leather. Looking to the others, he was glad to see he was not alone. They were all having the same trouble - everyone, that is, except old C. Norman Calhoun.

* * *

After several hours, Calhoun reined up. "We'll stop here for a break."

He didn't have to say it twice. All five men fell from their mounts, welcoming the feel of the hot sand on their raw rear ends.

"Geezz! Look at my skin," Ken exclaimed. "Burnt red!"

He wiped the sweat from his head and shaded his eyes with his hat as he looked up. "Now I know how the Indians got the name redskins. It was that miserable sun up there."

Calhoun sat in his saddle, a big grin on his weather-beaten old face. He looked over the sun burned city boys as they gulped down water from their canteens. After only a couple of minutes, he turned his attention toward the mountains and spurred his horse in that direction.

Startled by his sudden departure, the newly made cowboys jumped to their feet and quickly mounted.

Pushing his horse to catch up, Virgil yelled at Clay. "Sure glad he gave us that break, aren't you, Clay?"

"Break, my ass. That was a cruel thing to do. That sand was feeling pretty damn good on my rear!"

"I know just what you mean," Virgil answered, reaching back to rub his own.

Behind them, Rob and Brian struggled with the slow moving mules.

"You guys up there slow down a bit! These ornery critters can't move that fast," Brian yelled.

Calhoun stopped until they caught up, then headed out again, this time at a slower pace.

Treading their way through the mesquite bushes, the treasure hunters were thankful again for the chaps. The mesquite bushes had one and a half inch thorns as sharp as needles. In fact, Indians and early settlers had used them for that very thing - sewing clothing. The thorns scraped against the thick, tough leather without penetration.

Noon came and went as they continued on. Their shirts were soaked with sweat. There was no wind to cool them from the blistering sun.

Famished, Rob yelled at Calhoun. "Dammit, Calhoun, when does the noon whistle blow, anyway?"

Calhoun pulled his horse to a stop. "Hungry, are you?"

Virgil reined in. "Hell yes, we're hungry. Don't you ever eat?"

"Once in a while. When you live up here, you get used to one meal a day. Sometimes you get lucky and get two. Stay too busy for anymore." He paused. "Ain't no coffee breaks up here either. This ain't the city, boys. It's wild country and you better learn that if you plan to keep up with me."

Brian was getting angry. He dismounted, holding onto the saddle horn to relieve the pain shooting through his rear. "Dammit, Calhoun! You do what you want, but, by God, I'm going to take a break and get me something to eat. If you don't like that, you can go to hell!" he shouted, walking back to the pack mule.

"If I recall right, Calhoun," Clay said. "We don't need you, you need us. We're stopping." He got off his horse and flopped down in the sand.

"Okay! Okay!" Calhoun said, dismounting. "No need to get sore about it."

It was two o'clock in the afternoon, and for the first few minutes they sat soaking their handkerchiefs in water and patting their hot skin.

Brian wrapped his kerchief around his neck and started digging through the packs. Without being asked, he had designated himself camp cook.

He found the meat he and Rob had bought for the trip. The only thing he knew for sure would not spoil in the desert heat was canned Spam. He had purchased several cans of it and now set about opening a couple cans for sandwiches

Half an hour later, Calhoun, who had been staring at Brian off and on through out the break, picked up a dead branch from the sand and walked toward Brian. His face showed no emotions, his eyes never wavering from him.

Lying in the warm sand under a small Cholla bush, Brian watched him approach with apprehension. He braced himself, but did not move. *That crazy bastard doesn't scare me none. Just let he come right on.*

As Calhoun got closer to Brian, Virgil, who was watching, put his hand on the old peacemaker 45, slowly drew it from the holster, laid it across his lap pointed at Calhoun and waited.

Clay slowly got to his feet. "Calhoun," he said softly.

"It's alright, Morgan," Calhoun said, without taking his eyes from Brian.

"Now, city boy," he said to Brian. "Don't you move a muscle - just freeze. There's an old rattler wanting to share your shade."

Brian's eyes were open wide as Calhoun eased the stick downward then suddenly flung it upward.

Everyone stared at the dull brown, diamond shaped markings on the body of a huge rattlesnake as it went sailing through the air, its rattles now buzzing loudly.

Brian jumped to his feet and ran in the opposite direction.

Calhoun broke into a harsh laughter and didn't stop for several minutes. Afterwards he looked at Brian. "There!" he said, tossing the stick in the direction of the snake that was still rattling off in the bushes. "He's gone now. You can sit back down."

"No thanks!" Brian replied. "I think I'll stand."

Calhoun headed back toward his horse, turned to look at the five men staring at him and growled, "Can we move on now?"

With the big rattler on their mind, they were eager to get high in the saddle.

Virgil slipped the big gun back into the holster and stood up. Not a step was taken, however, without giving the ground a nervous glance for more snakes.

10

Big Alice and Laura were seated at the bar in the hot saloon. Laura wore a very loose-fitting, pastel blue sack dress and a pair of low cut shoes that looked like they had been casualties of the Civil War.

Laura sat staring at the bar. Though she had raised her voice several times, so far Big Alice hadn't harmed her in any way. In fact, she had given her the dress to replace the torn one. Laura wasn't happy about having to accept anything from her, but at least it was clean and she didn't have to hold it together. Big Alice had also let her take a bath. After scrubbing her skin raw to get rid of the feel of Rockford, she felt better. In fact, she felt grateful to Alice, but she was still determined not to become a prostitute for her.

Big Alice stared at Laura. Teaching her the ropes of being a good working girl had become a chore. Laura wasn't being very cooperative. "Now, you look here, girl. I'm about to lose my patience with you. You're gonna have to cooperate with me. You hear me, girl?"

Laura didn't answer. She stared down at the bar, refusing to give in to Big Alice's prodding.

A huge hand grabbed Laura's face hard and jerked her head around until she was nose to nose with her. "Once again! You see this man walk in. You're at the bar. What do you do?"

Laura began to cry.

Big Alice shoved her away. "I guess you'll just have to go to bed hungry again tonight. I'll not feed you until you decide to cooperate with me. Around here we earn our keep." She motioned for Padro. "Take this little wimp back to her room and make sure the door is locked."

Padro looked Laura up and down for a minute. He used his hand in an effort to smooth the tangles in his long black hair, his mouth drooling on his fu-man-chu type mustache. "Señorita Alice, give her to me. I will break her in proper. You know, like the last one."

Big Alice chuckled and shook her head. "No, Padro. Not yet. I want a healthy girl, not one you've ruined."

Padro grabbed Laura's arm with a huge hand and headed for the back room, dragging her behind of him. At the door, he gave her a violent shove across the room, causing her to go sprawling onto the bed.

Before she could react, he dove upon her, pawing and clawing at her dress. She struggled desperately.

Padro jammed a hand under her dress as he tried to jerk his belt loose with the other.

"PADRO!" Big Alice's great voice thundered through the room. "You heard what I said! If you touch her, I'll cut off your balls!"

Padro lost all interest in sex. He jumped from the bed, eyes wide with fear. He glanced at the door, then at Laura. He knew Alice meant what she said. He tried to straighten Laura's dress. Unable to get it right, he quickly scurried from the room, slamming the door behind him.

The sound of the padlock snapping shut echoed through the dark room as Laura started sobbing hysterically.

11

The small caravan of riders slowly made it's way toward the mountain. By dusk they had reached its base. They rode on, threading their way around the large boulders and the brush. They climbed higher and higher, following an animal trail barely visible in the sand.

Darkness set in fast. Unable to make out the trail, Calhoun called a halt. "No fires," he warned. "We don't want anyone to know we're up here. They might bush-whack us."

Too exhausted to care, the men slowly and painfully climbed from their horses. They stepped gingerly around, in case there were rattlesnakes lurking in the sagebrush. Satisfied the area was clear, the weary men marked their bedding down places in the sand.

When the horses and pack mules had been cared for, Brian and Ken managed to pull a couple more cans of spam and a loaf of bread from the pack. They made sandwiches for everyone. No one complained.

Sunburned, tired, and sore from being in the saddle all day, all fear of snakes, or anything else harmful, was quickly forgotten. Not even the distant yapping of coyotes bothered the men, who minutes after devouring the sandwiches, were sound asleep.

* * *

Loud laughter woke them long before first light.

Startled, Clay jumped from his bedroll, pulling his jacket around his neck to ward off the night chill as he caught sight of Calhoun standing off in the distance laughing as loud as he could.

Virgil stepped up beside Clay. "Something's wrong with that man, Clay. Sure as hell there's something wrong with him."

"Yeah, I think you're right, Virge. We'll have to keep a sharp eye on him from now on."

"You hear that crazy laughing out there?"

Startled by Brian's silent approach and unexpected voice and already spooked by Calhoun, Virgil and Clay jumped.

"Damn you, Brian," Virgil said, "You just scared me out of ten years of life."

Brian chuckled. "Sorry 'bout that. But I heard the noise and came to check."

Clay cupped his hands to his mouth and shouted. "Calhoun! How much further!"

Calhoun stopped in mid-laugh. Sober faced, he walked back to camp, not stopping until he had reached his already saddled horse. "Be there by noon today." Mounting his horse, he rode away.

Five men scrambled to get their horses saddled.

Higher and higher, they climbed, struggling to keep from being unseated by their horses as they stumbled over small boulders and slid on loose rocks. By mid-morning, even though they had been out of the lower desert for some time, it was scorching hot again. The men now knew the true meaning of *desert mountains*. There was no change in the plant life or the heat. Only the ground changed. The higher they went, the rockier it got.

Sweat poured and the canteens stayed busy. The only sounds were the squeaking of saddle leather and the clanking of horseshoes against rocks as the horses picked their way along the now steep, rocky trail.

Off in the distance below them, Clay spotted a large log building. He spurred his horse up beside Calhoun. "What's that place down there, Calhoun?"

Calhoun shaded his eyes with his hand and looked off toward the building. "That's Big Alice's saloon. Best stay clear of there. Bring you nothing but trouble."

Clay's interest was peaked. "What kind of trouble?"

"Been said many a man has disappeared right there. That big black lady has been suspected of killing 'em. Just can't nobody prove it."

"Why is that?"

"You'd have to understand the mountains. Her place is so far out in the wilderness, it's like stepping back into the old west. She's been running whores there for years and ain't nobody ever bothered her. Won't nobody tell the law on her either. She's got no electric or running water like in the Junction." Calhoun spit a string of tobacco juice into the sand. "Look around. Do you see anything for miles around that building?"

"Nope. Looks like it's all alone down there."

"Best stay clear," Calhoun said, spurring his horse ahead.

They rode on. Ever upward. Soon Alice's Saloon was nothing but a small speck below them.

The blistering sun was directly overhead when Calhoun reined to a stop and stepped from his horse. "From here we go on foot." He headed up the steep mountainside.

The boys sat on their horses, watching him climb.

He stopped and looked back. "Well, don't just sit there. Come on. It's just up the grade."

The would-be treasure hunters scrambled to dismount. Tying their horses to some brush, Brian, Ken, Rob, and Virgil scurried up the slope.

Clay was a bit slower. He grabbed a flashlight from his saddlebags, figuring he may need it if the cave was dark. He hurried after the others.

12

$\mathbb{F}$ar below at the log saloon, Big Alice sat on the porch staring through binoculars. She studied the mountains for a long time. Finally she took them down. "Gonzales! Get your ass over here! I got a job for you!" She raised the binoculars back to her eyes.

Gonzales ran to her. "What is it, Señorita Alice? What do you want me to do?"

Big Alice put the binoculars down. "I want you to get in that piece of shit pickup of yours and go to Mr. Rockford's ranch. Tell him there's a pack train of horses with riders heading up the mountain."

She stopped talking to look Gonzales in the face. "Did you understand what I said, Gonzales?"

"Sì, Señorita Alice, I understand good."

"Repeat it back to me."

"Get in piece of shit pickup and go to Señor Rockford - tell him many riders on mountain," Gonzales said proudly.

She shook her head and waved him off. "I guess that'll have to do. Now hurry along! You know Rockford always wants to know who is up here. Thinks he owns the whole goddamn mountain."

Gonzales scurried out to a beatup old pickup parked in the yard and jumped in. When it started, the blast of the exhaust without a muffler was deafening. The old truck went roaring down the sandy road, leaving in its wake a dust stream much like that of a high flying jet.

Big Alice put the binoculars back to her eyes. "I wonder what they're after up there?" she said aloud to no one in particular.

13

Climbing for five or ten minutes, the hopeful treasure hunters rounded a large outcropping of rock to find Calhoun sitting on the ground, waiting for them.

Clay flopped down near him, gasping for breath. "So? Where is it?"

"There." Calhoun pointed to a small, but very distinctive, opening just above their heads.

While they took a minute to catch their breath, Clay checked his flashlight to see that it worked. It did. They rushed to the small opening in the mountain.

This time Calhoun followed them.

Clay slipped his hand holding the flashlight through the opening, then his head. He could see the cave was shaped like a large bubble. He could not see what was in the rear of it. They would have to go inside. He turned to Calhoun. "You sure it's safe to go in there?"

"Sure, come on." Calhoun disappeared through the opening.

The boys looked at each other and hurried in after him.

They were amazed to find that they could actually stand up inside the cave. It was like a large dome, with what appeared to be a couple of openings in the back wall.

"Over there." Calhoun pointed to something on the floor. "There's the Spanish breast plates."

His heart pounding with anticipation, Clay turned the light beam in the direction Calhoun was pointing. It lit up an object lying on the floor. They eased closer. The light focused on several old, rusty tin cans. The pounding in Clay's ears eased. He looked at Calhoun. Surely that bastard knows the difference between a bean can and an armor breastplate, he thought.

"The skeleton is over by that large rock in back," Norman said.

Once again they advanced further into the cave. The light beam struck something white.

"Jesus! It is bones!" Clay said, casting the light around. "More bones!" He moved closer to get a better look at them. When he did, his heart sank. He could see they were too small to be human. Finally the light fell upon a skull. Clay looked up. "Well, this definitely is not human. Must be from a goat or sheep."

Clay glanced at Calhoun. He was standing back a ways watching them. He had a big grin on his face. Suddenly, it dawned on Clay that they had been made fools of. His face grew hot with anger. He lit Calhoun up with the light. "You bastard!"

Before anyone could react, a terrifying roar filled the cave. Clay swung the light upward just in time to catch the gleam of white teeth in the mouth of a mountain lion ready to pounce on them.

Screaming and yelling at the top of their voices, everyone ran for the cave opening.

The lion leaped and caught Ken, slamming him to the ground. Growling and clawing, it tore at his flesh. Ken screamed and beat the lion with his fists as he struggled to keep it from getting to his throat.

Clay had just started through the opening when Ken screamed. He spun around and rushed back, even though he was scared. He didn't know what he could do, but he knew he had to help. He also knew he didn't stand a chance against the big cat.

Ken was striking the cat with his arms and fists, but it kept trying to get at his throat. Struggling to remain clear headed, he threw his arms across his throat to protect it. The cat's front claws dug deep into his chest. Screaming in pain, he fought to keep his arms between his throat and the cat's long fangs. Ken tried to roll onto his side, but the cat sank its fangs deep into his right shoulder.

Virgil had rushed back behind Clay. He jerked his old pistol from the holster and pointed it at the cat, trying to get a clear shot without hitting Ken.

When Ken rolled the other way, the cat bit down on his left shoulder. He knew he was going to die. Far off in the distance he could hear someone yelling and see a flash of light now and then.

Clay was only a foot or so away from the cat. Shining his light into the big cat's eyes, he screamed at the top of his voice, hoping to either scare it away or blind it. It didn't work. As a last resort, he ran up and hit the cat on the head with the light.

The attacking cat slashed out at him with its claw, but Clay jumped clear. Turning its attention back to Ken, the cat once again tried to get at his throat. Ken's screams filled the cave as the cat bit into his arms.

Clay saw Virgil aiming the gun. "Shoot the damned thing! Shoot it, Virge!"

"I can't get a clear shot!" Virgil knew he had the only means to kill the cat. He had to get close. Ignoring his own terror, he ran right up to the cat, stuck the gun barrel against its head and pulled the trigger.

The explosion from the .45 peacemaker was deafening, but the big tawny beast fell on Ken's chest.

Clay stopped yelling, but continued to wave his free arm and hold the light steady on the cat. It didn't move. It looked dead.

Ken lay gasping for breath. He struggled to get the 200 pounds of dead weight off his chest. The cat's body flopped to the cave floor.

Virgil poked at the cat with the gun barrel. The gun was cocked and ready to shoot again if it moved. It didn't. It was dead.

Clay was scared. He dropped to his knees beside Ken. "Are you alright, Ken?"

"Hell, no. I'm not alright," Ken whimpered, with tears running down his face. "I'm clawed and bit all over my body." His voice got even lower. "Besides that, I think I've shit my pants!"

Clay let out a deep breath. He was relieved. Ken was talking. At least he wasn't dead. Not yet anyway.

By now everyone was back in the cave and trying to help Ken. Clay looked up. "Rob, run to the horses and grab the first aid kit! Hurry!"

Rob scrambled through the opening.

Clay bent over Ken, examining his wounds.

Ken knew he was hurt but didn't know how badly. He could only imagine what the lion had done to him. He had seen movies of mountain lions attacking people and animals. The lions had always made their kill. He was scared. He grabbed Clay by the front of his shirt and shook him. "I'm going to die, Clay. Oh, my God! I'm going to die."

"You're not going to die, Ken. Just relax. You'll be alright."

"No! I'm going to die!" He shook Clay. "Clay, please don't let me die way out here in this god forsaken wilderness!"

Clay grabbed Ken and shook him hard. "Shut up, Ken!" Clay pulled Ken's hands from his shirt. "Just shut up and listen to me."

Ken grew quiet. His eyes searching Clay's for the truth.

He pointed to the wounds. "Ken, I know they hurt, but most of the claw marks are just deep scratches. Oh, they'll need stitches, but you're not gonna die from them. You're gonna be okay. We'll patch you up and get you to a doctor."

Ken wanted to believe Clay. He settled down a little.

Clay examined his wounds. He found several deep scratches, almost like knife cuts, but no artery or large vein damage.

Brian gave Ken a nervous grin. "Scared the shit out of me, too, Ken. But don't you worry none, we won't tell a soul."

A burst of sadistic laughter came from Calhoun. He stood near the opening.

Jumping to his feet, Clay charged him.

Calhoun stopped laughing.

Clay stopped nose to nose with Calhoun. "You son-of-a-bitch! You knew all along that there was no gold here. You knew there were no Spanish breast plates or skeletons here!"

Calhoun chuckled. "That's right, city boy! I knew it. I find it great sport fooling you dumb boys from big city. Besides, you all look like you could use the sunshine and exercise!"

"You mean you've done it to others?" Clay was furious.

Calhoun danced about like a crazy man. "Hell, yes! Works every time, every time! Been doing it for years! It's my hobby! My hobby! Why do you think they call me Crazy Norman! Crazy Norman! That's me! The C in my name stands for Crazy!"

Calhoun's laughter was cut short as Clay's fist landed square in his face. Calhoun fell sprawling onto the floor. Before anyone could move, he sprang to his feet and pulled his pistol. "Get back! All of you get back or I'll kill you!" He pointed the gun at Virgil. "Give me that hog leg you got there, mister. Make the wrong move and you're a dead man."

Virgil entertained thoughts of trying to draw and shoot, but knew he wouldn't stand a chance. Besides, as crazy as Calhoun was, he might kill everybody. He slowly drew the pistol from its holster and handed it to Calhoun.

Rob crawled into the cave with the first aid kit. He stood up and looked around. "What the hell's going on?"

Calhoun pointed the pistol at Rob. "Get over there with the others! Now!"

Rob eased over to stand beside Clay.

Nervously, Calhoun swung the pistol from one man to the next. He chuckled. "Grab your friend and start walking to the rear of the cave. "Do it! Now!"

"He needs medical attention right now," Clay said.

Calhoun cocked the pistol. "He won't need anything if you don't get him and move back." He fired a shot into the roof of the cave. The concussion of the blast hurt their ears.

Clay and Rob helped Ken to his feet and they hurriedly made their way to the rear of the cave.

The cave was dark and they had to fumble their way along, feeling the walls. Ken was moaning from the pain. Clay stopped. He looked back over his shoulder. He couldn't see Calhoun. He had no idea what to do. The man was mad. Clay was sure he would kill them if they tried to resist. "Calhoun..."

"I said keep moving," Calhoun shouted. He fired a volley of shots. The blasts thundered in the ears of the greenhorns as they ducked low to avoid ricocheting bullets and scurried further into the darkness of the cave.

Calhoun stood listening to the sound of the men stumbling ahead. He chuckled and did a little dance. A loud growl broke the silence of the cave. Calhoun looked at the mountain lion. It was struggling to get to its feet. The lion had not been dead, only stunned. Calhoun dove through the opening in the cave and raced down the grade laughing madly.

As the sounds faded in the distance ahead of them, the greenhorns stumbled ahead, following the cave as it twisted through the mountain, branching off in several places. Which branch was the right one, they could only guess.

Clay stopped the others. "Listen up a minute," he cautioned.

Back the way they had came, they could hear the lion growling in the distance.

"Boys, we're in deep shit now, Clay said. "We've got either another lion back there or we just wounded that one and he sounds mad as hell. And that's not to mention a crazy man with a gun." He turned to look ahead. "I have no idea where this cave leads, but we're going to have to follow it."

Ken groaned. He cursed himself for changing his mind about coming on this trip. He should have listened to his mother. He would be back in L.A., enjoying all the girls around her swimming pool right now. Instead he was here probably dying from the mauling the mountain lion gave him. "What if it just dead ends? What do we do then?"

Clay looked down at him. "I don't know, Ken. We'll just have to cross that bridge when we come to it. Right now, we have to get you patched up."

"And cleaned up a little," Rob remarked, holding his nose.

Dropping his head, Ken muttered. "I can do the cleaning if you'll just give me a minute." He tore some strips from his shirttail and stood looking at Rob and Clay until they moved a little further down the cave.

Virgil walked over to glare at Brian. "C for *Crazy* Norman Calhoun. I hope we live to see that bastard again."

Shrinking away from his glare, Brian tried to explain. "How was I to know? He sounded straight - didn't he? You guys heard him. Didn't he sound straight?"

Ken walked back to them.

Rob sniffed. "That's better. Now lay down and let me and Clay patch you up."

When Ken got stretched out on the cave floor, Clay and Rob set to work on his injuries.

Brian was still at it. "Well, didn't he sound straight, Clay"?

Clay looked over at Brian. "Yeah-yeah, we heard him. Now get over here and hold this light for us."

Brian jumped at the chance to get away from Virgil's intense gaze.

With Brian holding the light, Clay stripped off Ken's shirt. Most of the bleeding had stopped. There were several nasty looking deep claw marks on his chest and shoulders. There were puncture marks from the cat's teeth on both his shoulders near the neck. *Close,* Clay thought. *Damn close.* He applied medicated ointment to each scratch and bite. He and Rob wrapped Ken's upper body in gauze and helped him put his bloody, shredded shirt back on.

They stepped back to look over their work. Clay shook his head. "Well, it don't look like much, but maybe it'll do 'til we get to outta here and back to town."

Virgil flopped down on the cool stone floor of the cave. As cool as it was he was sweating. He could feel the walls of the cave closing in on him. He closed his eyes. "I don't like this at all, Clay."

Clay sat down beside him. His eyes were more accustomed to the darkness now and he could see outlines of the others. "What's wrong, Virge, you sick?"

"Not sick. I have claustrophobia and I hate being cooped up inside this narrow ass hole in the ground."

Clay stared at him. *Virgil with claustrophobia? That's hard to believe. I've never seen him be anything but cool in any situation. Maybe he's experiencing the same feelings I get when I fly.* Clay looked both ways, but couldn't see anything. "Just relax, Virgil, we're gonna find a way outta here soon."

Brian sat against the opposite wall of the cave. He was visibly upset. His face was red and the veins in his neck stood out. Any other time, he would have used better judgement in dealing with someone like Calhoun, but this time, the thrill of being in pursuit of gold had diminished his good judgement. It was for that reason they were all now sitting on death's doorstep. "I'll kill that bastard when I catch up with him." He shook his fist in the direction they had come. "Calhoun! You son-of-a-bitch! I'm going to wring your scrawny neck! You hear me?" His voice echoed through the cave.

No one spoke for a few minutes. They listened intently. In the distance they could hear another echo of low growling. It could have just another echo of Brian's voice, or it could have been the lion, but they were convinced it was Calhoun.

Virgil opened his eyes and turned to Clay. "You hear that? I think that crazy bastard is still laughing at us."

"I'm telling you he is," Clay replied. "He's a damn lunatic!"

Ken moaned again.

Clay got up and rumbled through the first aid kit. He was glad Rob had managed to get it. He came up with some aspirin. He looked around. There was no water for Ken to take the pills with. He'd have to swallow them dry.

Looking over at Ken, Clay saw that he was still shaking. Either from fear or shock. Why in the hell did it have to happen to Ken? He was the only man who really didn't want to be here. The only one who was really afraid. Clay reached in his pocket and pulled out the pills he had gotten from Doctor Johnson. Maybe one of these would settle him down a little. Wouldn't hurt to try.

He walked over to Ken and handed him the pills. "Aspirin and a little something for your nerves, my friend. No water. Do your best to get 'em down in a hurry. Otherwise, they leave a foul taste in your mouth."

Ken managed to swallow the pills without too much difficulty.

Looking around at his friends, Clay knew they were in a pickle and he was responsible. He had gotten them into this mess and it was up to him to get them out. He glanced off down the cave. Nothing but darkness. He reached for the flashlight Brian was stilling holding. He flashed the light on the cave's ceiling of dark rough-pitted stone. It looked like a naturally formed, narrow cave probably carved through the rock by the molten lava of one of the many volcanoes that had given birth to these mountains maybe a million years earlier. It might meander for miles under the mountain. Clay knew they were in for a rough time, but at least the cave was cool. It felt good on his sun burned skin.

Clay was worried. He knew they couldn't go back the way they had come. The wounded mountain lion's growls could still be heard in the distance. Besides, there was crazy Calhoun to contend with. He might still be lurking around the opening of the cave waiting for them to come out so he could kill them all. Who would ever know? They'd have to try to find another way out. "We'd better get started looking for a way out. I'll lead the way with the light. Rob, you and Brian help Ken, Virgil you cover the rear. Better listen good for that damned lion. I got no idea what a wounded lion will do."

"Okay, but just bear in mind that we're roughing it," Virgil said, his voice a little shaking.

"Yeah, and don't forget we're having an adventure," groaned Ken. "Why in the hell did I ever let you guys talk me into doing this shit?"

Rob and Brian exchanged glances. They didn't comment. They pulled Ken to his feet and followed Clay, watching the floor of the cave for rattlesnakes, spiders, and such, while cautiously casting nervous glances over their shoulders for any vengeful lion.

Stumbling over the rough surface of the cave floor inside the bowels of a mountain without food or water, Clay, already miserable with sunburns, saddle sores, and lack of rest, began to realize just how dangerous the wilderness really was. He also began to realize for the first time that they might not survive this great American adventure he had so longed for. He shined the light back at Ken. He seemed calmer now, not shaking. The pills must be working. He turned back to the task at hand - finding a way out.

For hours, the men struggled along, cursing when they stubbed a toe or stumbled over a large rock in their path.

Virgil was having a hard time. Even in the coolness of the cave, sweat soaked his clothing. His heart pounded loudly in his ears and his breathing was labored. Claustrophobia had a grip on him. He fought to control the urge to break into a run - to get out into the open. He was near panic when Clay finally stopped.

"We'll stop here and try to get some rest," Clay said. He didn't have to say it twice. The others fell to the floor exhausted. Virgil leaned back against the wall of the cave and closed his eyes, trying hard to control his fear.

"I take the first watch while you guys try to sleep. Virgil, I'll wake you in a couple of hours. You wake Rob and so on."

Virgil didn't answer. He opened his eyes, looking around frantically.

Clay leaned closer to him. He could see Virgil was shaking and his eyes were wild with the look of fear. The claustrophobia! He had forgotten all about it, and he knew Virgil was not one to complain. Clay sat a minute trying to think. He knew there was nothing in the first aid kit to help what Virgil had. Then he remembered the pills in his pocket. Hell, they were for this very thing. He quickly fumbled in his pocket and pulled out the bottle. Shaking one into his hand, he reached over to Virgil. "Here, Virge," he said in a low voice. "Get this down. It'll take the edge off."

Virgil welcomed anything that might help. His hand shook as he struggled to retrieve the pill and get it into his mouth. It was another chore to get it swallowed. He looked at Clay, gave him a weak nod and leaned back, closing his eyes again.

Clay sat back, keeping an eye on him as best he could in the darkness.

Fifteen minutes later, Virgil had settled down and was sound asleep.

With the cave wall supporting his weary back muscles, Clay let his thoughts wander back to Van Nuys and his wife, Judie. They had been married nearly twenty years and already this was the longest time he had spent away from her. Would he ever see her again? What about the children? Both were in their teens. What would become of them without a father? What would become of Judie if he died here in this hellhole of darkness? Why had he ever considered undertaking such a foolish venture when he had absolutely no experience in survival tactics? He cursed himself for allowing Calhoun to persuade them to rush off after *his* lost Dutchman's gold mine. He should have recognized that Calhoun was not all there. Instead of using his God given common sense, he had let gold fever be his guide and now he and his closest friends were probably going to die.

Clay shook the thoughts from his head. *No. Hell, no. We're not going to die under this damned mountain. I'll get us out of here somehow.* He stared off into the darkness as the heavy snores of four miserable men broke the deep silence of the cave.

14

$\mathbb{A}$ thick dust cloud rose in front of the beat-up old truck as it slid to a halt in front of the hacienda of the Rockford ranch. Jamming gears and cutting the engine, Gonzales jumped out and headed toward the porch. Danny Wiscoff and Tom Davis, each one holding an automatic rifle, blocked his way.

"I must see Señor Rockford right away," Gonzales stuttered in his broken English, as he removed his hat.

"What business do you have with Mr. Rockford that makes you drive like that in his yard, Gonzales?" Davis demanded.

"Señorita Alice sends me, she say I must hurry."

"You just wait right here," said Davis, heading for the door. But before he could reach the door handle, it swung open.

Rockford strolled out. "What's all the excitement, Tom?"

"Gonzales here says Big Alice sent him to tell you something."

Pushing past Davis, Gonzales rushed onto the porch. "Señor Rockford! Señorita Alice say tell you there are many men on the mountain," His hands nervously fidgeting with his sombrero.

"Who are they?" Rockford asked.

"I do not know, Señor, but Alice say they have pack horses, too."

"Okay, Gonzales. Thanks for the message." He turned to Davis. "Tom, you and Danny get the chopper ready. We'll take a run up there come morning."

Both men rushed off toward the side yard where the blue helicopter was tied down.

Rockford turned back to Gonzales. "Go tell Alice that I'll handle the men on the mountain at once." He turned away, but stopped and called after Gonzales, who was running for the pickup. "Hold on there, Gonzales."

Gonzales stopped and looked back.

"Does Alice still have that little filly I gave her?"

"Sì, Señor. She is kept in the back room all the time. She gives Alice nothing but trouble. She's a stubborn one alright."

A wicked grin broke Rockford's sharply chiseled face. "Good. Looks like I'll see her again sooner than I expected," Rockford laughed.

15

Loud laughter echoed through the canyons. Silhouetted against the setting sun, Crazy Norman rode wildly down the mountainside with his head thrown back and mouth wide open. Five riderless horses and two mules followed the old man as he crashed through the thick brush. Without notice, he passed an old hand-painted sign partially covered by brush.

Had he been paying attention, he would have seen the name Riley at the bottom of the sign. It warned:

NO TRESPASN HER.
SHOT ON SITE.
FRED RILEY CLAIM.

Norman was still laughing when the first shot rang out. It ricocheted off a nearby rock. He knew at once what he had done. Reining up hard, he looked around, cupped his hands to his mouth. "Hold on there, Riley! It's me! Crazy Norman! I'm just passing through! I won't stop on your Claim!"

When no more shots were fired, Norman raised his hands high and clucked his horse into a walk. He continued his cautious position for several minutes. When he was sure he was off old Riley's claim, he spurred his horse into an easy gait.

Norman looked back over his shoulder. The other horses had caught up with him. He wondered where the greenhorns were. He knew they would follow his tracks. It was their only hope of finding their way back to town. He chuckled. Even city boys should be able to follow the tracks left by eight horses and mules.

Grinning his crazy grin, he wondered how they were going to like old man Riley's welcome when they crossed his place.

Lost in his thoughts of what he had done to the city boys, Norman had failed to stay alert. Suddenly, there was a swishing noise on a rock just above his head. He turned in time to see the bright glint of the sun on a huge steel blade as it swung at his head.

Norman felt a twinge of pain, then nothing as his head flopped to the ground, quickly followed by his body.

A loud scream from the rock above echoed through the valleys and spooked the horses into a dead run. Racing down the path, they headed for home.

On the rock, a wild looking man dressed in tattered buckskin danced a jig as he yelled in an unknown tongue and swung the huge machete around and around his head. His long, shaggy, white hair swirled about his white bearded face as he danced.

Just as sudden as his attack on Norman had started, the wild man stopped screaming and jumped from the rock. He grabbed Norman's head by the hair, lifted it high and danced away through the brush, chattering to himself.

Crazy Norman Calhoun had guided his last group of city boys into the mountain wilderness!

16

Clay was shivering when he opened his eyes and looked around. He was lying in a fetal position on the cold floor of the cave and his body ached all over. He tried to preserve his body heat by not moving. As he lay there he could hear Ken groaning and saw Brian standing against the wall of the cave, watching back the way that they had come.

Ken groaned again.

Clay pulled himself to his feet and stretched. God, he was thirsty. His stomach growled reminding him that they had not eaten since breakfast the day before. He searched around the floor for the first aid kit. He found it near Rob who was snoring loudly. Clay fumbled through the kit until he found the aspirins, and shook three into his hand. He pulled his own pills from his pocket and shook one out. He looked over at Virgil who was just waking up. Clay popped another pill from the bottle, made his way to Ken and knelt beside him.

Ken stared up at him. His eyes in pain.

"Got some more good dope for you, buddy," Clay said, handing four pills to Ken.

Tossing the pills into his mouth, Ken tried to swallow. He gagged, but managed to get them down his dry throat. "Thanks, Clay," he said, his voice shivering.

With the other pill still in his hand, Clay eased over to Virgil and slipped it to him. "Something to wake up to."

Virgil sat up and swallowed the pill. He hadn't asked Clay what it was. He trusted him enough to know it wouldn't hurt him to take it. Whatever he had given him last night had done the trick. He had slept like a log and felt much better this morning. With the one he just took, maybe, just maybe he might get through the day.

Clay knew he had to get Ken out of the cave some way. "Okay, you guys, let's get this show on the road."

Moaning and groaning, the others struggled to their feet and, with Virgil and Rob helping Ken, shuffled further into the cave, following the light Clay held in his hand.

An hour later, without warning, Clay's feet slipped on a downward slope on the cave floor. The flashlight flew from his hand and fell to the floor as Clay struggled to keep his footing. He found himself sliding downward into the darkness. He yelled out and fought to get a grip on anything to stop his plunge as he gained speed. His rear end and back burned with pain as he bounced against the rough stone. He splashed into something soft. Something like mud. He slid to a stop. There was a strong stench in the air. Like something dead and rotting. He lay still, afraid to move. There might be another drop off.

"Clay!" Virgil yelled from above. "Clay where are you?"

Clay opened his eyes. He could see Virgil's light dancing off the wall. Except for the burning on his back and rear, he felt okay. "Down here!" he yelled.

Instantly, a loud flapping noise and squeaks filled the cave as thousands of bats, frightened from their ceiling roost, frantically darted away from Clay.

As the light flashed on him, Clay looked around. He knew what he had slid into that felt like mud. It was bat droppings. *Bats! I'm lying in a pool of bat shit!*

Now the stink was extremely strong. He tried to hold his breath as he struggled to get to his feet. In seconds, the bats were gone and the cave was silent.

"Clay, are you alright?" Virgil yelled again.

"Yeah, just roughed up a bit," Clay replied, as he gained his footing. "But I smell awful." With the aid of the light dancing around, he was able to see that he was in a larger size cave. His mind raced as he searched the ceiling and walls and further down the cave. Bats! Bats! Bats had to have a way into the cave. His eyes fell upon a hint of light against the wall further down the cave. "Cut your light a minute, Virgil!"

Clay was engulfed in darkness. A few seconds later, as his eyes become more accustomed to the darkness, he spotted what he had been looking at. It really was light shining in the distance. "I can see light up ahead, Virgil! I think it might be a way out."

Virgil flashed the light down again.

Clay looked up. The cave floor sloped upward to where Virgil stood with the light. It looked to be some hundred feet or so. "Virgil, see if you guys can climb down here without falling. Bat crap is six inches deep."

Clay shook his hands and arms to get as much bat droppings off as he could, then waded to the cave wall and leaned against it, watching the slow downward progress of his friends as they picked their way to him.

"Jesus, it stinks down here," Rob remarked, as he neared Clay.

"If you fall, you'll find out just how stinky it can get. Better stay clear of me, I'm covered in it," Clay warned.

When everyone had safely made their way down the incline, they staggered toward the distant light and, hopefully, a way out.

Clay approached the small circle of light. The opening was about three or four feet in diameter and was partially covered by weeds on the outside. He pushed the weeds back with the flashlight, watching for scorpions, spiders, and snakes. When he was sure it was clear, he eased his head through the opening. A feeling of relief come over him. They were outside on the west side of the mountain, the same side they had entered on.

The sun was midway in the eastern sky when he climbed out and stood up. *Damn, as hot as it already is, it sure feels good.* "Come on out, boys, we've made it," he called back into the opening. He looked at his watch. It was nine o'clock. They had been in the cave only twenty-one hours, but it had seemed like days to Clay.

He helped pull Ken through the opening, trying not to cause him any more pain than he was already in.

The others followed close behind. When they were all out, they dropped to the ground to rest and began wiping the bat droppings from their boots with sage bushes and hot sand.

Almost completely covered with the bat droppings from his slide down the slope, Clay looked around for something to clean with.

"Clay, could you move a little further away from me? You smell like bat shit," Rob said, with a chuckle.

"Okay! Okay! I get the drift!" Clay stripped off his shirt and pants and stood in his silk boxer shorts, beating them on the bushes. When all the loose droppings were gone, he rubbed the clothes in the hot sand. Finally, he shook them and looked them over. "That'll have to do 'til we get back to town." He reluctantly put the stinking clothes back on.

"You can sit next to me anytime, Clay," Virgil offered. "You got me outta that damned cave into the open air. I don't think I could have survived very long in there."

Clay paid no attention; he was looking the area over. He shook his head and looked around again. "I don't believe this."

"What don't you believe," Brian asked.

"Look right up there about three hundred yards to the north. That's the hole we went in at noon yesterday."

Virgil jumped to his feet. He searched the mountainside. "The son-of-a-bitch took all the horses and the pack mules!"

"We gotta find that trail we came up on. It's our only hope," Rob remarked. "Was anyone paying any attention to the way we came?"

They looked at each other. No one had paid attention.

"Best we can do is try to find the horses' tracks and follow them backward," Clay said as he got to his feet and started searching the ground. Brian stayed with Ken as the others began a circular pattern search. A half-hour later, Clay found the first sign. "I think I have the tracks over here," he called out.

When the others, along with Ken and Brian, had joined him, Clay pointed out tracks that indicated the horses were running back down the trail. As the blistering sun beat down on them, they headed back down the mountain, following the tracks. At least now they had a chance to make it back alive.

17

Rockford stood looking off toward the mountains while Davis and Wiscoff climbed aboard the helicopter. When Wiscoff had the motor warmed up and ready to go, he climbed into the seat and motioned upward.

Once they were airborne, Davis, seated in the rear, checked his automatic rifle. The Uzi 9MM automatic had a fold out wire stock. Davis kept folding and unfolding it. He loved guns. They could make people do anything you wanted them to do. He grinned and slapped the side of the weapon. "Great piece, Boss. We going to use it today?"

"Maybe. But first let's see who they are. You know Alice; she might be setting me up. It might be the sheriff's own posse she wants me to fire on. No, we'll wait and see. I don't trust that woman."

Half an hour later, Wiscoff pointed down. "Look at that, Boss! Horses!"

Rockford leaned closer to the door and opened it. He stuck his head out and stared down at six horses and two mules making their way down the slope. The horses had empty saddles and the mules had loaded packs.

Rockford scanned the terrain. "Something sure got them spooked."

"Want to go after them, Boss?" Danny shouted.

"No, let's go up on the mountain and see if we can spot anyone. Those empty saddles tell me there are people on foot somewhere."

They flew on.

When Alice's place appeared in the distance, Rockford leaned toward Wiscoff and pointed. "Let's make a quick stop and see Alice. Maybe she's got more information by now."

Danny eased the stick back. The helicopter slowly slipped downward to a smooth landing in front of the saloon. The down wind from its rotor blades blasted everything and everyone near it with sand and brush.

Rockford climbed out. Bending over to avoid the swirling rotor blades, he headed for the porch where Alice was perched, fanning their dust away.

"Good morning, my big beauty," he called out cheerfully. "I came as soon as you beckoned."

"Bullshit, Rockford! You came 'cause you don't want nobody prowling them mountains but your own self. Now, get on up here so I don't have to look down at your nasty ass."

Rockford walked up on the porch and sat down beside her. "What we got up there, Alice? Think they're anyone to worry about?"

"Now, you know as much as I do about them people up there. I seen five - six riders and two pack mules headed toward old Weaver's Needle yesterday just befo' noon. Ain't seen 'em since."

"I saw some riderless horses heading down the mountain as I was coming up here, Alice. Had to be their horses. Bet they're on foot up there."

"Could be." Alice picked up the binoculars and trained them on the mountain.

"See anything up there now?"

"Not a movement."

"Let me have a look," Rockford reached for the binoculars.

Alice held the binoculars away from him. "You think your eyes any better than mine?"

"No, Alice. I just want to look. Please, may I have the binoculars?"

Alice handed him the glasses.

Rockford focused on the upper mountain terrain. He saw nothing. Rising from his seat he called to Davis, who was swooning around a couple girls hanging out a bedroom window. "Davis, get away from those whores and come here."

"Watch yo' smart mouth, Rockford. I done told you I got no 'hoes here," Alice scorned. "These gals are up-right working ladies, every last one."

Rockford looked at the girls, "Where's the new one?"

"Still in the lock up. Ornery little shit just won't give in. Gonna take some time, I reckon - but then I got all the time in the world, ain't I, Rockford?"

"Yeah, I reckon you have, Alice, all the time in the world," he answered. "Just make sure you turn her out, though. I promised her that."

Without waiting for her answer, Rockford turned to his pilot. "Danny, let's take a ride up the mountain."

The typical chop-chop-chop of the blue helicopter's motor echoed through the canyons as Rockford and his two men kept their eyes on the ground below, looking for any sign of life. They cruised several canyons and valleys but came up with nothing. Then Davis pointed out the window. "There's a bunch of people down there. Have a look, Boss."

Rockford could see several tiny specks moving slowly along a mountain path. "Dammit! Get this crate down close enough to see who they are!"

Within seconds, they hovered just above the heads of the five treasure hunters.

Rockford watched them start waving frantically. He could see one was heavily bandaged and being held up by two others.

Rockford let out an evil chuckle. "Well, I'll be damned. It's that same bunch of city guys from old Gus' Saloon."

Wiscoff flew the chopper past the group and then circled again. "Looks like they're heading toward old Fred Riley's claim, Boss."

"Want I should give 'em a little fire, Boss? Maybe pay 'em back for what they did to you at the saloon?" Tom asked eagerly.

Rockford glared at him, then chuckled again. "I ought to, but there's no need for us to waste bullets on 'em when old Fred'll likely shoot 'em before they get past his claim. That is if the heat don't get 'em first."

Below, Clay Morgan and his friends waved and yelled at the helicopter. Clay cupped his hands and shouted over the roar of the engine. "Help! We need help!"

Virgil pointed at the injured Ken. "We have an injured man here! Land that thing and help us!"

They could see three men in the helicopter laughing, but couldn't clearly make out their faces because of the reflection on the glass.

Clay stopped yelling and turned to Virgil. "It's no use, Virge. They're not going to help. Look at the bastards! They're laughing at us."

Virgil stopped waving and stood with his hands on his hips as the helicopter slowly slipped away and dropped off in the distance. "Well, what the hell you think their problem was?"

Clay watched the helicopter disappear. "I don't know, Virge. Just mean ass people, I guess." He turned to Ken. "I guess it's back in my arms, old boy." He took Ken's arm and put it around his neck. "Rob, you and Brian take the point. Just keep following this trail. Virge and I'll tote Ken."

* * *

The sun showed no mercy on the boys as they trudged on, ever downward. They had stopped sweating long ago, their bodies slowly dehydrating. Clay had read about people dying of thirst. He knew a man could live for 20 or 30 days without food, but only a few days without water under normal conditions. Out here, in the blistering heat, it would not take long. They hadn't had any water since early the day before and thirst was now their main concern. The only thing he knew to do was stop and rest in some type of shade as often as possible. He could see the others were barely able to struggle along. He called a halt.

Exhausted, their lips parched and cracked, they slumped down under any bush big enough to cast a shadow. "Virge, you remember seeing any water on the way up?" Clay asked.

Virgil thought for a minute. "No, can't say as I did."

Brian was still trying to make amends for getting them involved with Crazy Norman. He stood up. "You guys stay here and rest. I'll scout ahead for water."

"No, Brian. We'd better stick together. All we need now is for us to get separated out here," Clay said.

Brian dropped his head and kicked at the sand. "Well, you know I'll do it. I'd like to do something to make up for this mess I got us into."

"You didn't get us into this mess, Brian," Virgil said. "We got ourselves into it. We're big boys, you know. We could have backed out any time."

Brian looked up at Virgil. He had respect for the quiet man and felt uplifted by his words. "Thanks, Virge. Glad you feel that way."

"Whhoooooo! Whhoooooo! Whhoooooo!"

Everyone jumped at the hooting of the owl as it flew low over their heads.

Rob ducked. "What the hell...?"

Brian grabbed his hat. "Holy Shit! If that old bird had been any lower, he'd have been right in our laps!"

"If he gets close enough, we'll have some owl stew," Rob remarked. "I'm so hungry I could eat anything right now."

They watched the huge owl fly to a saguaro cactus some distance away and land.

"They say owls don't often fly around in the day time," Virgil said, settling back in the sand under a large sage bush. "I hear they taste like chicken."

"Yeah, well, right now, as hungry as I am, I'd trade a whole chicken for just a cup of water," Clay replied.

The owl was quickly forgotten as they each sought shelter from the scorching sun.

Clay shifted his body to move with the shadow of the Cholla bush. He looked around their dry, desolate, resting-place. Suddenly, a movement off in the brush caught his eye. *My God! It's an Indian!* He stared at the Indian for a moment. He couldn't believe his eyes. He rubbed them and looked again. It was still there. He looked around at his friends. They were paying no attention. He quickly looked back. *What the hell? It really is an Indian.*

The Indian was standing with his arms folded across his chest. He wore buckskin vest and loincloth over cloth shirt and pants, with high buckskin boot like leggings laced in place with rawhide strings. He also wore a cloth headdress. Clay was sure it was an Apache. He had seen pictures of them. This one also wore a beaded breastplate, which Clay assumed identified him as a chief.

Still in awe, Clay watched the Indian bend over and pluck something from a cactus. He straightened and held the object up for Clay to see. Then he began eating it.

"Hey! Hey, you!" Clay called out.

The Indian faded from sight.

Virgil looked over at Clay. "Who you yelling at, Clay?"

"Didn't you guys see that?" Clay asked, rubbing his eyes.

"See what?" Virgil asked.

Clay looked at each of them. It was plain they had not seen the Indian. "Nothing." He shook his head. "Must be the heat." He wasn't about to tell them he had seen an Indian and that it had faded right before his eyes. He sat for a minute staring at the place the Indian had stood. His curiosity got the best of him and he rose to his feet.

Walking over to where he had seen the Indian, he looked for tracks in the sand. There were none. He looked around. Nothing. His tracks were there, but no Indian tracks. *Something isn't right here.* He looked back at his friends. They were all there. He could see them and everything else clearly. The heat wasn't playing with his mind. Maybe he did see an Indian. He turned back to the spot where the Indian had stood. Still no tracks but his eyesight fell on a small cactus. It was spread out over the ground and had thick, flat leaves like Mickey Mouse ears with small yellow pear shaped bulbs.

"Well, I'll be damned," Clay said softly. "I'll just be damned! A prickly pear cactus!" He jerked his knife from its sleath and hacked away the prickly thorns that adorned the cactus near the bulbs. He cut off several bulbs and hurried back to the others.

"Hey! Hey, you guys! I got us some water and food too!" Rushing to them, he passed around the bulbs.

Virgil looked at the little plant in his hand. "What the hell is this?"

"Peel the outside and suck on the inside part for the moisture, then eat the pulp. It's nutritious!"

Skeptical, they sat staring at the yellow cactus bulbs.

Clay watched them for a second or two. "For Christ's sakes! It's a prickly pear cactus! I thought you guys were engineers! Hell's fire, boys, we studied about this little jewel in high school. Don't you remember that?"

"I've heard of barrel cactus being a source of water, but prickly pear . . ," Rob said.

"I had forgotten all about it growing out here until that...uh..." Clay paused and looked at his friends. "Uh...go ahead and try it. It tastes terrible, but it's safe to eat. The...uh...Indians called these little things pears. They lived on them for years."

"How do you know that?" Brian asked.

"I read about how these little cacti sustained the Indians and saved many a prospector from dying of thirst out here."

Clay took a long suck on the piece he held and enough moisture came out that some dripped from his blistered lips.

Seeing that, the others quickly bit into the plant.

"You're right, Clay. It does taste terrible," Virgil said, rubbing the wet plant against his cracked lips. "Thanks."

Brian ate his and hurried out to get more.

Ken shook his head. "I can't believe this shit. Sitting here on the side of a hot desert mountain, mauled all to hell by a mountain lion, sucking on some wild plant for life giving moisture." He paused. "I wish we were back in Los Angeles right now!"

Rob chuckled. "It's an adventure, Ken. Tell me where in Los Angeles you can find such an adventure?"

Ken knew it was no use to say more and he went back to sucking the cactus fruit.

Brian brought in several more and passed them around. "We might have a chance yet."

Clay watched Brian for a few seconds. Maybe he saw the Indian. "See anything unusual out there, Brian?"

"Unusual like what?"

"Never mind." Clay looked off into the desert. He stared at the place he had seen the Indian. *I think I just saw my first ghost. Had to be a ghost. But he showed me where to find the life saving cactus. How? Why? And why an Indian?* Clay glanced up toward the heavens. "Don't know why or how, Big Guy, but thanks."

"Talking to yourself again, Clay?" Virgil asked.

Clay didn't answer. He just grinned and turned his attention back to the cactus.

An hour later, Clay rose from the hot sand. He brushed off his pants and looked off toward the place he last saw the Indian. Nothing. "We better get a move on, it's still a long way back." He rummaged around in his pocket and came up with more aspirin and another nerve pill for Ken.

When he handed them to Ken, Ken grabbed his hand and pulled him close. "Don't let me die on this damn mountain, Clay. Get me back home alive! Please!"

Clay winked at him. "Ken, whatever gave you the idea you were gonna die up here? Hell, man, you got us. You'll be all right. Now stop worrying about it and swallow those pills."

Ken swallowed the pills and struggled to his feet with Clay's help.

"How about cutting some more cactus to take with us, Clay?" Brian asked.

"Good idea."

Virgil, Brian, and Rob went looking for cacti. They had their pockets stuffed with the little cactus pears when they returned.

Virgil and Clay each took one of Ken's arms over their shoulders as Rob and Brian led off down the trail.

Clay looked back over his shoulder. No sign of the Indian.

Their clothes had long since dried and turned white from the salts escaping from their bodies. It wasn't long before their mouths were dry again. Brian pulled out a pear. He took his knife and cut it. "What the hell...?"

The pear had no moisture in it. It had dried out.

Brian frantically tried all the rest. Every one had dried out. He threw them down. He was disgusted. He looked at Clay for help.

Clay shook his head. "I guess I didn't realize what this heat would do to 'em."

They looked around. There was no prickly pear cactus to be found.

Rob started searching the ground. "I read somewhere that if you're thirsty, you can put a small pebble in your mouth and it'll help keep it moist."

"Really?" Brian asked, as he began looking for a small pebble.

18

Apache Junction's Chief of Police, Dennis Blackhorse, had just poured his first cup of coffee of the day when his phone rang. Flopping his tall, muscular frame down in the large chair behind his beat-up oak desk, he snatched the phone off the hook. "Chief Blackhorse and I hope it's important."

"It is, Chief," Gus McAdams said.

Blackhorse recognized Gus McAdam's voice. "What's wrong, you old saloon rat? Bad night?"

"Bad day's more like it."

"What's up?"

"Got a missing girl, Dennis. I think my niece, Laura Pratt, has been kidnapped."

"What makes you think that?"

"She hasn't been home for days. Her mail is stacked up. She's never done anything like this before, Dennis. She would never miss work, and she hasn't been in to see me all week. No phone calls, nothing."

"When did you see her last?"

"She was in my saloon last Sunday night. Had a run in of sorts with Paul Rockford." Gus' voice broke. He waited until he had control. "He took her, Chief! Sure as hell that bastard took her!"

"Now hold on, Gus. You don't know that for sure. Maybe she's just visiting relatives or something."

"Not likely, Chief. I'm the only living relative she has left."

Blackhorse didn't answer for a minute. He had known Gus for years. All the years he had been a cop, Gus had owned the saloon. He knew Gus wasn't one to jump to conclusions too fast. "I'll be over to the saloon in a few minutes, Gus." He hung up the phone and sat looking out the window. He knew Laura Pratt. She was about as nice a girl as you could hope to meet. And she loved her Uncle Gus. Blackhorse reached for his coffee. "Maybe she just met her dream man and is spending a few days with him," he said aloud.

Taking a sip of the hot coffee, he stared at the cup and frowned. He was going to have to stop drinking that foul tasting stuff someday - but not today. He took another sip...it tasted better. He got up and walked over to the Bunn coffeepot on the windowsill for a refill. He stood staring out the window watching heat waves rise from the street below, despite the early hour. *Summer heat's getting to everyone. Maybe the girl just took a trip up north to cool off a bit.*

He thought about Rockford. He didn't like the man. He'd had dealings with him before. The slimy bastard had moved in on a cattle ranch just outside town from parts unknown. From the way he lived, with all his fancy cars, helicopters, and bodyguards, he had to get his money from sources other than the cattle ranch. Probably involved in some Mexican dope racket. Maybe Gus was right. Maybe Rockford did take her. At least it was a place to start.

Blackhorse grabbed his hat and headed out the door. He knew that if it had been Rockford he wouldn't leave any witnesses. Laura was probably already dead.

* * *

Gus set a can of Diet Coke on the bar in front of Chief Blackhorse. "This one's on the house, Chief. Anymore and you buy."

Blackhorse took a drink of Coke and grinned. Even with a missing niece, Gus was still good natured and easy to talk to. "Gus, tell me what happened between Laura and Rockford."

"Well, he was all fancied up and as usual had those two mean looking goons with him. Laura was sitting right over there and he spotted her. I was busy down at the other end of the bar when it started, but she said he just waltzed right up and sat down at her table without even asking. Then he made a pass at her. Wanted her to go party with him somewhere. She refused and tried to make him leave the table, but he got rough with her. When he grabbed her, she slapped him. He was about to hurt her bad, and that's when those boys from L.A. stepped in."

"What boys from L.A.?"

"Oh, I didn't tell you? There were these five men here from the big city. They were going up in the mountains to look for the Dutchman."

"Maybe they took her."

"No, I don't think so, Chief. They were real decent guys. Before old Rockford could hit Laura, they had all jumped up and kicked back their chairs. That's what caught my attention. One of them confronted Rockford, and before I knew it, had knocked him flat on his ass right there in the floor. Maybe there would have been real trouble, cause his goons had ran to help him, but I pulled out old Rosco and put a stop to it." He chuckled. "One of the boys called Rockford an asshole. I tell you, that man sure knows how to read people."

Blackhorse took a long pull on the Diet Coke. He put the can on the bar. "After you pulled the shotgun, what happened?"

"Rockford's two flunkies were pulling their guns when I got their attention. Rockford knew he was about to die. I would've killed him dead. He made 'em stop. Rockford said they were leaving, but made threats. You know, with his fingers, like he was shooting someone." Tears welled in Gus' eyes. "I tell you, Chief, Rockford took her. Made good on his threat."

"It's beginning to look that way, Gus."

Blackhorse stood up and finished the rest of his Coke. "I'll need a picture of Laura, Gus. Get one over to my office as soon as you can."

"Sure thing, Chief." Gus knew that Blackhorse would do everything in his power to find Laura. He had known Blackhorse since the young, energetic Apache Indian had first became a policeman many years earlier. Throughout those years, Blackhorse had gained the respect of most decent people around Apache Junction.

He had married a local girl, and they had two children. Course, both were grown now. Gus knew he was a very capable man and held him in high esteem. If Laura was out there alive, or even dead, Blackhorse would find her. "What can we do, Chief?"

"Right now I'm going out to see Rockford, and he'd better have the right answers."

Blackhorse walked out. From the information he had gotten from Gus, it sounded like he had a real abduction on his hands, and he also knew he had little chance of getting anything from Rockford. He would just have to play it by ear.

From his car, Blackhorse radioed headquarters to broadcast the information on Laura Pratt's disappearance nationwide as being an abduction with foul play suspected, and gave her description.

As he drove to Rockford's ranch, Blackhorse formulated the questions he would ask. What had happened at the saloon? Who saw what? Where did they go after they left the saloon? Did they see Laura Pratt?

Blackhorse turned onto the road leading to the ranch house. He passed under a huge sign with ROCKFORD RANCH on it. The huge hacienda appeared in the distance. Blackhorse like this place. He had dreams of some day having one just like it. But that was just a dream. He knew he would never be able to afford even the sign over the gate on his salary.

From his chair on the porch, Rockford watched the plain black sedan pull into the driveway. He knew it had to be a cop car. No one else would drive one like that.

Braking to a stop in the drive, Blackhorse sat looking around, reading the place for any sign. He saw Rockford on the porch watching him, and took his time getting out of the car.

"Come up here out of the sun and have a seat, Chief," said Rockford. "Too damn hot to stand out there."

Blackhorse nodded and walked up the steps. He pulled up a seat and sat down.

"What brings you way out here, Chief?"

"A missing girl. Laura Pratt. Know her?"

"Now why should I know her?"

"You damn near had a fight over her in Gus' Saloon the other night," Blackhorse replied, raising his brows.

Rockford thought for a minute. Damn. He already knew about that. No way out but to admit it. "Oh yeah. I remember her. Young girl. Related to Gus somehow."

"His niece."

Rockford waited for the Chief to go on. When he didn't, Rockford continued. "Well, go on. What is it you want to talk to me about?"

"Tell me how you know her. Tell me what happened that night."

Pondering the question a minute, Rockford finally replied. "Well, I'd like to help any way I can." He cut his eyes at the Chief. "I've seen the girl around. Kinda cute. I stopped in for a drink Saturday night, saw her sitting alone, and asked her for a date. Next thing I know these dudes were jumping my case." He stopped and looked at the Chief to see how he was taking it. "There was a fight, but Gus broke things up and I left. That's all I can tell you, Chief."

"Who was with you?"

"Oh, just my boys. You know, my pilot Danny, and Tom, my aid."

"You mean your flunkies."

Rockford chuckled. He couldn't fool this man. "Well, you could say that, but I wouldn't want them to hear it. They're kinda touchy about their title."

Just then an older Mexican woman walked out carrying a tray with two large glasses of iced tea.

Welcoming the interruption, Rockford jumped up to help her. "Margarita makes the best iced tea in the county. Sweetened while it's hot. That's the only way to make good tea. Right, Margarita?"

"Si, Señor Rockford. The hot tea melts the sugar better and gives the tea a good, even taste."

Taking the cold, water-beaded glass, Blackhorse rolled it across his hot sweaty forehead. "One thing about iced tea, it's good in more ways than one."

When the woman had gone back inside, Blackhorse went on with his questions. "Where'd you go after you left the saloon?"

"Came back here. Had a few drinks with Danny and Tom, played a few cards, as I recall. Yep, played most of the night."

Rockford got to his feet. "Let me call the boys out here." He stepped to the door. "Danny, you and Tom come out here a minute."

The door opened almost instantly, and Davis and Wiscoff stepped out.

Blackhorse knew they had been listening. Whatever they said now would only serve to support what Rockford had told him. He got to his feet and he let them go on.

"Boys, tell the Chief here what we did that Saturday we went to town."

"We went to town to get some drinks and pick up some girls," Davis replied.

Rockford whacked him on the shoulder. "Not that! Tell him what we did after we left Gus' Saloon."

"Oh, that. We came back here and played cards all night long. Didn't we, Danny?"

"Sure 'nough did. 'Til dawn."

Rockford opened the door and the boys, like trained dogs, filed back inside.

Blackhorse shook his head. It was quite obvious they had rehearsed the whole thing. He would get nowhere here.

Rockford took a sip of tea and grinned big. "Well, there you have it, Chief. Innocent as babes."

Blackhorse stepped closer to Rockford, his black eyes dead serious. "Rockford, I think you know more than you're telling me. I'll be back. You can count on it." Blackhorse walked down the steps and to his car.

As Rockford stood watching him drive away, Davis and Wiscoff came out. Rockford grinned. "Distrustful bastard, ain't he?"

They all laughed.

19

$\mathbb{C}$lay strained his eyes to see the trail. It was getting too dark to see. He had been following the horses' tracks along a small animal trail down the sloping mountain terrain. *I hope those horses are headed home, or at least taking a trail that would lead us to a road. Any road.* He motioned the others to stop. "We'll stop here for the night. I can't see the trail anymore."

Rob and Brian found a spot to bed Ken down. He was in pain. When they helped him to the ground, he laid back and closed his eyes. Rob felt his forehead. Ken was running a fever. Rob looked over at Clay and motioned with his head for him to come.

Clay crawled over and felt Ken's forehead. He nodded. "Get the aspirin."

Rob caught the small bottle that Brian had already retrieved from the kit and pitched to him.

Clay shook three aspirin from the bottle and tossed it back. He reached into his pocket and slipped out another nerve pill. "Here, Ken. Force these down. They'll make you feel better."

Ken opened his eyes and took the pills from Clay. He popped them into his dry mouth and struggled to get them down. "No moisture left, Clay. Like trying to swallowing rocks after snoring open-mouthed all night."

Clay nodded and patted his shoulder. At least he had swallowed them. The aspirin should lower the fever some, but Clay knew they had to get him to a doctor. The fever was caused by infection setting in, and he would be in dire trouble if they didn't find help soon. Clay stood and looked around to get his bearings. He recognized nothing. He looked at the sky. It was getting dark, but still too light to see the stars clear enough to pick out the North Star. He looked at his friends. Like him, they were exhausted. They sat in silence, catching their breath and letting their hearts slow to a normal beat, their eyes ever watchful for prickly pear cacti and ...rattlesnakes.

Clay sat down in the warm sand. He was tired and sore. All the years at the drafting board had taken their toll. He wasn't used to all this exertion.

Virgil crawled over to sit beside him. "Clay, you think we'll ever catch up with Crazy Norman?"

"As much as I hope we do, I doubt it," Clay replied. "He's probably back in Apache Junction by now. One thing for sure though, I'm going to find that bastard as soon as we get to town." He looked around at the others. "By the way, did any of you happen to catch the numbers on that helicopter? I'd like to talk to that bastard, too!"

Rob, Brian, and Ken all shook their heads.

"I was too damn mad to think to look for it," Virgil said. "Maybe the sheriff will know who it was."

"I hope so. I know there's no law that says people have to help others in trouble, but out here I can see a definite need for one," Clay said. "They could have at least been good Samaritans."

"They sure as hell didn't have to laugh at us," Ken said.

"Can we build a fire tonight?" Brian asked.

"I don't think we should, Brian," Rob answered. "Norman might have been right about someone robbing us."

"What the hell they going to get from us? We don't have anything left. Not even food or water," Brian said from his sandy bed.

"That's true, Brian," Clay said. "But they don't know that. Let's not forget that we *are* still alive and that could change if someone should try to rob us. We don't know these people around here."

"I'd say we're getting to know 'em pretty damn fast," Brian said.

Rob shook his head. "I've heard enough tales about Mexican bandits to know I don't want to send out an invitation."

Virgil was stretched out in the warm sand, his hands behind his head. "In that case, we'd better post a look-out tonight."

Clay nodded. "You guys crash and I'll take first watch. Brian, you relieve me in two hours. Rob, two hours after that. Then Virgil." He looked at Ken and grinned. "You lucked out this time, kid."

"You got it, Clay," Brian answered as he settled back and closed his eyes.

Clay watched as the four men each gave a concerned look into the darkness before dropping off into a troubled sleep. He noticed the foul smell of his clothing was not as bad as it had been. The heat had dried the dropping stains. Maybe tomorrow the smell would be completely gone. The cold camp fell silent, and Clay tried to divert his attention from the hunger pains gnawing at his stomach and the cotton-like dryness of his mouth to the only sound in the night - the distant howling of a coyote.

* * *

Clay opened his eyes to the pale hint of orange on the eastern horizon. Dawn was near. He stood, stretched and looked around. Virgil was standing watch. He walked over to him. "Any sign of life out there?"

Virgil shook his head. "Nothing at all. Not one movement. Yet, I have the feeling there is plenty of life out there in those bushes."

"I know just the feeling. Wish we hadn't lost your old gun, maybe we could shoot a jack rabbit or something." Clay said.

"I saw a lizard a while ago. It was looking pretty damned tasty."

"Lizards are good to eat. Why didn't you catch it?'

"Hell, weak as I am right now, that lizard would have run circles around me."

Clay nodded. "I'll go wake the others." He walked back to where Brian was sleeping. "Up and at 'em, boys. As the Duke would say - we're burning daylight."

Rob jerked from his sleep and looked around, startled by Clay's loud voice. "What the hell...?"

"It's daylight. We need to get moving while it's halfway cool," Clay said, bending down to help Ken to his feet.

Ken accepted the help, but insisted he was all right. "I can make it on my own today, Clay. Brian gave me a couple aspirins a while ago. I feel fine, honest."

Clay felt his forehead. It was still as hot as it had been the day before. It was just the aspirin and nerve pills that made him feel better. Clay decided to let him try to do what he could. Might keep him from being so depressed. "Okay, but let me know if you need help."

With Clay taking the lead, they headed out. The cool early morning mountain air helped, but didn't make them forget their desperate need for water.

· Two hours later, the mountain air had turned into a blast furnace, and Ken was back in the helping arms of Virgil and Rob.

Another two hours and, with agonizing thirst invading his exhausted body, Clay looked up to get his bearings. He could see they were getting near the base of the mountain. The stench of bat droppings had all but left his clothes, but the desert sand had invaded them and they felt like sandpaper on his skin. He was sure he had sand in his shorts as well. His feet hurt so bad he wanted to rip his boots off and expose his sore toes to the air, but he knew if he ever got them off, which he doubted he could, he would never be able to get them back on. He was totally miserable, but it was better to suffer the pain than be naked or barefoot out here.

"Clay!" Rob called out, pointing behind him, as he and Brian struggled with Ken.

Clay looked back. Virgil was lying in the shade of sage bush. "What's wrong, Virge?"

Virgil didn't answer, just waved them on.

Making his way back to him, Clay urged him on. "We've got to keep moving, Virge, or else we'll die out here."

"I think I'm dead already, Clay. I can't get my legs to work right."

Looking back at Rob, Clay could see he was struggling hard to keep going. "Hey, Rob! Let's take a break!"

They dropped in their tracks.

Flopping down under a sage bush, Clay took off his hat and mopped his brow. "Don't you give out on me now, Virge, we've still got a ways to go."

"I need water, Clay. I'm dehydrated nearly to the point of being incoherent. I'm weak."

"I know, Virge. I know. Maybe a little rest will help."

Clay laid back and closed his burning eyes. He fought sleep. He knew if he went to sleep in that heat he wouldn't wake up.

An hour later, Clay pushed himself to his feet and looked down. He shook his head and looked again. He didn't see any horse tracks. His heart pounded. His mind raced. *My god! I've lost the trail!* He searched the ground panic stricken. He looked at the others. They were paying him no mind. *When? How far back?* His heart racing with fear, Clay started walking in a wide circle around their position.

Suddenly, he stopped, chuckled and pointed to the ground. "There they are!" he said proudly. "Right under my feet. I didn't lose them at all!" They were only a few feet from where he had been. *Damn! I hope I don't scare myself like that again.* He motioned for the others to get started.

Moaning and using what little strength they had left, they struggled to their feet. Even Virgil had regained strength enough to continue - at least for now. They trudged downward again.

The plant life was taller and thicker down near the base of the mountain. The cholla and mesquite more plentiful, making the horse tracks harder for Clay to see. He kept his eyes to the ground. He didn't see Fred Riley's faded sign when they passed it. Neither did the others.

A shot rang out. The five men dove headlong into the sand, rattlesnakes or not. Now Clay was thankful for the plants; they offered the only cover. He even welcomed the hot sand that poured into his clothes as he lay waiting for the next shot.

Everything was still. No sound. No more shots. Clay belly-crawled over to Virgil. "Who in the hell can that be, Virge?"

"Think it's Crazy Calhoun?" Virge asked as he burrowed deeper under a cholla, despite its sharp needles.

Clay searched the brush with his eyes for the shooter. "You see anyone, Rob?"

"No," Rob whispered loudly. "But then I haven't raised my head high enough out of the sand to see anything."

Clay took off his hat and threw it up in the air. It jerked violently as a bullet struck it dead center. "Someone's out there, that's for sure!"

Several more shots rang out and bullets cut through the brush above their heads, dropping twigs down upon them. They burrowed in deeper.

Clay listened to the explosions of the shots. They sounded as though they were a good distance away. "Keep your head down or lose it, boys!" He cautioned.

"What are we going to do, Clay?" Virgil asked.

Clay looked up at the broken brush above his head. If he could just stay below that, he thought. He crawled over to his hat that now had two holes in it. "L.A. street shootings weren't like this, were they, Virge?"

"Well, at least on the streets we had good solid brick buildings to hide behind. Ain't nothing but twigs here," Virgil called back in a loud whisper.

Clay knew he had to do something. They couldn't just lie out in the sun all day. If he could crawl on his hands and knees and not be seen, maybe he could get out of range of the bullets. He had nothing to lose, except his life, and that would be gone soon if he just lay there. He crawled forward on his elbows. He got several yards without a shot being fired at him. "They can't see us if we stay low! Come on! Crawl this way!"

With Virgil and Rob on either side of Ken helping him along, they crawled to Clay's location. No shots were fired.

"Hell of a way to travel, but they can't see us when we're on our hands and knees. We gotta get out of range," Clay stopped and motioned them on down the trail. He watched each man as he passed. His thoughts drifted back to the day at the cafeteria when Ken had suggested they head back to L.A. Dammit, he should have listened, but hell no, he had to be tough and talk them into staying. Now look at 'em. They sure didn't look the same. He shook his head sadly. With Brian crawling in the lead, they scurried like animals, putting as much distance between them and the shooter as they could. Suddenly, Brian let out a yell and whirled around, crashing into Virgil and Ken in his haste to flee something he had seen.

As he started past Clay, Clay grabbed him to keep him from jumping up and getting shot. "Whoa, big boy! What the hell's the matter? What is it, man?"

All Brian could do was point to the trail ahead.

"You stay put. I'll check it out." Clay crawled past Virgil and Ken. He slowly eased forward, then froze in his tracks. He stared down at the body of Norman Calhoun for a few seconds, then scurried back. "MY GOD! It's...it's Crazy Norman. He's...his head is gone!"

Virgil crawled up and had a look. He quickly turned back, struggling to keep from vomiting. "Who in the hell could have done that? The one shooting at us?"

"I don't think so," Clay said, regaining his composure. "Bullets don't do that."

Fear was evident in each man's face as they strained their eyes, searching the brush for any sign of movement.

Clay could see his friends were scared. Hell, he was scared. He'd never in all his life seen anything like that. "We've got to get out of here." He took his hat off and stuck it on a stick he retrieved from the sand. Taking a deep breath, he slowly eased the hat up. He kept it low at first. No shots. He hoisted the hat higher. Nothing. He waved it back and forth. Still Nothing. Satisfied that no shots were going to be fired; Clay eased his head up and looked around. He could see nothing. He stood up and ran weakly down the path. He was scared. He could already feel the bullets slamming into his back. He tried to run faster. Still no shots. Finally he stopped, looked back and motioned for the others to follow.

They weren't trying to follow horse tracks now. They were just trying to get away from the shooting and Crazy Norman.

20

The sun was a huge red ball low in the western sky as the desperate men, having been without food or water for two days, sun burned so badly the blisters had already broken and were peeling, stumbled through the mesquite bushes hardly noticing the long thorns digging into their flesh. They had long since tossed their protective chaps away because of their weight and heat. If they made it, they would just have to pay Liege Blackhorse for them.

Clay, his eyes half closed, staggered through the brush, no longer watching the ground. He had long since lost the horse tracks and he was past caring. Behind him staggered the others. They were exhausted - near their end.

First Ken, then Brian, then Virgil fell to the ground and lay still. Rob stumbled along behind Clay. He looked back and stopped. He knew his friends had gone as far as they could. "Shit." He looked at Clay and pointed behind him. "Clay."

Clay stopped and looked over his shoulder. What he saw sickened him. His friends were dying and it was his fault. He felt the tears start to roll. He fell to the ground and beat the sand with his fist.

If only I hadn't talked them into coming along. If only they hadn't listened to me. If only...
"WHHOOOOOO! WHHOOOOOO! WHHOOOOOO!
The owl flew over Clay's head. He turned and watched it sail on a few feet before landing behind a tall cactus. He squinted his eyes to see into the heat waves rising from the ground. The owl was gone, but something moved near the cactus. It was the Indian. Clay pulled his hat lower to see better. It was him alright. The Indian turned and walked away a few feet. He turned back and looked at Clay.

Clay watched in disbelief as the Indian turned and walked a few more feet. *My God, am I losing my mind?* Clay forced himself to move. He struggled to his feet and step by step he staggered along behind the Indian. He stumbled and fell. The Indian waited until he struggled back to his feet, then walked on.

Behind him, Clay could hear Rob calling his name. He didn't answer. He was too busy keeping the Indian in sight.

Suddenly, the Indian disappeared. Clay stopped. He searched the brush for him. He was not there. Clay strained his eyes to scan the land ahead.

"Clay! Where the hell are you?" Rob called as he staggered closer.

Clay didn't answer. He was staring at something ahead. "What the hell...?" A dark line stretched across the horizon just ahead of them. *My God, can that be? Are my eyes playing tricks on me? Is that a mirage?*

Rob staggered up behind him. "Clay?"

Clay didn't look back. He just stared ahead and pointed. "Rob, Rob. Is...is...is that a road?"

"I think it is, Clay."

Summoning up strength from somewhere, Clay managed to push ahead. Now he could see it. It really was a blacktop road. "It is! It is a road!" He turned to Rob. "We've made it! We're safe!" He staggered past Rob. "Let's get the others."

The men helped each other struggle and stumble toward the road. Feeble cries of joy escaped their cracked, sunburned lips.

Staggering onto the road. Clay stomped his feet on it. They had walked so long in the soft sand, the solid surface felt good.

They looked for vehicles, first one way, then the other. There was no sign of civilization as far as they could see either way. It soon became obvious to them that it was still a long way to any town. They flopped down on the side of the roadway.

Clay studied the sun, the road and the mountains behind them. Disoriented, he had no idea where they were or which way to go. All he knew was they were on the same side of the mountain that they had went up on. To the south the mountains were higher. They had come from the mountains. Clay didn't want to follow the road back that way. They would take the road to the north. "Well, we can't just sit here. It might be a week before a car comes along this desolate road. Besides, it's going to be dark soon and unless we want to spend another night out here without food or water, we'd better move on."

"You sure it's the right way?" Virgil asked.

"According to my non-expert calculations, we go this way," Clay replied, staggering off down the black road.

The strong sense of hope now helped each man garner strength from somewhere. Moaning and groaning their protests, they slowly got up and trudged after Clay, hoping like hell that he had guessed right.

The sun was low on the horizon but it was still hot. There was no wind, and the blacktop road had waves of heat rising upward to blur the vision of the men as they strained their eyes to catch sight of any movement ahead. The appearance of what looked like large pools of water ahead in the middle of the road made it even hotter for the men. They knew it was nothing more than heat waves rising from the road and causing a mirage.

Suddenly, Virgil nudged Clay with his elbow. "Clay! Is it just my imagination or is that a car?"

They stopped. All eyes fell upon the blurry outline of a vehicle materializing out of the heat waves. As it got closer they could see it really was some type of vehicle.

Cheers erupted from the desperate men as they dropped down on the side of the road to wait for the car.

Ken lay watching Clay. Tears flooded his eyes and ran down his cheeks. "You did it, Clay. You didn't let me die up there."

Clay turned away to keep anyone from seeing the tears in his eyes. These were tears of joy. Tears for his friends who would not die because of him.

The vehicle grew larger and larger, until it completely emerged from the heat waves. It was a sheriff's vehicle, complete with overhead light bar.

The green and white blazer coasted to a stop on the road near them. A young deputy sat in the blazer looking the bunch over. With their dirty, blistered faces, tattered clothing and a week's growth of whiskers, they were a sight to behold. When his eyes got to Ken Smith and he saw all the dirty bandages, he jumped from the blazer and hurried to his side. "What happened to you?"

"Big old cougar jumped me up on the mountain," Ken replied.

The deputy looked at the hot, exhausted men. "Let me get you fellas some water, then we'll change those dirty bandages." He hurried back to his vehicle. He returned with a large canteen of water and a large first aid kit. He handed the canteen to Ken, who immediately started gulping it down.

The others waited patiently until he had finished and handed the canteen to Brian.

Brian looked at the canteen, then handed it to Clay. "Go ahead, Clay, I can wait."

Clay took the canteen and passed it to Rob. "You go next, Rob. I still got a little cactus juice left in my teeth."

While they were drinking, the deputy was peeling off Ken's dirty bandages. "I'm Deputy Jesse Richmond." He slowly worked a bandage from a huge claw mark on Ken's shoulder. Beneath it, the jagged cut was infected. The deputy looked it over, then reached for a bottle of alcohol. "Couple of you fellas hold him still while I wash those cuts with this alcohol. It's going to burn like hell, but it'll help slow the infection."

Clay and Rob held Ken still while the alcohol was poured on. Ken gritted his teeth and winced in pain.

After the first wound was treated, the deputy stripped off the other bandages without hesitation and poured on the alcohol. "That'll have to do until we can get him to a hospital. He's going to need a lot of work to close those wounds."

The water from the canteen had been a lifesaver and though exhausted, the boys felt much better as they sat watching the young deputy apply new bandages to Ken's injuries.

When he had finished, he stood and looked around. "Anyone else injured?"

No one said anything for a moment.

"Yes, but he's beyond help," Clay said, pointing back out toward the mountains. "Fella we met in Apache Junction. He was supposed to be our guide, but he ran off with the horses and left us on foot up there. We found him on the way out. Someone had cut his head off."

"That's not unusual around here. Who was he?"

"Fella named Norman Calhoun," Clay said.

"Crazy Norman, huh?"

"You know him?"

"Everyone around these parts knows Crazy Norman. He's left many a man stranded up there, pretending to be a guide or that he had found the Dutchman's mine."

Clay and his friends exchanged glances.

"You're lucky to get out alive. That old fool didn't realize how dangerous it was to leave people unfamiliar with the area stranded up there without water or food. We'd have stopped him if there had been any laws broken. Unfortunately it's not against the law to lie about finding the Dutchman." Richmond kicked the filthy bandages into a pile on the gravel alongside the road and set them on fire.

"How far is it to Apache Junction?" Clay asked.

"Thirty miles. You fellas walked a long way." The deputy pointed to his blazer, "Pile in and as soon as these burn, I'll get you guys to Valley Lutheran Hospital over by Apache Junction. You could all use some attention on your sunburns and those cracked lips." He looked at Clay's clothes and wrinkled his nose. "What the hell you been into?"

"Bat shit."

Deputy Richmond could only stare at him as they piled into the blazer. Within minutes they were on their way to safety.

21

The sterile walls and white tables in the emergency room of Valley Lutheran Hospital were a welcome sight to Clay, Virgil, Rob, and Brian, who had already been treated for their burns, cuts, and bruises. They leaned against one of the white walls drinking cool water from paper cups and watching the doctor apply the last butterfly bandage stitches to Ken's claw cuts. Already they were feeling much better, gaining strength by the minute.

"It was too late for me to put regular stitches in those injuries. After 10-12 hours, it only makes matters worse to use stitches that try to pull the lacerated flesh closed on the outside, when it has already started the healing process inside. These butterfly tape strips will do the job if you take care of them." He examined a deep claw mark on Ken's shoulder and placed a butterfly strip on it. He started applying the bandages. "You're very lucky, young man. A day or two more and that infection would have spread all through your body."

"A day or two more and the infection would have been the least of my worries," Ken replied.

The doctor nodded knowingly and went to wash his hands. "The antibiotics will kill the infection and lower the fever. I suggest you take it easy for a few days, and I want those bandages changed every day. There's a small medical clinic over in Apache Junction. They're pretty darn good out there, and a hell of a lot cheaper than here at this emergency room. The doctor will check the infection. There's a nurse named Brenda Carpenter. She'll take care of changing the bandages.

Ken nodded as he rose from the table and started to put his clothes on.

"Here! Here! Don't you dare put those filthy clothes on over my clean bandages. Put on some hospital gowns."

Even Ken chuckled at the doctor's remarks. He put on a gown and, after checking his exposure, put on another one backward and went wobbling out with his friends.

Deputy Richmond gave them a ride back to their motel in Apache Junction. On the way he assured them he would file a report on Crazy Norman. "It'll probably be me that goes up to get him anyway."

They watched the deputy drive away from their motel. Then the smell of food cooking coming from Will's Family Restaurant caught the starving men's attention. They started across the street, but looked back at Ken. He was standing on the sidewalk holding the hospital gowns closed.

"Okay, Ken," Clay said. "We'll wash up first."

They hurried into the motel to take a shower and change clothes.

Will Barnett was shocked at the sight of the five men. "My god! You fellas look like shit! What the hell happened up there?"

"Water!" Clay said. "Bring water! Lots of water!"

Will hurried to get the water while the boys gathered around a table. He returned with a large pitcher of ice water.

He stood watching as the water disappeared. He grabbed the pitcher and hurried for more.

When they had drunk their fill, Will pulled up a chair and sat down. He listened intently as they told him what had happened up on the mountain. "It's a damned wonder you're alive," he said, shaking his head.

There was silence around the table as they acknowledged him with nods.

"Young Jesse will tell the sheriff, for all the good it'll do. Jack Wilkins is not one of your better sheriffs, if you know what I mean. He's more interested in what the rich and politically inclined think of him than in doing his job."

"One of those, huh?" Virgil remarked.

"Scared of his own shadow, too. He won't be going up on that mountain tomorrow. It'll be young Jesse or one of the other deputies."

"It was Deputy Jesse Richmond that found us in the desert and took us to the hospital," Virgil said.

"He's a good man. Got more sense in his little finger than the sheriff has in his whole damn body. Wish he was sheriff. Things would be different around here."

"ORDER UP!" The cook rang a little bell.

Will hurried away.

The door opened and Police Chief Dennis Blackhorse stepped in. He glanced their way, nodded to Barnett and walked over to their table. "Howdy, Gents. I'm Dennis Blackhorse, Police Chief of Apache Junction. I understand you've just been through some tough times."

Eyeing the man up first, Clay finally offered his hand. "Pleased to meet you, Chief. Have a seat."

Chief Blackhorse shook hands with the five men and pulled a chair from a nearby table. As he sat down, Barnett returned with platters of food.

"I know you boys are hungry, so I'll just sit back while you eat. We can talk later." He looked at Will. "Maybe a little coffee, Will."

"Sure thing, Chief." Will hurried away.

Blackhorse watched as they hungrily attacked their food. "Deputy Richmond told me what happened to Crazy Calhoun. Been expecting any day to hear some city fella shot him up on that mountain for pulling his fool stunts, but didn't expect nothing like this. Where'd you say it happened?"

"Just above the base of the mountain. Maybe five or six miles up," Clay said.

"Then you guys were somewhere around old man Fred Riley's claim. Probably him that shot you."

"Then that man's crazy, too," Clay replied. "He damned near killed us."

"Old Fred has never hit anyone yet. He's a dead shot and hits only what he aims at. Just wanted to scare you off his claim."

Will placed Blackhorse's coffee in front of him. "I tried to tell these guys not to go up there, Chief. That makes five people over the years who've had their heads cut off."

Blackhorse didn't answer. He was watching the men devour the food. They paid little heed to manners as they stuffed the food down. Blackhorse had always been a good judge of character and he could see why Gus had said these were decent men. He smiled. They weren't the kidnappers.

Clay wiped his mouth and took a sip of coffee. He looked at Blackhorse. "You said we could talk later. Is it about Calhoun?"

"Not really. I'm more interested in what you fellas can tell me about Laura Pratt," Blackhorse said, watching each man's face for any reaction. He saw only a questioning look. "You know, the girl in Gus' Saloon that you helped. She was having trouble with some guy."

"I remember her now. What about her?" Clay asked.

"She was kidnapped that same night."

Blackhorse had everyone's undivided attention now.

"Kidnapped?" Clay said. "By who?"

"That's what I'm trying to find out. Suppose you tell me what happened that night."

Clay leaned back to think. "Well, there's not really much to tell. We were having a few beers when a lady yelled. We saw a man giving her a hard time. We stepped in and stopped it before it got out of hand."

"Did you know the guy?"

"Chief, we've only been in town a short time. I'd never seen him. Come to think of it, though, the girl called him Rockford, I think. Had two other men with him."

"Looked like maybe bodyguards, the way they acted," Virgil said. "They kept reaching under their coats like they were going for a gun or something."

Ken chuckled. "That's when Gus cooled them down with that big shotgun."

"Have you checked them out yet?" asked Clay.

"Yeah, but it was like talking to that wall. Get just as much from it as I did them. I will say they're my prime suspects right now." Blackhorse paused. "Can you remember what time she left the saloon?"

"She was still there when we left with Crazy Calhoun," Clay replied.

Blackhorse nodded. That was the same story Gus had told. If they were dickering with Calhoun at the motel that night, they couldn't have snatched Laura Pratt.

"Is she alright now?" Brian asked.

"Don't know. She's still missing."

Virgil shook his head. "Damned shame. She seemed like a nice lady."

"She was," Blackhorse replied.

"How many kidnappings do you have around here?" Clay asked.

"This is the first, actually. At least the first one I think is really a kidnapping. We had lots of missing people but they usually turn up...like you guys did. Some do end up being found up on the mountain dead. But this is the first kidnapping."

"And you think we did it?"

Blackhorse smiled. "No, not now. But I have to check out everybody who might have seen her that night."

"I see what you mean," said Clay.

"Gus doesn't think it was you; he is sure it was Paul Rockford."

Virgil leaned on his elbows and looked at the Chief. "You know, Rockford did make some threats that night. Pointed his finger like a gun at us and then at the girl."

Blackhorse nodded and pulled out his notebook and pen. "That's also what Gus told me. I'll need to get your names and addresses for the report."

While Will watched, each man gave Chief Blackhorse the information he wanted. He was just putting his notebook in his pocket when a blast of heat hit the room as the door burst open. They all looked up.

A heavy set man of fifty-five years or so in an expensive western cut suit, complete with a 10-X white Stetson hat strutted in. He stood looking around.

Chief Blackhorse pushed his chair back and stood up. "I'll leave you fellas now. But I may need to talk to you again. I'll look you up." He pointed. "That's Sheriff Jack Wilkins. He'll handle the Calhoun case." Blackhorse walked away. He only nodded at the sheriff when he passed, making it very obvious Blackhorse didn't care for the man.

Will pointed at him. "Boys, meet that Sheriff I was telling you about."

Wilkins spotted them and swaggered across the floor to the table.

"Jesse told me about your troubles, boys. Too bad," he said, flopping down in a chair. "Would've been here sooner, but had to eat supper first. It's a thirty mile drive over from Florence and that's a long ways to drive on an empty stomach."

Will rolled his eyes, got up and walked around behind the counter. He leaned his elbows on it, watching and listening to the sheriff.

"So tell me what happened up there," Wilkins said.

Clay once again told the events of the last three days. When he was finished, the sheriff broke out in a deep-throated laugh.

"Old Crazy Norman did it again, did he?"

All five men sat staring at the man.

Clay glared at him. "Don't it bother you that he's had his head cut *completely off* and is lying up there on that damn mountain *dead*?"

Wilkins looked puzzled. "What the hell, boy? After what he did to you guys, you should be happy he's dead."

"For what he did to us, he should have been thrown in jail or had his ass kicked. He didn't deserve to die for it."

Wilkins looked at Clay and narrowed his eyes. He didn't like people from big cities. They were always sticking their nose in where it didn't belong. And he especially didn't like this smart-ass. *Who the hell does he think he is? Coming to my county and talking to me like that.*

He gave Clay a nasty look. "Hell, boy, the man's dead. You told me that yourself. There ain't nothing we can do to bring him back and he ain't going nowhere tonight. Why should it bother me?"

Clay just stared at him.

Wilkins stood up. "You just let the law handle this mess, Mister. He narrowed his eyes at Clay. "I want you boys to go home. Back to the city. Don't go back up on that mountain."

He started to walk away, but stopped and turned back. "By the way. Did you fellas see anything else up there?"

Clay stared at the man for a minute. What the hell did he mean by that? Wasn't what they did see enough? "Like what?" he asked.

Wilkins shook his head. "Never mind." He turned to Barnett. "Barnett, I'll send young Jesse out there come morning to fetch Norman on back here. See you tomorrow." He turned and walked out without another word to the boys.

"By God, Will, I'd say you were right about that man," Virgil said in disgust, as he rose from the table. "He has definitely got a problem."

Rob stood, yawned and stretched. "I don't know about the rest of you, but I'm going to bed and sleep for a week."

22

It was late when the Sheriff Wilkins' car skidded to a stop in front of Paul Rockford's ranch house - almost too late to come calling. But Wilkins knew Rockford would want to hear about the men in town. He slid out from under the steering wheel and ambled up onto the porch where Wiscoff and Davis met him.

They both grinned. They knew he was Rockford's man - bought and paid for.

"Got any good news for us, Sheriff?" Tom asked.

"Got some for the boss, not you weasels," he said, pushing past them and going into the house.

Wilkins stood just inside the door waiting for Rockford. He looked around the room with envy. The inside of Rockford's house was like the outside - plush. All the luxuries of an extremely successful man. Nothing but the best of everything for Rockford. Wilkins didn't like Rockford, but he could put up with a lot of crap for the money Rockford paid him. He looked around. Some day. Some day I'll have one just like it.

"Well, well, well! To what do we owe the honor of your presence at this late hour?" Rockford asked, as he strolled into the room.

Wilkins nervously twisted his Stetson in his hands. Usually no one made him nervous, but for some reason, being in the presence of Rockford always made him nervous. Wilkins took the chair that Rockford waved his hand toward. "Been a bunch of city boys up on the mountain."

Rockford was all ears. "What do you mean, 'city boys'? Cops?"

"No, no, no. Real city boys. From Los Angeles. They're searching for the Lost Dutchman."

"You've talked to 'em?"

"Yeah, just a while ago. They came crawling out of the mountains near dead."

"But they weren't dead?

"No."

"Where are they now?"

"At the Junction Motel," Wilkins said, then grinned. "Asleep, I reckon. They hadn't slept for days."

"How come you don't have someone watching them? Come on, man. What's going on with you?" Rockford was getting excited.

"Just calm down, Paul. Nothing to worry about. They got hooked up with old Crazy Norman and he led them on his usual wild goose chase. You know, the one where he tells them he's found the Dutchman and needs help to get the gold out."

"You better hope it's alright, Wilkins. You know we can't afford to have people tramping around up there. They might just accidentally find our little business, then you won't be in charge of a jail, you'll be in one."

"Yeah, yeah, I know, Paul. Anyway, these guys were just about dead when we found them. One was clawed up bad by an old cougar. I guess old Norman left 'em stranded up there, then someone, probably the same bastard that did all the others, cut Norman's damn head clean off - so they say," he mused, then went on. "They had to walk out without water or food. They're at the motel now, and will probably be heading back to the big city tomorrow."

"I'd better have my people get on it, Jack. I don't trust your men. Some of 'em seem to have an honest streak in 'em that could be dangerous to us." Paul laughed at his own words.

Sheriff Wilkins, intimidated as usual by Rockford, dropped his eyes to the floor. He knew Rockford was not only a very wealthy man but also a very dangerous one. He had no intentions of crossing this man. Not a man who could either make him rich or kill him with the blink of an eye.

"If you think that's the best way to handle it, then send your men. If they need anything, tell them to call me," Wilkins finally said.

Rockford stared at the man. Wilkins was a wimp and he couldn't stand wimps. The very sight of him in his house was irritating. "What on earth could you do to help my men?" he asked, sarcastically.

"Well, you know..." Wilkins said, searching for words. "Maybe...maybe they might need some legal help along the way. I could get 'em out of just about anything like that, as long as they do what I tell them."

Rockford knew he was right about that. That was the only reason he had Wilkins along in the first place - to see that the law stayed away from his business. He changed his tone. "You're right, Jack. What was I thinking of? Of course, you can be of help. They'll call you as soon as they need something," He rose and walked to the door. Opening it, he stood looking back at Wilkins.

The sheriff knew the meeting was over and he was being dismissed. He shuffled out the door, hat in hand.

When Wilkins drove away, Rockford called his men inside. "I want you boys to go to town tomorrow and see what you can learn about that new bunch of men. They have to be the ones we saw up near the old Riley claim the other day."

"Want we should take the chopper, Boss?" Danny asked.

"Don't see any reason to, unless they go back on the mountain. If you get wind they're going back up there, then hotfoot it back here and get the chopper. For now, take the pickup. It's less conspicuous."

"Good thinking, Boss," Davis chuckled. "They'll never suspect the truck."

23

A loud knocking at the motel door jarred Clay from a sound sleep. Shaking his head to clear his mind, he wrapped a sheet around himself and opened the door just a crack. The sunlight was blinding. He squinted.

"It's just me... Deputy Richmond. Wanted you to know we were able to find Norman's body, and brought it down this morning. We didn't find his head, though."

"Geez. What the hell time is it, anyway?" Clay asked.

Looking at his wristwatch, the deputy replied, "It's half past two."

"In the afternoon?"

"That's right. You guys were really tired last night."

"You got that right, Jesse!" Virgil said from behind Clay. "Slept like a baby."

"Well, when you guys get up and around, we'll talk some more. In the meantime, if you need anything, just yell," said Richmond.

"How the hell did you guys get him out of there so fast?" asked Clay.

"Search and rescue helicopter from Phoenix and those good directions you fellas gave me. We only use the rescue helicopter for retrieval of bodies and injured people up on the mountain."

Clay watched the deputy walk away, then closed the door and fell back across his bed. He was still tired but knew he had to get up and get Ken to the clinic.

"Better wake the others," he said to Virgil, lazily reaching for the phone.

Ken yelled as the pretty, auburn-haired nurse ripped the bandage from the claw marks on his shoulder.

Clay, Virgil, Rob, and Brian cringed in sympathy.

"Want a piece of leather to bite down on while she finishes that, Ken?" Clay asked in a soft voice.

"I could use one," Ken answered, wincing in pain. "I think she's trying to finish what that old cat started."

The nurse, Brenda Carpenter, stood about five-six and was in her mid-thirties. She flashed her green eyes at Clay and chuckled. She was used to talk like that from the men she had treated over the years around Apache Junction. It was her experience that all men had a very low tolerance for pain, unless something had their adrenaline raging through their veins like oil through the Alaskan pipeline.

"I'm just about finished with you, Ken. Just hang in there for another minute or two," she said, ripping another bandage from a wound. When she had the new bandage on, she turned to Clay. "I can see by your remark about biting on a piece of leather that you're well versed in the medical field so I'll give you the report."

Clay felt his face flush. He grinned sheepishly. "I'm sorry about that little remark."

Brenda ignored his apology. "He's doing better than expected with those cuts being from the filthy claws of an animal," she said. "He'll heal okay but I'm afraid he's going to have plenty of scars to remember that old cat by."

Clay offered her his hand.

She shook it.

"Thanks, nurse," he said. "Like I said, I'm sorry about the remark. We really appreciate everything you've done."

The nurse looked him over. *My goodness. This man really is sincere. I think he really does appreciate me.* Most of her clients took her for granted. Oh, they muttered something like thanks, but there was very seldom any feeling behind it. She liked this man. "No apology necessary. That's the way they used to have to do it. But today we have painkillers galore. Just wasn't necessary to use them on Ken." She looked Clay in the eyes and smiled. "I'm Brenda Carpenter and I'll help you boys in any way I can. Feel free to call on me anytime, whether it's to repair your bodies or give advice. I'm good at both."

She turned to Ken. "I'll see you tomorrow, young man."

"Brenda, how soon do you think it'll be before he's able to be up and around again? You know - able to work?" Clay asked.

"Oh...perhaps four or five days, barring anymore infection."

"You hear that, Ken? Four or five days and you'll be good as new." Clay said.

Ken groaned aloud. "That'll give me enough time to heal before I have to face mom." He'd just as soon she didn't see him like this, but he didn't say it.

As Clay reached the door to leave, Brenda called after him. "Clay!"

Clay turned back. "Yes?"

"Take some advice and don't go back up there."

Clay looked her over. He wasn't planning to go back up there, but here was another person telling him to go home. "That's what Sheriff Wilkins told us last night."

"You watch out for that Wilkins. He's mixed up with some pretty shady people around here, and when they hear you guys are up there searching for the Dutchman, they'll pay you a visit. They don't want anyone messing around up there for some reason."

"We'll remember that. Thanks!" Clay said, quickly closing the door behind him so the hot desert air wouldn't warm the cool clinic room.

Brenda hurried to the window and watched them walk away. She knew that, even though they had been through a rough time, they were not likely to heed her warning about going back on the mountain. She felt drawn to this bunch of misfits. *What a nice bunch of men. Too bad they aren't local.* She went back to her work, making a mental note to keep tabs on them.

Brenda had married young while she was in nursing school in Phoenix. She had been happy until one day, after a twelve-hour shift at the hospital, she came home to discover her husband passed out in bed with a neighbor lady. Brenda had divorced him quickly and dove into her nursing career. As part of her training, she had been required to participate in the medical program at Apache Junction Medical Clinic. She liked the quietness of the area compared to Phoenix's heavy, noisy traffic. And she liked the people. When she earned her nursing degree, she left the Phoenix area to keep from running into her ex-husband. She had returned to work full time at the medical clinic in Apache Junction. She was happy now. At least in her work, she was happy. Her love life left a little to be desired. She dated some of the local men occasionally, but still had not found a suitable mate to settle down with.

She walked back to the window and looked out. They were gone.

* * *

Clay lay on his bed staring at the ceiling. He had planned to call his Judie as soon as they got back to the motel, but decided against it after he made his mind up that as soon as they could get some rest, they were heading back to Los Angeles. No one else had called home yet. There was no need to worry her when they would be there in just a few hours and she could see they were okay. The whole big adventure had gone wrong as soon as they landed. From the dirty motel to Crazy Calhoun. He rolled over and stared at Virgil lying on the other bed. Even his very best friend had nearly died because of him. Tomorrow - tomorrow they would go home. He closed his eyes and drifted off to sleep.

Hours later, Brian jumping on his bed, jarred him awake. "What the hell is going on?" he asked.

"Get dressed. We're moving!" Brian answered.

"Moving? Moving where?"

"Ken says he ain't staying another day in this run down dump. We're moving to the Holiday Inn down the street. They've got a swimming pool! Besides, we've already got the rooms reserved." Not one to argue about comfort, Clay quickly packed his gear.

* * *

Clay and Ken lay in chaise lounges beside the swimming pool of the Holiday Inn and watched Rob and Brian play in the refreshing water.

The water had felt good to Clay with his sunburned body totally submerged and surrounded by the coolness of it. He looked up at the sun just setting over the mountains in the west. He felt good for the first time in days. He turned to Ken, who couldn't get in the water because of his bandages. "So tell me, Ken, why are we here and not on our way back to Los Angeles?"

"Do you think for one minute I'm going to let my mother see me in this condition? Hell, man, she'd have me tucked away in some hospital for a month of Sundays. Wouldn't ever let me go anywhere. Might even have me locked away in some institution for the mentally handicapped."

"Well, maybe we are a bit mentally incapacitated," Clay replied, looking off toward the mountains.

"I figure we can stay here until I get all healed up," Ken said paying no attention to Clay's words. "Besides, it's not such a bad place if you have a clean place to stay and a cool swimming pool."

Clay nodded. "Hell, that's okay by me. I really wasn't ready to go back anyway. Nobody back in Los Angeles knows anything about our ordeal. Might just as well keep it a secret until we get home." Clay turned his attention back to watching Rob and Brian in the pool.

* * *

In Clay's room the following morning, they gathered to discuss their plans. Clay had already made up his mind. They were going back to Los Angeles when Ken got a little better. He was not going to be responsible for anybody getting killed searching for gold. He knew it was only by the grace of God, had no one been killed the over the last few days. "Okay, fellas, if you all agree, we'll stay here and enjoy a little peace and quiet for a few days while Ken heals up a little, but then we're heading home."

No one spoke for a minute or two. They were mulling the situation over in their minds.

"I don't care what you guys decide to do," Clay continued, "I'm going back to the city. I don't want to be responsible for one of you getting eaten by some damned mountain lion or God only knows what else. Ken knows what that feels like."

"You think that lion was trying to *eat* him?" Brian laughed. "Hell, after the first bite he was just trying to spit him out!"

Clay chuckled. "As a matter of fact, I think he was doing just that when Virgil shot him...right Virge?"

"Looked that way to me."

Ken tried to give them a nasty look but couldn't suppress a grin at their humor. He could see they were just trying to cheer him up. He stood and paced the floor, his mind racing. *Damn, they're going back because of me. What should I do? Just keep on being afraid of everything that comes along? I've been this way all my life.* He stopped and looked out the window at the mountains on the horizon. *Spooky looking bastards. Up there I was actually, in real life, attacked by a mountain lion and lived. Well, actually Virgil and Clay saved my ass. I was lost for days in the desert without food or water, but still I'm alive. Not a bad feeling.* He grinned to himself. *No, not a bad feeling at all.* He turned from the window and found all eyes on him. He looked from one man to the other. These were his friends. If he was in trouble they would help, just like they already had.

Finally he spoke. "You know, I feel good about living through that attack. Don't get me wrong; it hurts and I wouldn't want to do it again, but I feel good about it now. I don't know if it's that 'manly thing' you spoke of or not, Clay, but I've never in my life experienced such a feeling of self-confidence. Not a bad feeling at all." He paused to look out the window again. "Well, I honestly would like to stay and make another search for the Dutchman"

The others sat staring at him. They couldn't believe what they were hearing. Their old friend actually wanting to go back up there after what he had been through. Unbelievable.

"Now, what brought all this on, Ken?" Clay asked.

"I don't really know," said Ken. "I just don't feel like going back to the city right now. Back to mowing lawns, repairing the house, or maybe, just maybe, wet our feet at the beach once or twice. Man, you guys just don't know what it feels like to live in fear all your life, then have something like this happen to you and survive. I was always afraid of getting hurt. Hell, it isn't nearly as bad as I thought. I think we ought to stay right here just as we planned and finish that adventure Clay talked about. An adventure for men."

Clay walked over and felt of Ken's forehead. "No fever."

Brian got to his feet. "He might be right, you know. We give up now, maybe we'll hate ourselves the rest of our lives. We'll always be wondering if it was there and if we could have found it. To tell you the truth, I think I've developed gold fever! I wouldn't mind staying, either."

Clay walked to the window to stare up at the mountains. "I don't know, Ken."

"You wouldn't be responsible for anything happening to me now, Clay, it's my decision."

"The city could kill you just as dead as anything out here," said Rob. "Some crazy drunk driver could kill you crossing the street. How much different can getting killed out here be?"

"I doubt that getting killed by a car is nearly as scary as getting killed by a lion," said Ken.

Virgil, in his usual soft voice, said, "I think it's only fair that we let Ken make the decision. Who else do you know that has been attacked by a mountain lion, lived to tell about it, and wants to go back for more?"

"That's another thing! "Brian put in. "He has a hell of a story to tell his grandkids. What have I got to tell about? Sunburn and sore feet, that's what."

"If that bothers you, Brian, you can tell my story," Ken offered.

This caused a few snickers.

"What about you, Virge? Want to stay or go?" Ken asked.

Virgil thought for a minute, then said, "Well, I must admit we had a close call up there, but when you think about it, it's like Brian said. Every time you run across the street back in the city, you're chancing death from a fast moving Mercedes or Jag or something bigger, like maybe a cement truck. I like the feeling of freedom I've had out here. You don't realize just how crowded Los Angeles really is until you've spent the night out there in the wide open spaces." He looked around the room at each man. "Feeling that gold wouldn't be bad either."

The room was silent.

"Maybe Clay can go on home and the rest of us stay," suggested Brian jokingly.

Clay turned from the window and looked at the others in the room. "Okay, if that's what you all want, then we stay. Just remember that it was your own doing this time, not mine."

"No problem with that," Ken answered.

"In a way, I'm glad we're staying," Clay remarked. "That sheriff telling me to go home didn't set too well with me."

"Well, if we're going back up there," Rob said. "I'm buying me the biggest gun I can find."

Clay agreed. "Rob's right. We should each buy a gun and plenty of ammunition. I know we don't have much experience with guns, but with a little practice, we could handle 'em okay."

"Sounds good to me," said Virgil, getting to his feet. "Now let's go drink a few cold beers."

Hurrying toward the saloon, they paid no attention to the two men who got out of a new pickup and followed them down the street.

At a table in the same saloon where they had met Crazy Norman, Rob was getting tipsy as he downed beer after beer. "Clay," he said. "Supposing we do find the gold. What would you do with your share?"

Clay looked around. There was only a handful of people in the bar, but there were a couple of guys sitting too close for them to be discussing gold.

"Shhhh...." Clay placed his hand over Rob's mouth and whispered. "Not so loud, Rob. Any one of these guys could be listening."

Rob put his finger to his lips and grinned sheepishly. "Sorry."

Clay leaned closer, "Gonna buy me a small ranch somewhere with some horses and a few cows, then just sit back in my rocking chair on the porch and watch 'em get fat."

"That sounds great," Rob whispered back. "Maybe I'll do the same thing. I think I'd like country living."

Virgil was watching the two men at the next table. They seemed to be mighty interested in what Rob and Clay were talking about. He tapped Clay on the arm. "Let's knock it off until we get back to the motel. Too many ears in here."

Rob looked around and saw what Virgil was talking about. He raised his voice. "Sure hate to leave this beautiful country, but I got to get back to the big city. This place gives me the woollies." He leaned back to Clay and winked, "Think that'll work?"

Clay chuckled at Rob's humor. "I doubt it, but it sure sounded good."

A few minutes later, the two men got up and walked out.

Clay looked at Virgil, then back at the door. "Probably wasn't anything to worry about," he said.

24

Davis and Wiscoff stood in Rockford's living room, telling him what they had seen and heard.

"They're going back on the mountain, Boss," said Davis. "I heard 'em whispering about gold. One of 'em tried to pretend they were leaving, but he didn't fool me none. He was about half drunk and just thought he was whispering."

"When they leaving?"

"That we don't know, Boss. They didn't say."

Rockford puffed on his cigar and paced the floor. He stopped and pointed at Davis. "That means you two better get the chopper ready to go. Tomorrow you follow them again. Stay out of sight. I don't want you to bother them, or even let them think you're following them. See where they go and keep me posted. If it looks like they're going to leave, get back here to the chopper."

"Sure thing, Boss," Wiscoff said, as he and Davis hurried out the door.

Rockford quickly grabbed the telephone and dialed a number. Impatiently, he drummed his fingers as he waited for someone to answer.

"Hello, Sheriff Wilkins here."

Rockford shouted into the phone, "Dammit, Wilkins, I thought you said they were leaving."

"I thought they were, Paul. Only fools would go back up there after what they went through," Wilkins said on the other end.

Rockford lowered his voice. "You had better get this under control, Jack. I told you I don't want them finding anything up there."

"I will, Paul! I'll get right on it!"

"Just see that you do!" said Rockford. Slamming down the phone, he started pacing the floor, rolling the cigar from side to side.

25

Clay sat with the others eating breakfast at Will's restaurant, deep in his private thoughts. He shuddered. They had been back for more than a week now, but he could still see the mountain lion on Ken, and the body of Crazy Norman without a head, and hear the shots fired at them by old man Riley. It had finally struck him just how close to death they had come. He shook his head to clear the thoughts.

"I called Judie last night and told her everything was going according to our plans. Didn't mention anything about the trouble we've had or she would've been on the next flight out here. Told me to have a good time, that she was enjoying her new found freedom by shopping all the stores in Beverly Hills."

"She wasn't kidding either, "Virgil replied. "That's exactly what Pat said when I called her this morning, Sounds like she and Judie had this cooked up from the start."

"Well, maybe we'd better start having that good time," Clay said. "We've been here for a week now, and Ken's looking pretty darn good. I think we should try to find us some guns." He spied Will

Barnett coming out of the kitchen and called out. "Will! Got a minute?"

Will walked over to the table, wiping his hands on his apron. "What's up, Clay?"

Clay lowered his voice and whispered, "Two things, Will. First, do we need permits to go searching for the Dutchman; and second, where can we buy some guns? Reasonable."

"Well, first off you won't need a permit unless you are planning to go into a full fledged mining operation. Just to do some searching, no permit. As for the guns, try the outfitter store down the street. Talk to Liege Blackhorse. He owns the place."

"Yeah, we've met him," Virgil said, shaking his head. "I don't think he'll be happy to see us. We lost five of his horses and two pack mules."

"Is that where you got the animals?" Will asked.

"Yeah, why?"

"Well, those horses of his always come home," he said. "He has 'em trained to come home if they get loose. Yours came home three or four days ago. Happens all the time."

"You gotta be shitin' me!" Rob said, slapping the tabletop. "You mean we've been worrying all this time, dreading when we had to tell him, and his horses were home all along?"

"Looks that way, Rob." Will chuckled. He looked at Clay. "Liege has all kinds of guns and he's reasonable. He's a good man. Just likes a good practical joke once in a while."

"Their practical joke nearly got us killed," Ken said.

"Norman must have gotten mad at you guys. He would usually leave a little water behind for his victims. And no one has ever been attacked by a lion before," Will said. "Liege wouldn't hurt anyone intentionally. His brother is Apache Junction's Chief of Police, Dennis Blackhorse. And unlike Wilkins, the Chief's a decent guy."

"Good," Virgil said. "As soon as we finish here, we might just as well head over to the outfitter's place. Maybe he's in the mood for a practical joke. Somewhere out there, we threw away five pairs of his chaps."

* * *

Liege Blackhorse stood in the center of the store's floor with his big arms folded over his chest as he listened to Clay.

"We had to pitch the chaps. Weak as we were, they got too heavy. Just tell me how much they cost and we'll settle up with you," Clay said. "I heard the horses came home a few days ago."

"Sure did, son. Came charging right down that street hell bend for leather and skidded to a stop right out front." He shook his head. "Too bad about old Norman. He wasn't a bad sort - just a little crazy is all. Only fun he ever had was tricking the city boys." He started to laugh, but saw the stern expressions on their faces and changed his mind. "Uh, uh, well, anyway, I'll figure up the cost on the chaps. I'll have to replace them, you know. Now, what can I do for you fellas today?"

"Will said you might have some guns you'd be willing to sell," said Clay.

"What kind of guns? Handguns? Rifles? Shotguns?"

"Handguns," Clay answered.

Liege walked over to a wooden cabinet behind the counter. Unlocking it, he threw open the doors, exposing several handguns. He waved his arm across the guns. "Choose your weapons, my good men. Used, but every last one in excellent condition."

Stepping up to the counter, the boys looked the guns over.

Clay was first to speak. "Let me see that old Smith and Wesson 9 mm automatic."

Liege handed him a handsome black, semi-automatic pistol. "Holds fifteen rounds. Great gun for close range fighting when you're outnumbered."

Clay worked the slide on the pistol.

Rob and Brian chose .45 caliber semi-automatics.

Ken, not to be caught short again, took two of the 9mms.

Virgil, after looking the guns over good, pointed to a long barreled revolver. "That one, Liege. The big one, what's that?"

Liege retrieved the huge handgun. "This, my friend, is one terrific weapon. It's awesome. A real powerhouse. Smith and Wesson .44 mag with an eight inch barrel. Kill your ass from a mile away."

Virgil tried the mechanics of the gun and turned to Liege. "I'll take it and a holster. Better give us plenty of ammunition, too. I sure as hell don't want to run out up there."

Liege chuckled. "Well, if you did, you could beat 'em to death with the barrel of that pistol you got there."

Liege gathered everything the boys would need and began writing out the bill.

"Don't forget the prorate you promised if we didn't use your horses the whole week," Clay said.

Liege looked hurt. "You mean you're gonna hold me to that after all the weight my horses lost running back home?"

"Why not? We lost more than they did," Clay said.

Liege thought for a minute. He could picture the five men running after the horses. He shook his head and laughed. "You drive a hard bargain, son. How about I deduct the refund from the cost of these guns."

"That'll be just fine," Clay replied, relieved that the man gave in so easy. He hadn't expected to see any of the money refunded.

Liege motioned for the boys to follow him as he headed for the backdoor. "Let's go try those guns out. I got a little range set up out back. If you're like other city boys, you need the practice or you're likely to shoot each other."

The thunder of shooting echoed through the streets as the men shot targets and familiarized themselves with their weapons.

An hour later, Liege called a halt. "I think you got it. Not the best I've seen, but at least now you know how to operate the damn things. You come back in three days and pick them up."

"Three days? Why not now?" Clay asked.

"Federal law says so. The three days is a cooling off period. They hope by having this law, if you get mad at someone and decide to kill them, rush out and buy a gun, by the time the three days are up, you've cooled down enough to not to want to kill that person. I don't necessarily agree with it, but it's the law."

"Well, if it's the law, then we wait." Clay looked at the man with some respect now. "Thanks, Liege. Will Barnett was right when he said you were a good man."

Liege winked. "Just be careful up there. Them's killer mountains."

"So we've been told... several times now." Clay replied.

"By Godfrey, let someone shoot at us now," Rob stated, admiring his new pistol that Liege was putting away.

As they walked away from the store, a new pickup pulled away from the curb and followed a block or so behind, unnoticed.

* * *

Three days later, at the motel, Virgil stuffed his gun under the pillow on the bed and turned to Clay. "Get the boys and let's do a check of the helicopter. We need it ready to roll, come morning. Looks like Ken will be ready by then." He stopped for a minute. "That is if someone hasn't towed it to the pound for illegal parking behind that old motel."

"I'm sure it's still there," Clay answered.

"By the way, Clay, has Ken been to the nurse yet today?"

Clay jumped up and hurried toward the door, "Hell, no! I'd better run next door to his room and get him over there."

Brian heard the pounding and opened the motel door. Before he could say anything, Clay yelled past him. "Ken! You've got to get those bandages changed. Come on. Let's get going. The clinic will be closing soon."

Ken staggered out, running the fingers of one hand through his hair while the other was buttoning his shirt. They headed off down the street toward the clinic.

Brenda Carpenter was just locking the clinic door when they came running up.

"We too late?" Clay called out before they got there.

Brenda jumped, startled by his unexpected voice. "Uh - no-no. Not too late. I'll just unlock the door and we'll get Ken fixed right up," she said cheerfully, as she put the key back in the lock and opened the door.

Following her inside, Clay leaned against a wall and watched while she worked on Ken.

"I'd began to wonder where you guys were," she said. "Figured you'd left for the big city already."

"No, we've decided to head back up on the mountain in the morning," Clay said. "Think Ken will be okay to travel by then?"

"I don't know. Maybe you'd better ask the patient."

Ken was quick to respond. "I'm okay, Clay. I'm fine. I'll be ready. This is nothing."

Brenda started removing bandages. When she cut the last off, she examined the wounds. "The infection is almost all gone. I don't suppose the trip will hurt him if the wounds don't break open and cause another infection. Ken, I don't want you lifting anything heavy for a few days. Give your body time to heal." She put bandages on some of the deeper wounds, then turned to Clay. "Check the bandages every day for signs of drainage or blood. There shouldn't be any. If there is, put some of this antibiotic cream on it, then re-bandage." She handed Clay a tube of cream.

Ken started to give her some money, but she pushed it away. "There's no charge for this," she said. "I wish you guys weren't going back up there, but if you must, I want you to be careful. It's a wilderness, you know. Anything can happen. Try not to let my good nursing be a waste of time."

Ken put the money in his pocket. "Maybe you could have dinner with us tonight at Will's. We'll even buy!"

Brenda looked at Ken, then at Clay to see if he extended the invitation as well.

Clay smiled and winked. "Why not? Might be fun."

"Okay. Supper at Will's it is. I'll meet you there in one hour," she replied and shooed them out the door. "Now run along while I clean up - again."

They hurried out and strolled back to the motel.

Along the way, Clay said, "I think she likes you, Ken."

Ken laughed. "That wasn't the impression I got, brother. She was looking at you for the invitation."

"That's your imagination, Ken, I'm not her type. Besides, I'm a married man and don't consort with other women."

"Bullshit! You're just afraid you'll get caught!"

"Wrongo, my young friend. I'm a faithful man. Yes-sir, faithful as hell I am."

The smell of food cooking in the kitchen drifted across the large table in Will's restaurant to mix with the delicious aroma of Brenda's perfume as the treasure hunters studied the menus.

Clay put his down and looked across the table at Brenda. She was very pleasant to look upon.

She lowered her menu as though she could feel his eyes on her. "What're you having, Clay?" she asked.

"Probably the fried chicken. I doubt I'll have another chance at that for a while."

"I don't know, maybe we'll find us a little Señorita up there who can cook chicken," Rob offered.

"The only thing you'll find up there is trouble," Brenda replied.

"I take it you don't believe there is such a thing as the Lost Dutchman's Mine," Virgil said.

"I don't know," Brenda said, half-heartedly. "There's lots of stories around that would lead one to believe it's up there, yet no one has ever found anything positive."

Brian couldn't resist the chance to stir the pot. "I hear there's ghosts up there cutting off heads. Is that right?"

"Somebody's cutting off heads, though I doubt it's a ghost," Brenda grinned.

This started a long conversation about ghosts, gold, and killers that continued throughout the meal and still later at the saloon. Excitement built as they listened to Brenda's many stories. It was quite obvious that they had found a friend.

It was late when she finally glanced at her watch. "Damn," she said, "Look at the time. I have to go. I have to be at work early."

When she stood, chairs emptied as the boys jumped to their feet in true gentleman style.

"We'll walk you back to the clinic," Ken said.

"No. I have my car just outside. I'll see you guys when you get back." She quickly turned and left the saloon.

Clay got to his feet. "I wouldn't want her to get kidnapped, too," he said, hurrying for the door to make sure she got to her car safely.

"I think we'd all better hit the sack," said Virgil. "We have to leave early in the morning."

As they headed for the motel, each in his own thoughts, Davis and Wiscoff slipped from the doorway of the saloon and stood grinning at each other. Tomorrow they would be taking a chopper ride. In the dimly lit saloon, they had managed to get close enough to hear everything. When the city boys were well out of sight, they hurried to the pickup.

26

It was social security and public aid check day on the mountain and the recipients were in a spending mood. Cigarette smoke cast a thick haze in the saloon and loud music spilled from a windup piano near the dance floor where a drunken couple was trying to do the two-step. The tables were filled with dirty looking men just in off the mountain and whiskey flowed as they grabbled with women who hovered about them, trying to lure them into the back rooms to sample their wares.

At the back of the room, Big Alice sat at her table sipping wine and watching her girls work the lonely prospectors who had ventured in from the heat with money in their pockets. Money they would not have when they left.

Alice motioned to a young Mexican woman at a nearby table with one of the men. The girl hurried to her.

"Go back there and bring that girl out here. She needs to see this."

The woman hurried toward the back while her male companion yelled for her to come back.

She quickly returned with Laura in tow. Pointing Laura toward Alice's table, the young woman headed back to her impatient friend.

Laura walked slowly, head down, over to Big Alice's table and stood waiting for orders.

"Sit down, Girl."

Laura sat in a chair, but didn't look up.

"I want you to watch my girls work. You'll see that they're having fun."

Laura, not wanting to make Alice angry, raised her head and looked around the room. She didn't really see much in the hazy room, just a few blurry images of men and women laughing, talking, and snuggling at the tables.

"You could be having fun, too, you know. All's you have to do is get yourself cleaned up and grab one of those men flashing all that money."

Laura looked back down at the table. She shook her head. "I can't do it, Alice. I just can't do it."

"Well, you just suit there and watch. Maybe you'll learn something anyway."

27

$\mathbb{A}$s the first streaks of dawn escaped the horizon to spread across the vast sky in the east, Virgil was already at the helicopter, doing a routine run through of the mechanics.

Clay checked the supplies. They were prepared for what they had originally come here to do - go up to Weaver's Needle to start their search. He wondered if Crazy Norman had not sidetracked them, if they would have found the gold by then. He checked the last straps on the supplies and crawled out of the helicopter.

Virgil was standing by the door, pointing to his watch as Brian, Ken, and Rob arrived on the run. "You're late!" he scorned good naturedly and chuckled as they threw their gear inside and scrambled aboard.

Out of sight behind the helicopter, Clay slipped the bottle of pills from his pocket and gulped one down. He felt one was enough this time, seeing as how they weren't going very far. At least he hoped it would be enough. He jumped inside and took the co-pilot's seat again.

Virgil came aboard and, after doing a final cockpit check, pushed the starter. The engine whined and coughed as he pushed starter continuously. Finally, it caught and slowly gained power. Virgil's eyes constantly scanned the control gauges for any signs of a problem.

Clay once again had a death grip of the sides of his seat as the craft slowly rose from the ground, gaining altitude fast. Though, the pill was slowly taking effect, Clay's heart was still in his throat. He forced himself to look out the window. Far below he could see the motel getting smaller and smaller as they gained altitude. Off in the distance rose the haunting forms of the Superstition Mountains. He closed his eyes.

Behind them, a small blue helicopter rose from the horizon and followed. Inside the chopper, Wiscoff and Davis were doing Rockford's bidding - following the city boys to see where they were going.

When Virgil reached the desired altitude, he leveled off the craft and settled back to enjoy the ride. Glancing out the window, he could see the mesquite, cacti, and sand of the desert lying peacefully as in the lull before a storm. The early morning sunrays had not yet reached a boiling point. He watched the desert give way to small foothills and finally to sharp upheavals of solid rock. They had entered the mountain range. He marveled as he thought back to a few days earlier, when they had traveled the same route on horseback. It had taken the better part of two days to get this far. The helicopter turned that same trip into mere minutes.

As Virgil was enjoying the view below, he caught a glimpse of Big Alice's saloon. He tapped Clay on the knee and pointed downward. Clay was slow to respond, but Rob, Brian, and Ken all grabbed a window to see what Virgil was pointing at.

"We'll have to check that place out sometime!" Rob yelled from the rear, "Might be there's a good time to be had there!"

Virgil nodded and busied himself, trying to trim the ship as he felt the first tug of a crosswind blowing between the two huge peaks forming the canyon they were flying through. A smile creased his face as the chopper reacted to his touch.

Beside him, Clay still clutched his seat, his head down, eyes closed.

Virgil gave him a quick glance and yelled over the roar of the engine. "I thought you were going to navigate for me. You know where the Needle is, I don't."

Clay opened his eyes at the sound of Virgil's voice. "I have to check the topical map," he nervously replied.

"Then you'd better get a move on or we'll be back in L.A.," Virgil chuckled.

Forced to turn loose of his seat, Clay reached for his briefcase. He retrieved a map. Unfolding it, he felt himself relaxing a little as his eyes searched it for their location. Running a finger over the lines, Clay stole a quick look outside. Off in the distance to the right rose a spear of solid rock. He pointed to it and yelled, "Over there, Virge! There's Weaver's Needle!"

Virgil glanced at the sheer walls of rock that rose straight up to the heavens. It stood alone, an unusual formation for these mountains. Virgil could understand where it got its name. He slipped his right hand slightly to the right and the huge green ship banked around and headed for the peak.

The sudden direction change caused Clay to grab for his seat with both hands, dropping the map. He managed to lift one hand and point out the window. "Land on that flat plateau to the north of the Needle!"

Virgil nodded, then pushed down slowly on the collective control. He felt the chopper slowly start to descend. At the same time, he felt the strong pull of the crosswinds grab hold. The helicopter shuddered slightly. He enjoyed the feeling that rushed through his veins, a feeling he had not felt since his missions over Vietnam.

With the chopper at an angle and drifting downward, Virgil spotted the plateau Clay was talking about.

It was a beautiful sight. It was about three hundred yards wide and maybe three miles long, tapering off at one end to a narrow trail that led downward, twisting around to the canyon floor. The other end fell away in a gentle slope to another plateau some two hundred feet below, easily accessible by horseback.

On one side, a steep rock wall rose a couple of hundred feet straight up. At it's base, nearly hidden among a stand of scrub pine and scattered cottonwood and sycamore trees, a swift, mountain stream cut its course thirty feet wide through solid rock. The clear swift water churned around large boulders before cascading down through the trees to plummet into a beautiful falls over the south rim.

The other side of the plateau was a sheer drop off of two hundred feet with scrub sage and other small desert plants growing along it's edge.

Gently, Virgil maneuvered the big whirly-bird and set it down near the mountain stream.

28

While Virgil was setting his craft down on the small plateau, Wiscoff was turning his away. "I think that's where they're going to land!" he yelled. "We'd better get back and tell Rockford. That's pretty damn close to his holdings!"

Davis nodded his approval as the LOH slowly descended the mountain toward Big Alice's. "Why don't we stop there and tell Alice to keep a watch up here. She might see something," he said.

"You just want some whiskey, or maybe have a go at one of Alice's whores," Wiscoff laughingly replied.

Within minutes he was setting the chopper down in the yard near Alice's favorite chair. Shutting off the engine, both men headed for the saloon and something cold to drink.

In the rear bedroom, Laura, pale and weak from the lack of food and water, worked feverishly to get the hinge pins to move, but was having very little luck. She had no idea who it was, but she had heard the helicopter come in and wanted to get out. Maybe they would help her. Laura was weak but she was still determined to escape.

Padro was standing just inside the door as Davis and Wiscoff entered the dimly lit saloon. "What you two doing way up here, gringos?" Padro asked. "Señor Rockford got you running errands for him? What does the big man want this time?"

"Padro, sometimes you piss me off with that smart mouth of yours," Davis said. "One of these days, I'm going to shut it for you." He tried to walk around the big Mexican.

Padro blocked his way. "How about now, gringo? Want to shut it right now?" he said menacingly, squaring off at Davis.

Padro's attention was intently on Davis, and he did not see Wiscoff pull his 9mm pistol.

"Maybe you'd like me to shut it, Padro - permanently," Wiscoff said, cocking the pistol and sticking it out toward the big Mexican.

Seeing the gun, Padro threw both hands in the air. "No, No, Señor Danny! I like you! I don't want no trouble with you. It is only this gringo who make me angry."

"Padro!" Big Alice yelled from behind the big man.

Padro jumped and looked around.

"Padro! Get your taco ass back here and let the company alone!"

"Sì, Señorita! I come now," Padro answered. He turned to Davis. "You had better be very careful around me, gringo. Someday, I think I will have to kill you," his voice was low and threatening. He hastened toward the rear of the saloon.

Davis and Wiscoff stood laughing at him.

"I wouldn't be too hasty to laugh, gringos," Alice said. "You both almost met your maker."

Wiscoff and Davis looked up to see Alice pointing a double-barreled shotgun.

"Now, don't be messing with my man anymore, you hear me?"

The two men stood looking at her to see if she was kidding or not.

Alice had never liked these two men. They reminded her of two Doberman Pinscher dogs lunging at the end of a chain held by Rockford. She cocked both barrels of the shotgun. The sound of the metallic clicking echoed across the porch.

"We heard!" Wiscoff said quickly and eased his pistol back into his pocket. They stood stock-still waiting for the woman to make the next move.

Alice lowered the shotgun. "That's more like it. Now, why did old Rockford send you up here?"

"There's some men up on the mountain," Wiscoff was quick to answer. "Same damn bunch as before. Only this time they're in a helicopter. The boss wants you to keep a close watch, so they don't go near his place. Wants you to send a runner if they start flying around up there."

"I saw 'em go in up there. But you tell Rockford it'll cost him dearly for me to keep that close a watch," she said, motioning for the two men to follow her inside.

Pouring them a drink of whiskey at the bar, she continued, "If he don't like that, tell him to get his own ass up here and watch them folks. I can't be looking up there too damn long anyways. Hurts my neck, you know, looking up through them binoculars like that. Ain't young as I used to be."

"We'll tell him just that, Alice," Wiscoff said, gulping down the whiskey and heading for the door.

Davis was close on his heels. They wanted no part of her and that damn scattergun. Rumors had it she'd killed many a man with that very gun.

Laura stopped prying at the hinge pins when she heard the roar of the helicopter as it started. She hurried to the window and watched as it flew away. Reluctantly, she returned to her bed to wait for another time.

Half an hour later, the LOH set down in Rockford's yard. Davis scrambled out as Wiscoff let the engine wind down then shut off the power.

Rockford sat on the verandah watching their approach.

Davis hurried to him. "They're all the way up near Weaver's Needle, Boss. Looks like they plan to set up a camp."

Rockford didn't answer for a minute, but sat deep in thought. Finally, he slammed his right fist into his left palm. "By God, they don't scare off easy, do they?" he said, more to himself than to Davis. Getting up from his seat, he walked to the edge of the porch and stared off toward the mountains barely visible through the haze. "I want you two to set up a camp near them. Use whatever means necessary to discourage them from staying!" He turned to look Davis straight in the eye. "Tom, you're in charge of this little mission. If you think you need any more help, take one of the Mexicans with you." He pointed his finger in Davis' face. "You fail, and I'll have your ass! Comprénde?"

"Yes, sir! You know you can count on me, Boss!" Davis answered quickly.

Wiscoff, who had joined them, spoke up. "Want us to take the chopper, Boss?"

"How are you going to get it up there without drawing attention to yourself? No, I want you to take horses and pack mules. Take one of our radios, too, just in case I need to contact you in a hurry. I have the base station in the house."

"Okay, Boss. We'll leave at first light," Davis said.

"You'll leave today. I want you on them as soon as possible."

"Yes sir."

"You check in with me every few hours by radio."

"Yes, sir!" Davis called over his shoulder.

Davis scurried for the corral, yelling to Wiscoff. "Danny, you get the supplies together. I'll get Josè Diego to go with us. He can take care of the camp and cook."

Rockford stomped inside and grabbed the telephone. He dialed a number and waited impatiently. "Wilkins!" He shouted into the phone. "Rockford here! Listen up! There won't be any deliveries made for a while."

"Why the hell not, Paul?" Wilkins yelled back. He had banked on this last sale. He needed the money. "You know we made a deal the other night with some big money people. Don't go screwing it up now!"

Rockford's temper flew out of control. "Look, you fat, bald-headed, two-bit tin star, dope pusher bastard! Don't you give me a hard time or I'll send Tom and Danny to pay you a little visit. Or better yet, I'll come pay you a visit."

Wilkins' attitude changed drastically. "Okay! Okay! Settle down, Paul. Shit, man, you just caught me by surprise, that's all. I got other people to deal with, you know. They sure ain't gonna like this!"

"I don't give a damn what they like, Wilkins. Now listen to me, you weasel. I run this operation, not you."

"I know that, Paul."

"Just don't you forget it again. You understand me, chubby?"

Wilkins winced at the word chubby. *Hell, I'm stocky built, not fat. He's just trying to piss me off.* "Yes, sir, I understand."

"There's a bunch of men up on the mountain looking for the Dutchman. I don't know how long they're going to be there, but I have an eye on them. We're trying to run them off without having to kill them."

"You mean those bastards went back up there, after me telling them to stay away?"

"Sure as hell did. This time in a helicopter."

"What if they find your operation?"

"Then I'll have to see that the Dutchman claims some more victims, won't I, Wilkins?" Rockford slammed the telephone down and stood deep in thought. He couldn't stand that man. He was nothing but a fat, greedy pig. "One of these days I'm going to have to kill that bastard," Rockford said out loud, as he walked out to watch Davis and Wiscoff leave.

29

Virgil sat quietly staring out at the surrounding area, mentally marking out his lift off pattern should they have to leave in a hurry - a habit he had gotten into while in Vietnam. He looked at Clay, who still clutched the sides of his seat, his eyes closed. "We're home, Clay. You can open your eyes now."

Clay opened his eyes. "I knew that," he said, turning to look out at the rugged terrain around them.

Behind him, Rob, Ken, and Brian scrambled to get out of the helicopter, eager to set up their base camp.

Slowly, Clay unbuckled his seat belt and followed them out. When his feet hit the ground, he felt much better, though he swayed slightly from side to side as he tried to walk. It would take a minute to gain his footing.

Clay squinted his eyes to see Weaver's Needle. It looked farther away now that they had landed. "How far away do you think that is, Virgil?"

Virgil walked over to where Clay stood and looked off toward Weaver's Needle. "I'd say a good six miles, maybe a little more."

"I thought we were closer, but this'll do just fine. I figure the Dutchman is somewhere on or near this plateau."

Taking a stroll around the plateau, Clay searched for a place to set up camp. Sucking in a deep breath of the hot, but refreshing, mountain air, he decided on a spot just inside the stand of cottonwoods along the stream. They would shade the whole camp most of the day. This area was far enough away to keep them clear of any falling rocks from the ledge above and still afford them some cover, should they be attacked. He looked back. He was alone. The others were already wandering along the creek bank looking for gold. He grinned. Eager damn bunch. "Rob!" Clay yelled. "You guys grab the gear and let's set up camp before we get too involved in prospecting!"

The rest of the morning passed swiftly as the men labored in the stifling heat to set up two large tents. When they finished, they stowed away their gear in the tents and paused for a few minutes to catch their breath and grab a snack.

"Good eye, Clay. I like this spot," Virgil said, leaning against a large boulder, eating a spam sandwich. "We'll have to gather plenty of wood for a fire, though. I have a hunch it gets colder'n crap up here after that sun goes down."

"Sure couldn't tell it now," Ken said, sliding his fingers across his forehead to sling away the sweat. "Hotter'n hell right now."

Ken pointed at a large cottonwood tree. "How in the hell do those trees grow out here in the desert?"

Clay looked at the tree, then the area around the camp. "I'd say there's water here year round. Either above or below ground. That stream feeds 'em while it's full and there's probably under ground pools down deep. Cottonwood trees have long tap roots that can reach them."

Brian crawled over to where Clay sat against a tree. "We going to start searching for gold right away - this afternoon?"

"There'll be plenty of time for that, Brian," Clay said, looking around. "I think we'd better check the area out for anything that might prove to be dangerous, before we get too engrossed in searching for gold."

Rob, lying under the shade of a tree with his hat pulled down over his eyes, called out, "I think we should take along one of the conventional metal detectors just in case."

Clay gave the suggestion some thought. "I don't see how that would hurt. Who knows, might latch onto a nugget along the way. Each group can take a detector along."

Something a few yards away caught Clay's eye. He shook his head as though to clear his eyes as he stared off toward the stream. Standing near a large cottonwood, his arms folded across his chest, was an old Indian man, complete with buckskin clothing, beaded breastplate and full headdress.

Clay couldn't believe his eyes. He didn't know what to do. He sat up slowly so as not to scare him off. Stuttering, he pointed in the Indian's direction. "H-h-hey, you guys! Look over there." He glanced over to see if they had heard him.

All four men were looking toward the place Clay was pointing. They turned to look at him.

Clay looked back and the Indian was gone. He jumped up. "I saw him! He was standing right over there by that big cottonwood tree!"

"Who was standing right over there, Clay?" Brian asked.

"An old Indian man! A Chief!"

Brian grinned, "Sure, and I see Wild Bill Hickok standing right over there, too."

"I tell you it was a real Indian," Clay said, glaring at Brian.

Clay wondered why they couldn't see the Indian. It was the same one he had seen when they were walking out of the mountains. "He had on buckskins and a full head dress." Clay said, searching the cottonwoods for signs of the Indian. Had to be him. Disappeared just like before. But why was he watching them?

The others sat staring at Clay. "Come over to the stream with me. I can show you his tracks. He was standing right at the edge of the stream not twenty feet from us."

They all reluctantly rose and followed him to the stream. But try as they might, they found no sign of any moccasin tracks, only the boot tracks left by them earlier while they explored the stream for gold.

"I know you don't believe me, but he really was there for a second," Clay said, as they headed back to their food.

Brian chuckled, "Old Clay being part Apache and all, maybe it was one of his Apache ancestors come to pay him a visit. "

Clay grinned. "Could be," he said.

"Whhoooooo! Whhoooooo! Whhoooooo!"

Ken sprang to his feet. "What the blue blazes was that?"

"Hey, you guys!" Brian said, pointing to a branch of a nearby cottonwood tree. "Look at the size of that owl!"

"Biggest damned owl I've ever seen," said Virgil.

Rob studied the owl for a minute. "You know, they say when an Indian dies he comes back as an owl," he said. "Think that's our Indian Chief, Clay?"

Clay didn't reply. He sat watching the owl.

It stared silently down at them, opening and closing first one eye then the other, as though winking at the misfits.

After their meal, Clay called a meeting. "Look, fellas. I propose a few rules here. We don't know who," he paused to look at the owl, "or what is up here, so we'd better be prepared for anything. There should always be two or more of us together when we're moving around. Always keep your guns handy, and I would suggest we each carry a canteen of water and maybe a length of rope."

"What's the rope for, Clay?" Ken asked.

"Just in case we have to tie that old Indian up," said Clay. When he saw the blood drain from Ken's face, he chuckled. "I was only kidding, Ken, but I'll bet we'll find a hundred uses for a rope out here."

Ken recovered a little and nodded his head. "Makes sense to me," he said. "I packed plenty of hundred foot lengths of that new mountain climbing rope. Even got some hookups for repelling, if we need 'em."

Each man took a length of rope and shoved it up under their gun belt letting it hang out over it.

Clay looked around at the camp. The tents were up, the gear stowed, and the wood for the fire was in place. He was satisfied with it. "Let's go do some exploring," he said.

"Ken," Brian said, "why don't you and I check out the south end of this plateau, while the others check out the north."

"Let's get it done," Ken answered.

"Couple more instructions," Clay said, holding up his hand to stop their departure. "We meet back here at, or before sunset, and if anyone gets into trouble, fire three shots into the air."

The five treasure hunters set off to find their fortune.

Ever watchful for rattlesnakes, Rob, Clay, and Virgil picked their way along the outer edge. The sage bushes were nearly waist high in this area with a sprinkling of chollos. Scrub pine was scattered here and there, where they could find enough dirt in the rocky soil to grow. An occasional lizard would dart across a rock and disappear from sight.

The only sounds were those of the wind whipping through the dry sage brush and the constant buzzing of the metal detector Rob swung over the ground as he walked.

The sudden rattling of a snake disturbed by the vibrations of their steps stopped all movement.

"Holy shit, Clay! That's a rattler!" Virgil said, one foot still held in the air

"Yeah," Clay answered, trying to determine where the creature was. He stomped his foot.

The snake buzzed loudly.

"Coming from behind that rock," Clay said. "Step over this way and we'll ease around him."

The three men stepped lightly sideways until they were far enough away to pass safely.

The rattling stopped.

"Damn!" Rob exclaimed. "Gotta be on your toes all the time, don't you?"

"Looks that way," Virgil answered.

Running the metal detector, Rob began lagging a little behind, sweeping the large loop from side to side, hoping to hear the much sought after alert tone indicating the presence of metal. Fickle alert tones sounded weakly as the loop passed over mineralized rock. These were distracting but quite distinguishable from the real thing. They indicated to Rob that the area was loaded with mineralized rock - a good sign for the presence of precious metals.

Rob eagerly worked the detector, paying little attention to anything else. Moving slowly and using the loop to brush aside the sagebrush and weeds as he went, Rob moved closer to the edge of the plateau, the hum of the detector filling his ears.

Stepping into a thick patch of desert weeds, Rob suddenly felt himself falling. "A-a-a-a-e-e-e-e!" he screamed, automatically throwing out both arms. The metal detector went sailing across the rocks.

His arms slammed hard against the top edges of the hidden crevice he had fallen into, causing him great pain and slowing his fall only a bit. His arms were forced upward by his weight and he continued sliding downward. Screaming, clawing and grabbing for anything to break his fall, he suddenly slammed to a jolting stop.

Eyes clinched shut from pure terror, Rob froze in place. He waited for the inevitable - the smashing of his body against the rocks below. When that did not happen, he slowly opened his eyes and looked around to find himself wedged between two solid rock walls, some twenty feet down, in a huge crack in the plateau. "Oh, my God! Oh, my God!"

Feeling an updraft of air in his pant legs, he twisted his head to steal a glance past his shoulder and down. His stomach rolled and he almost vomited. "Oh, God!" He snapped his eyes shut as sweat poured from him. He had wandered out onto an outcropping of rock and fallen into a crack. Now his feet and legs dangled two hundred feet above the valley floor.

His breath came in short gasps as the walls compressed his lungs. He opened his eyes and looked around. He was shaking violently. *I have to get a hold on myself. I have to stop saying oh, God, oh, God. I have to scream for help.* He clamped his eyes shut again and screamed at the top of his lungs, "Clay! Virgil! Help! Please help!"

The scream had taken the air from his lungs and caused him to slip deeper into the crack. His heart jumped into his throat. He clawed at the rock walls for a handhold. Anything that would stop him. There was nothing. He sucked air into his stomach to expand it. He stopped sliding. He found that by taking short choppy breaths, he could hold enough air in his stomach to keep him wedged. Maybe he could hold this until his friends got to him.

Clay and Virgil had heard the scream and were running around searching it out. Spying the detector lying on the ground, Clay ran to it, nearly falling into the crevice himself.

Dropping to his knees, Clay gazed down into the huge crack. "How in the hell did you manage that, Rob?"

Rob didn't answer.

"Well, don't worry, we're here. Just hang on and we'll get you out!"

"Hurry, Clay! Hurry! I'm slipping!" Rob whispered desperately.

Yanking the rope from his shoulder, Clay quickly made a loop in it and began feeding it down to Rob.

Virgil ran up and looked down the crack. He grabbed the rope behind Clay and set himself to start pulling.

"Grab the rope and put it over your head and under your arms!" Clay yelled down at him.

"Okay, Okay!"

Rob reached for the rope before it got to him. The stretching caused him to slip even farther down. He screamed. He felt himself stop again. "I can't do it! I'll fall!

"No, dammit! You won't fall!" Clay snapped back. Then added calmly, "I know you're scared, Rob, but you have to stop your screaming. Take in a deep breath and hold it while you ease your hand upward. The air will keep you wedged in. This time don't stretch so far!"

Rob's arm trembled as he reached up and came into contact with the rope. He had it over his head and under his arms in the blink of an eye.

As soon as it was in place, Clay jerked the rope tightly - it held.

The rope made Rob feel better. At least he wouldn't fall on through the crack.

"Pull, Virge!" said Clay. "Pull hard!"

Muscles bulged, sweat popped out, and the rope cut into their hands as they strained to pull Rob up but he didn't budge from the crack.

Clay looked around frantically for Brian and Ken. They were nowhere in sight. Still straining on the rope, he yelled as loud as he could. "BRIAN! KEN! COME QUICK! HELP!"

Behind him, Virgil, gripping the rope hard with one hand, pulled his .44 magnum and fired three quick shots into the air.

The sudden, deafening explosions directly behind him, startled Clay. He nearly dropped the rope. "Jesus, Virgil! You could have warned me!" Clay yelled.

Putting the pistol away, Virgil shrugged. "Didn't have time, Clay."

Clay eased hand over hand on the rope to the edge and peered down to see that Rob was still stuck solid. He looked the walls over, and then saw that a few inches to Rob's right the crack was a little wider. If he were there, he would swing free and they could pull him up. "Rob, we can't pull you up from where you are. Try to force your body to your right a few inches. It's wider there. Use your feet to help push up."

Rob shook his head. He really didn't want to move. "I can't move, I'll fall!"

"Bullshit, Rob! Move your ass or we'll leave you right there," Virgil shouted.

Rob knew he had to move or die where he was - or on the rocks below. His mind raced. How the hell had he gotten himself into this fix? He took a deep breath. "What the hell," he whispered. "If I have to die, then so be it. May as well do it like a man." He looked up at Clay, "If I don't make it. Thanks for trying anyway."

"Knock off the shit, Rob. We'll get you out of there," said Clay.

With fear in his heart and determination in his mind, Rob closed his eyes, wiggled his body and pushed hard against the walls with his hands and feet. He slowly let out his breath. He felt himself sliding over and down at the same time. Suddenly, he fell free and slipped almost all the way through the crack.

The sound from his voice was neither scream, nor whisper, but some weird thing in between. Just when he thought he was gone, the rope jerked him to a stop. He dangled there, two hundred feet in the air, swinging back and forth.

Over his head, his friends were pulling with all their might.

The heels of Virgil's boots dug into the hard soil as he struggled to keep from losing ground. He strained on the rope, ignoring the searing, burning pain in his hands as the rope slid through them.

Both men pulled with all their strength, their faces red - the muscles in their bodies bulging. They were losing ground.

His eyes clinched shut as he strained, Clay felt his boots slide on the rock at the very edge of the crack. *My God! We're going to lose him.*

Suddenly, his forward movement stopped. He was making headway again. He opened his eyes. He didn't have to look back, he knew that Brian and Ken had grabbed the rope. It was easier now. With all four of them pulling, they were actually gaining ground. The rope inched upward.

Without looking around, Virgil gave a sigh of relief. "Thank God you guys got here in time. We would have lost him for sure," he said.

Slowly, Rob began to surface. First his hands, then his head came above the lip of the crack. He looked terrible. Finally, he was completely out, and flat on the ground, his head buried in his folded arms. The only movement was his heaving shoulders as he cried tears of joy.

Clay and Virgil flopped down on the ground and turned to thank Brian and Ken. Their mouths dropped open. Brian and Ken weren't there. There was nobody around.

Virgil was flabbergasted. "D-d- did you feel that? Did you feel someone on the end of the rope?" he asked.

"I sure as hell did!" Clay replied, in a whisper. "I thought it was Brian and Ken."

Still staring at the spot where Brian and Ken should have been, they stayed sprawled on the ground catching their breath.

When Rob got to his feet, he went to join them. "Thanks, fellas. I owe you my life," he said, shaking each one's hand.

"I don't know, Rob. We were losing you," said Clay. "Something else happened here and I'm not sure what."

"That's a fact," said Virgil. "But don't ask me what."

"Whhoooooo! Whhooooooo! Whhoooooo!"

Jerking their heads up toward a rock ledge some hundred feet away, they saw the huge brown owl.

"Sure makes you wonder, doesn't it?" said Rob.

"It sure does," replied Clay. "Damned spooky out here if you ask me. Let's get the hell back to camp before something else happens."

Rob stood for a minute, looking first at one, then the other. His voice trembling, he said, "Seriously, boys. I really don't know how to thank you for saving me."

"Don't have to, Rob," said Virgil. "Thank that old owl up there, or whatever it was. Like we told you, we couldn't have gotten you up without some kind of help."

"You may get a chance to save both of us before this trip is over," said Clay. "Now come on. The walk back'll do you good."

Rob still hung back. "There's one other little thing, boys."

Virgil and Clay looked at him

Hesitantly, Rob muttered, "W-w-would you two not mention about me crying and all. You know it wouldn't look good for me in front of Brian and Ken."

Clay and Virgil looked at each other for a second, then burst into laughter.

"Our lips are sealed, Rob," Virgil promised.

The walking eased Rob's tension, and he felt confident Clay and Virgil wouldn't say anything to the others.

Half way back, they met Ken and Brian coming at a run, pistols drawn.

"What happened? We heard the signal shots and came running," Brian asked.

"Jesus, Brian, you guys should have been there," Virgil replied. Rob nearly got killed."

"We were back at camp, and came as soon as we heard the shots," Ken said.

"Thanks, guys," Clay said. "We managed to save him - with a little help from someone."

They walked on toward the camp, with Virgil filling them in on what had happened.

It was dusk, and a pleasant surprise awaited them as they walked in. Brian and Ken had hung Coleman lanterns around in the shorter trees, set up the Coleman stove, and had dinner cooking. The smell made their mouths water.

"What's that you're cookin', Brian?" Rob asked.

"*I'm* cooking it," Ken corrected. "It's some of the best stew you've ever tasted and it's ready when you are."

"I gotta wash up first," Clay said, heading for the stream with Virgil and Rob close behind.

The cold mountain water felt good on their hot, aching hands. They splashed it over their heads and necks.

Hurrying back, they sank their teeth into the stew, and like Ken had said, it was the best they had ever tasted.

Ken and Brian had also prepared fried potatoes with onions as well as the old standby - canned pork-&-beans. A meal fit for a king.

As they ate, Rob told Brian and Ken again what had happened to him. They listened in awe as he told each step of the incident, adding a little here and there to juice it up, but making sure he steered clear of the crying part. He told them about the owl being there. The same one they had seen before. When he was finished, he looked to Virgil and Clay to substantiate his story.

They both nodded their heads.

Brian and Ken turned to glance around the camp towards the darkness beyond the camp lights. The night noises became louder. Even the crickets seemed louder.

Brian stood up and looked around. "Think we should post a watch? You know, just in case that Indian Clay says he saw comes back?"

"I think that owl is really the Indian," said Clay.

"No doubt in my mind now," Virgil chuckled. He hadn't seen any Indians, but he knew Clay. Unless he was cracking up, there was something to his story. Something happened back there today. Something helped them pull Rob from the crack.

"You guys remember when we were almost dying of thirst and I found the prickly pear cactus?" Clay asked.

"How can we forget?" Ken stated.

"Well, I know it's hard to believe, but that owl flew up and landed on a cactus, then an Indian appeared and showed me the cactus."

"Aw, come Clay," Brian said. "You don't believe in spirits and that crap, do you?"

"Whether I believe in it or not, it's true. He even picked one and ate it while I watched...damn amazing. I thought the heat had gotten to me, but now I wonder."

Virgil stood and brushed off the seat of his pants. "Well, I know I saw the owl, and I still don't know if it turned into an Indian, but I do know something happened out there today." He looked around the camp. "I don't think we need a guard for the owl, I think it's friendly, but I think I can rig up a little alarm, just in case someone besides it comes to pay us a visit."

He took a length of rope and stretched it around the camp, tying it to trees and rocks or whatever he could find. "Grab those empty tin cans you had from supper, dump a few rocks in 'em and bring 'em to me."

When the cans were ready, Virgil tied them onto the rope a few feet from each other. He stood back to admire his work in the light of the Coleman lanterns. "There! Ken, how about you testing it. This was very helpful during Vietnam."

Ken walked out of the camp, then back into it, pretending he didn't see the rope. When his legs hit the rope, the cans started jerking and the rocks rattled loudly in the still night.

"Well, Brian. Think you can sleep with that around you?" Virgil asked.

"If it worked for you in Vietnam, it'll work just fine for me," Brian grinned.

They sat around the fire and talked late into the night about everything that had happened to them so far, and about what they could expect tomorrow when they started the search with all the metal detectors. When the men finally laid down, it was to a troubled sleep, their minds still on Rob's accident and the owl, or Indian, or whatever it was, that had helped them.

30

Big Alice sat gazing through the binoculars, trying to catch sight of the helicopter or the men up on the mountain in the fast fading evening light. She laid the binoculars down on the table beside her and called out, "Padro! Come here!"

Padro hurried out of the saloon to her side as she picked up the binoculars and once again gazed up at the mountain. Without taking them from her eyes, she pointed toward the mountain. "Padro, I want you and Gonzales to take the horses and go up there. Find those city folks and keep a close watch on 'em. If they find anything, send Gonzales back to tell me. I'll let you know what to do after that."

"What do you mean 'find anything', Señorita Alice?"

"Dammit, Padro. What do you think I mean?" She snapped angrily at his stupidity.

"Uh, uh, maybe something - maybe some gold, huh?"

"Now you got it, dummy! G-O-L-D!"

"Sì, Señorita Alice, I leave right away."

Laura lay curled up on the bed, groaning. She was sick. Too, sick. Weak from lack of food, sharp pains shot through her stomach. Her head hurt and the bed seemed to roll as though it were a boat in rough water. She had to do something or she was going to die. Self-preservation set in and she rolled off the bed and staggered to the door.

Outside, the last rays of daylight had slipped away when Laura began pounding on the door of her room.

It was opened and Big Alice stood with hands on her hips glaring at her. "Now what?"

"Alice, I'm sick. I am really sick."

Alice looked her up and down. "What'da you mean, you're sick, girl?"

"I feel like I'm dying, Alice. I really need a doctor."

"Now looky here, girl. There ain't no doctors up here on the mountain, and you know I can't take you to town. That'd be too risky for me, don't you see?"

"Please get one to come up here," Laura replied.

"Well, sometimes there's this nurse who comes up here to check on these girls. She's due anytime now," Big Alice said as she examined Laura closely. "I don't think you need her or a doctor, girl. I think the only thing wrong with you is that you ain't been eating nothing. If you were to eat, I know you'd feel better."

Laura dropped her head and shook it. "I'm not going to be a whore for you, Big Alice," she said, as tears began to build in her eyes. "I know that man told you I was one, but that wasn't true. If I had been, I would have no objections to being one here."

"I'm beginning to think you're telling me straight," Big Alice said, thoughtfully. She didn't know what was wrong with her. Suddenly, here she was getting soft. This little wisp of a girl was growing on her. She found herself caring. After a minute of silence, she went on. "Look here. If I said you wouldn't have to be one of my working girls, would you eat a little something?"

Laura looked up at the big woman. The tears broke, and ran freely as she nodded hastily, "Y-yes. If I don't have to be a whore."

Big Alice took her hand and walked her down the hall and into the saloon where she sat down at her favorite table. Laura, bent over with weakness and pain, stood waiting.

Big Alice sat for a long time, staring at Laura. Then she looked around the room at her other people. She could see Juan the bartender, watching from his stool behind the bar. The cook, Juanita, stood leaning against the kitchen doorframe. Two or three of Big Alice's working girls sat at tables. They waited. Waited to see what her decision would be. She knew what they would like her to do, though they would never say it aloud.

Laura didn't move. She watched Alice's every movement.

Big Alice wondered if she was getting weak in her old age. There was something about this girl that she liked. Maybe it was the way she fought so hard against being turned out, even though she was alone up here. Maybe it was because she was so defiant, even in the face of sure death. Then again, maybe it was because she reminded her of herself when she was young. Big Alice wasn't sure what it was. She turned back to Laura. "Okay, girlie. You don't have to be a whore like Rockford said. Now, you go clean up a little and we'll get something to eat."

Laura started sobbing louder and deep sighs of relief could be heard around the room.

Crying and laughing at the same time, Laura quickly nodded her head to Big Alice and hurried back to the room where she had been kept prisoner for the past few days. For the first time since her abduction, someone was showing compassion for her. Laura only hoped it was real.

After she had gone, Big Alice turned to see a big smile on Juan's face. She shook her head. "Juan, you know I'll probably live to regret this." Then she chuckled deeply. "One thing for sure. Old Rockford gonna throw a fit when he hears about this. Maybe he'll do something to give me cause to kill his mean ass!"

Juan grinned. "That would make me happy, Señorita Alice. Señor Rockford, he is a bad gringo. It would be a fitting end for him, I think."

Big Alice looked around the dimly lit saloon, thinking over the situation. Her girls at the tables were talking excitedly among themselves. She knew they were glad she was helping the girl. All the girls were Mexican or Indian. Rockford had brought her a couple of the girls, but they had already been prostitutes wherever he had found them and they had no objections to turning out for her. Nor had they ever shown a desire to leave her saloon. Big Alice glanced down the hallway toward Laura's room. *Not so this little white girl from Apache Junction. No. Not even after a whole week of being locked up and not eating. She is losing weight and does look sickly, that's for sure. All 'cause she won't be a working girl for me. Stubborn little thing.*

She turned to Juan. "No need to have her die just because she didn't want to screw every filthy bastard on the mountain. I'll deal with old Rockford when the time comes."

"Juanita!" Big Alice yelled toward the kitchen.

An ageless Mexican woman rose from a table near the kitchen door, stuck her head out and answered, "Sì, Señorita. What can I do?"

"Fix something to eat for Laura. I think she'll eat now."

A pleased grin creased the wrinkles on the dark face as the woman hurried off to the kitchen. She, too, was happy. She had been watching the young girl get worse day by day, but there was nothing she could do. Her own experience had proven that. Years ago, her husband, a prospector, had gone into the mountains. He never returned. Meantime, the young, innocent Juanita ran out of food. She was near death when the big black lady kicked open her cabin door and found her on the floor.

Big Alice took her to the saloon and nursed her back to health. When Juanita's husband was found dead, she had also stubbornly refused Big Alice's offer to work as a prostitute. Alice must have felt sorry for her, because she had let her be the cook instead.

"Sì! I will fix very good food!"

"Don't get carried away, Juanita. Just something to fatten her up a little."

In the dirty, barren room where she was kept, Laura was stripping off her baggy dress when the door swung open. Panic-stricken, she jerked the dress down to cover herself.

It was one of the girls carrying a wash basin of water. "Alice said you should wash up a little."

Relieved it was just the girl and not Padro, Laura nodded and retrieved the water. After the girl left, she soaked a piece of cloth torn from her old dress and hand-bathed herself as best she could. She hoped Big Alice was not lying to her about her not having to be a whore. She was starving. The smell of food cooking filtered into the room as it had every day while she lay refusing to eat. *Tonight, maybe it'll be different. Maybe tonight I'll get to eat.*

Hastily, Laura pulled on one of the dresses that Big Alice had brought to the room while she was trying to entice her to become one of her working girls. This dress fit much better. She even had a pair of shoes that actually fit. She managed a slight smile as she stood, running her hands through her hair to untangle it before she hurried from the room, following the aroma of fried beans.

Big Alice's eyes lit up when she saw Laura walk up to the table. "Well now, look at you, girl! You look just like a lady should. Sit down and let's eat, I'm starved."

The smell filling her nostrils was so overpowering that Laura thought she was going to be sick. She held her stomach and sat down just as Juanita hurried to the table with a large tray stacked with enchiladas, tortillas, refried beans, burritos, and some sort of soup that Laura had never seen. The sick feeling passed and her mouth began to water. The food smelled delicious.

Laura tried to hold back, but couldn't. She grabbed a spoon, filled it with soup, and dumped the hot liquid into her mouth. It burned all the way down. She grabbed for water to cool her throat.

Big Alice reached over and patted her hand. "Easy there, young lady. You'll really be sick if you don't take your time and let your belly get used to having something in it. Go slow, now."

Laura knew Alice was right. She stopped a minute, then spooned the soup more slowly. Tears welled up in her eyes as she ate portions of the other food on the table. It was delicious. It had been so long since she had eaten. In an amazingly short time, she felt stuffed. She hadn't eaten half of her food.

She stopped and sat quietly watching Big Alice eat. Even though she was this woman's prisoner, she felt beholden to her now. If only she would keep her word.

31

Rockford paced the floor, puffing on his cigar. His stomach churned and his face was hot as his temper rose. He hated to wait on anything or anybody. His men had been gone all afternoon and he hadn't heard one word from them on the radio. They should have checked in by now. Something had to be wrong. Davis knew better than to go against his orders.

He paced until his fury got the best of him and he dashed to the table holding a transmitter. Grabbing the microphone, he shouted into it. "For Christ's sake, Davis, where the hell are you guys?"

He waited a second or two. No answer came. He shouted louder. "Damn you, Davis, I'll have your ass for this!" Still getting no answer, he threw the mike across the room and rushed out the door.

* * *

The truck's engine roared as Rockford rammed it into gear, making a turn off the main road and heading it out toward the mountains. Even the new truck rocked and bounced over the rough desert road. Rockford had calmed down somewhat during the drive, but he was still anxious. He drummed his fingers on the steering wheel. He was going to see Big Alice. Maybe she had seen his men or at least those city men up there.

A coyote slunked onto the roadway, its eyes flashing bright yellow in the truck's headlights. Rockford grinned and swerved the truck to hit the gray animal. It leaped back just as the front wheel brushed its fur. Rockford pounded the steering wheel and laughed. His thoughts wandered from the coyote to that pretty little Laura Pratt. His mind conjured up the scene in his bedroom again. He felt a sudden rush of heat through his loins, and his lips spread into an evil smirk.

The truck's headlights lit up a sign that read:

BIG ALICE'S LAST CHANCE
SALOON - 20 MILES

* * *

A few miles ahead in the desert darkness, Rockford's men struggled with the mules. "Dammit, Tom! These stinking mules are wearing me out. We have to stop for the night!" Wiscoff yelled.

"Pretty soon, Dan. Pretty soon we'll be at Big Alice's."

Wiscoff reined up his horse. "What'd ya mean, Alice's? You know damn well Rockford will skin your hide if you stop there. We've been pussyfooting around all afternoon as it is. We're to get up to the Needle as soon as possible."

Davis pointed ahead. "Come on, Danny, it's right up there. Damn, boy, you worry too much."

"Maybe you should call him on the radio and tell him the pack animals slowed us down a lot."

"I've already tried that. The radio's not working right. Batteries must be bad. Now let's get moving."

* * *

Covering the twenty miles in short order, Rockford slid the truck to a stop in front of the saloon. When he got out, he stopped and looked off toward the peak of the mountain for a minute. *Where in the hell are my men? What in the hell are those damn greenhorns doing up there? Why am I having so much trouble keeping tabs on these guys?* Finally he turned and hurried up the steps.

"Big Alice!" he yelled as he stepped inside the door. He stopped to accustom his eyes to the dim interior. "Where the hell are you, Alice?"

At her table with Laura, Big Alice watched Rockford without answering.

Fear seized Laura as she recognized Rockford. She glanced at Big Alice, who sat staring at him. "Oh God, Big Alice! Please don't let him get me!" she whispered in terror.

Big Alice jerked her head toward the back. "Git to your room, girl."

Laura quickly shielded her face, jumped to her feet and ran full out for her room. She could not let this man see her. She could only pray that Big Alice would not let him get to her. She couldn't live through another of his attacks.

Only after she heard Laura's door slam shut did Alice speak. "What you want now, Rockford? Trouble?"

From the doorway, Rockford strained his eyes. *Wise ass bitch. Some day. Some day soon.* He spotted her at the rear table and strolled in his usual cocky manner back to her and flopped down in a chair.

"Didn't nobody ask you to sit down. I asked what you wanted," Big Alice growled.

"Now, Big Alice, don't be such a bitch. How come you always got to talk to me like that? Anyone else, I'd kill outright."

"You wanta try killin' me, sucka?" she snapped, her black eyes quickly narrowing.

"No, no!" Rockford replied, holding up both hands. "Jesus, Big Alice! I just came up here to see if you had seen anything of my boys. They headed up the mountain on horseback this morning and I haven't heard from them. Thought they may have stopped by here."

"Ain't seen 'em, Rockford. Now you can git!"

"Dammit, Alice! I'm losing my patience with you. Now lighten up a little. After all, we're partners - you and me."

Big Alice turned back to her tequila. Sprinkling salt on the web of her hand between her thumb and forefinger, she licked it off, then tossed down the tequila. A slice of lemon found it's way to her mouth, and she bit into the bitter fruit. Still she said nothing to Rockford. When she didn't speak or offer him a drink, he yelled at the bartender. "Juan! Bring me a bottle of tequila!"

Juan looked at Big Alice. She gave him a nod and he fumbled around under the bar and finally came up with a bottle. He shuffled over to the table and set it down, holding his hand out for money.

Rockford looked at him, then at Alice. "Well, hell's fire woman, I'm good for it!" he snapped in disgust.

Big Alice grinned and nodded her head again. Juan shuffled away.

"Damn! You'd think I was a total damn stranger or something. What's got into you lately, Big Alice?"

"Nothing. I just don't care for the way you treat people, Rockford. You treat everybody like they'se dirt under your feet. Some of us ain't, you know. I don't take none of your crap."

Rockford opened the bottle, poured his glass full, and gulped it down. He quickly poured another and gulped it down. He looked up at Big Alice. "So you haven't seen Danny or Tom."

"Ain't been here yet."

"Seen anything of those city boys up there?"

"I didn't figure those two dummies of yours would be able to find that big green helicopter, let alone the five little city boys, so I sent Padro and Gonzales up there this afternoon."

"Now look here, Big Alice, those boys do just fine. It's just a long ride on horseback."

"Could'a saved a hell of a lot of time if they had trucked the horses up here, then set out, don't you think?"

"Didn't think of that."

"See what I mean?" Big Alice chuckled.

Rockford guzzled down more tequila right from the bottle. He was already beginning to feel its effects. He looked around at the girls. He grinned wickedly at Big Alice. "Say, where's that pretty little girl I brought you, Alice? I don't see her anywhere."

"She's around," Big Alice answered. "Rockford, you're going to get us both thrown in jail." Big Alice tried to get his mind off the girl. "The money you pay me for keeping watch up there ain't worth it."

"Money? Money?" He almost screamed. "Is that all that's wrong with you? Hell, Big Alice, I can up your take. How much more you want?"

Big Alice looked him in the eyes. "It ain't money, Rockford. It's jail - prison, dammit. I ain't going to prison 'causea your mean ass."

Rockford leaned toward the woman. "You ain't going to jail, Big Alice. Nobody knows you're helping me. Nobody knows that girl is here. Nobody knows nothing."

"What about your people?"

"Hell, honey. They're involved up to their necks. They can't say anything. Besides, they know if they said anything, I'd hunt 'em down and kill 'em." Rockford looked around the saloon. "What about your help here?"

"Don't you go worrying none about my people. They's just fine."

Rockford looked around. Nobody was paying any attention to them. "That's good. The fewer people involved, the less chance of a leak." He looked across the table at Big Alice and grinned again. "Now about that girl."

"That girl *is* something to worry about, Rockford! She ain't no whore like you said. Why did you lie to me 'bout that?"

"I didn't lie, Big Alice. If you'll remember, I said I wanted you to turn her out as a whore."

"For your information, she ain't never been no whore nowhere. You kidnapped that girl, raped her, then dumped her here. Don't you know that kidnappin's a federal rap, dumb shit?"

"Don't worry, it's under control. I'll take care of her so nobody knows."

"Now don't you start that. I got no qualms 'bout killing someone who deserves it, but she don't deserve it."

"But someone who gets too near your precious Dutchman does, huh?" Rockford interrupted.

"That's different! They was all cheats and was trying to rip me off. It was like self-defense." She narrowed her eyes at Rockford. "Don't you piss me off, sucka."

Rockford knew he had gone as far as was healthy. "Okay, okay, but stop worrying. I'll take the girl off your hands."

"No, you won't. I'll figure something out."

Rockford's temper flared. "What do you mean, 'no'?"

Big Alice locked eyes with him as she slowly mouthed her words. "N-O! Spells NO, Rockford. You gave her to me. You don't get her back."

"Bullshit, Big Alice!" Rockford glared at her. He was angry. He knew she was at the present without her huge Mexican bodyguards, Padro and Gonzales, but still he had to be careful. This was her little kingdom, and he knew all she had to do was snap her fingers and everyone here would jump to do her bidding. Besides, he knew she was very capable of killing him with her own hands. He gulped down more tequila. The bottle was almost empty now. "Okay, Big Alice, I won't kill her. I'll just go back there and visit with her a little, then. Surely you can't object to that!"

"Let her be, Rockford," Big Alice warned. "She's not your type. If you're that horny, take one of the other girls."

He swayed as he stood up. "Not this time, Big Alice, I want her," he growled, as he headed down the hallway toward the room where Laura was hiding.

When he reached the door, he tried the knob. It was locked. Everything was against him tonight. His temper already high, he reared back and kicked the door. It crashed in with a loud bang.

Laura screamed.

Like a bull in heat, he charged into the room and grabbed her. "Hello, my lovely! Aren't you glad to see me?"

Blood rushed from Laura's head as she nearly fainted. She was crying loudly and struggling hard to get away from him. *Oh, no! Not again! Oh, please, God, not again!* She was weak from the lack of food, but she kicked with her feet, and fought for all she was worth.

Rockford just laughed. "Fight, bitch! Fight!" Pulling her near, he crushed his mouth against hers so hard she felt blood oozing down her chin. She bit his lip. Hard!

He yelled and jerked his head back. He flung back his fist to hit her.

A deafening blast erupted in the room.

Startled, Rockford jumped, but froze when he saw Alice standing in the doorway holding the smoking sawed-off shotgun. She didn't speak. Her eyes told Rockford all that was necessary.

He pushed Laura away from him. "Now go easy there, Big Alice," he said.

Laura hurried away from the bed and pressed against a wall in fear.

Big Alice cocked the other barrel of the shotgun.

Fear struck Rockford. He started to plead. "Please, Alice, put that thing down. You don't want to hurt me." He was slowly reaching under his coat for the pistol he kept in his belt.

Big Alice was having no part of that. "Keep them hands where I can see 'em or I'm gonna blow your balls off," she snapped at him, lowering the shotgun to point directly at his crotch.

"Okay, okay," he said, shoving his hands high over his head.

"Girl!" Big Alice snapped at Laura. "Get that gun from under his coat and bring it to me. And watch the sneaky bastard. He's liable to do anything."

Trembling with fear, Laura eased back to the bed and reached for the gun under his coat.

Big Alice watched her carefully to see that she didn't decide to use it on her.

When Laura had the pistol, she eased around Rockford, sliding along the wall of the small room to do so. She stopped just a few feet from Big Alice as she contemplated her chances with the pistol against the woman. It took only seconds for her to decide she wasn't that stupid. Laura stepped on over to Big Alice and handed her the gun.

"Boy, you sure as hell don't listen, do you? I told you she wasn't yours. Now get your ass outta here or, so help me, I'm going to kill you right here tonight." Alice ordered.

Rockford was slow to move.

"I said now! Right now! Git!"

Rockford still didn't move fast enough.

"Juan! Go get the shovel and start digging me a hole out back!"

"Now, there ain't no need for that kind of talk, Big Alice. I'm leaving. I promise. I'm sorry I didn't listen to you. Please, Big Alice!" He walked ahead of her, this time truly in fear for his life. When they got into the saloon, Rockford glanced up to see Juan aiming another shotgun right at his head.

"Want I should shoot him first, Señorita Alice?" Juan asked.

Big Alice chuckled. "Maybe in a minute, Juan. Let's see if he means what he says."

Rockford headed for the door with Big Alice right behind him.

When they reached the door, she stopped him. "Rockford, you may scare hell outta everybody down in the valley, but up here, I'm boss. I don't scare. Understand?"

"Yeah, Big Alice. Sure. I understand," Rockford said. "I'm sorry."

"Don't let this little girl cost you the sweet deal you got up here, Rockford. You hear me?"

Rockford looked at her for a second. He could get another woman if it was sex he was after. Like she said, no need to blow things here. Inside he was boiling mad, but he tried not to let it show. *I'll get even with you, bitch. If it takes forever, I'll get even.* Rockford knew that for right now it was better to leave on her good side. He dropped his eyes to the floor. "I hear you," Rockford answered. "And you're right, Big Alice. I guess I was letting my dick do my thinking for me. I won't bother her again."

"Best you go now."

Rockford stepped out the door and hurried to his truck. Leaning across the seat, he reached for the glove box. Slamming the door open, he grabbed another pistol and turned back to look at the saloon. Big Alice and Juan were standing on the porch with their shotguns still trained on him. He kept his gun hand low.

Big Alice smiled and waved at him.

He tossed the gun back in the glove box, slammed the truck into gear and roared off down the road.

As Big Alice stood watching him drive away, she wondered what she was going to do with the girl. One thing was sure, she wasn't going to do what Rockford wanted - kill her. She had never killed, or had anyone else kill, a woman and she wasn't about to start now. She had to draw the line somewhere. Maybe she could figure something out. Maybe Laura would get to like the place if she didn't have to be a whore. Maybe... maybe...maybe...

* * *

A hundred feet from the front of the saloon, Wiscoff, Davis and
Josè Diego sat on their horses in the dark and watched the activity. As
the pickup truck roared past, only twenty feet or so away, they could see
it was Rockford driving.

Wiscoff stared after the vanishing truck. "I'm not stopping here,
Tom. You do what you like, but Diego and I are going on. I want no
trouble with the boss."

Reluctantly, Davis nodded in agreement. "He must have come
looking for us," he said, turning his horse toward the mountains and
squirming to get comfortable in the saddle. "Guess you'll want to ride all
night now," he grumbled.

"No, Tom, I don't want to ride all night. Just away from here.
Then we'll get some rest." He pointed an accusing finger at Davis,
"Besides, it was your idea to ride straight through or we would have
been asleep hours ago."

* * *

Laura heard the pick-up truck roar away. Still shaking with fear,
she stared at the door. It was unlocked. Taking a deep breath, she got up
from the bed, reached under the mattress, and pulled out the bed slat.
Holding it like a club, she eased to the door and peeped out. Everyone
was still on the front porch. She had but a few seconds to make a try for
freedom. Laura dashed from her room, running full out for the back
door. She slammed through it and out into the night air.

Once outside, she ran for her life, ignoring her pain as the sharp
needles of the bushes tore at her flesh. Sand filled her shoes, and rocks
jabbed her feet through them. They were dress shoes, not mountain
climbing shoes.

Laura was free. She didn't know where she was or where she was
going, but she knew she had to get as far away as possible before they
missed her. She ran as fast as she could in the darkness and brush. She

was scared. Big Alice might get mad enough to kill her if she was caught.

* * *

Back in Laura's room, Big Alice stood with her hands on her hips, looking down at the bed. "She done run off," she said, shaking her head. "Can't say I blame her."

She walked back to her table and took a long pull on a tequila bottle. *Maybe it's best this way. Maybe it was meant to be. I won't feel so bad if she dies up on that mountain. At least, I won't get caught with her, and one thing for sure, that damned Rockford won't ever touch her again. I'm glad she left. Rockford would have found a way to kill her anyway.* She took another pull on the bottle and looked out the window toward the mountains. "Poor little thing won't last 'til morning out there." She said aloud.

32

$S$and in her shoes rubbed blisters on her feet, and blood ran down her arms and legs from the many scratches. Her dress was torn in several places. Finally, out of breath, she had to stop. Her eyes wide with fear, she looked back. She could see nothing. She listened. Nothing. Not a sound. Nobody was following her. She gave a sigh of relief.

She stood using the bed slat as a prop until she could breathe again. She had to move on. But where? It was pitch black around her. She had no idea what direction she was going. Which way? Which way must I go to get help? She had no sense of direction. She started walking. Any direction away from the saloon was good enough.

For hours, Laura stumbled along in the darkness. She was exhausted. Her dress was now in shreds, and she had long since lost her shoes. Sheering pain shot through her feet with every step. Blistered, cut and bleeding, she could hardly walk. Without warning, she fell headfirst down an embankment to the bottom of a gully. Landing hard, the breath was knocked from her. She lay gasping and wheezing for air.

Finally, she caught her breath and lay trying to determine if she had broken anything. She felt no pain, except the cuts and bruises.

Rolling over, she got to her hands and knees. The bed slat was gone. She searched for it, but couldn't find it in the darkness. She crawled up the opposite bank. Reaching the top, she struggled to her feet and looked around. It was still dark, but her eyes were now accustomed to the darkness; and she was able to make out images of plants and some of the larger rocks.

The hooting of an owl close by caused her to jump. A distant coyote let out a long lonesome howl. She shivered. She was scared. She sat down, dropped her head, and started crying. The owl called for its mate again. The coyote howled. Laura cried. She didn't know what to do. Maybe she should just stay where she was until daylight. At least until it was light enough to see. *Maybe I can see something. A house maybe.* Her eyes closed and she drifted off to sleep.

A loud scream filled the night air, causing Laura to jerk awake and leap to her feet. It was a cougar, and it was close. She tried to determine where it was by listening. The cat screamed again. It was behind her. It must have picked up her scent while she was sleeping. She started running. She had to stay ahead of it.

Struggling up a large sandy dune, she reached the top and was startled to see a red glow in the distance. It looked close, but at night in the desert, distance is deceiving. *A fire! It's a fire!* "Oh my God!" she said aloud. "I've made it! I'm safe!" She stumbled ahead. Behind her the cat screamed again. Closer this time. Laura broke into a run toward the red glow in the sky.

33

"Clay! Virgil! Get over here, quick!" Brian shouted from the edge of the stream.

Thinking he was in trouble, everyone scrambled from the tents, their guns at the ready, and ran toward him.

Brian yelled again, "Clay! It's gone!"

"What's gone!" asked Clay.

"The water! All the water's gone!"

Stopping beside him, Clay stared down at the streambed. Only a trickle was left.

Virgil had stopped beside Clay and was trying to catch his breath. He was angry. "Is that what you were screaming about?" he demanded.

"I wasn't screaming, Virgil. I was yelling. And yes, that's what I was yelling about. Yesterday that was a raging white water stream; today it's bone dry. What's going on here?"

"It rained somewhere up in the mountains yesterday, or the day before," Clay answered. "What we saw yesterday was the run off of that rain. There won't be any more water here until the next time it rains up there."

"That's a hell of a thing. How are we going to bathe and get drinking water?" Rob asked.

"Drinking water, we have. Bathing is something we'll just have to do without until the next rain. Roughing it, remember?" Clay answered.

"Clay's right," Virgil said, turning back toward the tent. "Now that you have us all wide awake, Brian, how about you fixing breakfast?"

By the time the sun poked it's head over the peak of the mountain, Clay had all the metal detectors out and was giving crash courses on the operation of each one. The long-range detector would be used to try to locate the gold mine, while the two conventional detectors would be used to detect any gold nuggets or other metal, such as tin cans, that would tell them that men had been there before - other men like Don Miguel Peralta or Jacob Waltz.

Clay conducted some dry runs for them, and they were able to see how the detectors worked and what to expect in the way of detection noises.

Two hundred yards away, an exhausted Laura stumbled blindly along in the early dawn light. Though she had prayed for daylight, now that it was here she could no longer see the glow from the campfire. She wanted to lie down. Every muscle in her body hurt. Pain shot from every scratch and every bruise. She needed sleep, but she knew she must force herself on toward the fire. It was her only chance for survival.

She stopped and squinted her eyes in the direction she had last seen the red glow. Smoke. She saw smoke - campfire smoke. Now she was really close. She brushed her hand though her tangled hair and wiped her eyes with her dress hem. She started walking faster now.

Within minutes, she saw the rotor blades of a huge helicopter above the brush. She started crying. Tears of joy ran down her face and she hurried her pace. She started to run. She was safe. She slammed hard into the huge outstretched arm of Padro Sanchez. The blow knocked her to the ground. She screamed.

Clay and his friends jerked their heads toward the scream. "What the hell was that?" Ken asked.

"Sounded like a woman screaming to me," Virgil answered.

"Probably another mountain lion," Clay said. "They say the cry of a mountain lion on the prowl sounds just like a woman screaming."

Clay looked around at his friends. "You know what happened to Ken and then with Rob yesterday, so don't take any chances today. I don't think we should go out of voice range of each other."

"And watch out for Clay's kinfolk up here," Virgil chuckled. "You know - that old owl or Indian or whatever it is."

Rob glanced up at the branches of the trees in the area. "You shouldn't make fun like that, Virge. It might be listening."

"That's true, Rob. That is true," Virgil answered, he too watching the tree tops as they left camp.

Padro was upon her before she could move, his huge hand covering her mouth.

Laura kicked and struggled, but she was no match for the monster of a man.

Padro motioned with his free hand, and Manuel Gonzales stepped out of the brush.

Gonzales looked toward the treasure hunters' camp, and seeing no movement, nodded to Padro.

Padro picked Laura up and carried the struggling girl to their horses tied in a gully a ways off. He grinned as he laid Laura on the ground and lay down beside her, still keeping his hand over her mouth. Her eyes showed her terror. "Too bad, little one. You almost made it. But since you have run away, now you must pay the price." He started feeling Laura's body with his free hand.

Manuel Gonzales watched. "Padro, Señorita Alice will not like this thing you are doing."

"She ran away, Manuel. She must be punished. Besides, Señorìta Alice need not know of this."

Gonzales chuckled. "She will know, my friend. I am loyal to her. I must tell her what you have done."

Padro stopped his pawing and looked up at his friend. "I haven't done anything yet. But you must also be loyal to me, Manuel. I am your friend."

Si, but you do not pay me like she does. So I must tell her. She will blow your balls off with her shotgun." Gonzales chuckled. "Then I will have to service your woman back at the saloon."

Padro glared at Gonzales for a moment. He grunted his disgust with his friend and ripped a piece of Laura's dress off to stuff it in her mouth. Securing the gag, he got to his feet. He picked Laura up and threw her over the rump of his horse. He mounted, and placed a huge hand on her back to keep her in place. He looked at the grinning Gonzales. "Some friend you are," he said, as he spurred his horse toward the saloon.

Laura lay across the rump of the horse, looking back at the smoke lazily making its way into the sky. She went limp as tears filled her eyes again.

34

Like the day before, the greenhorns set out in two different directions, slowly sweeping the buzzing machines over the ground ahead of them.

Virgil and Clay worked as a team on the long-range detector, while Rob ran the conventional one, keeping a close watch on where he was at all times.

Clay continuously swept the antenna over the terrain. The sun beat down and sweat soaked their clothing. By Clay's calculations, the heat index at high noon was about 120 degrees, and the strong crosswinds felt like a blast furnace hitting their faces. He wiped the sweat from his forehead and thanked the Lord for their old western hats, even if his did have a hole in it. Just the shade from the brim cooled the air at least ten degrees or so.

By late afternoon they had not found one single gold nugget, nor for that matter, anything else made of metal.

Consulting his watch, Virgil called out, "Think we should head back, Clay? It's 6:30 and we're an hour or so from camp."

Clay hated to leave. They were just getting to the area he figured the Dutchman was in. But he knew Virgil was right and reluctantly shut off the switch on the metal detector and pushed the antenna in. "Guess we'd better, Virge. Sure don't want to get caught away from camp come nightfall."

As they walked back, Clay glanced over at Virgil and Rob. "Do you think we'll be lucky enough that they'll have supper ready again today?"

"I wouldn't hold my breath. They may not be back in camp yet," Rob answered.

Rob had been right. When they arrived, Brian and Ken were just putting down their packs.

"Do any good?" Ken asked.

"Not one single hit," Clay replied. "Thee haven't been any men up here, or we would have at least found their discarded garbage."

"Tired as I am, I think a light sandwich and a hot cup of coffee is all I want for supper," Virgil said. He pulled off his boots, rubbed his sore, hot toes, and leaned back against a rock.

"Anything but Spam. I don't want any Spam tonight," said Ken, eyeing Brian. He knew Brian was a great one for Spam sandwiches and remembered hearing him say once that he could eat Spam for every meal. He had already pushed his Spam off on the rest of them several times during this trip.

Brian took the hint and rummaged through the packs 'til he came up with a small canned ham. He sliced it into five equal pieces and threw it into a skillet. "Hot ham sandwiches tonight, boys!" he announced.

This met with everyone's approval.

After eating, Clay and Virgil cleaned up the remnants of supper, while Rob walked the rope alarm to see that it was in good working order. The rattle of the rocks told him it was, and they would be warned if anything got too close.

Exhausted from the long day's work, bedtime came early. And despite the eerie night sounds of the wilderness and the distant flashes of heat lightning, the five treasure hunters were soon sound asleep.

35

Big Alice sat at her table, staring down at the food on her plate, when the back door burst open. She looked up as Padro pushed through it with the battered and tattered Laura slung over his shoulder. She felt relief sweep her body. She grinned. "I see you have found my little runaway."

"Sì, Señorita. We found her high in the mountains. She almost made it to the camp of the gringos."

"Did they see you or the two of you?"

"No, Señorita. They saw nothing."

"Well, put her down, Padro."

Padro slid her from his shoulder, and helped her to get her balance on the floor. As he took off the gag, he glanced back at Gonzales to see if he was going to say anything to Big Alice about what he had almost done to Laura. Gonzales grinned at him and hurried to the bar.

Big Alice pulled out a chair next to her and patted it. "You look terrible, girlie. Come sit here and have some food."

Laura looked at Big Alice.

Big Alice patted the chair again. "It's okay. I'm not going to beat you."

Laura dropped her head and slowly walked to the chair and sat down.

Big Alice glanced up at Padro. "You two get back up on the mountain."

Padro rushed to the bar and grabbed the glass of tequila that Juan had placed on the bar for him. He gulped it down and hurried after Gonzales, who was already going out the door. Padro pulled the door closed behind him and let out a sigh of relief that Gonzales had not said anything to Big Alice.

Reaching over and brushing some hair from Laura's face, Big Alice shook her head. "Laura girl, whether you believe me or not, I'm glad to see you. You could have been killed out there."

A hopeless feeling came over Laura. Tears welled in her eyes and spilled down her cheeks. "I almost made it," she said. "I was almost safe."

Big Alice nodded. "I almost wish you hadda made it, girl."

36

The violent clanging and banging of Virgil's tin can alarm jerked them all from their sleep.

Clay sprang from his cot, grabbed his gun, and ran outside. He could hear loud, weird, beast-like roaring coming from the bushes - sounds he had never heard before. Scared out of his wits, he pointed the gun first one way, then another, as he jerked his head from side to side trying to see what was out there and where it was. "Holy Shit! What are those things?"

The others, all armed and ready immediately joined him.

"What the hell is it, Clay?" yelled Virgil.

"Don't ask me!" Clay answered, his eyes wide with fear. "My God, I don't know what it is!"

Several large shadows were scurrying about at the very edge of the light cast by the campfire.

Imaginations ran rampant - attacking Indians, wild headhunters, and man-eating animals. Anxiety got the best of them, and they opened fire in all directions. The sounds echoed though the mountains in a deafening roar.

"My God, what is it? What are those things?" Rob yelled, firing his pistol at the moving shadows.

No one had time to answer. They were too busy blasting away at the beasts.

Clay saw one of the beasts charge out of the brush and straight at him. He pointed his pistol and took quick aim. Then he stopped. In the dim light of the fire, he realized he was aiming at a little burro. He stood there, shocked at what he saw, and the burro nearly knocked him down as it darted past.

"Hold it! Hold your fire! It's just a herd of wild burros!" Clay shouted in an attempt to be heard above the roar of the guns and wild braying of the burros.

Within seconds, it was over. When echoes of the gunshots stopped bouncing off the canyon walls, only the sound of little hooves against rock could be heard as the burros hastily made their retreat. Luckily for them, the scared men were shaking so badly that none of their bullets had found their mark.

As the last hoof beat faded from hearing, total silence filled the camp.

For a couple of minutes they stood, each one eyeing the other, each one trying to keep from laughing. It was useless. They all erupted into laughter. They had survived yet another killer attack on Superstition Mountain.

Rob threw a couple of logs on the smoldering campfire as they all gathered around it as though it would provide them some sense of security.

Virgil looked at the others to see if they had been as scared as he had. He shook his head, "I have to be getting pretty holy about now. That's about the fourth time I've had the hell scared right out of me."

Clay laughed, "From the way they were braying, I think they were just as scared as we were."

"By God, we had a right to be scared," Rob said. "I never knew little burros sounded like that."

"I never knew they could bray that loud," Ken added. "Never in my life have I heard anything like it."

"I had no idea what those things were," Brian said, letting out a long sigh of relief. "I thought they were going to eat us alive!"

"All I could think of was that old cougar that tried to eat me," said Ken, staring into the glowing fire.

"Whhoooooo! Whhoooooo! Whhoooooo!"

They glanced up to see the owl perched on a branch, just above their heads, at the edge of the firelight. He was moving from one leg to the other as though he was dancing - or maybe laughing at them.

They stared at him for a minute, mouths agape.

Clay decided to talk to it. He held up his hand in the universal peace sign. "How!" he said. "Welcome to our camp!"

The owl stared down at him a second more, then unfolded its wings and dove off the branch, flying away into the night, leaving the boys baffled once again.

"Who the hell are you anyway?" Clay yelled.

"Don't ask that too loud, Clay," Rob said, leaning in close as he whispered. "He just might be the devil himself."

Brian shook his head. "You think that owl's really a dead Indian's spirit, Clay?"

"I don't know if it is or not, Brian, " Clay shrugged, "but I *do* know that I'm not going out there to find out." He turned back toward the tent. "Nope, I'm going back to bed."

They headed for their tents, casting quick glances around the shadows, each with a death grip on his gun. Creeping back into their tents, they lay awake listening to the distant hooting of the owl.

Dawn found all five men standing around the fire drinking coffee and talking about the night's events.

Brian chuckled, "Man, this is something. There sure isn't a dull moment around here, is there?"

"Not so you could tell," Ken replied, "One thing's for sure, Brian; now you have your very own story to tell. Not many people can say they've been attacked by killer jackasses and lived."

Laughter erupted, relieving any tension left.

"Well, come on," Clay said, tossing the remains of his coffee on the fire. "We might just as well start searching again. I don't feel like breakfast anyway."

Rob started gathering his gear. "Me neither," he chuckled. "With Brian fixing it, it would be Spam anyway."

37

José Diego speared the strips of bacon in the skillet with his fork and flipped them over. Diego had been working for Rockford ever since he met him in a saloon down in Sonora, Mexico. Rockford had given him enough money to feed his family for a few months, then put Diego in his helicopter and flew him up to the ranch. He was in the United States illegally. Rockford had assured him that as long as he worked for him, no one would ever know. Diego was pleased. It was a good paying job, and he would do whatever Rockford wanted. He wiped his hands on his pants, then pushed another piece of wood on the fire.

Across the fire, Tom Davis sat staring through the binoculars at the camp on the high plateau across the valley. He could just make out the helicopter and tents in the dim light of dawn. "I wonder why the hell they were doing all that shooting?"

"Maybe they were just doing a little target practice," Wiscoff replied.

"In the middle of the night?"

Diego handed Wiscoff and Davis a plate with bacon and beans on it. They ate as the sun rose higher. Glancing through the binoculars again, Davis spotted the five men when they were leaving camp. Turning to Wiscoff, he snapped orders, "Dan, get the pack and that worthless radio the boss sent along. We're going to pay those guys a visit." He turned to Diego. "Josè! Get the horses saddled."

Diego hastened to do his bidding while still trying to eat his own breakfast. When the horses were ready, they slowly made their way across the valley and up the backside of the plateau, staying hidden as much as possible.

By mid-morning they had circled around and gotten on the ledge above the plateau the treasure hunters were on. Tying their horses to some scrub pine, the three men walked toward the edge of the ledge.

"You guys wait here," Davis said. Dropping to his knees, he crawled to the rim and peeked over it. Not more than two hundred yards away to his left and directly below the rim, he could see three men slowly making their way toward him.

He held up his hand. "Keep quiet! They're not far away." He eased back away from the rim of the ledge. "We'll keep a watch on them from here."

Their search took the treasure hunters from gully to gully along the plateau until they reached the solid rock wall rising a hundred feet straight up.

A few feet from the dry creek bed, Clay made several sweeps with his detector. He was just about to change locations again when the antenna suddenly locked onto a target. Clay looked around for Virgil and Rob. They were several feet away, poking around some rocks. "Virge! Rob!" he shouted, "Over here! Hurry!"

They hurried to him. He swept the area again so they could see the machine do its job. When it locked on target, he turned to them. "There's something metal right over there, boys!"

Virgil made a mental notation of the general direction the detector was pointing, then placing his foot in front Clay, he pointed his toe along the antenna. "I've got the direction marked, Clay. You can move over and take another reading."

Clay quickly paced off several feet to his left and stopped. He looked at Virgil and Rob to get his bearing and for a little moral support. He slowly lifted the long-range detector and swept the area ahead of him. Holding his breath to balance the machine as perfectly as he could, he watched the antenna ease across the terrain. He broke into a grin when he felt a strong tug as the machine locked onto a target. "That's it, Virge!" he shouted.

Virgil checked the triangulation of the two hits. Slowly, he shook his head. "There nothing there but sheer rock wall, Clay."

"Move in closer to it. Maybe there's a cave or something."

Both men moved forward, making sure they kept on the same points the machine had locked on. When they reached the wall of stone, they were standing together, but there was nothing but sage bushes and a pile of small boulders that had fallen from the rim above.

"Mark the ground right here, Virge," Clay said. "Use a stone or something. Then we'll use the conventional detector. Maybe it's underground."

Clay took the conventional detector and slowly worked the ground at the base of the rock wall. There were large cracks in the ground. He sidestepped them as he searched.

Meanwhile, Virgil and Rob began a close search of the rock wall.

Easing along step by step, Virgil suddenly stopped and used his foot to push back several thick clumps of sagebrush. Behind the bushes was a large crack in the rock wall. "Rob, look at this!" he said.

Rob checked the crack, then quickly started clearing away the dry vegetation.

"Better make sure there aren't any rattlers or scorpions lurking around," Virgil warned.

Rob jerked his hand back like he'd been burned. He looked up at Virgil and nodded. More slowly now, he worked the sagebrush loose and started moving some loose rocks.

"Clay! We found something over here!" Rob shouted.

Clay hurried to them. "What have you got, Rob?"

"Might just be a crack in the wall. It's filled with loose rocks and brush. Going to take some work to get it open enough to see." Rob said.

Clay could see that the rock wall sloped inward slightly at the point where Virgil and Rob were digging. Quickly, he jumped in to help. Soon the dust was thick as they struggled to clear the opening.

Above them, Davis' eyes followed their every move. He eased back from the edge. "They're digging against the wall right below us." Davis said, looking around. He grinned. There was an abundance of loose rocks as big as a man's head. "Let's just set a little trap for the boys down there," he said. "We'll arrange those rocks so they'll fall over the edge with a little push. Then when we're ready, we'll give 'em a little heave."

Wiscoff frowned. "Boss said scare 'em, not kill 'em."

"They'll have time to get out of the way - if they're quick enough. If not, it'll just be another accidental land slide that killed 'em - not us."

Working quietly, the three men gathered rocks and stacked them in a pile. Before long, Davis called a halt. "I think that's enough. When these rocks fall, they'll break loose others and what happens should be very interesting. Let's do it."

So engrossed in their labors were Clay, Virgil, and Rob, that they failed to hear the three men above them. The three men who were busy moving rocks, too - over the edge and right down on top of them.

As the first rocks struck the ground near them, all three men instinctively dove for the cover of the small over-hanging wall.

"Rock slide!" Clay yelled. By pressing close against it, most of the rocks were missing them. Dust filled the air. They couldn't see anything at all.

Clay felt fear once again set in. *A rock slide! My God! People have been killed up here by rockslides!* Clay knew there was nothing they could do but try to protect themselves from being crushed to death by the rocks. "Press the wall and cover your heads," he shouted to Rob and Virgil.

They pressed even closer against the wall and crossed their arms over their heads for protection. Still, some rocks struck them on their arms, shoulders and back, causing yells of pain.

It was over in seconds. The rocks stopped falling. The air was thick with dust. There was an eerie silence.

The treasure hunters were buried to their waists, mashed against the wall by the rocks, but they were alive.

Clay listened without moving. He was sure he heard something. It sounded like someone laughing way off in the distance. The sound faded. "Don't move!" Clay whispered. "That slide didn't start by itself. I heard someone up there."

They waited. No sounds above them.

After several minutes, Clay slowly began pushing the rocks away from him. He groaned with pain.

Rob and Virgil were struggling to get free.

Finally all three were free.

"You guys okay?" Clay asked.

"Yeah, I think so," Virgil said.

"I hurt like hell, but no bones broken," Rob said.

Grimacing from the pain in his shoulders, Clay jerked his gun from the holster and raced along the wall, searching for a way to the top. Several hundred feet away, he came upon an animal path leading to the ledge above. His pistol cocked and ready, he raced up the rocky slope to the top. It was vacant.

Gasping violently for breath, he stopped with his hands on his knees, trying to suck in air. By the time he got his wind, Virgil and Rob had joined him.

They began a search.

"Over here," Rob shouted.

Where the rocks had been pushed over, there were boot prints in the dust. They stood looking down at them.

"Well, by God!" Clay exclaimed. "We've finally found someone up here that actually leaves tracks."

"Yeah, too bad whoever left 'em is already gone," Virgil said.

"Don't see any sign of that old owl, do you?" Rob asked, as he craned his neck looking for the big hooter.

"I don't think it was the owl, Rob," Clay said. "Last I heard, owls don't wear cowboy boots."

Halfway across the valley, Rockford's three men reined up behind a clump of palo verde trees. Using binoculars, they watched the treasure hunters searching the ledge where they had just been.

Laughing, Davis reached for the radio. "Big Daddy! Big Daddy! This is Little Daddy, over!"

Davis tried several more times to raise Rockford. A long wait and nothing. "Shit! Might just as well not have the damn thing. It don't work." He stuffed it into the saddlebags and headed for camp.

38

At the other end of the plateau, Ken Smith and Brian Speller were having their own problems. As they struggled to search an unusually thick, brushy area, loud grunting and squealing erupted from the bushes. Both men froze for a second, their eyes scanning the brush as they listened to the strange noises getting louder.

Ken, not about to be caught off guard again, dropped the metal detector and drew both his 9mm pistols. He poised for action as he slowly backed away from the sounds.

Brian drew his pistol and eased backwards beside Ken.

Several squealing, snorting javalinas exploded from the brush, charging straight for the two men.

Emitting screams as loud as the wild pigs, both men, their eyes wide with astonishment and fear, spun on their heels and ran full out, trying to out distance the javalinas. Racing just ahead of the pigs, Brian pointed at some large boulders. "Head for those rocks!" he yelled.

The huge javalinas were slashing at their legs as they leaped upon the boulder. Jumping from one boulder to another, they gained as much height as they could. When they reach the last boulder, they stopped. They were breathless. Bracing their hands on their knees, they stood, bent over, staring down at the wild animals that were still lunging and slashing at the boulders.

"Jesus Christ!" Brian exclaimed, raising one hand to wipe the sweat from his forehead. "Everywhere you go there's some kind of creature trying to kill you. And there's nothing superstitious about it. Those damn things are real!"

"What in the hell do we do now?" Ken asked, still out of breath.

Brian noticed that Ken was still holding onto his two pistols. He shook his head. "Why didn't you shoot the bastards, Ken?"

Ken, his hands still braced on his knees, looked down at the guns, then over at Brian who was still holding his pistol. He grinned. "Same reason you didn't. Too damned scared to think of it."

Brian held up his weapon and looked at it. He grinned. "Lot of good this does if we can't remember to use it."

A noise behind them caught their attention.

Both men spun around.

A huge porker with long tusks was charging straight at them.

They both opened fire at the same time. The javalina's front legs buckled and he slid to a stop at their feet - dead.

The roar of the shots had made the rest of the javalinas change the tone of their squealing from anger to fear.

Brian and Ken turned in time to see them flee back into the bushes.

"I didn't see the back side of this rock," Brian said.

"There's a path leading right up to us."

"That pig knew about it, that's for sure." Ken said.

"He sure did."

"Well, we dispatched him in short order, huh, Brian?" Ken remarked cockily, twirling his pistols and dropping them into the holsters much like a western gunfighter would.

Brian grinned. "Shore did, Wyatt. He's deader'n a doornail."

"You really think he's dead?"

"Let's check him out."

"Not yet! Better wait to see if those other devils come back first. They may be regrouping for another attack." Ken warned.

The two men stood watching the bushes for any sign of movement. After five minutes they had neither heard nor seen anything of the pigs.

"Looks like they're gone," Ken said.

Rob still had his gun trained on the downed pig.

Ken pulled his guns again and slowly stepped over toward the unmoving pig. He squatted in front of it and pointed both pistols at its head. "Now check it," he said.

Brian eased around to its side and nudged the pig with his foot. It didn't move. He looked it over very closely. There were seven bullet holes in it that he could see. He figured the rest of the shots most have missed.

"Looks like it's really dead," he said.

"Now what?" Ken asked. "You know it's against the law to shoot wild animals in a Federal Wilderness Area, don't you?"

Brian put his pistol away and stood looking around. "Only if you get caught. Besides, we had no choice but to kill this old tusker. It was strictly self-defense!" He looked down at the dead animal and grinned. "I've got it! We'll eat the evidence," he looked at Ken. "Ever butcher a pig?"

"No, can't say I ever have," Ken replied. "As a matter of fact, I've never even seen a dead pig 'til now."

"Well, you're going to today, my friend!" Brian said, excitedly. Yessireebob! There's gonna be a pig roast in the old camp tonight!"

Brian started searching around in the brush. "Come on, help me find a pole to carry it with."

They came up with a dead tree branch that looked strong enough to hold the pig.

Brian pulled his large survival knife from the sleath on his belt. He was glad he had thought to strap it on before leaving camp. He cut two short lengths of rope from the one he had looped through his belt and approached the pig. He kicked it again with his foot to make sure it was dead. Satisfied, he bent over the pig and neatly tied its front legs together with one piece of the rope. He turned and tied the hind legs in the same manner.

Grabbing the pole, he slid it between the legs of the pig. "Saw this in a jungle movie once," he said. "Grab that end and let's head for camp. We're bringing home the bacon today!"

Hoisting the pole onto their shoulders, they held it with one hand and carried their pistols in the other. When they got to the hastily discarded metal detector, Brian secured it between the pig's legs. Now they had a pig and a metal detector to carry back to camp. They headed out again, their guns ready and their heads jerking around at every little sound like a couple of scared Barney Fifes.

Walking into camp, they found Virgil, Clay and Rob already there.

"Hey, fellas! Look what we have. We're going to have a pig roast tonight!" Brian said.

"So that's what all the shooting was about," Clay said. "We were just about to head your way. Thought you might be in trouble."

Brian noticed that their hair and clothing was dust covered and they had several scrapes and bruises. "What the hell....?"

They quickly dumped their load on the ground.

"What happened to you guys?" Ken asked, as he hurried from one to the other, checking to see if they needed any medical attention.

Neither he nor Brian could find anything worse then minor scrapes and bruises.

"Looks like you'll make it. Now tell us what happened," Brian said.

"You go first, Brian," Virgil said "Tell us about that pig."

For the next few minutes, they listen as Brian gave graphic details of their narrow escape from the killer pigs.

When he was finished, Virgil told them about the rockslide someone had started above them.

"Someone wants us off this mountain, that's for sure," said Clay.

"Yeah, but who? That's the big question," Rob relied.

Clay shrugged. "I've got no idea. Maybe it's the crazy man that cut off Calhoun's head. But this seems a little out of his territory. Besides, he uses a knife, not rocks."

Virgil looked around at the sad sack bunch. "We came out here to find the Dutchman, not get killed. You guys think we ought to take their warning, pack it up and head back to the city?"

There was a long silence, and then Rob spoke. "Life in the city is nothing like this," he said. "Oh, you might get killed, but at least, by God, you know you aren't going to be eaten alive. Out here that could happen at any minute."

Another long silence.

Clay got up and walked over to get a view of the valley below. His eyes scanned the terrain for signs of movement. Nothing.

Silence.

"We killed a wild pig today," Brian stated, matter of factly. "Can't do that in the city."

"That damned pig almost killed us today," Ken retorted. "Would have, too, if those rocks hadn't been handy."

Silence.

"We almost got killed by a rock slide today," Rob said.

"Someone pushed those damned rocks down on us," Clay replied.

Silence.

Virgil sat staring down at the ground. "I saw some strange markings on the wall back there just as the rocks started falling," he said softly.

Clay jerked his head up. "You never told us that. What kind of markings?"

"I don't know. A turtle or maybe a snake and some letters...O-R or something like that."

"Jesus, Virge," Clay almost shouted. "Those are Spanish signs. Why didn't you say something before now?"

"Didn't have time; I was trying to stay alive."

Clay was excited. This could be it. This could be what they had come for. "The Spanish always carved signs in rocks around their mines so they could identify the place later, no matter how long they were away. It was like trail blazing."

"That damned rock slide buried it today, remember?" Rob said.

"We'll dig it out again tomorrow," Clay replied.

Silence.

Rob jumped to his feet. He wasn't ready to leave just yet. Not with Spanish markings within reach. "I thought we were going to have a pig roast!"

Brian grinned, "By God, we are." He looked around at the others. "I personally think it's great. Where else can you get the shit scared out of you one minute, and enjoy a luau the next?"

Getting up from the ground, Ken brushed off his rear end and snapped orders. "Brian, looks like you and I have got a pig to butcher. The rest of you guys get whatever it takes to make this luau work."

Clay grinned. He watched Ken struggling with the pig. He could see a change in him since the injuries inflected by the cougar had healed. He was no longer the whiner. He actually seemed to be enjoying himself for a change.

"Hey, fellas," Rob said. "How about me giving you guys a hand with that pig? I've never seen one butchered, either." He hurried to lend a hand.

"Need any more help cutting up that pig?" Clay asked.

"Nope!" Brian answered. "With all the hands we already have in it, someone's liable to lose a finger or two as it is."

Virgil stood up and stretched his back. "From the looks of things, I guess my question about leaving is answered. Looks like we're going to stay and continue having all this fun and adventure."

Clay grinned. "Looks that way," he said. "I say we break out the booze. I think we've earned a good drunk."

Virgil looked up at the sky. It was still a long time before dark. "While they're getting the pig ready, what say you and I take a little run down to that saloon and see if we can dig up some good old Jack Daniel's whiskey?"

Clay stood staring at Virgil. There he was again, trying to get him on that helicopter. Clay wanted to tell him to go to hell, but if he did, he knew they would all laugh at him and he couldn't stand that. "Okay, let's go." He turned to the others. "You guys need anything?"

"Girls!" Rob shouted from the tree near the stream where they had hung the pig up to butcher. "Bring girls!"

"Might pick up a bottle of white wine to go with the roast pork." said Ken.

"How long you gonna be gone?" Brian asked.

Virgil looked at the sun again. "We should be back in an hour or so."

"The pig should be ready for the spit by then."

Walking to the helicopter, Clay slipped the pills from his pocket and gulped one down. He knew it probably wouldn't have time to work, but the thought was still comforting.

Virgil cranked up the engine and made his usual checks under the close supervision of Clay.

"What's that red light?" Clay asked. "Something wrong?"

"Will you relax, Clay? One would think you were afraid to fly from the way you act," Virgil said with a knowing grin.

Clay gave him a nasty look and settled back in his seat as the helicopter lifted off the ground. He stole a glance down as the blast of air from the rotors whipped up dust and debris, causing the three men below to shield their eyes. *Damn pig will probably be full of sand now.* By the time he turned back to the front, they were high in the air.

Virgil yelled above the roar of the engine, "I think we should have a look around up here. Maybe spot whoever it was that pushed those rocks down on us!"

Clay nodded and, though his confidence in Virgil's flying was growing, he still had to force himself to look out the side window as they circled around the Needle.

Cutting across one valley and over a tall peak, they came upon a box-canyon.

Clay stared down at it. It had green plants growing in it. *By God! That looks like a farm.* He reached over and tugged at Virgil's arm. "Hey, Virge! Look at that! A farm of some type, way the hell up here."

Virgil nodded and dropped the helicopter sharply down into the valley, causing Clay to grab his seat and clinch his eyes shut. He let out a low, continuous groan until the helicopter leveled out again, then shouted, "I wish to hell you wouldn't do that, Virgil. It makes me sick."

Virgil laughed softly as he watched Clay struggling to compose himself.

When Clay dared open his eyes, he could see row after row of tall green plants. Glancing off toward the side of the field, he could make out the outline of a building. He pointed. "A building! And look over there! A water tower with irrigation pipes running to the fields."

"How in the hell do you think they got water way up here?" Virgil asked.

"Probably hauled it in by helicopter. No way to get a drilling rig up here, let alone into that box-canyon."

The building was long, wide and low. A smaller building was a few yards away.

Virgil made a slow pass over it. Looking down, he saw three men run out of the long building with guns in their hands.

Clay saw them at the same time. His heart jumped. "They got guns, Virge! Get the hell out of here!"

Virgil's old wartime reactions automatically took over as he yanked at the controls and twisted the throttle hard. The chopper rose sharply.

Clay caught a glimpse of the first spurts of fire escaping from the gun barrels. He clenched his teeth as he waited to be hit by the slugs.

The helicopter climbed upward and away. It was soon out of range of the bullets. When they passed over the canyon wall, both occupants breathed a sigh of relief.

"What the hell was that all about?" Virgil shouted, fighting the controls with both hands and feet to stabilize the craft.

Clay was having trouble answering and trying to catch his breath at the same time. His stomach was still in his throat.

Finally, he managed to squeeze out, "An educated guess would be that it's a marijuana plantation and that building is where it's processed into pot and hashish. That's one big operation. Must be twenty-five acres of weed down there. Worth millions on the street."

The cockpit was silent as they thought about what they had just seen.

Clay sat staring at the controls but not seeing them. He was thinking about the marijuana farm. Now it was starting to make sense. That explained a lot about what was happening on the mountain. He turned to Virgil. "Now it all makes sense. That's why there's so much killing going on up here. It's not because of the Dutchman's gold, but because of the damn dope they're growing."

Virgil's eyes lit up. "That's why someone tried to kill us this morning. They didn't want us to find their damned illegal dope farm."

"It's sure in a good location," Clay said. "I doubt anyone on foot or horseback would find it. It's pretty well hidden in that box canyon."

"That's true," Virgil said. "But from the air it's pretty obvious. It's the only green on the whole mountain. Everything else is brown."

They went back to their thoughts as Virgil headed the helicopter back toward Big Alice's saloon.

39

On the ground behind them, the three shooters stood watching the big ship disappear in the distance.

"Son-of-a-bitch!" exclaimed Jack Stockard, the heavily bearded, dumpy man in charge of the farm. "Rockford sure ain't gonna like this crap!" He headed back for the building. "Might as well radio him the bad news and get it over with."

"What the hell do you mean you shot at them? That was just plain dumb!" Rockford's voice screamed over the radio receiver.

"Yeah, I guess it was," Stockard tried to explain. "I thought we could knock 'em down. No one would have ever known about it if we had."

There was a long silence over the radio. Rockford was furious. Stockard knew the farm was to be a secret. He knew better than to draw attention to it, especially from someone in a helicopter. Someone who might have the knowledge and means to report it to the federal authorities. Stockard had been with him for many years. He was the farm manager, and he was an expert at cultivating good marijuana in any type of soil. But what Rockford really liked about Stockard was how cold-blooded he could be. Stockard could kill a person without batting an eye. Maybe he ought to get him to kill that damned girl up at Big Alice's place. Oh, well, he knew too much about the operation for Rockford to piss him off. "Well, hell! What's done is done, I guess. We'll have to harvest early or lose it to the Feds."

"Maybe those people won't know what we have here - maybe they won't tell anyone," Stockard said.

"Bullshit, maybe! We're out of business up there. Now get things ready to harvest that damn green crop! You can bet they'll run to the law. Just hope it's the local law. Just hope it's Wilkins they go to."

40

$\mathbb{V}$ irgil set the helicopter down in front of Alice's place.

As they jumped out of the chopper, Clay stopped Virgil. "Best not mention what we saw up there while we're in here," he whispered. "We might not get out alive."

As they approached the saloon, they could see several old pickups, a couple horses, a donkey complete with pack, and a new blazer parked around the building. The windows of the saloon were full of faces staring out at the helicopter.

"Must be check day," said Virgil.

"Come to think of it, I have no idea what day it is, do you?"

Virgil looked at his watch. "According to my handy, dandy Timex, it's Saturday, June twentieth, 1600 hours."

"According to my figures, we've already been here the better part of two weeks."

"My, how time flies when you're having fun," Virgil said.

Stopping just inside the dim interior, figures began to appear as their pupils dilated. Almost every table was full of men, with a sprinkling of women here and there.

Clay walked over to the bar. "Cold beer."

Virgil ordered his favorite drink. "Jack Daniel's - black."

Juan, the bartender, shuffled off and returned with only a beer. "We got no Jack - what you say - black." He said dead pan.

"No Jack Daniel's black label whiskey?" Virgil asked.

"At least not behind the bar," said a woman behind Virgil.

Startled at the voice, Clay and Virgil turned to see Nurse Brenda Carpenter standing with her hands on her hips and a smile on her face. Her white nurse's uniform brightened up the dull surroundings.

Brenda was happy to see them. "What the hell are you two doing here? I thought you were way up there on the mountain."

"We are, uh, were," Clay stuttered. "We just dropped down to get some wine and Jack Daniel's."

"Come on over to the table and meet Alice. She can probably get you Jack Daniel's, or anything else you want," Brenda said, nodding her head toward the girls sitting at the tables. She led the way to a table at the rear of the saloon.

Big Alice sat staring at them.

"Alice," said Brenda. "I want you to meet Clay Morgan and Virgil Patton. Friends of mine. They want some Jack Daniel's black label whiskey. Think you can help 'em?"

"Why sho, honey," Big Alice's eyes lit up. These were the men from the mountain. Maybe she could wrangle a little information from them. "You boys sit down here, and I'll have one of the girls fetch the Jack. I got to keep it hidden, you know. How many bottles you want?"

"Better make it at least two," Virgil said. "We've got three more thirsty men waiting back at camp."

Big Alice snapped her fingers and a Mexican girl hurried to the table. "Get me two bottles of Jack Daniels. Black label."

The girl hustled away.

"Where you boys camped at?" Alice asked, nonchalantly.

"Oh, up about ten miles or so, not too far. At least not by chopper," said Virgil.

"What 'cha looking for - gold?"

Clay looked at her. He knew she was already fishing for information. He wasn't about to tell her anything. "We're looking for anything we can find. Mainly just getting away from the big city to have an adventure of sorts."

"You've already found that, haven't you, Clay?" Brenda asked cheerfully.

He looked at her. Damn it sure is nice to hear her voice again. "You haven't heard the best of it yet." He grinned. "I've never seen anything like it. Things happen all the time up there."

Virgil spoke up, "Yeah, just today we almost got killed. Someone sh...."

Clay had quickly kicked him under the table. He didn't want anything said about spotting the marijuana operation.

Virgil glared at Clay. He had painfully gotten the hint. "...some rocks shook loose above us. Caused a rockslide that almost buried us alive. Not to mention nearly braining us."

Clay winked his approval from across the table.

Big Alice eyed them both suspiciously, "Nearly ever' body that comes up here is lookin' for the Dutchman."

"Yeah, that's what I hear, but I don't believe it really exists, or someone would have found it by now," Clay said, taking a long pull on his beer. Big Alice was asking too many questions. He had to change the subject. He turned to Brenda. "Brenda, what are you doing here?"

"Oh, I come up here once a week or so to see if they need any medical attention. I check temperatures, blood pressures, cuts for infection, venereal disease, and just about anything else," she said. "Most of these people are so obsessed with finding the Dutchman they won't even come out to see a doctor; and most doctors I know won't come in here to see them."

"You're truly a humanitarian," said Virgil.

"Yes, it's nice of you to care, Brenda," said Clay.

Brenda looked around at the people in the saloon. "Someone has to care, I reckon," she said.

Virgil turned to Alice. "You wouldn't happen to have any good white wine around here would you, Alice?"

"Well, I might be able to find you something. How about some white port or muscatel? Maybe some Thunderbird or Twenty/Twenty? They're all good according to the locals."

"I had a Chardonnay or White Zinfendel in mind."

Alice chuckled. "A Chardonnay in this hell hole? I think we can dig up something. Not a Chardonnay or Zinfendel, but maybe a white Christian Brothers."

"That'll do."

Brenda was now curious. "Roughing it in the mountains and ordering white wine? Now that's strange. What's the wine for?"

Clay looked around and spoke in a low voice. "We had a bad day up there, today. Ken and Brian got attacked by wild pigs and had to kill one, so they butchered it and we're having a little party tonight; a luau, as Brian calls it."

"Now that sounds like fun."

"How about joining us?" Clay asked.

"How am I going to join you way up there? There are no roads up where you guys are."

"Fly up with us." Virgil said, "We'll bring you back."

"Oh, I don't think so," Brenda said hesitantly. She would really like to go, but didn't want to intrude. They were just asking to be nice.

"I know you don't know us very well," Clay said. "But we're all pretty decent guys. You'll be safe with us."

"That's not what I'm worried about, Clay. I know I'd be safe with you guys. But it'll be dark when the party's over and you can't fly at night."

"Wrongo, little nurse. This man here can fly that bird anywhere - anytime. Right Virge?"

"That's right, Brenda. If you want to come, we'll see you get back safe and sound."

Brenda thought for a moment, "Well, I should have a look at Ken's injuries... might just as well do it. Besides, a real pig roast sounds like fun." Brenda turned to Big Alice. "Will my blazer be okay parked out front, Alice?"

"Ain't nobody 'round here gonna bother it, Brenda," Alice grinned. "They know I'd skin 'em alive if they did! You just go on up there and have some fun."

In the little room at the rear of the saloon, Laura Pratt worked feverishly at the hinge pins. She had one of them almost out. She had been working on them since Big Alice had seen the nurse coming and quickly locked her in her room. Laura was eating well and her injuries from the long run in the desert had almost healed, so Big Alice saw no need for her to see the nurse.

Laura knew it was because she didn't want her to talk to the nurse, for fear she might tell her that she was being held prisoner. And Big Alice was right - she would tell if she could just get the chance. Laura could hear the pleasant voices of the men talking to Big Alice. She knew it was her big chance to escape. *If I can get out of this room, that nurse and those men would help me get away. Surely Big Alice isn't stupid enough to try to stop me with them watching. Nothing will happen to me once they see me. I have to let them know I've been kidnapped.* Laura pushed against the hinge pin. Her mind raced and sweat rolled from her face as she labored with the bed slat.

When they had finished their drinks, Clay went to the bar and ordered a case of beer. "I don't suppose you would have any ice up here, would you?"

"Sorry, Señor," Juan shook his head.

"I figured as much," Clay replied. He turned to Virgil and Brenda. "You guys 'bout ready?"

Laura heard them talking about leaving. She threw down the slat and started beating on the door and yelling.

At the table, Virgil looked toward the hallway behind him. "What's that?"

"Just one of my girls," Big Alice said. "No need to worry, she does this all the time. Mad at her boyfriend - old Padro. He's gone away tonight." She looked at Brenda. "You know how Maria is, Brenda, always fussing about Padro. When he's here, she's fighting with him; and when he's gone she's screaming and crying for him to come back."

"I remember her. Tried to help her a couple of times, but she wouldn't talk to me."

"I think she enjoys throwing little temper tantrums," Big Alice said, as she rose from the table. She called to the girl who had fetched the whiskey, "Child, you get Mr. Virgil a couple of bottles of that good white wine from the back room!" Turning back to the table, "I'll just go calm her down a little. She'll be alright."

They watched Big Alice make her way down the hallway, and then they joined Clay at the bar where the girl had placed two bottles of white wine. Tossing money on the bar for their drinks, they took a last look down the back hallway and walked out.

At the door to Laura's room, the knob turned and it opened a little. "Best settle down, girl. I can't let them know you're here. I'd go to jail and you know that. So you best be still in there." Big Alice slammed the door shut and clicked the lock.

Laura stood motionless in the middle of the room. She didn't make another sound. She was still afraid of Big Alice. She listened to her walk away from the door.

Suddenly, she heard the whirring of the helicopter engine. It was too late. The helicopter was gone. She slumped into a heap, beat her fists against the floor, and sobbed.

41

As they cruised high in the mountains, Virgil pointed toward the north. "Looks like it's storming somewhere up north," he yelled over the roar of the engine.

Clay stared off at the distant thunderheads forming at the very top of the mountains. "The stream will be running full, come morning. That means we can finally have a bath."

Virgil nodded.

Brenda sniffed the air then held her nose. "You could sure use one," she said mockingly. She sat looking at the back of Clay's heads. *Why do I feel so relaxed around these guys? Why am I not even a little bit leery of them? It's like I've known them all my life. Good people. I just sense they are damn good people.* For the first time in ages she actually felt good. She was enjoying her newly found friends.

The helicopter was gliding slowly across the valley toward their camp on the plateau.

Virgil slapped Clay on the shoulder and pointed downward. He swung the helicopter in a tight circle.

After Clay caught his breath, he looked down at a small campsite on the slope of the mountain, across the valley from their own. Hidden almost from view among a patch of scrub juniper trees, Clay could make out at least three horses, some mules and a tent. He could also see two men standing beside the tent watching them.

Virgil made a couple of low circles to let them know he had seen them. He then headed for camp. Virgil yelled over the engine's roar, "Bet they're the bastards that pushed the rocks down on us!"

"I think you're right," Clay said. "We'll keep an eye on 'em now that we know where they are."

The helicopter settled easily onto the ground. Virgil jumped out and Clay passed the refreshments out to him.

Then Brenda stepped out.

A loud whistle burst from Rob's lips. "You did it! You did it!" He yelled. "You brought us a girl!" He ran to meet them. "Hi, Brenda. Didn't expect to see you way up here."

"You're a welcome sight, Brenda," Ken said. "Looking at these ugly guys all the time gives one a complex."

Brenda smiled. "I came to see if you were healing properly, Ken," she said. "How're the injuries?"

"They're fine, Brenda. At least they don't hurt anymore."

Brian watched their arrival from where he was keeping close tabs on the pig roasting over the hot fire. It was on a homemade spit - one that had to be turned every few minutes by hand. Not an easy chore. He yelled to the newcomer. "Welcome to our camp, stranger. Come share our luau!"

"Hi, Brian," Brenda called back. "Looks like you're the chef tonight!"

"Most all the time, Brenda. Most all the time I have to be chef."

Virgil looked over the homemade spit. He nodded his approval. "By golly, Brian," he said, "that looks like a professional job. When will it be ready to eat?"

"Oh, 'bout two, three more hours. Had to borrow one of the tent poles to use as a spit, but we won't miss it unless it comes a hard blow tonight."

Gathering around the fire, the group of friends talked and drank Jack Daniel's and warm beer while they watched the pig cook. They told Brenda what had happened to them since they had last seen her. They even told her about the owl and the Indian Chief.

Brenda shook her head. "There haven't been any Indians living up here for years. There are some Apaches and Pimas down below, but they don't dress like the one you describe. The way you describe him, it sounds like the way the Apache Indian dressed years ago. They wore a mix of buckskin and cloth clothing, with a cloth headdress."

Clay lifted his cup in a toast. "What can I say, Brenda? I saw him. Now let's drink to finding the Dutchman!"

They lifted their drinks. "Here! Here!"

"If we don't get killed first." Virgil added.

"You really think someone pushed those rocks down on you?" Brenda asked.

Clay cast a glance across the valley. "Damn right someone pushed 'em. We found their boot tracks up there," he said, pointing toward the ledge above. "And the bastards are right over there." Now he pointed across the valley.

"Think they could be Big Alice's men?" Virgil asked.

Brenda thought about it for a minute. "No. I don't think it's Big Alice. You haven't found the gold yet. That's when you have to worry about her."

"If she's that bad, why do you go there?" Rob asked.

"As black-hearted as she is at times, Big Alice can be a pussycat at other times. She has never been out of line with me. In fact, she helps her girls a lot. Oh, she's gruff and sometimes mean talking, but with her, they have a home and someone to watch after them. She asked me to come up and check on them every so often, in case they get sick or something."

She looked at the boys. "Now don't get me wrong. According to stories I've heard, she'd kill you at the drop of a hat if she thought you had found the Dutchman's gold. As rumor has it, she's already killed several men up here."

"Sounds like a nice lady to stay away from," said Clay. He looked at Brian, Ken, and Rob. "Boys, we have to keep a close watch on those men across the way. They're the ones who are trying to get us off the mountain. See 'em around here, fire a shot over their heads. Maybe that'll scare 'em off."

"How do you figure it was them, Clay?" asked Brian.

"We stumbled onto a hidden marijuana farm a little higher up," Clay replied. "Big operation. Damn near got killed. Those bastards shot at us when we flew over their processing plant."

"You know," said Virgil, "as easy to see as it is from the air, it looks like the sheriff or someone should have found it by now."

"The only way in to it is by helicopter. It's in a box canyon," said Clay.

"Hell, Sheriff Wilkins flies over these mountains all the time," Brenda said, with disgust. "He has to know it's there. He has use of a helicopter any time he needs it. Belongs to a rancher named Paul Rockford. When something comes up, Wilkins calls Rockford, who puts the helicopter and pilot at his disposal."

"What color is it?" asked Rob. "I'll bet he's that son-of-a-bitch that wouldn't help us when we were half dead carrying Ken down the mountain. Came right down to us and laughed in our faces, then flew off!"

"It's light blue. Small one - holds about four people, I'd guess," Brenda said.

"That was him!" Virgil remarked. "An LOH - light observation helicopter. Made for use by the military, but now the pride of most big business men for transportation and status."

"Rockford's an evil bastard," said Brenda. "I never did care for him. Always undressing me with his eyes. Always trying to get me to go out with him. I never would."

"Good for you," Ken said, opening another hot beer.

"He makes a lot of money, and it's not from selling cattle," Brenda added. "Probably drugs. He and the sheriff are close friends. They're probably both involved in that marijuana farm. All that flying around up here is just to check on the farm."

"It's no wonder it hasn't been found," said Ken.

"If the sheriff's mixed up with that marijuana, we'll have to watch our step around him," Clay said. "We'll stay away from up there and confine our activities to searching for the Dutchman around here. No need to antagonize 'em any more than we have to."

The sun had long disappeared beyond the horizon when Brian announced, "Pig's done! Let's eat!"

They gathered around Brian as he cut huge slices of roast pork and dropped them on their plates. Ken served up fried potatoes with onions and hot beans. Coffee, wine, beer, and Jack Daniel's completed the feast.

With heaping plates, they ate in silence, staring into the flames of the fire and listening to the thunder from the big clouds to the north. A chorus of howling coyotes and the occasional roar of a cougar as it caught the scent of the cooking pork, added to their peaceful setting.

It was peaceful, alright, and Clay wondered how long it would last. He hoped they didn't have any more trouble, at least while Brenda was still in camp. He glanced beyond the camp, across the valley. He could just make out the faint glow of a fire.

He knew they were probably being watched right now. Perhaps even now they were conjuring up another plan of attack.

Clay didn't know two more pairs of eyes had been watching them all day. Padro and Gonzales sat quietly on their perch of large boulders, not more than a hundred yards away.

Padro watched through binoculars. He had seen Davis and Wiscoff earlier when they had nearly killed the three men with a rockslide. He would have to tell Alice about that. She would be plenty mad. She didn't want the treasure hunters killed, or even scared off. She wanted them to find the gold first, then she would kill them, if necessary. He watched the greenhorns as they cut hot meat from the pig over the fire. His mouth watered for some of that roasted pig. Putting down the binoculars, he pulled a cold burrito from his pack.

Gonzales sniffed the air. He could smell the hot meat. He rolled his eyes and shook his head sadly. He bit into his own cold burrito.

Padro knew they couldn't risk a fire, for fear of being detected. He knew Alice would skin him alive if they were discovered. Padro stuffed the cold burrito in his mouth and put the binoculars back up to his eyes.

42

$\mathbb{P}$olice Chief Dennis Blackhorse stepped into the dimly lit room of Gus' Saloon. He found a table and dropped down into a chair. He was tired and disgusted. He had been working for days on the Laura Pratt case and was no closer to learning what happened to her than he was when he first started. Checking his watch, he saw it was six o'clock in the afternoon, and it was Saturday. This was one of those cases where he couldn't just go home on Friday at four. He had to stay on it or risk finding a dead girl. He sat pondering the case.

Gus had seen him come in and poured a large glass full of whiskey. He walked over and sat down, placing the glass in front of Blackhorse. He looked at Blackhorse. "Here's something strong to help you relax a little."

"You know Indians can't handle whiskey, White man."

"Yeah, but you look like shit."

Blackhorse nodded and lifted the glass. "I feel like shit."

"Anything on Laura yet?"

"Hell, no and it's been two weeks now. I can't seem to get a break in it. She's just disappeared into thin air."

Gus shook his head. "Maybe we'll never find her. Maybe no one knows anything."

"No," said Blackhorse, "I won't accept that. Somewhere, somebody saw, heard, or knows something. Always do. Every case I ever worked, clues were left behind. There's a saying in police work, 'if you've been there, you've left something behind'. Maybe just trace evidence, but something. I just have to find it." He looked into the sad face of Gus. "I've sent out hundreds of flyers on her, Gus. Maybe something will turn up. Let's not give up just yet."

Gus knew the man was just trying to cheer him up. He also knew Blackhorse was truly worried. Gus knew what kind of man he was. He wouldn't rest until he found Laura. "Yeah, can't give up hope yet," Gus replied. Someone tapped an empty glass on the bar and he hurried off to serve them.

Blackhorse stared after the man for a minute. He took a drink of whiskey and sat staring into the glass. *Where am I missing it? What have I over looked. Okay, let's see.* He held up a hand. *Number one - she was last seen leaving this saloon by Gus two weeks ago on a Saturday night. Two - she had trouble in the saloon with Rockford and his men. Three - they left before she did. Four - she was last seen getting into her car by Gus. No one was around her at the time.*

He stopped. "Car", he said aloud. "Where the hell's her car? Why haven't we found her car yet? Did the abductors take it?" *I don't recall seeing anything on it. Maybe the information on it was never entered as missing. She was, but maybe the car wasn't. I'll check that as soon as I drink this beer. If not, I'll get it entered into NCIC pronto.*

Blackhorse took another snort of whiskey. He knew it was important to get the car's description entered into the National Crime Information Center, the national clearinghouse for Wanted People, Criminal Histories, Missing People, and Officer Safety Information. If the Pratt car showed up anywhere in the United States and was checked out, it would be red flagged as a kidnapping involved vehicle. They would get the word within minutes.

43

As the fire burned lower, the treasure hunters and their guest crowded closer. It was getting late, and the night air was beginning to take on a chill.

The heat of the fire felt good to Clay. He stood and turned his back to the fire, rubbing his rear. "The only bad thing about a camp fire is that your front burns and your rear end freezes."

The luau had been perfect. They had eaten their fill, and then drank their fill, while swapping tales with each other.

They sat quietly now, listening to the distant rumbling of thunder, and watching the sky light up as the storm moved closer to them.

Clay looked around at his friends and smiled. *Now this is the way to have an adventure. Under the open sky, sitting around a warm fire with all my friends.* He took another sip of Jack Daniel's. He was getting slightly drunk. He looked at Brenda. It was getting late and they had to get her back to Big Alice's. He leaned toward her.

"Brenda, if we leave now, we'll beat that storm. It's sure to hit here before long."

"Thanks, Clay," said Brenda, "but I haven't enjoyed myself like this for so long, I want to stay as long as I can."

Clay looked at her. Her face showed how relaxed she was in their company. He smiled at her. "Stay as long as you like."

Brenda looked around the fire from one man to the next. *What a great bunch. It's been a long time since I've been with a bunch of men and didn't have to be constantly fighting them off. I'm being treated as an equal and the conversation has not once turned to sex. Where in the hell have these guys been hiding all my life?*

A sudden explosion of thunder jerked them all from their thoughts. The storm was upon them, yet there was no rain. The sky lit up as brightly as day. Huge blue streaks of lightning shot across it and wrapped around the entire mountaintop, emitting crackling sounds as it continued to stay visible. Spears of lightning branched off the main streak and plunged to earth. Some bounced back skyward as huge, round, red and blue balls of energy, before dissipating a few hundred feet up. Thunder rolled for miles and miles through the mountains.

"My God!" Clay said, unable to take his eyes off the phenomenon. "I've never seen anything like it. It just seems to go on forever."

"What a beautiful sight! It's breathtaking!" Brenda exclaimed. "I've never seen it from up here. It's so clear!"

Rising from her seat beside the fire, Brenda staggered a little before gaining her balance. "This is the only place in the world where the lightning lasts so long. Caused by the collision of the cool ocean air above the mountains with the updraft of hot desert air."

"Ocean air?" asked Clay. "Where the hell do you see an ocean way out here in the desert?"

Brenda laughed. "Not out here, silly. The ocean air comes all the way from the Pacific Ocean. Rides the jet stream, I would guess."

"Well, whatever causes it, it sure is a sight to behold," said Virgil.

"Yeah, when there's a storm like this one, people come from miles around to watch and photograph it," said Brenda. "Sometimes there're a hundred cars parked along the desert roads below with people taking pictures of the lightning." She watched the awesome sight a moment. "The Indians are very superstitious about these mountains. To them, they are sacred grounds. They believe the fireballs in these electrical storms are their ancestors showing their displeasure with something they've done. Some say that's how the mountains got their name."

When the lightning did stop, it plunged the plateau into darkness. But it was only a minute or two before the next flash appeared.

"I'm an engineer," said Ken, "and I still don't understand how the lightning lasts so long without clouds anywhere near here."

"It's in the air currents, Ken," Brenda said. "Sometimes it doesn't rain anywhere in the mountains - even where the clouds are."

"What a way to end our luau!" Brian said. "A fireworks show! Almost like it was planned."

"Beautiful sight!" Virgil said, "But you know we won't be able to fly you out of here until it's over."

"That's okay, Virgil. I'm in no hurry to leave. I'll just stay up here for the night." She started to walk and staggered a little more. "Damn! I think that last drink did something. I think I'm 'bout half looped."

The boys all stood, each one weaving as much as she had.

"If staggering is an indication that you're drunk, then I guess we're all drunk," Clay laughed.

"That's right," Rob said, "and now it's time for bed."

Clay looked around the camp for a decent place where Brenda could sleep. "Brenda, we can fix you a bed in the helicopter if you like. It'll give you more privacy."

"If you don't mind, I'll just throw a blanket on the ground in your tent. The helicopter is just a little further from here than I care for."

"That's fine," Clay replied. "My cot is the one on the left. You take it. I'll crash on the ground. Go ahead and climb in the tent and when you're settled in, you holler for Virge and I."

"My-my, I've never seen such gentlemen," Brenda laughed, as she started for the tent.

WHHOOOOOO! WHHOOOOOO! WHHOOOOOO!

Everybody stopped and stared up at the huge owl perched in a tree at the edge of the camp lights.

"There you have it, Brian," Clay said, pointing at the owl. "It was all planned by him for Brenda's benefit!" Clay stood up. "Thanks Chief!" he called out. "And a good night to you, too!"

Brenda shook her head. "Indian Chief! Spirits! You guys are crazy. That's just an old horned owl," she laughed, as she disappeared into the tent.

"A lot you know!" Clay called after her. "Wait 'til later, maybe you'll get your mind changed!" He looked at Virgil. "I sure hope it goes well tonight," he said. "We don't need to get attacked by burros or pigs again. I wouldn't want anything to happen to her while she's here."

"Me neither, Clay. We'll have to keep her under close guard."

"Okay, fellas, it's safe to come in now," Brenda yelled from the tent. "The honor system applies, right?"

Both Clay and Virgil muttered yes and slipped into the tent. She was lying under a blanket on the floor between their cots.

"Why didn't you take my cot?" Clay asked. "I told you I'd sleep on the floor?"

Brenda lay still a minute thinking of snakes and bugs. She sat up. "I believe I will." She quickly slipped from the floor to his cot. "Ahhhh," she sighed. "This is much better. Thanks, Clay." The alcohol she had drunk was having its effect. She was almost in tears. "No one's been so nice to me in years. Thanks for asking me to come up here."

"We've enjoyed your company, Brenda," Clay said, making himself as comfortable as possible on the hard floor. There was only the tent canvas between him and the rocky ground.

"That's right," Virgil added. "You sure brightened up this sad sack bunch. Now get some sleep."

Both Clay and Virgil slept in their clothing out of respect for her.

The tranquillity of the evening, the rumble of thunder, the distant howling of coyotes, and the drinks worked as sleeping pills for them all. Within minutes, the sound of their snoring blended nicely with the wilderness night choir.

Breaking glass, the rattle of the tin cans tied around the camp and the clanging of metal horse shoes against rocks brought Clay running out of the tent, gun in hand.

It was pitch black outside. The lanterns were out. Only a small glow from the dying fire gave light.

Clay was quickly joined by the others, guns ready.

"What the hell is it?" asked Virgil.

"I don't know yet," Clay replied. He looked around. "There," he said, pointing at a broken lantern lying in the light of the smoldering fire. "Someone's destroyed our lights!"

"By God, it looks like they rode right into camp and did it," Rob said.

"Yeah," Virgil said, "they must have been watching us and thought we would be too drunk to hear them."

"But why break our lanterns?" Ken asked. "What does that prove?"

"They're trying to scare us out of here," Clay said, searching the night with his flashlight. There was nothing he could see or any sounds he could hear beyond the camp. "Well, it's too damned dark to go prowling around in these rocks. We'll wait 'til morning and have a better look."

The boys weren't happy. Once again, someone who wanted them off the mountain had disturbed their peace.

Clay mumbled, "This shit keeps up, damned if I won't have to pay a little visit to that camp across the way!"

"Why wait? Let's go do it now!" Rob said, waving his pistol.

Virgil motioned for him to put his pistol away. "We're up here to find the Dutchman, Rob, not to kill people."

Brian and Ken were busy pulling the remainder of roasted pig from the fire where it had fallen.

"Dirty bastards!" Ken said, when the pig was secure. "I'll keep watch the rest of the night." He pulled both pistols out and sat in the shadow of a nearby bush.

At dawn, Clay slipped out of the tent. He looked at Ken, who was still on guard. Damn, he thought. Bet he's been out here all night. He must be worn out.

"You want to get some sleep, Ken?"

"No. I'm okay," he said, standing up and brushing off his pants. He pointed to the stream. "Looks like we'll be able to take a bath today, the stream is running full again."

"Good!" said Clay. "I'll put the coffee on." He grabbed the big coffeepot and headed for the stream.

Sure enough, roaring white water filled it bank to bank. Squatting, Clay scooped water into his face with his free hand. It felt good. It had been days since they had enough water to bathe properly. Maybe later, when the current slowed a bit he would bathe. It was much too dangerous now. He knew raging waters of flash floods accounted for many a death in the mountain and desert areas. With the coffeepot filled, he headed back to the fire.

Clay was just putting the pot on the Coleman stove when Brenda came out of the tent. "Is that ready yet?" she asked, holding her head. "I could sure use some."

"Not just yet. Ten - fifteen minutes, it'll be steaming hot," Clay replied.

"Did I hear you guys up last night?" she asked.

"Some bastard rode through the camp and broke our lanterns. Just another little problem for us, but nothing to worry about."

"I was too tired to come out of the tent," Brenda answered. Yawning widely, she ran her fingers though her hair and looked at the coffeepot. "Ten-fifteen minutes, huh?"

"Yep. But no longer than that."

"Well, I need to wash up a little, anyway. I'll just take a walk to the stream."

"Watch yourself out there, that water's running awfully fast," Clay warned.

Brenda headed off to the stream.

Brian, Ken, and Virgil joined Clay around the fire.

"Toss on another log, Brian. We'll heat that pig up a little for breakfast and sandwiches," said Clay. "Most of it'll spoil in the heat later anyway."

"Good idea," Brian replied. He put some logs on the fire.

Clay examined the meat closely. "It's still warm from last night. Might be a little gritty with sand, but then this ain't the Waldorf."

Suddenly, a scream filled the air.

Clay jerked his head toward the stream. Oh, shit! She's fallen in! He headed at a dead run for the stream. He got there in time to see Brenda being swept down stream by the raging water. He raced along the bank. Brenda was grabbing at anything she could. She grabbed a rock that slowed her a little, but the force of the water ripped her grip on it loose.

The thought of her drowning caused Clay's heart to jump into his throat. He shook the thought away and sprinted along the bank, dodging trees and boulders. He was slowly gaining on her.

"Aaaaaaaaeeeeeeeee! Help, Clay! Help! I'm going to die!" Brenda yelled.

"No, you're not!" Clay yelled, now running alongside her on the bank. He didn't know what to do except go in after her. Maybe the two of them could grab a handhold somewhere.

Running just ahead of her, he clenched his teeth and jumped into the wild stream. He was instantly grabbed by the swift current and pulled along. He managed to grab ahold of Brenda, then got his arm around under hers. He held on tightly. They were both being washed further downstream. He could hear the others crashing through the brush along the bank, yelling at him.

"Grab that rock, Clay!" Brian yelled.

Clay turned his head to look, but they were past it before he had time to react.

"There's a tree up ahead! Grab a limb!" Virgil shouted.

Brenda and Clay were tumbling over and over as they were swept along faster than the others could run. They were swept past the tree before Clay could get turned. Soon they were ahead of the others.

Clay knew it was up to him. He had to do something, and do it quickly. Turning to face downstream, he dug his heels in the bottom. It was like bulldogging a huge steer, but it slowed them a little. Every time he got turned so that he could see something coming up to grab, the force of the water on his back spun him around again. He felt helpless.

Without warning, the pair was swept over a waterfall four or five feet high. They sank from sight below the surface of a large pool, being forced to the bottom by its power.

Still clutching Brenda, he struggled to hold his breath. Setting his feet flat on the bottom, he squatted and pushed upward with all his strength. They broke the surface. Gagging and choking for air, they were instantly swept along again, but at least they could breath.

Fighting so hard to gain a foothold was wearing Clay out. He was losing strength fast. A loud roar of water filled the morning air. Clay looked. It was another waterfalls. *Oh, shit! This a big one! This is it. We're going over. We'll never survive this one.* He struggled harder, trying to get the current to work in their favor and push them toward shore. The current was too strong.

The roaring ahead of them got louder.

Grabbing the side of a boulder with his free hand, Clay felt them slow down a little, but again the rushing water broke his hold. There was nothing he could grab. It was too late. He got a firm grip on Brenda and waited for the end to come.

Then he saw it - a tree along the bank with its huge roots exposed and in the water. If he could grab it, they might have a chance. They were headed straight for it. Brenda had a death grip on him so he let go of her with one arm and kicked his feet hard against the bottom to force them closer to the bank. He stretched his arm and made a grab for the closest root.

They jerked to a stop, and before the current could force him to lose his grip, he wrapped his legs around another root. It worked; they had stopped. The waterfall was only feet away.

With a death grip on the limb, Clay regained his breath and some of his strength. "Brenda, put your arms around my neck and hang on tight," he said.

When she had a firm grip on him, he slide one hand after the other along the root, never turning it completely loose at any time, until their feet touched the rocky bottom in a small eddy. Without the force of the raging water against them, they managed to crawl up on the bank, where they collapsed.

Clay lay with his eyes closed. He could feel pain from scrapes caused by the jagged rocks. *Pain? I feel Pain? If there's pain, I'm not dead.* He eased his eyes open and nudged Brenda.

Brenda didn't move a muscle.

"Brenda, are you okay?"

She struggled to get the words out. "Yes. Yes, I think I am."

Crashing brush caused him to turn his head. It was Virgil and Rob, huffing and puffing for breath. Ken and Brian were right behind them.

"Are you two alright?" Rob asked. He was truly worried. He had thought they were going to die.

Brenda said nothing. Now she was sobbing.

Clay looked at her, "Brenda, you sure you're okay?"

She nodded her head.

The others pulled her and Clay to their feet and checked them for injuries. Nothing but a few bruises and scrapes.

"How did you manage to fall in, Brenda?" Brian asked.

"I didn't fall in," she gasped between sobs. "I was pushed."

"Pushed? What? Who did it?" Rob demanded. "I'll kill the bastard!"

"I didn't see 'em. They were behind me."

"They?" Virgil asked. "How do you know there was more than one?"

"Because I heard them laughing."

Virgil, Ken, Rob, and Brian drew their guns and fanned out in the brush, looking for any sign of the men. They searched as they made their way back to camp. They saw nothing.

Not far away, Wiscoff and Davis lurked in the bushes, trying hard to keep from being heard as they laughed at the city folks, stumbling around with their guns drawn. Finally, when they had moved far enough away, Davis motioned for Wiscoff to follow him. They slipped quietly away. He felt this would surely persuade them to leave the mountain. The boss would be happy.

A hundred yards in the opposite direction, Padro sat on his boulder, watching them through binoculars. He cursed. "By God, Gonzales, Alice will kill those two gringos when she hears they tried to kill Miss Brenda."

Gonzales nodded and reached for the binoculars.

Clay and Brenda sat around the warm campfire. As hot as it had been, they were chilled from that long ride in the cold water.

A heavy fluttering of wings caught their attention and they watched as the huge owl landed in a nearby tree. "Whhoooooo! Whhoooooo! Whhoooooo!"

Clay smiled as he watched the bird twist its head around from side to side. "Where were you when I needed you, old friend? Whoever you are."

Virgil shook his head. "Maybe the owl and the Indian are two different things."

"I think they're one and the same," Clay replied.

Rob kicked the ground. "How long are we going to put up with this shit? Let's go kick some ass."

Brenda looked up at Rob. "I can understand your feelings, but that's just what they're trying to get you to do. Up here, if you invade another camp, you're fair game."

"We'll find a way."

After an hour had passed and Clay had regained his strength, he stood up. "Brenda, you ready to head back to Alice's?"

Brenda didn't move. She was sitting with her knees drawn up under her chin and her arms wrapped around them. "Do I have to? I kind of like it up here. I haven't had this much excitement since I was a kid."

"You almost got killed, Brenda," Ken remarked.

"I know we almost got killed, but what a way to wake up in the morning!"

Everyone stared at her in disbelief. More coffee was poured.

Brenda looked at Clay. She had suddenly been drawn closer to this man. A warm feeling swept through her body. She would be dead right now, if he hadn't jumped into that raging water and saved her. "Thanks for saving me, Clay," said in almost a whisper. "I would have gone over those falls if you hadn't jumped in and grabbed me. I'd be dead right now."

Clay waved it off as nothing and poured himself a cup of coffee.

Brenda sat watching him for a minute then spoke. "Why don't you guys do some searching, and I'll stay in camp today and sleep. I took a few days off work and I don't really have anything else to do. Besides, I need the time away from all that suffering... you know, sick people."

"Brenda, you know how dangerous it is up here. And it's much more dangerous being here with someone out there trying to kill us. You'd be better off with those sick people right now."

"Clay, if you don't want me to stay."

"It's not that, Brenda," Clay said, quickly. "I'd really like for you to stay, but I'm just worried you'll get hurt."

"Besides, won't someone miss you?" Brian asked.

"Who? I have no one to worry about me."

The boys looked at each other and shrugged.

"Okay," Clay finally said. "Why not, lady. It'll be a pleasure to worry about you for a while." He stood up. "Right now, we have to go do some digging." He looked over at Ken. "Feel up to it, Ken?"

"You bet. I'm anxious to see those signs that Virgil saw." Ken replied. He walked over to Brenda and handed her one of his pistols. "Here, Brenda. Something to protect yourself with while we're out of camp."

Brenda took the gun and holding it in both hands, examined it, checking its action and to see if it was loaded. It was obvious she had handled guns before. She looked up at Ken. "That's sweet of you, Ken. Thanks."

Clay interrupted the conversation. "Brenda, we're going to be just about a mile to the north. All five of us will be there digging out an old cave we found. You see or hear anyone or anything, just yell or start shooting and we'll be here before you can catch your next breath."

"That's awful fast," she said, smiling.

Looking at her standing all alone and thinking back to earlier, Clay shook his head. "I think one of us should stay with her."

"Oh, no you don't. I can take care of myself. If it's that damn Rockford you're worried about, he won't mess with me. Especially with me holding this pistol. Now off with you. Go find the Dutchman."

The sun was already high and scorching hot when the treasure hunters filed out of camp. Each one took a last look back at Brenda. They were worried about her safety.

Brenda knew she would be safe with these guys around. She went into the tent and laid down. Sleep didn't come quickly, however. She was too up tight. Up tight, and as excited as a little girl at her first carnival.

44

After returning to their camp in the juniper trees, Davis grabbed the radio and tried to reach Rockford again. The radio was worthless. He had to contact Rockford. He turned to Diego, "Josè, you ride hard for the ranch house and tell Mr. Rockford that those guys took a ride in the helicopter yesterday and that we think they spotted the farm. Find out what he wants us to do now."

"Maybe the boys up at the farm have already told him. They do have a radio, you know," Wiscoff said. "And it probably works."

"That's true, but we'd better tell him anyway. You know how mad he gets if we aren't on top of things," Davis said. He could still hear Rockford's warning about having his ass if something went wrong.

"In that case," Wiscoff said, "suppose I go instead of Josè. That way, if Mr. Rockford wants to come up here, I'll be there to fly the helicopter. You know he can't fly it."

"That sounds logical. But just don't forget that I'm still up here," Davis said.

He watched Wiscoff saddle his horse and tie his bedroll to it. It had been a two-day ride with the slow pack mules, but Wiscoff could make it in about a day on his horse, if he really pushed it.

45

Rockford paced the floor at the ranch house. He glanced at his watch, then charged out the door to stand on the porch, glaring off toward the mountains. Grabbing his binoculars, he looked for any sign of Davis or Wiscoff. It had been four days since he had heard anything from them. He already knew about the treasure hunters flying over the farm and being shot at. Stockard had told him that. He wondered where the hell Davis, Wiscoff, and Diego were. Things were falling apart, and his men were nowhere to be found.

There was too much clutter and haze between him and the mountain to see anything as small as a man on horseback.

Rockford looked over at the helicopter parked in the yard. He wished he had learned to fly the thing. If he had, he would take it up into the mountains and see what the hell was going on up there.

As Rockford paced the porch, his mind whipped back and forth between killing Davis, the nasty scene with Big Alice, and the last telephone call he had had with Sheriff Wilkins. He had to take his anger out on someone. *Now there's a son-of-a-bitch who pissed me off. I think it's time to pay him a visit. Set his ass straight about who yells at who. Besides, he'll have to make arrangements for the sale of the green marijuana. Maybe the trip to Florence will help pass the time until Davis checks in with me.*

Rockford tossed the binoculars down on the table and hurried out to his truck.

Driving the thirty-odd miles to Florence, Rockford calmed down somewhat. He even laughed at the thought of how Wilkins' face would look when he walked in on him today. He rarely went to Wilkins' office. But a personal appearance always seemed to work wonders when he had a tendency to forget who paid him.

Rockford thought about how he had first gotten involved with Sheriff Wilkins a few years back. Wilkins had always hung around him, bragging about how he had connections with the mob, even if he was the sheriff of Pinal County. He said the mob would buy all the dope he could supply. Rockford hadn't taken him seriously until a while back when he had bumped into Wilkins over in Phoenix. He had been with some men Rockford knew to be connected to the mob. After that, he had struck up a deal with Wilkins and several sales were made. It had been quite lucrative so far. Rockford knew he still needed Wilkins, otherwise he would have disposed of the fat bastard years ago.

An hour later, Rockford parked the truck in the lot of the county jail where Wilkins' office was. He strolled inside.

Rockford slipped into Wilkins' office without being seen. Wilkins sat at his cluttered desk reading a report. Sweat poured from his pudgy round face. A large cigar rolled from one corner of his mouth to the other, almost as though it was on automatic pilot.

Rockford stood glaring at the man for several seconds before Wilkins sensed his presence. He looked up. Startled, he jumped, his eyes popped open wider and the cigar dropped from his mouth onto the desk.

"Rockford!" he exclaimed, quickly grabbing the cigar and brushing the hot ashes from the papers. "Paul! What brings you here?"

Rockford waited until he had cleaned up the mess. "You, Wilkins. You're what brings me to town."

Wilkins stood and extended his hand to Rockford.

Rockford ignored the feeble gesture and pulled a chair over to the desk. He sat down and leaned back, looking up at Wilkins until the nervous man flopped back in his own seat.

"You might call this a personal visit, Wilkins," Rockford said, cocking one eyebrow. "I just wanted to hear you say again what you said to me on the phone."

"What was that, Paul? What did I say?"

"You don't remember yelling at me, Wilkins? Demanding in a threatening voice that I had better not screw this deal up with the big money people?"

Wilkins grinned nervously. "Now, Paul. You know I was just excited and you know how I get when I'm excited. I didn't mean anything at all by that remark." He tugged at his tie, his top shirt button already loose. "You're not mad at me, are you, Paul?"

"You think I would drive alone into this God forsaken hellhole of a city if I wasn't mad at you, Wilkins?" Rockford said. His eyes narrowed and his voice icy.

It was obvious the sheriff was deathly afraid of Rockford. He pulled a handkerchief and mopped his baldhead before stuttering, "I-I-I g-guess not. But you don't have to worry, Boss. I'm fine now. I understand that you're the boss. I guess I was talking too big for my own britches, huh, Boss?"

Rockford recognized the whimpering as an apology and softened his voice. "If you ever talk that way to me again, I'm going to come here and shoot you right between those little weasel eyes of yours. You understand me?" He emphasized his question by pulling out his 9mm pistol, leaning across the desk, and pointing it right between Wilkins' eyes.

Wilkins felt his bowels roll and loosen. He shut his eyes and tightened his muscles to keep from losing control of his bowels. Even though he had a gun on his belt, he knew not to touch it. He was terrified. "Yes, sir, Boss," he whined in a whisper. "I hear you, Boss. It'll never happen again."

Rockford put his gun away. "Got a drink?" he asked as though nothing had happened.

Wilkins opened his eyes. He was happy to get up - alive. He was shaking as he scurried over to a small dry bar, where he grabbed two glasses and a bottle of tequila. He hurried back to his chair, sat down, and poured the glasses full.

"I want you to make arrangements for an extra large shipment, right away," Rockford said, taking the tequila Wilkins offered.

"I thought you said there wouldn't be any shipments for a while."

"That was before that damn city trash up there found the farm."

"My God! You mean they know where it is?"

"Hell, yes," Rockford said. "Especially after those nitwits of mine shot at 'em." He stopped to stare into the glass of tequila. "One good thing, though. They haven't been off the mountain, so chances are they haven't told anyone about it yet."

"What'll we do?" Now Wilkins was scared for a different reason. Any lawmen finding the farm would find evidence of him being involved.

"I think we still have time to harvest the crop and get it packaged."

"But Paul, it's still green."

"You think I don't know that?" Rockford shouted angrily. "God dammit man, I know there're twenty-five acres of green marijuana growing up there that's worth millions when it's ripe. But if I don't get it out before the law gets there, I'll lose it all." He lowered his voice. "At least by cutting it green, I'll be able to get maybe fifty cents on the dollar for it."

"Green marijuana will mold and rot if it's packaged."

"I know that, you dummy! It'll just have to be taken somewhere else and hung out to dry. I know it'll mean extra care, and I know that makes it more dangerous to hold on to. I also know that's why I'll get less for it."

"Well, maybe we can swing it," Wilkins said, not wanting to anger Rockford any more than he already had. He drummed his fingers on the desk as he tried to think of someone to sell it to.

Finally, he looked at Rockford and grinned. "I think I know someone who might take it. How much you asking?"

"Just what I said, fifty cents on the dollar of market value of dry marijuana. It's worth every penny of that, and you know it. Even cut green, my marijuana is the best in the damn country!"

Deputy Jesse Richmond knocked at the open door. They stopped talking to look at him.

"Yes, what is it, Richmond?" asked Wilkins, curtly.

"Just wanted to tell you we have a bunch of new warrants, Sheriff. Thought maybe you'd want to see them before you left for the day."

"Okay, Richmond, you've told me. Now close the door behind you."

Deputy Richmond looked at Rockford. Something didn't smell right about those two being together. Without another word, he backed out, closing the door.

Wilkins turned back to Rockford. "Okay, Paul. I'll make the arrangements. When can we deliver?"

"Five days."

"Damn, man, you sure don't give a man much time, do you?"

Rockford sat his glass down, stood up, put his hands on the desk and leaned over into Wilkins' face. "We don't have much time, Sheriff," he said in a deadly, but calm voice. "We have to get moving on this now. It's quite possible several people may have to be killed just to keep things quiet for those five days." He narrowed his eyes. "Don't you be one of 'em."

"I - I won't, Paul. I won't. But what about my share?"

"Your share will be fifty cents on the dollar of your usual cut," Rockford said. He turned and walked out without looking back.

Wilkins stared at the empty doorway. *By God. Any other man talk to me like that, I'd kill 'im.* He chuckled nervously. He wasn't going to argue the point with Rockford. He would get plenty of money, even at fifty cents on the dollar, and that would be much better than a bullet between the eyes. He jumped to his feet and headed for the restroom, unbuckling his belt as he hurried out the door.

Outside, Rockford climbed into his truck and sat looking back at the sheriff's office, wondering what he was doing. He laughed out loud. Wilkins was probably already in the toilet. He looked like he was about to go when the pistol went between his eyes.

Rockford needed a drink, and maybe some female company as well. That always lifted his spirits. Seems every time he came into town, his sexual urge took over. His perversion to pick up women in small, dingy, neighborhood bars was beckoning. There was just something about the type of women found in sleepy places that excited him. Perhaps it was because they were mostly married women starved for love. Perhaps it was because of the excitement and danger of it all. The danger of it killing him someday - either a jealous husband or a case of AIDS. But whatever it was, when the urge hit, Rockford couldn't resist. It was like a magnetic force pulling him along. Forcing him to search out those little neighborhood bars.

* * *

Rockford drove for several minutes before spotting an old Lone Star Beer sign hanging over the sidewalk. This wasn't Texas, but it looked like someone sure like Texas beer. Rockford knew it was still a little early for many women to be out, but he parked and went inside anyway.

* * *

The bartender tapped his fingers on the bar to the tune of the music as he watched the man walk in. There was something vaguely familiar about him. But then again, there was something familiar about everyone in his bar. The handful there were regulars - local men and women who came in to listen to a little music, have a few drinks, and unwind.

"Seven and Seven," Rockford said, looking around the bar at the women.

The bartender filled his order and sat it on the bar.

Rockford downed the drink and snapped his fingers for another one. This one he sipped. He looked around for women.

Staring the man in the face this time, the bartender knew there was something about him. "Don't I know you?"

Rockford turned his gaze from the women to look at him. "I don't think so. I've never been here before," he said. He turned back to the women. He spotted a lone female sitting at a table. He hustled her way. Flopping down in a chair at her table, Rockford grinned his best. "Say honey, wanna go out to my ranch and party a little? Got some really wild music out there."

The slim, blonde woman, about twenty-one or twenty-two years old, looked him in the face. "I don't think I know you, Mister. What's your name?"

"Who cares about names?"

"Well, I do."

"Just call me Paul."

Taking a sip of her drink, the woman eyed him. She shook her head. "I don't go out with strange men."

"Why not?"

"Because of that girl that got kidnapped over in Apache Junction a while back. They say she was snatched right from a saloon. Didn't you see all those flyers on her up at the bar?"

Rockford stole at glance at the bartender. He was still watching him. He looked at the girl. Maybe the flyers had his picture on them. Maybe he was wanted. But how could that be? Wilkins would have known. Maybe he was one of the new warrants Deputy Richmond had.

"So what's your real name?" she asked.

Downing his drink, Rockford felt a shiver go through his body. Something was wrong. The bartender was coming his way. He had to get out.

The bartender walked over to the table. "I know where I've seen you. Over in Apache Junction. Seen you at the cattle auctions. You're Paul Rockford. Own a big ranch over there somewhere, don't you?"

Now Rockford was sweating. He stood up. He had to do this right. He made himself relax a little. No one had seen him snatch the girl that night. He'd left the bar before she had. He glanced at the bartender and walked out without answering.

"Hey, Rockford! What's wrong?" yelled the bartender.

Outside, Rockford took long strides to reach his truck. He got in and drove off as fast as he dared, wanting to avoid drawing attention. He cursed himself for being so jumpy. *I shouldn't have reacted like that. What the hell is wrong with me? Losing my nerve?* He pounded the steering wheel. He knew the reason. He couldn't help himself when it came to women. He had to have them and preferred to force them. *Damn, that was close. I was about to do the same thing. If I had gotten that girl out of there, she would have been mine and I would have been caught. They knew me back there.*

Driving back to his ranch, Rockford thought about Laura Pratt. She could hang him. Now he had her to worry about. She had to go. He had to find a way to dispose of her properly without Alice being around.

His mind drifted to the greenhorns and all worries they were causing him. They were the cause of all this trouble. He clenched his teeth. He yelled out the truck window. "You'll pay, you bastards! You'll all pay! I'll see to it you pay!"

46

W atching through the binoculars, Padro doubted they would
ever find the gold. Rockford's men were going to kill them first. He
had to tell Alice what was happening. He took the binoculars from his
eyes and rubbed them sleepily. He turned to Gonzales. "Manuel, you
ride like the wind down there and tell Señorita Alice what we have
seen. Tell her what Rockford's men are doing. Maybe she will have
something to say. Hurry, man!"

Crawling through the brush to the clump of trees where they
had stashed their horses, Manual mounted and quietly rode off. As
soon as he was far enough away not to be heard, he spurred his horse
into a gallop, letting the horse have its head to pick its way along the
winding mountain trail in the dark.

* * *

Within four hours, he was bounding through the front door of
Big Alice's, out of breath and thirsty.

"Señorita Alice!" he shouted.

Big Alice waddled from the back room and sat down at her table while Gonzales downed some water. "Señorita Alice! Padro sent me to say that Señor Rockford's men are trying to kill the treasure hunters up there. Padro wants you to tell him what we should do."

Big Alice drummed the table with her big thick fingers as she gave the matter some thought. "Ain't a hell of a lot I can do right now."

"Señorita Alice, I think maybe the treasure hunters have been to Rockford's farm in the mountains. I believe that is why they are trying to kill them!"

Big Alice thought some more, then looked at Gonzales. "When you have rested a little, Manuel, you take some tequila back to Padro. Tell him that I said to keep watching, but do nothing. Maybe they will outlast Rockford's men. I have to know if they find the gold. When they have found something, you two come on back."

"Sì, Señorita," Gonzales replied.

"One other thing, Manuel, don't you and Padro tangle with Rockford's men. They're dangerous and would just as soon kill you as not."

"Sì! That I already know," Gonzales said, as he headed for the bar to get the tequila.

Laura walked out of her room and sat at the table with Big Alice. She was feeling better. And once again she was allowed to come and go from her room, as long as there were no strangers in the saloon. Though she had not accepted the role that Rockford had planned for her, Laura had, for the time being anyway, accepted the fact that she was there to stay. She didn't try to run away. Where would she go? She had decided to make the best of a bad situation. Laura found that it was best to agree with Alice. When she did, Alice would not only allow her all kinds of privileges, but talk to her about her troubles as well.

"You look worried, Alice," Laura said. "What is it?"

"Nothin' for you to worry about, chil'," she said. "I just got me some thinking to do."

"You aren't going to give me back to that monster are you?"

Big Alice laughed, "No, chil', he gave you to me, and he gets nothing back. Rockford is too mean. He'd kill you if I gave you up."

Big Alice started drumming the table with her fingers again. "No. This is about those men up on the mountain. What to do about them."

Laura nodded her head. She really didn't understand what she was talking about, but it had to do with those guys in the helicopter, and she did understand them. She knew they could help her escape.

"Who are those men up there?" Laura asked.

Big Alice looked up from her thought, "Oh, they's just a bunch of treasure hunters from the big city." She chuckled. "You never give up, do you girl?"

Laura smiled. She would never give up. Even though she had settled down after Alice's promise, she was just biding her time until the right moment. A moment when she could escape.

Gonzales returned with two bottles of tequila and a sack of food. He nodded at Big Alice. "I go back to watch gringos now, Señorita Alice."

47

Rocks flew through the air and crashed down upon other rocks as Clay, Rob and Ken hurled them one by one over their shoulders and away from the mouth of the cave.

Above them, perched on the ledge, Brian and Virgil kept a close vigil of the plateau. When they set out earlier in the morning, they had decided to have two men watch while the others worked. That way the ones working would not have to keep watching for that bunch of men below. They switched off every hour or so to allow each man to get a little rest.

The three men worked feverishly. They were slowly making headway, but it seemed that the Spaniards or someone had filled the whole cave with rocks. The recent rockslide hadn't helped matters either.

Clay stopped to wipe the sweat from his brow and check their progress. He looked up. The sun dropping lower in the sky was near the mountain peak in the west. Once it passed it, darkness would set in fast. It would be dark soon and they still had not reached the opening, nor found the signs Virgil had seen. He knew it would be at least another day - maybe two, before they would be able to see inside. "Okay! That's it for the day! Let's head for camp!"

* * *

Tired as they were, the men's spirits soared when they saw that Brenda had prepared a hot supper for them.

"Well, I don't see any gold," she said.

Clay managed a weak laugh. "Not today, Brenda. Not today."

After washing up in the cool clear water at the now calm stream's edge, they joined her at a makeshift table. The food smelled delicious, and without fanfare, they began eating. There was little conversation.

Shortly afterwards, when the supper dishes were cleaned, the three younger men said their goodnights to Brenda, fell into their beds, and instantly dropped off to sleep.

Clay, Virgil and Brenda soon followed.

In the large tent, Brenda felt so relaxed that she had no trouble at all falling asleep.

The hours slipped by peacefully, but at midnight trouble appeared. A skunk slipped under the guard rope and entered the camp. It prowled around the campfire looking for scraps of food. Sniffing the ground, the skunk scurried along, following a scent, and finally slipped under the flap of the tent in which Rob, Ken, and Brian were sleeping.

Interested only in the smell of food, the skunk scurried around, paying no attention to the snores of the three men. A partially eaten sandwich that Brian had left beside his bed was its prey.

The skunk was having a feast when the sleeping Brian rolled over and his arm fell from the cot. It landed squarely on back of the little skunk.

The skunk had no recourse but to strike back the only way it knew how. Lifting it's tail, it sprayed Brian fully in the face.

Screaming out, Brian jumped from his bed, fighting for breath and trying to see what was happening.

Rob and Ken sprang to their feet, guns ready, when the skunk hit them both dead center. By now all three were choking and gagging.

Yelling and stumbling around blindly, they succeeded in collapsing the tent.

The loud commotion brought Clay, Virgil, and Brenda running. They stopped short at the first whiff of a pungent smell they instantly recognized.

"Skunk!" Virgil said, swiftly running away from the tent.

Brenda and Clay were hot on his heels.

They could see three large lumps struggling beneath the canvas, as the skunk found an opening and slipped out. It scurried for the brush.

Clay yelled, "Easy in there, fellas. It's just a little skunk!"

"Oh, God! I can't see!" Brian yelled back. "Oh, God! Oh, God!"

Under the canvas, the three men kept bumping into each other and yelling as they groped blindly for the opening.

Finally, Clay could not watch his friends suffer any longer. He summoned up his courage, held his nose, and ran to the tent. Lifting the section where the door flap was, he threw it open, exposing Rob and allowing fresh air to get in. Clay beat a hasty retreat back to safety.

In seconds, the three men scrambled from under the tent and stood staring at their laughing friends.

"It's not so damn funny," Brian snapped, rubbing his burning eyes. "Suppose you come over here and let this rotten smell get on you."

"No, thanks!" Clay chuckled. "No reason for all of us to smell that way."

Brenda held her nose to ward off the strong smell. "Nothing medical will help right now, boys," she said. "Better head for the creek. The water won't wash away all the smell but it'll wash off the fluid. There's not much else to do."

They ran for the stream. Flopping headlong into the cold water, they began splashing it on themselves. In no time, the water had them shivering in the cold night air.

"Dammit to hell!" Rob shouted angrily. "Why are all these crazy things happening to us? I'll bet that damn Dutchman never had these problems!"

"No, sir!" Brian interjected, "I'll bet he walked right in here, picked up the gold nuggets, and walked right back out, without being attacked every damn night by some damned man or wild varmint!"

"I don't know about that," Clay replied. "Maybe he was just lucky. Maybe they didn't grow marijuana back in his day."

"Whhoooooo! Whhoooooo! Whhoooooo!"

The camp fell silent as they watched the silhouette of the owl land in a tall tree nearby.

"Damn!" Rob whispered. "I think that old buzzard's laughing at us. Wouldn't surprise me if it was him causing all our troubles."

"You boys better take off those clothes and throw 'em away. The smell will never come out," Clay said. "Bury 'em somewhere down wind from camp."

"Yeah, then get over by the fire before you catch cold," Brenda said.

* * *

Daylight broke through the dark skies over the mountain peaks to shine upon Rob, Brian, and Ken sitting by the fire, wrapped in blankets.

Clay threw more logs on the fire. "Coffee will be ready soon, boys!"

Grumbling was all he heard from the tired men as he put the coffeepot on the stove.

When it was ready, it didn't take a second call for them to grab the steaming brew. A slight smell still lingered on them, but it was livable - if they stayed down wind.

"It looks like you're gonna have to wear that perfume off, boys," Brenda said cheerfully, as she walked up to the fire. "Personally, it's not one of my favorite brands."

Clay and Virgil laughed.

Rob, Brian, and Ken frowned.

"If you're going to insult us, least you could do is cook breakfast," Ken said. A faint smile broke across his face. He stretched and yawned big. "Ain't it great, living in the country?" he added. "Still want to live out here, Rob?"

"I recall saying I'd like country living. I said nothing about being a wilderness family!" Rob snapped, then looked at Clay. "Great adventure. Right, hotshot?"

Clay was trying hard to hold back more laughter and could only nod his head.

"How can you think about eating with that smell all over you?" Brenda asked.

"My stomach can't smell it and it's growling like a caged tiger," said Rob. "It wants something to eat before we start throwing rocks again."

Brenda and Clay started breakfast.

* * *

Across the valley, Rockford's men, watching through binoculars, did not see the skunk, nor could they smell the scent. They failed to see why everyone was laughing so early in the morning. Davis figured that as much trouble as they had been having, they should be crying.

* * *

Closer to the camp, Padro and Gonzales were still watching. They had seen it all.

"Serves the dumb gringos right," said Padro. "They should have stayed in the city!"

48

C hief Blackhorse sat at his paper-littered desk, swiveling his chair first one way, then the other. He was deep in thought. He stopped, picked up the phone and dialed a number.

"Sheriff Wilkins. What can you tell me about the two men Rockford has working for him?" Chief Blackhorse asked into the phone. "You know, the bodyguard and the pilot."

Taken by surprise by the Chief's phone call, Wilkins was caught off guard. "Well...uh...not much really. What do you want to know?"

"Oh, who they are. What they do for him. Where they really were the night Laura Pratt disappeared."

"Golly, Chief. I really don't know that much about 'em. They been with that rancher for a few years now. What's up anyway? Got a lead on the girl?"

Blackhorse grinned. He didn't have a thing, and if he did, he damn sure wouldn't tell Wilkins. He was just planting a bug in his car. "No, just going over the case. Needed a little background. I think Rockford and those two old boys know something about the girl."

"Look, Chief, I've known that man for many years," said Wilkins. "He's one of the most respected, civic-minded men in the county. No way he was mixed up in grabbing a girl. Hell, man, he can afford to buy dozens of them at a time. Rockford is a very wealthy man."

"Yeah, I know."

"Wish I could help you, but I can't. Need anything else give me a call."

Blackhorse hung up the phone and grinned. That son-of a bitch! He's worried. It's in his voice. Bastard will be on the phone to Rockford before I get out the door. Blackhorse grabbed his hat and headed out. He was going to see Rockford again.

Driving the country around Apache Junction had always been one of Chief Blackhorse's favorites. The view, with all the mountain ranges and the Lost Dutchman State Park lying to the east, was great. It was midmorning and the sun was just breaking over the Superstitions as he drove along the blacktop road toward Rockford's ranch. He wanted to talk with that man again. This time he would ask about his two goons and see what reaction he would get.

Blackhorse turned onto the road and passed under the Rockford Ranch sign.

49

Wilkins looked at his watch. He stretched and yawned. Then it hit him. He had forgotten to call Rockford. He grabbed the phone and dialed. "Paul! Wilkins here! The Police Chief from Apache Junction is on his way out to talk to you.

"God dammit! He's already been here once. Why's he coming again?"

"Thinks you or your boys are involved in snatching a girl a few days back. A kidnapping or something."

"Why didn't you handle him like you're supposed to?"

"I tried, Paul," said Wilkins, "but he's a good cop. Can't get to him. I have no control over him, nor connections in Apache Junction."

"Damn! ...What should I do, Jack?"

"Same as you did last time. I doubt he has anything else to go on. Just dummy up."

"What if he wants me to be in a line-up, or take a polygraph test? What'll I tell him?"

"Well, if you're guilty of what he says, don't take the polygraph test; and if you were seen, don't be in the line-up." Wilkins paused, then said, "Hope you didn't give him cause, if you know what I mean."

"Say what you mean, dammit! These lines aren't recorded."

There was a long silence. Finally, Wilkins spoke. "Paul, you didn't do it again, did you? Not right now. Not when we have so much going for us and have to be so careful."

"Screw you, Wilkins! You know I can't help myself."

Wilkins knew he had done it. *The son-of-a-bitch did kidnap that girl. He's gonna get us thrown right into my own jail.* He cleared his throat. "That's gonna be your downfall sure as hell."

"Get off my ass, Wilkins, or I'll be your downfall! Understand?"

"Sure, Paul, sure."

"Now shut up a minute and listen. I want you to make sure I don't go to jail. Understand?

"Dammit, Paul, there's only so much I can do."

"I know that, you dummy. But maybe you could find the time to tip me off if he gets a warrant for me!"

"Now Paul, get serious. You know I'd do that. And in plenty of time for you to get away."

There was a long silence. Wilkins knew Rockford was thinking. He was right now devising some plan to cover his ass.

"Jack, if he gets too close perhaps we - or you could place the blame on someone else."

"Someone? Someone like who, Paul?"

"Someone like - maybe Tom Davis. He'll no doubt be asking a lot of questions about Davis today. Maybe we could give Davis some money and send him down to Mexico City for a while." He paused. "If this thing gets out of hand, I might have to head for the border myself. I sure as hell ain't going to prison."

"Okay, Paul, I'll see what I can do. You don't tell the Chief anything. If he asks you to take a polygraph, tell him yes. You'll change your mind later, of course, but for now, tell him yes. And Paul."

"Yes?"

"You stay the hell away from any more women for a while."

"Do you think I'm stupid?" Rockford slammed the phone down.

Sheriff Wilkins placed the phone back on the cradle. "Yes, I think you're stupid, Rockford," he said aloud. "And I hope they catch your ass."

After he said it, Wilkins looked around to see that none of his deputies had heard. He sat down pondering his fate. Things were not looking too good. He had been planning to move to the Pacific coast after he made enough money, but maybe he would have to go there sooner. Until he did, however, he was stuck with Rockford.

50

"A little out of your jurisdiction again, aren't you, Chief?" said Rockford, as the man walked up on the porch.

"My jurisdiction covers the whole state in a case like this, Rockford," Blackhorse replied.

"Yeah, reckon it does. What can I do for you?"

"Just want to ask you and your boys a few more questions."

"You suspect anyone out here in particular?"

"No, should I?"

Rockford didn't answer. He looked out at some cattle that were grazing nearby. He wanted to tell him to go to hell and get off his property, but instead he replied, "No, but you act like it." He waved to a chair.

Blackhorse pulled the chair close to Rockford and sat down. It was a lot cooler in the shade of the porch. He sat eyeing the man up and down. Finally, he looked out at the cattle, too. "What do you raise out here, cattle or horses?"

"Both. Damn good ones, too. You interested in buying some livestock?"

"I live in the city. No room for house pets, let alone a horse or cow."

Rockford turned to Blackhorse. "Now, about those questions you want to ask me. . . "

"I believe Laura Pratt was grabbed just outside the saloon that night." He watched for Rockford's reactions.

Rockford's face had a deadpan look. "So what's that got to do with me?" he asked. "I've already told you where me and the boys were."

"Tell me about you personal goon - this Tom Davis fella, Rockford."

This caught Rockford off guard and he stuttered a little before gaining his composure. "T-Tom Davis?" he asked, searching his mind for a quick response. How in hell could he know about Tom Davis so fast? I just spoke with Wilkins about the man. No need to lie, I guess. He already knows Davis works for me. "You met him last time. He's one of my top hands. Why? You think that rascal did it?"

"I just need to talk to him."

Rockford gave Blackhorse a knowing look. "Wouldn't put nothing past that man. Good at his job, but he's as mean as they come. Bet he's got a record somewhere long as your leg."

"Is he here?"

"Unfortunately, no. He's out of town looking at some blooded stock for me. Been gone quite a few days now. I expect he'll be back soon, though."

"Where is he?"

"Fort Worth. Big live stock auction down there this week."

"What about your pilot? This Danny Wiscoff."

Rockford chuckled and looked at Blackhorse. "He's not here either. He's with Davis." Rockford looked at him. "I think you're grabbing at straws looking at me, Chief. Maybe you should be looking at Davis."

"But you told me you were all three together that night."

"Yeah, I know, but you know how it is. You hate to tell on one of your own men. Just don't set right."

"Then tell on him."

Rockford looked away again. He watched the cattle a second, trying to make Blackhorse think he was struggling with his mind over telling. He looked back at Blackhorse. "The truth is, Davis stayed in town that night. I can't say he did anything, but he has been acting funny ever since."

"How's that?"

"You know, nervous. Jumpy about everything. Keeps watching the road like he expects someone to come."

"I see," said Blackhorse. "You say he's in Fort Worth right now?"

"Yes, sir."

Blackhorse studied Rockford for a minute. *The man was guilty as hell otherwise he wouldn't tell me nothing. He's trying to throw the blame onto someone else.* Blackhorse looked out at the cattle again. He knew he didn't have enough to arrest Tom Davis or Rockford - yet. He had to talk to Davis and Wiscoff alone. Out of earshot of Rockford. The only way he was going to solve this case was to get one of them to talk. Maybe the fear of the death penalty would flush out one of them to save his own hide.

He rose from his seat and stepped in front of Rockford, looking him right in the eyes. "Rockford, I told you before, I was going to find out what happened to that girl. I meant it. I also know that you're somehow involved in it up to your chin. You remember this, if that girl is dead, I'm going to arrest you and see that you get the death penalty. Do I make myself clear?"

Rockford couldn't find his voice for a second or two. He could see that Blackhorse knew something. "I told you, I didn't have anything to do with that girl. You better take a closer look at Davis."

"When he gets back, give me a call."

"Sure thing, Chief. You can bet on it," Rockford stood up and offered his hand. "Next time you want to buy a cow, come on out," he said with a smile.

Blackhorse walked back to his car. He stopped and looked back.

"Rockford, if it comes right down to the wire, would you be willing to participate in a line-up and take a polygraph test?"

"Why sure, Chief. I had nothing to do with it. Anything to help. You just call me anytime." Rockford said, walking to the edge of the porch with a big smile on his face.

Blackhorse drove away. He grinned. He considered himself good at reading people and he had read Rockford very well. He was the right guy, alright. Blackhorse was sure of it. Now he just had to prove it. Time was running out for finding Laura alive.

Rockford, on the other hand, was falling apart as he watched Blackhorse drive away. He jumped from his chair and rushed inside to grab the telephone. Jabbing his fingers down on the buttons hard, he punched in a number.

"Hello, you have reached the Wilkins' residence. Please leave a message and I'll get back to you as soon as possible."

A damned answering machine! Rockford gritted his teeth in anger. He yelled into the phone. "Damn you, Wilkins, pick up that telephone. I know you're there!"

Rockford waited for a minute, then heard a click.

"Hello, Paul," Sheriff Wilkins said. "Good to hear from you so soon."

"Cut the crap, Sheriff. I'm in a hurry," Rockford growled.

"That Chief give you problems?"

"Yeah! He knows, Jack. He knows."

"What did he say?"

"It wasn't what he said, it was how he said it. He knows something."

"Paul, for God's sakes, tell me what the man said."

"I gave him Davis. Told him Davis was in Fort Worth buying stock, but that Davis had stayed in town that night."

"Good. That'll get you some breathing room."

"Jack, he wants me to take a polygraph."

"Did he say when?"

"No, just asked if I would take one."

"An old ploy of cops. They ask that to make you worry. Make you think they have something. I doubt he has shit right now."

"You know I can't take a polygraph test."

"You won't have to."

"I told Blackhorse that Davis had been acting strange ever since that night. Now we have to make sure Davis is never found."

"Think it'll work, Paul?"

"Might cost some money, but I think we can give Davis money to head for Mexico. While they're chasing him all over the country, I'll be forgotten."

"Don't say anything more now. Let the Chief do his work. By the way, Paul, what did you do with the girl?"

Rockford's mind raced up to Big Alice's Saloon. *The girl! Damn! What can I do about the girl? Something has to be done and quick.* Finally, he answered Wilkins. "She won't be a problem."

"Oh shit, I don't want to hear anything else."

Rockford hung up, grabbed a tequila bottle, and guzzled down a quarter of the bottle without stopping.

51

$\mathbb{F}$or the second straight day, the treasure hunters labored at moving the rocks from the entrance of the cave. It was getting late. The sun was low.

Brian dropped to the ground to rest. "My God, this heat is stifling. Ever seen anything like it, Clay?"

"Not in my lifetime," Clay answered. "I knew it was going to be hot, but, man, this is almost too much to bear." He looked over at Virgil. "Damn, Virge, you sure you saw a sign and cave under there?"

"Sure, I'm sure," Virgil replied, stopping to rest a minute. "Don't know if it's the Dutchman or not, but it's signs of some sort. And there does appear to be a cave here."

"Maybe we'll break though sometime tomorrow," said Clay. "I've had enough for today."

Rob sat down on a boulder, mopping the sweat from his forehead and neck with a large bandanna. Suddenly, he stopped. "Clay!"

"What is it, Rob?"

"Dynamite! Dammit, dynamite! Why didn't I think of it sooner!" he shouted. He jumped off the boulder. "We'll blow the cave open!"

"You'll blow it shut, nutty!" said Clay. He pointed at the ledge above. "There's enough rock hanging loose up there to cover this whole plateau."

"Not if it's done right!" Rob said, excitedly.

"So who can do it right?"

Rob proudly thumped himself on the chest. "Me! Hell, man, when I was in college I used to blow stumps, boulders, and drainage ditches as part of my engineering course. Got credits for doing it. I know just how much it takes to blow that hole."

Clay shook his head. "Well, that ain't a stump or a drainage ditch."

"Same difference," Rob said and chuckled as he remembered his explosives instructor. It had been a long time since he had thought about that old guy. The way he talked always reminded him of Walter Brennen. 'Just use a little, son.' that old instructor would say. 'Don't want to blow mom's windows out, you know.'

Clay turned to look at Virgil.

Virgil shrugged. "Who knows, maybe he can do it."

"What if he blows the cave shut again?" asked Clay. "We've just spent the better part of three days trying to dig it out."

"Well, if the boy's as good with dynamite as he says he is, then we'll just blow it open again," said Virgil, peeling the skin off several blisters on his hands. "Besides, I don't think my hands can take much more stone grinding."

Clay sat thinking the matter over. He looked down at his own blistered hands. What the hell. They had plenty of time. "Okay!" he said, "Let's do it. But let's wait until tomorrow, just in case. If it were to blow shut tonight, I think I would cry until the wee hours of the morning. I'm bushed." He got to his feet. "Let's go back to camp."

Gathering their equipment, they headed back. each man so tired he struggled just to keep on his feet.

Brenda once again had supper ready for the hungry treasure hunters. They applauded her when they entered camp.

"You are a lifesaver, lady," said Clay, as he headed for the stream to wash up. The stream was now not much more than a trickle.

They flopped to the ground around the makeshift table. Sitting Chinese style, the men wolfed down delicious ham and beans, potatoes, and cornbread. Warm beer and hot coffee topped off the meal.

"How'd you manage the cornbread, Brenda?" asked Clay.

"Like they did back in the old days, Clay. Cut the end of that five-gallon water can on three sides, bent the end up, put in the cornmeal mix, closed the lid and put it on fire. Done in twenty minutes. Home-made Dutch oven!" she said proudly.

She was applauded again.

There was not much conversation after the meal. Exhaustion had taken it's toll. Each man said their thanks and good nights to Brenda, slipped into their tent, and flopped wearily into their bed. Sleep came quickly.

Brenda quietly eased onto her bed. She lay listening to the snores of the men and a shiver of pure pleasure passed over her. It had been a long time since she had lain in the dark listening to a man snore. She looked around to make sure Clay and Virgil were not awake. She felt like a spy as she lay listening. But soon, the steady sound of their snoring caused her to drift off into a pleasant sleep.

Clay bounced out of bed at the first loud explosion of gunfire. Gun in hand, he flipped back the tent flap and stepped cautiously outside.

Suddenly, bullets struck all around him. Clay dove for the cover of some boulders.

The tents emptied quickly as everyone ran for cover.

"Who the hell is it now?" Brian yelled, "Another damn nut up there?"

More shots rang out.

Clay spotted the muzzle flashes on the ledge above. He opened fire at them. He was instantly joined by all other guns in the camp. The sound of the shots and bullets ricocheting against the rocks echoed for miles through the canyons.

A shot rang out closer. The muzzle flash was on their level, in the brush. All five men opened fire at it. The loud scream of a man in pain was heard as one of the bullets found its mark.

"We hit one of the bastards!" Rob shouted. He raced toward the bushes.

Clay ran behind him, darting from side to side, making himself hard to hit in case someone lay in ambush out there - something he had seen in the movies.

They both stopped and listened. In the distance, they heard a horse running through the dry brush, its shoes clanking on hard rocks.

"Someone's riding off," said Clay. "It's blacker'n hell out here. Get a light and let's see who we killed."

Ken ran to his tent for a flashlight and headed to Clay's location.

With the bright beam of the Mag-light, they searched the clump of bushes. They didn't find a body, but they did find a few drops of blood on a rock. They had hit someone.

Clay shined the light out into the darkness and around in a circle. Nothing. "Well, at least they weren't ghosts." he said. "Ghosts don't bleed."

Clay reloaded the clip to his automatic pistol and headed for the helicopter. "Virgil, you guys get some sleep. I'll be able to see all around the camp from the helicopter cockpit. It sits high and gives a better view than the ground."

"Okay," Virgil said, as he strained to see his watch in the dim light. "It's one o'clock. I'll relieve you at three."

Clay crawled into the cockpit and slowly swept the camp with his eyes. He had been right. He did have a good clear view of the camp. Nothing moved now. Laying his pistol across his lap, he settled in for a long stay. A noise outside caught his ears. He jerked the gun from his lap.

"Whhoooooo! Whhoooooo! Whhoooooo!"

The owl landed on a saguaro cactus nearby and stared in at Clay.

Clay smiled and relaxed. He had company. Another set of sharp eyes to help watch.

Brenda lay on her cot and listened to Virgil's even breathing. She knew he was asleep. She eased out of bed and slipped through the tent's flap.

Outside, she glanced around the camp and walked to where she could see the helicopter. She wondered if she dared go keep Clay company. She had been drawn to him since the first time they met and now she owed him her life. The more time she spent around him, the more he was in her thoughts. He had saved her life. *Boy, he was really something in that raging water.* Brenda had not been this emotionally attracted to anyone since her divorce. She stared into the cockpit. He looked so alone up in that big chopper. She walked closer. She wondered if he cared for her. *What's on his mind. Would he reject me if I told him my feelings?.. Would he....* She stopped. *No. He's married. I'd better not start something that has nowhere to go.*

She stood for a long time watching him. She could see him looking down at her. He didn't move. She longed so to go to him.

Inside the helicopter, Clay could see Brenda watching him. He was getting mixed emotions about the girl. *Damn, she's attractive. And such a pleasant person to be around. She seems to like our company. Why is she staying with us? What am I talking about? I gotta stop this.* He quickly turned his head to look the other way.

Brenda shook her head, turned back, and hurried into the tent. She laid down. It was going to be a long night. Her thoughts of Clay had put her hormones in gear, and she was wide awake.

52

The concentrated firepower on the ledge had overwhelmed Tom Davis. He lay flat, fearing to even raise his head. He heard a man scream. It was Diego. He had been on the lower plateau. It had to be him.

Davis scooted back away from the rim. When he felt he was safe, he scrambled to his feet and ran to his horse. He mounted the bewildered animal and headed back for his camp. Maybe he would run across Diego along the way. He was out there somewhere. Probably dead. Davis watched for him as he let his horse pick its way through the darkness.

When he hit the flat canyon floor, he spurred his horse into a run. He had not covered a hundred feet when he heard a groan. He reined up and looked around. "Is that you, Diego?" he said in a loud whisper, hoping the greenhorns did not hear him. "Where the hell are you, Josè?" He heard nothing. "Hope that scream back there don't mean you're dead."

No sooner had he got the words out, when Josè Diego's horse stepped out from behind a boulder. Diego was slumped in the saddle, his arm bleeding.

"How bad is it, Josè?"

"It is the arm, Señor Davis." Diego moaned. "It is broken and bleeds badly."

Davis quickly dismounted and tied a bandanna around it. "That'll hold it 'til we can get to a doctor."

The two men rode on to camp.

53

It was long past dark when Dan Wiscoff rode his weary horse into the corral behind the Rockford ranch house. Wiscoff was tired. He had ridden all day and half the night. Giving his horse to a ranch hand, he headed for the house.

Rockford, who had heard him galloping up, met him on the porch. "Where the hell you guys been? I've been trying to reach you for days."

"The damned radio don't work, Boss. That's why I rode out. I think we got troubles."

"More than you know. I got a call from the farm," Rockford said. "Come on in. I'll tell you about it while you have a drink."

"Just make it water."

Inside the house, Rockford paced the floor. "We're going to have to do something about those guys up there," he said. "Can't let 'em go tell anyone about that farm."

He thought for a minute. "Is Davis still up there watching them?"

"Yes, sir. He's waiting on your orders. We've harassed those guys day and night, but they're stubborn, Boss. They're scared, but stubborn as hell." Wiscoff drank down his water. "I came out to see if you might need the chopper, me being the pilot and all."

"You did right. Get a few hours sleep and we'll get the chopper and go up to the farm. We have to get the crop harvested as soon as possible."

"But it's still green, Boss."

"I know that!" Rockford snapped. "Damn! Does every one have to keep reminding me that it's green? Just do as you're told."

"Yes, sir! I'll have the chopper ready at daybreak," Wiscoff said, hurrying to the door.

"Dan," Rockford called.

Wiscoff stopped.

"I think the law is on to us about the girl we snatched."

"Shit!" Wiscoff exclaimed, walking back to him. "How in the hell did they get wind of us?"

"I don't know. Chief Blackhorse is hot on our tails. You better watch what you say and do from now on."

"What about the girl, Boss? She's still up at Big Alice's."

Rockford paced the floor and puffed on his cigar. "We'll have to figure some way to get to her. We can't let her live to point a finger at us."

"What about Big Alice? She's liable to start blasting away at us with that damned shotgun."

"That's not a problem. We'll just shoot that bitch, too."

"That would be a pleasure!" Wiscoff said. "But right now, I need some sleep."

Rockford nodded.

Wiscoff headed for the bunkhouse.

* * *

At 2:00 am, the helicopter was in the air carrying Rockford, Wiscoff and two ranch hands. Rockford had brought them along to help harvest the crop.

Flying at 90 miles an hour, the trip was short. In less than half an hour they were above Tom Davis' camp.

Rockford pointed down. "Take her down."

Wiscoff dropped the helicopter down into the camp.

Tom Davis rushed out to meet them. "Am I glad you got here, Boss!"

"Why? What's wrong?"

"Earlier tonight, when we were trying to scare those bastards off, Diego caught a bullet. It ain't bad, but he needs medical attention."

"What are they doing up there?"

"Digging around the face of the cliff is all I can see. We tried to bury 'em under a rockslide, but missed. Damned fools! They just came right back. This time they posted guards."

Rockford looked over at Diego with the bloody make shift bandage on his shoulder. Damn! Just something else to hold us back. If the law sees this, and they will, there will be more questions to answer. He walked over to Davis, reached into Davis' jacket and pulled out his pistol. Turning quickly, he fired a shot into Diego's forehead. Diego dropped to the ground before the horrified eyes of the others.

"Had to do it or we'd all be in jail by morning," Rockford explained as he handed the stunned Davis his pistol. Davis could only nod.

"I'll leave these two Mexicans here to help you with the body. Better drag it off in the bushes somewhere."

Rockford headed for the helicopter. "After I check out the farm, I'll come back for the rest of you," he shouted over his shoulder.

The helicopter lifted off and gained altitude. Rockford had Wiscoff swing out over the camp of the greenhorns. He wanted a look at the men he was going to kill, but all he could see was the big green helicopter and two tents. There were no people around. He didn't have time to look for them now. He had to get up to the farm. He motioned for Wiscoff to head on up to the farm.

When their helicopter landed, three men carrying automatic rifles greeted them.

"Morning, Boss!" Stockard called out.

"What's been going on up here, Stockard? You got things in gear for the harvest?"

"Yes, sir. All ready," Stockard replied. "I sure thought that old helicopter was going to land the other day, Boss. We took a few shots at it and scared the bastards off."

Rockford stared at the man. "Yeah, and because of that you have cost me a fortune."

Stockard dropped his head like a scolded kid.

"Well that's history now. How many men do we have to harvest the crop?"

"Well, there's three of us here and Wiscoff."

"Wiscoff don't harvest crops, Stockard. He's my pilot," Rockford snapped.

"Okay, that gives us three men," Stockard said.

"I have two more men down at Davis' camp. That should be enough to get it done."

"For twenty five acres?"

"That'll just have to do. Can't risk getting more men." Rockford walked to the door and looked out at the field.

"How long will it take to harvest all twenty-five acres?"

"With only five men - three - four days, and that's working sun up 'til sun down."

"Work nights if you have to, Stockard. I want that grass bundled and ready to haul out as soon as possible. Wiscoff will rent the big cargo helicopter and bring it up when we're ready to load. On the day you're ready, he'll fly it in about dawn so he's not noticed."

"Okay, Boss. Will he be bringing in a load of water?" Stockard asked.

"Not this time. We may not be coming back up here for a while."

When Stockard went out, Rockford walked to the office and sat down at the desk. He pulled out a bottle of tequila. "Dan, let's have a drink. Come morning, I want you to go back for Davis and the two Mexicans."

54

After being relieved by Virgil at three, Clay Morgan laid awake thinking about all the things that were happening to them. He didn't know if Rockford's men were trying to kill them, but it was damned obvious they were trying to scare them. As bad as he wanted to find the Lost Dutchman's gold, he hated taking chances and putting himself and his friends at risk. He decided he had had enough.

The sound of a helicopter caught his ear. It was coming closer. He rose from the floor and looked out through the tent flap. He saw the lights of Rockford's helicopter as it passed overhead. It circled, then headed up toward the farm.

When it was gone, Clay stepped out of the tent. Looking around, he could see nothing out of place. Spotting Rob in the chopper, he motioned for him to join him at the fire.

"You see that chopper, Clay?" he asked when he got to the fire. "They looked us over pretty good. I didn't move so they didn't see me. It was that Rockford guy."

"Yeah, I saw him," Clay replied. "Looks like they're heading up to the farm."

By now everyone was awake.

Clay waited until they had gotten a cup of coffee. "Because of last night," he said, "there's a change in plans this morning. Instead of blowing the mine this morning, we're going to pay those guys down there a visit.

"YAAHOOOOOOOO! It's about time," Rob said, eager to go.

"Maybe we'll find out just why they want us away from here." said Ken.

"That's easy," Brian said. "They know we're onto the Dutchman and they want it for themselves."

"I don't think so," said Clay, "it's the pot farm up there."

Virgil checked his pistol and headed for the Huey. "Let's get it done. We don't have all day. There's a cave to be blown, you know."

Clay turned to Brenda. "Why don't you wait here, Brenda. We don't know what kind of people these are. Could be dangerous."

"And miss all the fun? No way! Besides, I'm a nurse. What if one of you get hurt?"

Seeing it was useless, Clay nodded.

They all climbed aboard and buckled in.

Virgil cranked the engine. Sputtering and coughing, it finally caught. When it smoothed out, Virgil eased the stick up and they lifted off the ground.

The trip to the other camp would have taken most of an hour to hike. The chopper was there in seconds.

Virgil set the craft down in a clearing a few yards away from the camp.

"Brian," said Clay. "You and Ken stay here with Brenda. You'll be our back up. If we have any trouble, don't be afraid to shoot."

Brian and Ken nodded and drew their pistols.

Clay, Virgil, and Rob jumped out of the helicopter and walked toward Tom Davis, who stood alone by the tent.

Clay looked the camp over. He could see three horses. He knew there were more men, but he saw no one. He figured they were watching them right now, probably with guns cocked and ready. The hair on the back of his neck stood up as his senses told him he was in danger.

"Hello there," Clay called out to Davis, as he approached.

"What do you guys want in my camp?" Davis demanded.

Clay looked him over and again looked around the camp. *Friendly bastard. I can see right now this isn't going to go well.* He forced a grin. "Been having a little trouble up on the plateau. Seems someone's trying to kill us or scare us away. Got any ideas who it might be? Anyone harassing you guys?"

"Nope, nobody bothering us and we ain't bothering you, so git off this claim."

"You mean you guys have filed a claim here?"

"That's what I said," Davis answered.

"This is a Federal Wilderness Area. You can't file a claim here. Besides, you don't look like you're mining to me. But then, what do I know?" Clay said.

"That's right! What do you know? You're nothing but a bunch of stupid greenhorns come out here to cause trouble. You don't belong on this mountain," said Davis.

Rob started for the man.

Clay held him back. "It's not worth the trouble, Rob."

Davis stomped his foot. "Git!"

"You take warning, Mister!" Clay said through clenched teeth. "We catch you around our camp again, we're going to shoot you on sight."

Davis laughed and raised his hand.

A shot rang out. Dust kicked up nearby.

The boys jumped and looked around, hands on their pistols.

As Clay had suspected, the other men were in the bushes. "Come on, guys. Let's get out of here before we have to kill someone."

Davis pulled out an automatic pistol and fired a few rounds into the air. "The someone getting killed just might be you. I said git!"

Suddenly, bullets struck the ground all around them and they ran for the chopper, drawing their guns as they went.

From the helicopter, shots rang out. Ken and Brian returned fire over their heads as they ran.

Davis dropped to the ground and crawled behind some bushes. Dust kicked up in his face.

Brian and Ken kept up the heavy barrage as Virgil jumped into the helicopter. Clay and Rob stopped and turned around. They fired on the camp.

Leaves and branches jumped and jerked. Many fell to the ground around Davis. He and his men were pinned down for now.

Virgil gunned the chopper. Clay and Rob jumped in under the steady fire of Brian and Ken.

"Go! Go! Go!" Clay shouted at Virgil.

The Huey lunged upward.

Virgil prayed that a bullet wouldn't hit the fuel tanks or oil lines.

Suddenly, the helicopter slammed to a midair stop. It swerved violently from side to side.

Inside, the passengers grabbed anything they could to hang on to.

"My God, we're hung up on something!" Virgil yelled, struggling with the control to keep the craft from crashing. "What the hell is it? I've never had a helicopter do this."

Clay was sprawled out on the floor, hanging on to the back of his seat to keep from sliding out.

Virgil quickly lowered the chopper a few feet and put it into a hover. It stabilized.

Clay twisted around on the floor, stretched out toward the door. Getting a firm grip on the doorframe, he stuck his head out and looked down. *My God! A rope! Someone has tied a rope to the landing skid.*

"It's a rope!" he shouted. "It's a damn rope!" He sat up quickly. "Virgil! They've tied us to a pine tree down there."

They were sitting ducks for the shooters on the ground. Clay had to do something quick. *This time, we're in deep shit. We set the chopper down and those guys will shoot us. If we don't, we'll crash. Damned, there's got to be something I can do.* Quickly looking around the chopper, Clay spied a machete on the floor. "Rob!" he shouted. "Hand me that machete - there by the seat!"

Rob quickly responded and pushed the machete out to Clay.

With the big knife in hand, Clay laid down again.

Brian and Rob grabbed his legs.

Clay stretched out as far as he could and swung the machete at the rope. He missed. His reach wasn't long enough. He tried again. He still couldn't quite reach it. He looked down in time to see several puffs of smoke coming from gun barrels. He ducked his head inside.

A hail of bullets hit, one coming through the open door and going out the front windshield.

Virgil ducked and struggled with the controls, but the helicopter heaved hard to one side.

Rob and Brian were thrown back against Brenda, the force ripping their hands from Clay's legs.

With a scream, Clay vanished out the door.

Brenda tried to get to the doorway, screaming hysterically.

Brian grabbed her and pulled her back to the seats. "NO! NO! You'll fall out yourself. Sit with me."

"My God, Virgil!" Rob yelled. "Clay fell out!"

Diving to the floor of the leaning helicopter disregarding the bullets that whizzed past his head, Rob looked out. He couldn't see Clay anywhere. He must have landed in the thick bushes on the ground, a hundred feet below.

Rob crawled sadly back to his seat. All eyes were watching him. He shrugged. "He's gone."

With tears in his eyes, Virgil had his hands and feet in constant motion trying to keep the aircraft from crashing. He yelled over his shoulder, "Get back in your seats and hang on or we're all going to die! I'm going to try to break the rope! It's the only chance we have!"

He eased the helicopter down a few feet to gain better control in hover mode.

Another hail of bullets hit the metal craft, slamming their way through the hull, barely missing them. Virgil had been through this many times before, but the Hueys he flew had armor plate. At the first sight or sound of shots, he usually just darted away, listening to the thuds of the slugs hitting the armor. But this time was different. This time he didn't have armor. This time he was tied down like a goat. He couldn't dart away.

He looked back at his remaining friends. "Here we go! Better hang on and start praying!" he shouted, jerking the stick up and twisting the throttle as hard as he could.

The big workhorse lunged upward, hit the end of the rope, and faltered as the motors roared and strained hard against the rope.

Suddenly, it jerked free and shot straight up at a high rate of speed.

Virgil battled to regain control. Sweat popped out on his face as he struggled to get the craft leveled off.

Behind him, the grief-stricken occupants struggled just to hold on. Virgil slowly brought the chopper under control.

Everyone regained their seats and buckled in. They sat in silence. They had just lost a good friend.

Rob sat with his face buried in his hands, shaking his head.

Brenda sobbed uncontrollably. A nurse gets hardened to her work, but to see a friend sucked out of a helicopter and fall to his death was too great a shock. She couldn't help herself and finally broke into loud crying.

"Can't we go back and get him?" Brian yelled.

Ken patted Brian on the shoulder. "That's at least a hundred foot fall, Brian. It would have killed him instantly."

"No need to get the rest of us killed trying to get his body," Virgil said. "We'll go get the law and come back for him."

Virgil gave the chopper more fuel. The chopper was sluggish. "That damn rope is sure causing a drag on this chopper," he said.

"Want to set down somewhere and cut it loose?" Rob asked.

"No, I'll manage. I'm heading for Apache Junction! We're only minutes away now.

The speed of the craft caused silence inside the craft. Only Brenda's soft sobbing could be heard.

Suddenly, Ken held his hand over Brenda's face. "Quiet, Brenda!" he said, as he listened.

Startled, Brenda held her breath. She nearly choked, struggling to subdue her sobs.

"There!" Ken shouted. "You hear that?"

"Help!"

The sound was very faint and sounded far away.

Rob jerked off his seat belt and dove to the floor by the door.

Ken and Brian jumped up and each sat on a leg.

Stretching out his big frame, Rob looked under the helicopter. He was stunned. Clay was clinging to the rope tied to the runner.

"It's Clay! Virgil! He's alive!" Rob shouted.

Clay yelled out feebly. "Help!" Slowly, he slid down toward the small uprooted pine tree at the end of the rope. He had his eyes clenched shut. He had felt himself falling and had started grabbing at anything he could. He felt the rope hit his hand and grabbed it. He jerked to a stop, but fire shot through his hands as the rough rope slid through them. He was able to tighten his grip. He could hear Rob shouting something. He was far away.

"Hang on, Clay!" Rob shouted, "We see you!" Rob jumped to his feet and yelled at Virgil again. "Virgil! Clay's down on the rope! He's alive!"

Virgil blinked his eyes several times to get the tears from them. A big grin broke across his face as he slowed the craft's speed and started looking for a place to set it down. "Hang on, Clay," he said. "Please hang on." He maneuvered the helicopter closer to the ground, just in case Clay lost his grip.

Rob dropped back down and shouted at Clay. "We see you, Clay! Just hang on, buddy! We'll land this thing as soon as we can!"

A hundred feet below, Clay, his eyes still clenched tightly shut and clinging to the rope with all his strength, heard the sweet voice of his friend, but he couldn't answer. He was too scared. His hands burned like they were on fire. He felt himself slide further down. He couldn't look. He knew he was nearing the end of the rope.

Suddenly, he felt pine branches brushing his legs. Then he came to an abrupt stop. He had straddled the main truck of the small tree. He locked his legs around it and settled between branches. Despite hanging below a helicopter hundreds of feet off the ground, Clay now felt a sense of security - something solid under his rear end. He tried to open his eyes, but fear got the best of him and he kept them shut. He hadn't taken his pills before they got in the helicopter. For the first time since he fell, he dared to think there was hope. His hands burned furiously from sliding down the rope, but he paid them little attention. He was busy trying to keep a death grip on the rope as sixty miles an hour winds blasted his face.

Rob stuck his head in the cockpit. "Virgil, we got to land this thing. Clay is down on the tree we uprooted, but he could fall at anytime."

Virgil slowly lowered the helicopter toward the ground. "Okay, Rob," he said, "I can't set the helicopter down because of the rocks and vegetation, but I'll try to set him down here. I can't see him so you'll have to guide me."

Rob flopped back on his belly and started giving Virgil instructions. "Easy now, Virge," he yelled. "It's just a few more feet 'til the tree touches the ground.

Virgil hovered the helicopter above the ground, slowly easing it downward.

The tree touched the ground and gently laid over, but Clay didn't move. He refused to turn loose of the rope. He was frozen in shock.

"Clay! You have to turn loose! Just release your hands!" Rob shouted.

Clay still refused to turn loose.

Rob turned to the cockpit. "Virgil, we'll have to think of something else; Clay won't turn loose."

"Damn! We can't land here. The terrain is too rough. You watch him closely! I'm going to try to make it to a road near Apache Junction. We'll use the road to lay him and the rope down, then we can land. We need at least a hundred feet of flat surface to do it without killing him."

"Well, he's about a hundred feet down, so calculate that when you're flying low. We don't want to smash him into the bluffs," Rob said.

As the chopper started to gain altitude, Virgil used the radio for the first time. "Mayday! Mayday! Mayday! This is Virgil Patton in a chopper above the Superstition Mountains. We have a dangerous situation here and need a road cleared at Apache Junction for an emergency landing!"

The radio crackled and a man said, "What is your emergency, Pilot?"

"I have an unstable load."

"What's the load?"

"You wouldn't believe me if I told you!" Virgil replied. "Right now, just get me a road clear."

"Okay, Pilot. We'll notify Apache Junction Police and they'll close off a road for you. Stay in contact with us and good luck!"

Minutes later, Virgil pointed. "There's Apache Junction!"

Rob nodded his approval as he lay looking out the door, watching Clay.

Brenda was trying to cry and laugh at the same time. She was happy he was alive, but she knew he was still in grave danger of falling. The rope might break. The tree might come loose. He might simply let go, unable to hang on any longer. She didn't know what to do - cry or laugh.

Below, Clay could hear Rob yelling down to him. It was comforting to hear his voice. Now he knew what Rob must have been going through when he fell into that crack in the ground.

"Just keep hanging on, Clay," Rob shouted. "We're approaching Apache Junction now." Rob glanced a little ahead of the chopper to see if he could see the road. What he saw shocked him. "GET IT UP, VIRGIL!" he screamed. "GET IT UP! THERE'S A RIDGE COMING UP HE WON'T CLEAR!"

Virgil pulled the control back and the craft rose quickly, the dangling tree narrowly missing the top of a rock ridge.

"Control to Chopper!"

"Go ahead, Control," Virgil replied.

"The police have a road at the east side of town secured for your landing. You should be able to see their emergency lights by now. Proceed with caution."

Virgil looked out the side window. He could see two police cars with flashing lights several hundred feet apart on the ribbon of black road. More cars were racing toward them. "10-4, Control. I have them in sight and we're heading in now. Thank you!" Virgil slowed the helicopter and then hovered it above the blacktop road.

The huge green machine had already attracted the attention of several people, including Chief Blackhorse, who stood watching the strange sight. Hell of a way to haul a tree.

As the craft came in lower and the tree got near the ground, Blackhorse stared in disbelief. "My God! There's a man hanging onto that tree!"

Virgil couldn't see the tree. "Rob, I have to rely on your signals. Tell me something. Quick!

"Just a little more down. . . come on . . . a little more," said Rob. "Keep coming . . . easy. . . now!" he signaled. "The top of the tree is touching the ground. Lay it down slowly."

Virgil eased down on the stick ever so slightly, letting the helicopter inch forward and down. He knew if he moved any faster he would drag Clay along the pavement.

Dust from the rotor whipped around, blasting everything around, but Clay still clung to the rope for dear life, oblivious to the flying debris.

Gently, Virgil eased the chopper forward and down. He laid the rope on the roadway until finally he felt the runners touch the solid surface. Easing the stick all the way down, he cut the power and collapsed back in his seat, letting out a long sigh of relief. He dropped his head in his hands and shook uncontrollably for a moment. The shouts of people running to Clay's aid helped him regain his composure.

Brenda had already jumped out and was running back toward Clay. She was followed closely by Brian, Ken, and Rob.

When Virgil had fully gained his composure, he climbed out. There was a large crowd around the tree. Hurrying to it, he discovered Clay, still clinging zombie-like to the tree.

Rob and Brian tried to pry his hands loose, but he refused to let go. They stopped and looked at Virgil for help.

"He looks okay, but he won't turn loose. He's in shock." Brenda said, patting Clay's arm.

Virgil had seen this kind of shock in Vietnam and knew a cruel but quick cure for it. He hurried back to the helicopter and returned, unscrewing the top from a large jug of water. "Everybody move back," he said. "I have no idea what he might do."

The crowd took Virgil at his word and moved to the side of the road.

Virgil splashed the water in Clay's gaunt face and stepped back himself.

Clay, sputtering and spitting, swung out at him with one hand, then grabbed the rope again.

Virgil poured more water on him and watched as his friend lay quietly for a moment.

Clay relaxed his grip.

Rob and Brian quickly pulled him to his feet.

The crowd cheered.

Clay was unsteady on his feet.

Virgil watched intently.

Clay's face suddenly filled with rage. He snatched his pistol from his belt and pointed it at Virgil.

Rob and Brian turned him loose and joined the crowd running for cover.

"Virgil, you son-of-a-bitch!" Clay shouted.

Virgil could see that Clay was still out of his head. He knew he was serious. Looking around for cover, he spotted Chief Blackhorse' car and dove over it's hood. He yelled at Blackhorse as he flew through the air. "Take cover!"

Landing hard on the ground, Virgil scooted up against the wheel for cover, just as Chief Blackhorse slammed into the ground beside him.

Huddled behind the wheel, Blackhorse looked at Virgil. "Jesus Christ, man, I think your friend has flipped out," he said, drawing his revolver.

Virgil pushed the pistol down. "No. He ain't flipped, he's pissed!" He looked at the Chief. "Don't worry, he won't shoot anyone - unless it's me. Just give 'im a minute and he'll be okay."

Blackhorse nodded and slowly eased away from Virgil. He didn't want to be too close just in case.

When he didn't hear any shots, Virgil eased his head up.

Clay was standing in the middle of the road, his gun on the pavement.

"Hey, Clay! You okay now?" Virgil yelled.

"Yeah, I'm okay."

Heads popped up from behind all sorts of cover.

Clay's friends approached him.

When Virgil was close enough, Clay grabbed him in a big bear hug. "God, man," he whispered. "I thought I was dead for sure." Tears came to his eyes. "Thanks, old buddy. You saved my life."

Cautiously, Chief Blackhorse eased over to the two men. "Gentlemen, you might remember that I'm the Police Chief around here. Would someone please tell me what the hell is going on?"

"We had a little trouble up there, Chief," said Virgil.

Blackhorse saw Brenda. "Hello, Brenda. You can tell me later how you managed to get involved in this thing." He turned to Virgil. "I got a call from the airport control tower saying you were in trouble. I didn't know what kind, I just cleared the road for you."

"Thanks, Chief," Virgil said.

"When we get the rope off the helicopter, you can fly it over to our headquarters. We have a heliport there. Now suppose you fellas - and gal - come along with me to headquarters and tell me if something really happened to you up there, or if you were just trying out a new type of thrill ride."

Chief Blackhorse and his men hustled Clay, Brian, Rob, Ken, and Brenda away in their cars.

Virgil flew the helicopter off the road and to the City Police Department.

* * *

In the station, Brenda applied a soothing ointment and bandages to the palms of Clay's hands as Chief Blackhorse listened to the bizarre story about Rockford and the marijuana farm. He sat for a long time before he said anything. "I wish this was my case," he said. "But it seems it belongs to Sheriff Wilkins. I've sent for him. He should be here soon."

Brenda liked the Chief. He was a decent man, but she couldn't resist saying, "He won't do a damn thing, Dennis. You know that. Rockford is involved with Wilkins right up to his eyeballs."

"Now, Brenda, that's just a rumor. You don't know that for sure. Besides, he *is* still the sheriff," Blackhorse said, staring at his desk. He didn't like Sheriff Wilkins himself, but he couldn't go around telling people he thought he was a crook.

"Maybe there are other people who would be interested in Mr. Rockford," Blackhorse said. "Maybe I'll just make a few calls." He stood up. "In the meantime, you guys get to the motel and get some rest. I'll tell the sheriff where you are."

As they neared the helicopter, Clay stopped. He stood staring at it.

Virgil walked up to him. "Got to get back on the horse, Clay, or you'll be afraid of it forever."

Clay looked at Virgil, who was so confident about flying, and wished he felt the same way. Unfortunately, he didn't. "Would you mind terribly if I just took a cab this time?" he asked.

"Okay, but tomorrow you're getting back in that chopper. Right?" Virgil asked, raising his eyebrows and looking Clay squarely in the eyes.

"I was thinking we ought to stay in town a couple of days and get some rest," said Clay.

"Suits the hell right out of me," Virgil replied.

"Maybe that's what we need," Rob said. "Some peace and quiet. Things might cool down up there by then."

* * *

Will Barnett sat at the big table with the boys and Brenda, listening to Rob talk about their encounters. "Sure glad to see you boys are still alive," he said. "Damn, Clay! I wish I'd been there to see you come riding in on that wild pine tree."

Even Clay laughed at that remark, but the laughter was cut short when Sheriff Wilkins walked in.

He strolled over to the table, pulled up a chair and sat down. "Seems every time I turn around you boys are mixed up in something. I hear you had some more trouble up there."

"Yeah, well it isn't our doing," said Brian, looking Wilkins straight in the eyes. "Someone up there's trying to kill us, Sheriff. Now what are you going to do about it?"

"Whatever I can, boy!" Wilkins snapped. He turned to Clay. "Now, Chief Blackhorse has already told me you almost got killed up there. I've sent some men to see if they can find these guys that shot at you. If they do, we'll arrest them and see what they have to tell the judge." He looked around at Brian. "Does that suit you, young man?"

Brian wasn't satisfied, but what could he say. "Sure," he replied, "if your men can find them."

Clay hadn't said anything yet. He'd been listening. The sheriff hadn't mentioned the marijuana farm. Maybe Chief Blackhorse hadn't told him about it. Or maybe he was just keeping it back for later.

"Sheriff," Clay said, "we know someone up there is trying to kill us or scare us off. We think it's the man who owns the blue helicopter - the one we told you about before. You know, the one who refused to help us when Ken was attacked by the mountain lion. I think that man is involved in something illegal up there."

Surprised, Sheriff Wilkins asked, "Like what?"

Now Clay knew Blackhorse hadn't told him. He spoke quickly, before anyone else could say anything. "I don't know what. But it's enough to kill over."

"We'll get to the bottom of it, you can be sure of that," Wilkins said, standing up.

Brenda couldn't hold it back any longer. "Bullshit, Wilkins! You're not going to do one damned thing about it, 'cause it involves your buddy - Paul Rockford. You're going to do just as you always do - exactly what he tells you."

"You'd be wise to watch that smart mouth of yours, young lady," Wilkins glared at her. "It's going to get you into a world of trouble." He slammed his white Stetson on his head, stomped to the door, then stopped and looked back. "I want you people to stay off that mountain or I'm going to arrest you," he ordered angrily. "Just go on back to your big city where you belong." He turned and stormed out.

"I think you pissed him off, Brenda," Clay said, with an approving smile.

"Why didn't you tell him about the marijuana farm?" she asked.

"If Chief Blackhorse didn't tell him about it, I sure as hell wasn't going to. Besides, I don't like that man."

"I don't trust him, either," Ken said. "He reminds me of that weasel-eyed supervisor we used to have at the plant. You know, the one that always buttered you up to your face and then tried to get you fired behind your back."

Clay chuckled. "I remember him. He finally got fired himself, didn't he?"

"That's right," Rob said. "Got mixed up with a girl in the office and she ratted him out. What with all the sexual harassment charges that have been flying around lately, they sent him packing in short order."

"Never could trust that man, and now that you mentioned it, he *was* just like the Sheriff here," Virgil said, "I think I would much prefer to deal with Chief Blackhorse."

Clay stood up. "Let's head for the motel." He turned to Brenda, "What are you going to do, Brenda?"

She tried to hide her feelings as she answered. "Oh, I'll just go back to work, I guess. But first I have to get my Blazer from Big Alice's place."

"Want us to give you a lift up there in a couple of days?" Clay asked.

Her eyes lit up. "Hey! That's a great idea. That is, if you're going back up there."

Virgil looked at her. "Oh, we're going back up there, alright. Nobody's going to run us off that mountain until we're damned good and ready to go."

"That's right," Clay said. "Besides, we still have a cave full of gold to pick up."

They said their good-byes to Will and headed out the door.

"See you here for breakfast in the morning," Brenda yelled, walking away. "That is, if I don't sleep all day."

55

Chief Blackhorse sat staring at his desk deep in thought. He had not told Sheriff Wilkins about the marijuana farm. He was saving that for the Federal boys. He knew a Drug Enforcement Agent over in Phoenix who would jump on the chance to destroy such a big farm. Agent Charles Basker had been a friend of his for several years. Blackhorse picked up the telephone and dialed.

"Federal Building."

"DEA office for Agent Charles Basker."

"Who may I say is calling?"

"Chief Blackhorse of Apache Junction."

Blackhorse drummed his fingers on his desk as he waited for the connection.

"Well, hello there, Chief. How're things in your neck of the woods?" asked Charles Basker.

"Not so good right now, Charles."

"What the problem?"

"I have a little project for you if you're interested. Something you can help me with."

"Anything for you, my friend. What is it?"

"It seems some treasure hunters, city boys from Los Angeles, spotted what they think is a big marijuana processing farm up near Weaver's Needle in the Superstition Mountains. Said they'd been shot at by three men with automatic weapons. Even saw a big building up there. It appears to be a big operation, Charles."

"Hell, Chief, nothing can grow in that desert hellhole. Besides, who'd be stupid enough to start up a farm in a Federal Wilderness Area. Think they're imagining things?"

"No. They're not the run-of-the-mill prospectors. They're all engineers at some automobile manufacturing plant in California. All except one, that is, and he's the company pilot. As far as it being a desert, they say the field is being irrigated. There's a water tower up there. Bullet holes in their helicopter attest to some of their story."

"Helicopter?"

"Yeah," Blackhorse chuckled. "Would you believe it? They're flying an old Huey gunship. Makes 'em damn good transportation and saved 'em a hell of a lot of time."

Blackhorse paused for a second, then went on. "No, Charles, they're not imagining it. These guys are really having problems with someone up there. They were shot at just today by one of Paul Rockford's goons. Then someone tied a rope to their helicopter and to a tree. When they took off, they almost crashed while the man was shooting at 'em all the time. Came flying in here with one of 'em astride the tree, dangling a hundred feet down. Claims he fell out of the chopper. I believe these guys, Charles. There's something up there, alright."

Basker laughed at the thought of the man riding the tree into town. "Riding a tree tied with a rope to a helicopter. They're either pretty good men or crazy. They say how big a farm it is?"

"Said it looked to be twenty-five acres or so. Like I said, these guys are engineers. They would be able to judge land size."

"Wheewee, that's big bucks!" Basker exclaimed.

"You bet - considering one plant will produce from one to four pounds of marijuana. You can imagine how many plants they could grow on twenty-five acres. That's why I thought we might get you fellas interested."

"Damned right, we're interested, Chief. Can we meet at your place tomorrow?"

"Sure. The sooner the better. I think if we work this right, I might be able to find the person who kidnapped a girl here a few weeks ago."

"I heard about that, Dennis. Wish you luck."

"Thanks. See you tomorrow." Blackhorse hung up the phone and leaned back in his chair. Now maybe the shit will hit the fan for Rockford and I'll get a break before that girl ends up dead - if she isn't already.

"Those criminal histories are back, Chief," said one of Blackhorse' officers.

"And?"

"Rockford's clean as a whistle. So's Wiscoff. Davis has only minor charges like assault, battery, things like that. No felony charges. Best we can figure, the two have been working for Rockford for about three years now."

"Damn!" said Blackhorse. He had hoped something in the histories would show a pattern.

"Sorry, but that's all there is, Chief," said the officer.

56

Rockford stood in the doorway of the office of the farm building high in the mountains, watching his men cut and process the marijuana. He had laid out the plans for the building. Besides being a processing factory and warehouse, it contained the office and bunk area as well. He had even built a water tower and had the water hauled in by helicopter. Rockford kept three men at the farm around the clock. They served as field hands as well as guards.

Rockford watched them bring in a load of green plants. The plants had reached their mature size, but were still a long way from being harvest-ready. He sniffed the air. The fresh cut grass smell filled the building. He took another deep breath and grinned. It was an unusual smell here in the mountains.

The men scurried about in their attempt to get the green marijuana pressed into bails small enough to fit the cargo hull of a helicopter. An electric motor, used on the press and powered by a gas generator outside, roared to life as one man pressed a button.

Rockford grinned. *All the luxuries of the big city. Who in hell would ever suspect such an operation this high in the desert mountains?* His grin vanished as he thought about the greenhorns.

Only stupid luck. Only by the stupid luck of greenhorns did they discover my farm so soon. Discover it and put me out of business. He turned up the bottle of tequila he had been holding and took a long pull on it. *Someday - someday soon they'll pay.*

He glanced up at the empty hooks dangling from the ceiling. It was usually late fall when the mature plants were harvested. They would be hung from those hooks upside down to dry. The leaves, seeds, and stems were then separated and used in different ways. The leaves were pressed into 2.2 pound kilos, wrapped in waterproof paper, and sealed with tape. The seeds were used for replanting, and the stems were ground into a fine powder and chemicals added so it could be formed into cakes and then hardened. The cakes were wrapped in waterproof paper and shipped out as hashish - a prized form of marijuana, the strongest form available.

Rockford watched Tom Davis carrying a bundle of huge green plants over his shoulder. Rockford hadn't yet told him that they were suspects in the kidnapping. He decided now was the time. He yelled and waved Davis over.

Davis came into the office and shut the door, blocking out the noise of the motor. "Yeah. What's up, Boss?"

"Tom, something came up and you're going to have to leave the state for a while."

Tom looked puzzled. "What came up?"

"That girl we snatched in Apache Junction. The law is hot on our tail."

"How? What happened?" Tom asked.

"We don't know, but Chief Blackhorse is checking us out."

"But why just me leave, Boss? As I recall there were three of us involved."

"I know, Tom. But don't you worry none. I'm going to give you plenty of money and send you on a vacation down to Mexico City. How does that sound?"

Tom walked around the small dirty office as he pondered what Rockford had said.

To help him decide, Rockford added more fuel. "The police were asking around for you. I think someone saw you grab her from the car that night."

"I don't see how. It was pitch black that night."

"Well, all I can tell you is that Chief Blackhorse has been to my ranch twice now asking all kinds of questions. He is extremely interested in you. I told him you were in Fort Worth, Texas, buying livestock."

Tom stopped beside the desk. "Okay, Boss. Whatever you say. Maybe if they can't find me, they'll leave you alone."

"That's the spirit, Tom. That's the way to think. Now, there's just one more little matter I need you to handle for me before you go."

"What's that?"

"Dan and I will fly you down to the base camp today and you can pick up the horses we left there."

"Yeah, they might be getting hungry 'bout now," said Davis. He looked at Rockford. "Boss, what about those treasure hunters down there? What are you going to do 'bout them if I leave?"

Rockford laughed, "After what you did to them the other day, they're all the way back in Los Angeles by now." He turned in his chair, bent down, and opened a floor safe. He pulled out a large bundle of money and counted it out on his desk. Neither spoke until he had reached ten thousand dollars. "There!"

Davis' eyes got big. "Geez, Boss, that's a lot of money."

"Well, half of that is your money for the vacation, and the other half is your bonus."

"Bonus?"

"Yeah, I thought I'd let you have a little excitement before you go away, and give you a bonus for doing it," Rockford said.

"So what's this excitement I'm supposed to have?"

"I want you to take the horses back to the ranch, but on the way, I want you to stop by Big Alice's place and get rid of that girl we snatched." He studied Davis' face.

"You mean ....?"

"Yes. I mean kill her! Kill her before she can finger you and me for kidnapping and raping her."

"I didn't rape her," said Davis.

"You get the point. Just remember, Davis, kidnapping's a federal offense. You'll get life in prison if she talks."

Davis nodded, but he was still somewhat reluctant - not about killing the girl, but about killing her at Big Alice's. He was scared to death of that woman. "Look, Boss. You know that Big Alice bitch is crazy. She'll kill me if she catches me."

"Scared of her, are you?" Rockford laughed. "In that case I wouldn't let her catch me if I were you."

Davis sat thinking for a minute. He looked at Rockford and grinned. "Boss, you think I could. . . could. . . well you know."

Rockford realized what he meant. He laughed. "Why not?" he replied. "You're going to kill her anyway."

He stopped laughing and frowned. "Just do it before you kill her, man. Guys who do it after make me sick."

"What do you think I am, a pervert?" Davis asked indignantly. He grabbed up the money and stuck it in his pocket.

"Davis, about Big Alice. . ." He tossed another bundle of money on the desk. "Here's another five thousand and your chance to get even with her. I want you to kill that big bitch while you're there."

Davis' eyes lit up. He snatched up the money. "I'll take care of her, Boss. Don't you worry."

Rockford was suddenly anxious to get it over with. "Tell you what, Dan and I will take you down there now. No need for you to help with the crop. Might get dirt and sweat on all that new money."

"That's great!" Davis said.

57

Big Alice sat in her favorite chair on the porch and gazed through her binoculars. She watched a small dark speck high on the mountain. It was a blue helicopter. She put the glasses down and turned to Laura, who was sitting in a chair nearby. "Girl, that's Rockford's whirlybird up there. I'm not sure if it's coming here, but you best git back to your room."

Laura jumped up. She looked around like a scared doe. She glanced off toward the mountain but couldn't see anything. "Oh, Alice! Please let me go! Please! He's going to kill me if you keep me here! Please! I won't tell anyone about you," she begged.

Big Alice sat for several minutes without answering. She knew if word got out that she had kept Laura locked in her saloon, she would be considered just as guilty of kidnapping as the men who snatched her. No matter how bad she wanted to let the poor girl go, she couldn't, if she wanted to stay out of prison. Big Alice knew she could survive in prison, but who needed the hassle. *Hell, I get in there, I'd have to start all over again showing them gals who was boss. That damned Rockford done got me in this mess, now I gotta watch out for my own self. The longer I stay outta that place, the better.* She also knew prison was exactly where she was destined if she was caught with Laura. She had been trying to think of a way clear, but so far had come up with nothing but blanks.

She gave Laura a sad look and replied, "Look, girl, I've been pondering and pondering on how I could let you go without going to jail. But for the life of me, I can't figure a way out. Now, you go on to your room in case that Rockford shows up here. While you're there, put your own mind to work and see if you can come up with a way that I can let you go."

Alice snapped her fingers at Juanita, who was serving as Laura's guard while Padro and Gonzales were gone. "Take her on inside, Juanita."

Laura looked down at the big woman for a minute, then turned and went to her room. She knew Big Alice was right. There was no way she could let her go without going to jail.

As the door slammed on Laura's room, Padro and Gonzales rode up to the porch. Dusty, hot and tired, they dismounted and tied up their horses.

"Señorita Alice! They're gone!" said Gonzales.

"Gone? What do you mean they're gone?" Alice demanded.

"Si! It was yesterday the boys from the city went in the helicopter to visit with Rockford's men. There was shooting and they flew away with a man on a pine tree tied to the helicopter!"

Big Alice gave Padro an inquisitive look. "Either the sun got to you or you've been drinking too much tequila. Which is it?"

Padro was quick to answer. "Manuel is telling it right, Señorita. With the man on a tree they flew over the mountain. I think they are gone for good."

"Damn!" Alice remarked to herself. "Did you see them take anything else? You know, like gold?"

"No, Señorita. They didn't even take their tents. They're still up on the mountain."

"They left their tents?"

"Sì, Señorita."

"Then they'll be back," she said. She smiled and stared off toward the mountain. "I didn't think they were quitters. They'll find that gold and I'll have it yet."

She pointed at Padro. "Padro, I want you to get cleaned up, get something to eat, and then keep a close watch on that girl. There's something in the wind. I've spotted Rockford's helicopter moving around up there too much." She shivered even in the heat of the day. "Besides, I have this weird feeling."

Big Alice got up from her chair and walked over to look Padro in the eyes. "You see that nothing happens to that girl. You hear me, Padro? Nothing at all."

"Sì, Señorita," Padro said, shrinking from her meaningful glare.

Big Alice picked up the binoculars and took another look at the mountain. "Damn you to hell for bringing her here, Rockford," she muttered.

* * *

A full moon lit the night as Tom Davis tied all the horses and mules to trees a few hundred yards from Alice's saloon. He looked toward the log building. It was still a ways off. *This far out no one will notice them. I'll just slip in, grab the girl, have my fun, then kill her. Maybe I'll cut her throat - no. I couldn't cut a pretty girl's throat. I'll strangle her. Yeah, that's it. I'll choke her to death. Then I'll slip outside and shoot old Big Alice through a window. That way I can get away clean.* He mounted his horse and rode on down toward the saloon. Easing his horse into the bushes behind the dark building, he reined up. He sat looking and listening. He neither saw anyone nor saw anything.

Checking his pistol to make sure it was loaded, he eased off the horse and tied the reins to a bush. He had to be extremely careful or Big Alice would sic those two giant Mexicans on him. Davis knew the girl was kept in a rear bedroom that was locked. He would need tools to break the lock.

Poking around in his saddlebags, Davis came up with a hammer used for mending fences. It would do to twist the lock off the bedroom door. Sweat popped out on his forehead and ran down into his eyes, more from the anxiety that gripped him than from the heat. I've never killed a woman before. *I ain't sure I'll like it, but what I'm going to do to her first, I do like.* He looked around and took a deep breath. He was as ready as he would ever be.

Creeping though the yard, he made it to the back porch without being seen. He stood in the darkness of the porch, watching and listening, his heart thumping wildly in his throat.

Just a few feet away, inside the saloon, Padro sat at the very last table. He kept an eye on the bedroom door while engaged in deep conversation with his girlfriend, Maria.

The tequila flowed as Padro sweet talked the girl. She was trying to get him to go to her room and make love, but he was afraid to drop his guard on Laura.

After much persuasion, Padro could resist her squirming on his lap no more. He glanced around for Big Alice. She was no where to be seen.

He and Maria rose from the table. Padro was trembling. He cast an anxious eye around the saloon. He still didn't see her. He figured she must have already gone to bed.

Stopping at Laura's room, Padro checked the lock. It was still secure. He hoped nothing happened for a few minutes anyway; Maria had built a fire in him that only she could extinguish.

Giggling, the girl pulled him into the room across the hall from Laura's and closed the door.

Six feet away, the rear door slowly opened an inch or so. Davis eased his eye around the edge of the door and peeped inside. He saw nothing. Pushing the door open wider, he quietly stepped into the silent, dimly lit hallway, leaving the back door open just a crack so he could make a fast getaway. Flattening himself against the wall, he listened. Music came from the saloon, but all else was quiet. He could hear giggling coming from the room across the hall. He would have to be quiet.

Davis eased along the wall to the only door with a padlock. He slipped the hammer claws into the loop on the lock and twisted. He knew most locks would spring open if given a swift hard twist, but when you have to be extremely quiet, it's much harder. Davis strained as he put all his power into a slow twisting of the lock.

Suddenly, it came loose and fell to the floor with a crash. Davis quickly stepped back out the back door and froze against the outside wall, his hand going to his gun.

Inside Maria's room, she and Padro were on the bed clawing at each other's clothes. When he heard the crash, Padro froze. He listened. Nothing. He pushed Maria away and sat up. She was unaware he had heard something and wanted to get on with her love making. He struggled with her as he tried to listen. Hearing nothing more, he figured it must have been his imagination. To Maria's delight, he turned back to her.

When no one noticed the noise, Davis opened the door and tiptoed back to the door to Laura's room. He quietly opened it and slipped into her room. Easing the door closed behind him, he walked to the bed and looked down at the sleeping Laura.

Moonlight coming through the window splashed down upon the young body lying on the bed.

Davis' heart raced and the blood flowed through his loins as he eased closer, spellbound by the whiteness of her shoulders. He listened for a second, but heard only the sound of her soft breathing. The only movement in the room was the rise and fall of her bosom as she breathed. Unable to control himself any longer, Davis was upon her. His big hand clamped tightly over her mouth and nose.

Laura woke and struggled against him. She pounded him with her fists as she tried to breathe.

This only served to excite Davis, and he held her that way until she went limp from lack of air. Only then did he release her nose to allow her to suck in a long, deep breath.

His filthy body covered hers. He pulled a large knife from his belt and shoved it hard against her throat. "One sound out of you, bitch, and I'll cut your head completely off," he whispered.

Laura stared at him with terrified eyes. She knew she was going to die if she didn't do as he said. Her instinct to survive took over and she once again resigned herself to the fact that she was going to be raped. She stopped struggling.

Davis grinned from ear to ear as he released her mouth and crushed his own mouth down on it. He was violently struggling to get his pants down and force her legs apart at the same time. He stopped and put his hand back over her mouth.

"Spread those damned legs!...Now!"

Laura felt she had no recourse. Tears brimmed her eyes as she slowly spread her legs. Davis fell between them. The knife dug into her throat as he worked hard with his free hand to get his pants down.

In his struggles, the hammer he had stuck in his belt dropped out and struck the wood floor with a loud bang. The noise echoed through the saloon. Davis froze. Fear rushed through him. He was terrified.

Davis spun around with the big knife in his hand as a huge dark shadow fell across the bed, but Padro was faster with the machete.

Davis' right hand, still holding the knife, flew through the air, bounced against a wall and struck the floor with a dull thud.

The attack came so swiftly that Davis couldn't scream. He could only gurgle. He grabbed his stub of arm and struggled to get to his feet.

As he straightened, Padro drove the long blade through his stomach.

This time a horrifying scream escaped Davis' lips as he fell to the floor.

Padro stood over him. "Did I not tell you only a little while ago to be careful around me, gringo?" asked Padro, watching the squirming man on the floor. "Did I not say to you that someday I would have to kill you? Well, gringo, someday is here. Today you have been killed by me." Padro turned to look down at Laura. "You okay, Señorita Laura?"

Laura was trying to stifle a scream. She could only point at Davis.

"I know," Padro said understandingly. "He will bring harm to you no more."

A deafening blast spun Padro around.

Big Alice stood in the doorway - a smoking shotgun in her hands. It was pointed at Davis.

Padro looked down.

Davis lay dead now - a very large hole in his chest. He gripped a cocked pistol in his remaining hand.

"You're getting careless, Padro," Big Alice said, softly. "She was trying to tell you that he was about to shoot you."

Then Big Alice lashed out at him. "Damn you, Padro! I told you not to let anything happen to her. Where were you? In the sack with that little girl of yours?"

Padro knew not to lie to her. He spoke quickly, "Sì, Señorita, but right there! Right across the hall. No one could come near her without I hear him, Señorita. Forgive me, please, for my foolish ways. It was just that I have been up on the mountain for so long, away from my Maria."

Big Alice glared at him in anger for a minute, then her face softened and finally she chuckled. She could understand a man's needs. "Okay, you hot-blooded chili pepper. Go back and finish the job so you'll be useful to me again. I'll take the girl to my room."

Padro wiped the sweat from his forehead and glanced down at himself. A sad look came over his face. He shook his head. "I think I am finished, Señorita."

Big Alice had started to leave, but now stopped. "Well, if that's the case, you can take that dead bastard up on the mountain and toss him in the brush." She motioned with her hand toward Davis' head. "You might want to make it look like that old head hunter got him."

Padro knew what she meant. He held up his machete. "Sì, Señorita."

Laura followed Big Alice to her room.

Big Alice pointed at a small cot in the corner. "You sleep there, girl. You'll be safe here. Nobody ever comes in here unless I invite them."

Laura, still in shock, sank down on the bed. Tears started to roll. She lay sobbing softly.

58

"Rise and shine, boys," Clay shouted, as he pounded at the door of Rob's motel room. "If we're going back up on the mountain today, we gotta get a move on."

Rob rolled over and stared at the door. "Wish he'd go away. I didn't get much sleep last night."

Ken laughed and sprang out of bed. "You got loaded last night, Rob. You've just got a little hangover. Now come on! That fresh mountain air will cure you in no time."

Brian stepped out of the bathroom, already dressed. "See you guys over at the restaurant," he said, heading out the door.

The bright yellow of the egg yokes drew a thoughtful eye from Virgil, as he poised to slice his knife through them. "You think eggs are really as bad for you as they claim, Clay?"

Clay took a bite of hot ham. "Who cares how bad they are for you? We'll probably all get killed anyway, so stop staring at 'em and eat the damned things."

Virgil laughed and cut through the eggs, just as Rob and Ken came in to join them.

Ken looked around the room. "Seen anything of Brenda yet? Wasn't she supposed to go with us today?"

"Yeah, she should be along soon. I told her it would be around eight before we left," Clay replied.

Will Barnett was standing by the table wiping his hands on his apron. "I don't think you guys ought to go back up there. My God, boys, look at all that has happened to you already. Anyone with one eye and half-sense would run as fast as he could from that place."

Virgil stopped eating and laid his fork down. "Look, Will, we have to dig out that cave up there, or I'll never rest again. I know I saw carved signs on the rock wall."

"Carved signs are found all the time up there," Will said. "It don't mean shit. There are so many rocks up there carved on, they're selling them for souvenirs down at the outfitter's store."

"We're still going, Will," Virgil said, stubbornly.

Will shook his head and looked at Clay. "Clay, talk some sense into that man, will you?"

"I'm afraid he's right, Will," said Clay. "We have to do it."

Will threw up both hands and headed back to the kitchen.

"Just make sure we have our guns loaded," Brian said.

Rob sipped his hot coffee and groaned. "Guess we're going to start pitching rocks as soon as we get there, huh? No resting first?"

"Just as soon as our feet hit the ground, we're going to blast the hell out of that opening. I'd like to get off that mountain as soon as possible - with some gold, of course," Clay answered.

"Morning, fellas!" Brenda called out as she entered the restaurant. "Got room for one more?"

"Brenda Carpenter! Come on down!" Brian announced loudly, sounding a lot like Bob Barker on the Price Is Right game show.

She was in good spirits as she sat down. "Coffee, Will. Lots of it!"

After all the usual good mornings, Brenda turned to Clay. "I had another week's vacation coming and I just took it. Hope you guys don't mind if I tag along."

Clay was pleased, yet worried. "Brenda, you know how dangerous it is up there. You could get hurt."

"I still want to go."

"It could get even worse," said Virgil. "Sure you're up to it again?"

"I'm up to it, Virgil, but if you don't want me along. . ."

"It's not that," Virgil said quickly. "We just worry about you getting hurt."

"Well, I'm a nurse and I can help if any one does get hurt. I could have a job. Besides cooking, I could be your lookout. That way, all of you can dig."

Clay looked at Virgil, then at each man at the table. They all nodded their approval.

Looking back, Clay smiled. "Well, Lookout, looks like you're in. Might even cut you in for a share of the gold - if we find it."

"That's not why I'm going. Like you guys, this is an adventure for me, too. I've never felt so good. No, it's not the gold. But then again, if you were to insist, I would have no choice but to accept, would I?"

"No," Clay answered. "Now drink up and let's get going."

* * *

As they checked their guns and prepared to board the helicopter, Clay held back a little. He remembered his earlier ride. "Virge, I have never been so scared in all my life."

"You've got to do it, Clay," Virgil replied. "Otherwise, you'll never get over it."

Clay took a deep breath. He knew Virgil was right. He reluctantly climbed into the aircraft.

High over the mountains, the now six treasure hunters looked down at the scenery.

Even in their dried up brown state, the mountains were awesome. Palo verde trees, small, fuzzy cholla trees, and a duke's mixture of other desert plants were scattered among the giant saguaro cacti. The saguaro, some as tall as fifty feet, cast lonely shadows upon the brown background.

Virgil spotted their campsite and circled it.

He could see their tents were still standing and nothing seemed to be disturbed.

Clay nudged him and motioned toward Davis' camp. "Let's see what the bastards are doing now," he said.

Virgil swung the Huey around and headed for the camp, but this time staying well out of gun range.

They saw no sign of the men, horses, or tents.

Virgil dropped lower for a closer look. There was no one there. The camp was gone. The only movement was a few buzzards that burst from the brush as they flew overhead.

Relieved, Virgil slapped Clay on the shoulder. "Looks like the buzzards are cleaning up their mess. They must have packed up and left."

Clay nodded. "Let's hope so."

Smiling, Virgil whirled the helicopter around in midair and headed back to their camp.

The buzzards settled back down to finish their role as a cleanup crew on what Rockford's men had dragged into the bushes and thought they had hidden.

Piling out of the craft at their camp, they all set about getting things into shape. They built a fire, set up the rope alarm, and checked their bedrolls for critters.

When they were satisfied their camp was up to par, they prepared to head for the mine.

Earlier, Rob had buried the dynamite to keep it safe from the extreme heat as well as a stray bullet. Now he dug up the box, took out two sticks, and re-buried the rest. He stuck the two sticks of dynamite in his back pocket.

The others filled their canteens with water, packed some food, checked their guns, and headed for the rock wall where the cave was located. This time Brenda was with them.

At the cave, everyone kept their distance as they watched Rob prepare the dynamite. He carefully looked over the rocks that were still blocking the cave. *Probably a half stick will do.* He pulled out a stick of dynamite and his knife. With care, he cut the stick in half.

He started to put a primer in it, but walked over and looked once more at the cave. *Better not use that much in one place. Quarter stick at the top and the bottom will be better.*

He cut the dynamite again. This time it was just a fourth of a stick. He smiled, satisfied that he had made the right choice. He inserted a primer and fuse into both quarter sticks. Digging around in the opening, he poked the dynamite as far into the rock pile as he could get it. He made sure the dynamite was well covered with rock and sand.

When he was finished, he stood up and looked back at his friends. "Well, let's see what happens." He lit the two fuses and walked calmly back toward the others.

They had already run for cover. Squatting behind rocks, trees, or whatever they could find, they stuck their fingers in their ears and waited for the explosion.

Two soft pops were heard - hardly more than a firecracker.

They still waited.

"You can come out now," Rob called.

The air was filled with dust. When it cleared, they could see a small dark opening in the crack, but it was still too small for a man to crawl through.

Rob stood rocking back and forth, grinning. He was proud of himself.

Virgil walked closer, then pointed at the wall. "Looky there! I was right!" he said excitedly. "Good work, Rob."

The faint outline of a mark shaped like a turtle shell could be made out. It was carved into the wall. "You thought I was making it up, didn't you?" said Virgil, grinning.

Clay examined the sign. The turtle shaped carving had a cross in it. This was not a turtle, or even a cross, but a Spanish sign of an oval with the letter "T" inside it. Clay knew that sometimes this sign meant treasure, but sometimes it only meant the starting place for a journey. Regardless what it meant this time, he knew Spaniards had carved that mark in the solid rock wall hundreds of years ago.

Spaniards had definitely walked on this very spot. He was beside himself with excitement. Could this be the Dutchman? Could we really be lucky enough to find it? He turned to his friends and grinned. "Boys and girls, this could mean anything from a buried treasure to the start of a new trail. I don't know. But one thing's for sure. That sign was made by the Spaniards hundreds of years ago," Clay said.

"Let's get that opening enlarged!" Ken said.

Rob was smiling. He was proud of himself. "I can blow it bigger."

"No thanks, Rob," Clay replied. "We're too close now to chance blowing it closed again. We'll dig by hand."

By mid-afternoon, the small opening was large enough for a man to crawl through.

Virgil stuck his head in and, even though it was dark, he could make out that the inside was a tunnel or cave. He yelled over his shoulder, "This is it! There's a cave, for sure! Someone get a light."

Ken ran for a flashlight.

Clay was antsy. He couldn't wait for the light. "It's dark as hell in there, but I'm going in." He wiggled his way through the opening. Standing just inside, he looked back out. "I can't see anything without some light."

While waiting for the light, he leaned out of the opening and grinned at the excited faces of his friends. "My friends, I think now we are having a true adventure. How could you ever have doubted me?"

Ken came rushing up with the light. He quickly passed it in to Clay.

Clay clicked it on and looked down at it to make sure it was working. He turned, screamed, and disappeared.

"My God! Where'd he go?" Ken yelled.

Virgil rushed forward and dove headfirst into the opening. "Quick! Get another light!" He squirmed his way into the cave, stopping just inside when his feet touched the floor. He couldn't see Clay's light or hear any noise. Not even from Clay. He was scared. He didn't move.

"Here!" Rob shouted, handing a flashlight though the opening.

Virgil stood in place and clicked it on. He eased himself around until he was facing the inside of the cave. He moved the light beam around and downward. He could see he was standing on a small ledge about a foot or so wide. His heart jumped into his throat. Just beyond the ledge was a huge hole in the floor of the cave. It looked at least twenty feet deep and maybe twelve feet square.

Inching his way around its rim until he had plenty of room, Virgil dropped to his knees to peer over the edge. He choked up as the lights rays fell upon Clay sprawled on his back on the floor of the hole, unconscious.

Virgil shined the light around the floor. It was just a large square hole twenty feet or so deep.

"Rob!" Virgil called out.

"Yeah?"

"Grab some rope and get in here. Clay fell in a hole. He's hurt. Hurry, but watch your step at the opening, there's very little room to stand."

Rob, with the rope over his shoulder and a flashlight in his hand, slipped through the opening.

Skirting the hole, he dropped down beside Virgil, peering over the rim at Clay. "Jesus, he's dead! He couldn't survive a fall that high?"

"No, I've been watching him closely. He's breathing," Virgil said, jumping to his feet.

"Here, help get this rope around me." Virgil turned to the opening, "Brian, you and Ken better get in here, too. We'll need all the help we can get."

Almost before he was finished saying it, there were lights bouncing all over the cave as Ken, Brian, and even Brenda wiggled through the opening.

Brian lit a lantern they had brought to the site just in case it was really a cave. The inside of the cave was illuminated like daylight.

A feeling of dread swept over Brenda as she looked down upon Clay's prone body. Her heart raced. She had to get to him. *Please, God, don't let him be dead.*

"Lower me down!" said Brenda. "I have to examine him before he's moved! He may have a broken back."

Virgil flashed his light around the bottom of the hole. There was debris from sage bushes, blown in by the wind over the years, small rocks, and the bones of animals everywhere. "I'll go down first and make sure there are no snakes," he said. He slipped the loop in the rope under his arms and sat on the edge of the deep pit. He turned around and slipped over the edge until he hung by his arms.

"We've got you," Rob said.

Letting go, Virgil gripped the rope and Rob, Brian, and Ken lowered him to the bottom.

Once on the floor of the pit, Virgil shined his light around and listened for the buzzing of any rattlesnakes. When he heard nothing, he eased the rope from his arms. "Okay, send Brenda down."

When Brenda was beside him, they began to slowly examine every inch of Clay's body. Brenda checked his pulse and breathing. Both were good. She eased her hand under his head without moving his neck. When she removed it, there was a small amount of blood on it. "No broken bones that I can find, but there is a small cut on the back of his head. It's bleeding a little, but all in all he seems in pretty good shape for a man who just fell twenty feet."

A moan escaped Clay's lips. He slowly opened his eyes. "What happened?" He tried to move.

Brenda held him down. "Lay still for a minute," she ordered. "Do you feel pain anywhere?"

Clay lay for a second or two. "Just my head," he said, putting his hand up and rubbing it.

"Try to move your legs."

Clay managed to move both legs.

Helping him sit up, Brenda examined the bloody area. "Looks like you only got that small cut and lump on the head."

"What happened?" Clay asked again.

Virgil grinned. "Remember telling us how the Spaniards really knew how to set booby traps on their mines? Well, you just stepped off into a pit they intentionally dug just inside the entrance. Anyone who didn't know it was there would fall in and either get killed or become a prisoner until their return - something like the pit traps they use on tigers in India."

As they cast the flashlight beams around the floor, they could see there were bones of many animals that had been trapped and starved to death.

Virgil froze his light beam on some bones in a back corner. He could make out the bones of a human skeleton. "Holy shit, guys," he exclaimed. "Look at that!"

Brenda and Clay stared at the bones.

"Poor devil," Brenda said. "Wonder who he was."

"I don't know," Clay replied, "but he's been there quite a spell from the looks of his gear."

Virgil looked up at the three faces staring down at them. "I'll tie Clay on the rope, you guys pull him up."

"No! I'm fine," said Clay. "I want to have a better look at that skeleton."

Brenda carefully examined him again to make sure he wasn't injured. She stepped back and shook her head. "I don't see how, but you made it through that fall in good shape."

Clay flexed his muscles. "It's all those Spam sandwiches I've been eating. Strong as a horse."

The loud fluttering of wings interrupted their conversation and they looked up to see a huge owl fly out of the pit and through the opening of the cave. Even with them shining their lights all over the place, they hadn't seen it before now.

"WHHOOOOOO! WHHOOOOOO! WHHOOOOOO!"

No one dared to speak.

"Spam sandwiches be damned," Virgil finally said. "There goes the reason you didn't get hurt in that fall."

"You think so?" Clay asked. "I don't remember a thing."

"Something saved your ass down there. So why not the old Indian you keep telling us about?" Brian said from above. "Now can we get on with finding the gold?"

"We found a skeleton down here," Clay called up. "But it's so cluttered with debris, we'll have to clear some of it away to see more." Clay started walking around the pit as Virgil held the light.

Virgil whistled softly, "Look at that!" His light beam on the skeleton against the rear wall settled on the remnants of leather that formed a circle around what had been its waist. It was a gun belt and the remains of a holster. Beside it lay a rusty pistol - a model that dated back into the 1800's.

"He is an old timer, that's for sure," Clay said, moving in for a closer look. He shined the light on the skeleton's leg bones. Each one was in two pieces. He could actually see the jagged breaks. "This poor fella never had a chance. Broke both legs when he fell in." His light fell upon what appeared to be large leather pouches.

"Look there! Saddle bags!"

Virgil took a look at the saddlebags, then reached down and tried to pick them up. The leather was so rotten, it came apart, cascading large, yellow nuggets of gold to the floor.

There were shouts from above as everyone's light beams danced off the nuggets. There were hundreds of them.

"Tell me I ain't seeing things from up here," Rob said.

"You're not seeing things, Rob," Virgil answered. "We see gold, too!"

There were remnants of two saddlebags. At one time they had been completely full of the nuggets. These were not rocks with gold in them. These were pure gold. Bright yellow metal chunks - some nearly an inch in diameter. They now lay in the dust beneath the bags.

Clay stood staring down at the beautiful metal he held in his hand. He was excited. He shook his head. "Hot damn! Gold! We've really done it. All my life I've dreamed of this. Even planned for the day I would find it," he said. "Now I don't know what to do." He grabbed his handkerchief from his pocket and picked up a double handful of nuggets and tied them in it. "Here!" he yelled. "Catch this! Have a feel of it. That's what it's all about." He tossed the bundle up to his hungry looking friends.

For what seemed like hours, they played in the gold nuggets.

Finally, Clay looked up at the three men hanging over the edge of the pit. "We've got to get something strong to put this gold in," he said. "Ken, there're some canvas coin bags in the helicopter, under the last seat. I packed them just in case. If you guys will go get 'em and toss 'em down, we'll bag it."

"How are you feeling now?" Brenda asked.

"Never better!" Clay answered with a big smile. He fingered the gold nuggets. "Beautiful stuff, isn't it?"

No one answered. They were too busy looking at it.

In record time, canvas bags started raining down on their heads, and Virgil and Clay stopped admiring the gold and started bagging it. As each bag was filled, it was tied to a rope and hauled out of the pit. It took six bags to hold all the nuggets.

"Hope that old boy don't mind too much," Ken said from above.

Rob looked down at the skeleton and shook his head. "He won't. I'd say it's been more'n a hundred years since he cared about anything."

"Think he was Peralto or one of the hundred men killed with him? Maybe one of them ran in here to hide from the Indians and fell in."

"I don't think the skeleton is that old," Virgil said. "Could be Peralto Junior though, or maybe the Dutchman's partner, Wiser."

Clay looked the skeleton over. "His clothes say American, but then we don't know what Peralto Junior or Wiser wore. Could be either one. Or maybe it was just some unlucky bastard who found his gold, and stumbled in here to get out of the weather."

"He's one of those you were talking about, Clay. One that fell in and couldn't get out," Brenda said.

"Yeah," Clay replied. "Even if you survive the fall and don't break your back or your legs, these walls are so straight and smooth, there's no way to get a finger or toe hold to climb out. You fall in here alone, you're history." He passed up the last bag. "Now pull us up, before you guys get greedy and decide to leave us down here."

Before he was hauled up, Virgil took the rusted old gun and, searching the debris, found a pair of spurs. "No need leaving them down here; he won't be using 'em."

When everyone had been pulled out of the pit, they started slapping Clay on the back.

"Great work, Clay!" Brian exclaimed. "I never doubted you one minute. Did I, Clay? Did I ever doubt you once?"

All Clay could do was grin.

Brenda threw her arms around him and gave him a big kiss. "There! You deserved that. You stuck to your guns and found the treasure. I think that's just great."

"Nothing like it on earth," Ken said. "It has the power to make good people kill." He looked down into the pit. "I still wonder who he was - a miner or a claim jumper."

"Like I said, he was probably just some poor soul who struck it rich and died before he could spend it," Clay said.

"Well, I hope he don't mind too much if we spend it," laughed Rob. "Now, let's have a look around this cave."

The cave was like a large bubble inside. The roof was domed and high enough to stand in. They spied another opening at the rear of the cave and eased along toward it. It was another large empty room.

"Plenty of sign that this cave has been mined. Look at all the chisel markings along the walls." Brian said.

"It was productive at one time. That's why they went to the trouble of digging that big pit. You know, the Spaniards occupied this area for over three hundred years, mining everything they could find to take back to the old country for the queen," Clay said.

"Well, it looks like they took everything with them. I don't see anything here."

"There was something here," Clay said. He pointed to the bags of gold. "But I don't think it was from this mine. Those are nuggets. This mine was following a gold and quartz vein and would have been different - would have had quartz in them."

Virgil walked over to stare back down into the pit. "I still think we'd better check the cave over good with the detectors before we leave. Maybe the Spaniards missed something. Maybe the detector picked up on a large vein of gold farther back or deeper."

"I think it picked up the nuggets," Clay said, as he walked back to the others. "We'll check it again before we leave for good. Right now let's get back to camp and figure out what we're going to do with all these gold nuggets."

Brian lifted one of the bags he was carrying and looked it over. "Clay, I know we don't just take the gold into a bank and say cash this in. Just what do we do with it, anyway. Don't we have to turn it over to the government for payment?"

"Other than putting it in a safety deposit box, banks don't take it. If we want to cash it in, which we do, we have to take it to a federal assay office and have it graded and weighed. They take it from there."

"I'm for keeping back a few of the nuggets as souvenirs, "Virgil said. "You know, something to remember this adventure by."

Clay nodded. "We can do that."

Back at camp, the happy treasure hunters talked most of the day away. They sat around the fire, eating supper and tossing an occasional glance up at the huge owl perched high above them in a nearby cottonwood tree.

Virgil got up, walked over to the helicopter, and climbed inside. He reappeared, carrying a big bottle of champagne. "Gather round, friends," he said. "I've been saving this for the right time. Grab your cups and fill 'em up!"

When their cups were full, Virgil raised his in a toast. "To treasure hunting and our good fortune today!"

"Hear! Hear!" everyone said in unison.

Moving his cup toward the owl perched in a cottonwood tree, Virgil continued. "And to you, my feathered friend, whoever you are!" Turning back to his friends he said, "Now a confession. Being a skeptic, I didn't bring this along to celebrate the finding of gold, but to cheer you guys up when we failed."

"What a friend!" Clay said. "No trust!"

The adventurers were six happy people. The bottle was empty in minutes.

Clay looked around the camp. It was the first time he felt like they were really having the kind of fun they set out to have. He reached over and stroked the pile of canvas bags. "Boys, this is not all of the Dutchman's Gold," he announced. "It is only the tip of the iceberg. The rest is still somewhere out there." Clay pulled his hand away from the bags and stared off into the mountains.

For a long time everybody sat staring off in the same direction as Clay, letting dreams of finding the mother-lode flow through their minds.

Rob walked over and sat down near Virgil and Clay. "I got an idea," he said.

"What's that?" Clay asked.

"You know there's still a lot of daylight left. Why don't we get in that damn big bird over there and go down to that saloon and really tie one on tonight?"

"I thought you had a hangover from last night?"

Rob chuckled. "The one good thing about a hangover is that hard work and a lot of sweat will cure it every time."

Virgil looked at Clay and shrugged, "Why the hell not? That champagne was just enough to whet the appetite." He tapped Brenda on the arm, "How 'bout you, nurse? Want to go get loaded?"

"You promise not to take advantage of a girl when she's drunk?"

"You have my word as a gentleman," Virgil answered, bowing to her.

"I wouldn't trust that man as far as I could throw that helicopter," Clay said, laughing and getting to his feet.

"Well, the last one in the bird is a rotten owl egg!" Brian yelled, already on his way.

"Hold on," Clay said softly, his finger to his lips.

"We have to hide the gold. We certainly can't take it with us, you know. We have to be careful. Someone may be out there watching and listening to us."

Secretively, they selected a spot behind a tent and concealed Rob's digging by standing around him in a circle. They stood with their backs to him, watching every direction for any sign of movement or reflection in the sunlight.

After Rob buried the canvas bags, he and Brian wrestled with a huge boulder to roll over the freshly dug soil.

Standing back to admire their work, Rob boasted, "Never in a million years would anyone look there."

Clay held up a finger for attention. "Another thing we had better not do is tell anyone about it while we're down there," he said. "There's people in that saloon who'll cut your throat for a silver dollar and not think anything about it."

Brian looked at Clay. "Now can we go, father?"

Virgil was already cranking the engine on the Huey as they climbed in and took their seats, laughing and joking with each other. They had something to be happy about - gold. The helicopter lifted off the ground and roared off toward Alice's saloon.

59

The loud chopping noise of the big helicopter caught the attention of everyone around Alice's saloon as the Huey dropped from the sky into the front yard.

Big Alice, sitting in her usual chair, had to shield her eyes from the stinging blast of sand and debris. When the blades finally ground to a halt, she took her hand down and watched the passengers get out. She recognized Brenda Carpenter and the two men who had been with her a few days back. Now there were five men. Just as she had told Padro, the city fellas had returned.

"Hello, Alice!" Brenda called out, approaching the porch.

"Thought you had eloped with all those beautiful men," Big Alice replied, cheerfully. "You folks come to party?"

Jumping up on the porch, Rob danced a little jig. Laughing, he replied, "You got that right, lady. Just show us the way to the saloon."

"Right through that door. You'll find all you ever hoped for in there. Now go have a good time," Alice said. She eyed each man up and down. They seemed awfully cheerful for all they had been through lately. Maybe they had found something up there. She'd have to keep close to them tonight.

As the treasure hunters crowded through the door, Big Alice motioned for one of her girls. "I want you to stay very close to them. Listen to what they're saying and when they say something you think is important, run to me with it."

The girl nodded and hurried inside.

Two hours later, the party was still going strong. Virgil, Clay and Ken sat at a table by the hallway at the rear of the room and watched Rob dancing with Brenda and Brian with a pretty little Mexican girl.

"They sure know how to have a good time, don't they, Virge?" Clay said, without taking his eyes off the dancers.

"Ah, to be young and foolish again," Virgil replied, tipping his whiskey bottle up to pour a drink.

"Kinda makes you want to go find a girl of your own, don't it?" Ken asked.

Both men stared at him.

"Well, hell, man," Clay said, pointing out two or three girls sitting around tables with men. "There they are. Just sitting over there waiting for you to ask them to dance."

"They're already spoken for," Ken said, downing his tequila.

Behind them, in a dark room, Laura was working frantically at the hinge pins. She had been listening to the men talk. She knew they were not Rockford's. She could only hope they were decent people. She struggled with the wooden slat, and pushing hard, felt one of the pins give way. It toppled to the floor with a clatter. She froze.

There was no movement outside her door. She started to work on the other one. It must have been her lucky night because it, too, soon gave way and came loose. She grabbed it before it could fall. She eased it to the floor and started prying at the door with the slat until it opened an inch. She stopped to think about what she would do when she was out. She couldn't let Alice or Padro see her, or she would be put back. But she had to talk to those people.

Laura pulled the door open a little more and looked out. At the table just ten feet away sat three men. She shook violently with anticipation. Would they just laugh at her and tell Alice? Would they want to rape her, too? She clenched her eyes shut as tightly as she could to settle her nerves. When she felt better, she opened them. "Hey!" she whispered as loudly as she dared.

The men didn't look back.

"Hey, mister!" she whispered again, this time a little louder.

Clay turned his head to see who had called. He couldn't see anything but a dim hallway with several doors off it. He started to turn back when he caught a glimpse of movement from a door opened just a crack. A hand motioning for him to come. *What the hell? Is that one of Big Alice's girls trying to get me in bed?*

Clay looked back around. No one was paying any attention to him. He turned back and watched her motioning again. He saw how frantic she was acting. She had eased out the door enough for him to see that she was not a Mexican girl. Something was wrong.

He rose slowly from his chair and, making sure no one was watching, stepped back into the dimness of the hallway. He leaned against the wall to block her from anyone else's view. Without looking back, he whispered, "What's wrong?"

"Help me! Please!" Laura whispered. "I was kidnapped and I'm being held prisoner here."

Clay swallowed hard. He couldn't believe what he was hearing. He was nervous. Could she be telling to truth, or was she just trying to lure him to her room? He eased back another step. Still no one paid any attention. He stole a look at the girl. Her face showed pure terror. He looked more closely. *I know this girl. I've seen her before.* Suddenly, it hit him like a bolt of lightening. *My God! It's the girl from the saloon. It's that missing Pratt girl.*

Watching the front all the while, he eased into the room and quickly shut the door.

"Oh, my God! Oh, my God!" she sobbed, tears falling down her rosy cheeks. "You're my only hope!" She threw her arms around his waist. She hugged him tightly. "Oh, Please! I heard 'em talking. They know I can send them to prison if I tell," Laura said frantically. "I think they're going to kill me. Please help me!"

Clay looked around. "Who's holding you prisoner?" he whispered.

"Alice!" Laura said. "A man named Rockford kidnapped me and brought me to her. He wanted me to be a whore, but I won't. Please help me get away! I just know they're going to kill me!" Laura begged, sobbing heavily against his chest.

Rockford! That son-of-a-bitch. Just like Chief Blackhorse suspected. Hesitantly, he reached up and rubbed her head softly. "There, there. It's alright now. Is your name Laura Pratt?"

Laura leaned back and looked up at him. How did he know? Surely he isn't one of Rockford's men. She studied his face. *Oh, my God, it's the man who punched Rockford in the saloon.* "You're the guy who got into it with Rockford that night in Uncle Gus' saloon! You helped me!"

"Yes, I remember you. Chief Blackhorse has been searching for you since you disappeared." Clay continued to rub her head. He held her until he could feel her relax. His mind raced. This is really the kidnapped girl. We have to get her out of here. But how? We have to think of some way to get her out without Big Alice seeing.

He took her shoulders and held her at arm length. "Now listen to me. I'm going to help you, but you must do *exactly* as I tell you. And I do mean *exactly*! Understand?"

"Yes! Yes!" she replied quickly. "But we have to be very careful. They just killed one of Rockford's men tonight in this room. He tried to rape me. They carried his body off into the mountains."

"How did they bring you here?"

"By helicopter. Rockford has a helicopter."

"That bastard!" Clay peeked out the door. No one had noticed him missing. He turned to her. "Laura, I want you to stay in this room with the door shut. When you hear someone in the hall say O.K. L.A., I want you to open the door and no matter who it is, follow them. Wherever that person goes, you go."

"What are you going to do? They watch me all the time, and if they see you with me, they'll kill you too."

"I'll think of something," Clay replied. "You just be ready to run like hell." He turned to leave, then looked back. He smiled at her. "Okay, Laura Pratt, get ready."

As he stepped out the door, Laura closed it tightly and leaned against it. Her heart raced. Her face felt like it was on fire. She was scared, yet she felt good. At last someone had come. Someone would help her. She was so relieved, she almost fainted.

Clay slipped back to his seat. He motioned for Ken and Virgil to lean toward him. "Boys, I sure wish we hadn't left our guns in the helicopter," he said.

"Why, Clay? Is there gonna be trouble?" asked Ken.

"You're not going to believe this." He took a quick peek around to see who could hear him. "Remember that girl who was kidnapped over in Apache Junction that Chief Blackhorse talked to us about?"

"Yeah," Virgil replied. "I remember her. Laura, or something like that, wasn't it?"

"Yes, Laura Pratt. She's right back there. She's being held prisoner." He looked around the saloon. "We've got to get her out of here before they kill her."

Virgil looked closely into his eyes, then reached over and felt his forehead. "No fever. Too much tequila, Clay?"

Clay gave him a get-serious look. "I wish it was, Virge, but I'm dead serious."

Now Virgil knew Clay wasn't kidding. "Where's this girl now?"

"In a bedroom not ten feet from here, waiting for us. It was locked, but she worked the hinge pins loose. She says they watch her every move. They know she'll hang the lot of them when she talks to the law. They're going to kill her. They're just waiting for the right time."

Clay looked around again. There were a few men in the saloon who must have been regulars by the way Big Alice treated them as she moved around among the tables, talking to them as she went.

"Let's get the others and go out the back door," said Virgil. "She can slip right in among us and nobody will notice."

"That won't work," Clay said. "You know they'll be watching us leave. If they should see her, we might all get killed."

"In that case, we'd better come up with an alternative plan," Virgil said.

Clay sat for a few seconds. Finally, he stood up. "We have to get her from that room into the helicopter," he said. "Just watch my signal."

"Where you going?" Virgil whispered.

"You and Ken make sure nobody other than one of us gets back there," said Clay. He walked out to the dance floor, staggering and laughing as if he was drunk. When he got to Rob and Brenda, he eased his arms around both their waists and danced along with them. "We have a problem," he whispered, with a broad smile as he looked around the room.

"What kind of problem?" Rob asked.

"Laura Pratt, the kidnapped girl, is in a back room."

"You've got to be kidding!" Brenda exclaimed.

"She has been a prisoner here for weeks. We have to get her away. They're going to kill her."

Rob started to say something, but Clay shut him up. "Don't talk. Just listen. "

The three people spun around as they danced. Clay laughed loudly to attract attention. He whispered again, "Brenda, you go back to the table with Ken and Virgil. When you see the signal, go down that back hallway to the last door on the right. Say the words O.K. L.A.. When the door opens, grab Laura and run like hell out the back door. Head for the helicopter and don't stop for anything."

"What about you guys?" she asked.

"We'll be along."

Brenda nodded. "What's the signal?"

"You'll know."

"What you want me to do, Clay?" Rob asked.

"Stay right behind me and do as I do," Clay whispered

Clay groaned and stepped backward hard. He bumped violently into Padro, who was dancing by with Maria. He grabbed the giant of a man by the arm and bellowed. "Hey, what'd you hit me for?"

Rob got the hint and set himself for battle.

Brenda stepped clear and darted toward the back of the saloon.

"I didn't hit you, gringo, but I think I will now," Padro said, planting a fist in Clay's face, driving him backward across the floor.

Rob gave a rebel yell and struck Padro in the face.

It barely fazed him. Padro shook his head and glared at Rob.

Grinning sheepishly, Rob dove into Padro's belly, hammering away with his fists. He drove the giant back and over a table full of card players. The table crashed to the floor along with Rob and Padro.

Clay started back to help Rob, but Gonzales blocked his way. His huge fist struck Clay in the face, driving him back again.

Brian, who had not been told what was happening, saw the action, made like he was rolling up his shirtsleeves. He yelled at the top of his lungs. "Yaahooo! Just like old times in the city." He struck the nearest man, who was doing nothing but watching the fight.

This didn't set well with the man, and he attacked Brian full force as the floor became a war zone, with tables and chairs flying through the air and people fighting everywhere.

Virgil quickly shooed Brenda down the hallway.

She ran to the bedroom door and looked back into the saloon. Everyone was watching the fight. "O.K.L.A.!" she whispered.

The door opened slightly. Brenda grabbed Laura's arm and pulled her along, as she bolted for the back door.

Virgil and Ken stood blocking the hallway. They could see Clay, Brian, and Rob were outnumbered on the dance floor. They anxiously fidgeted about, waiting for Brenda to get outside.

Big Alice had jumped into the fight and was trying to break it up. She tossed men left and right.

As soon as the back door slammed shut, Virgil and Ken ran to join the fight. They pulled men away from Rob and Clay, who were for the moment losing their battle. Now that the odds were even, the fight turned in their favor for a minute.

Then the door swung open and four more men ran in. They had not come to help the treasure hunters. They joined Padro in battle.

Virgil took a blow that drove him over the bar and into a heap behind it. Regaining his footing, he shook his head and started counting the number of men they were fighting. Somehow the odds had changed drastically.

He jumped back over the bar and fought his way to Clay. He motioned for him to head for the door. "It's done!" he shouted. "Let's get the hell out of here!"

Clay looked around. Brian, Ken, and Rob had their eyes on him. He motioned to the door. He didn't have to do it a second time. They struggled toward it, trying to shake off their attackers as they went.

Virgil shot through the door first and ran full out for the helicopter.

Ken, Brian, and Clay were close behind, with Rob bringing up the rear. He struggled free of one man, only to be grabbed by another. He planted a huge fist into the man's face. The man lost his ambition to fight.

Until then, the battle had been man-to-man and nothing life threatening, but Padro pulled a huge machete from somewhere and waved it over his head. He was trying to get to Rob. Rob kicked loose from a man and ran for the Huey.

Virgil had already cranked the motor into motion and had the craft hovering a foot off the ground when Clay jumped in. He grabbed his pistol and turned to the door. He could see the machete swinging close to the back of Rob's head as he sprinted for the chopper.

Clay aimed a few well-placed shots over their heads. Everyone stopped, except Rob. Padro had skidded to a halt, but then bolted after Rob again. The shots had slowed the crowd just enough for Rob to jump for the door.

Clay's hand clamped around Rob's wrist and jerked upward as Rob jumped. He landed hard inside, just as the machete blade struck the edge of the door.

"Go! Go! Go!" yelled Clay.

Virgil yanked on the stick and the helicopter shot straight up.

Rob lay on the floor gasping for breath and laughing at the same time. He crawled to the door, leaned his head out and yelled down at the raging men. "Good fight, men! We'll be back another time!" Then he gave them the finger.

Rob rolled over on his back and shouted over the engine, "Damn, boys! That felt good! Just like old times!"

Brian sat staring at Clay. "Son-of-a-bitch, Clay. I thought I was crazy, but you got me beat by a mile. What the hell was that all about back there? I thought we were having a good time."

Clay was still trying to catch his breath. He looked up. He couldn't see Brenda. My God! I hope they made it. "Brenda!" he called out. "You in here?"

"Back here, Clay. We're okay," Brenda said, crawling from under a tent canvas in the rear compartment.

"To answer your question, Brian, we were having a good time," Clay said, pointing to the back of the helicopter, "but she wasn't."

Brian looked back as Laura crawled out from under the canvas.

"Boys, meet Laura Pratt," said Brenda. "You just rescued her."

"No shit?" Brian asked. He looked over at Clay.

"No shit," Clay answered.

Brian shook his head at Clay. "Never a dull moment with you, old buddy. Should have known you had a good reason."

"Hey, Clay!" Virgil shouted. "Get up here a minute!"

Clay struggled to get into the cockpit. "What's up?" he asked, buckling himself in.

"Where we going? To town or back to camp?"

"Well, it's near midnight now. I think we'd better go back to camp until we can see how she is doing and get this thing figured out. Come morning, we'll take her in."

"Maybe we can get ourselves put back together while we're at it," Virgil replied, wiping blood from his nose.

"Yeah," Clay chuckled. He winced as he touched his sore mouth. "Maybe Brenda can fix up our battle scars." He looked over his shoulder at his friends. "Hey, back there! How many of you guys got hurt?"

"Me!" Rob shouted, "but I loved every minute of it."

"I did," Brian said.

"Just my face!" Ken yelled.

"Nothing like a good tavern brawl after all these years of peaceful living," Brian answered. "I only wish you had waited 'til *after* I had taken that sweet little Mexican gal to the back room."

The men laughed.

A few minutes later, Virgil set the helicopter down on the plateau beside their tents.

When Laura got out, she stopped and waited for Clay. When he emerged, she threw her arms around his neck and gave him a kiss on the cheek. "That's for saving my life," she said. "All I can say is thank you, thank you, thank you!" Tears filled her eyes.

"Come on, Laura, let's go into the tent and I'll have a look at you first. These guys can wait."

They disappeared into the tent as Rob and Brian set about building a fire.

Clay walked off to the edge of the camp light and stared off toward Big Alice's. He doubted Alice's men would come up here after them. They'd figure the first place they would take the girl was the sheriff. But still he was worried. He walked back to the now blazing fire. "I think we should keep watch on that trail tonight. If they come after us, they could be here in a few hours."

Inside the tent, Brenda sat Laura down on a cot and examined her. Except for a few bruises and cuts that were already healing, she appeared to be okay.

"I know you've suffered terribly, both physically and mentally, Laura, but physically you appear okay. That's about all I can do right now. We'll get you to a hospital as soon as we can.

"What can they do, Brenda?"

"They can do whatever is necessary to make sure you didn't get some disease - or pregnant. "

Laura buried her face in her hands and started sobbing again.

Brenda put her arms around the girl and held her close. "Honey, I know you've been through a lot, but you're gonna make it. It may take a long time, but you're gonna put it behind you and go on with your life." Brenda had seen rape victims before and knew they heal physically, but they never really heal mentally. "You must keep in mind always that this was not your fault. You're a victim. What happened was beyond your control. It happened. It's over. It's history. There's no turning back the clock. You must forge ahead and not let it bury you."

Laura raised her head and nodded. She wiped her eyes. "Is there someplace I can take a bath? I feel so dirty."

Brenda knew most rape victims needed to have an examination by a physician before they took a bath to allow for the collecting of evidence. She also knew that, for Laura, the time for that examination was long past. Her wanting a bath as a good sign - the first step in the healing process. Brenda grabbed a few things from her bags, including an extra pair of jeans and a shirt that would fit Laura, and a flashlight. She held out her hand. "You just come with me. I think we can arrange that bath."

Laura took her hand and they slipped through the tent opening.

Outside the tent, Brenda led Laura over to where Clay stood with the others by the fire. "We're going down to the stream, Clay. Listen for me to yell if anything goes wrong."

Clay pulled his pistol and checked it. "Got you covered, girls. Go do your thing."

After the bath in the cold stream, Laura felt refreshed. Her spirits were much better. The jeans and shirt felt good on her as she found a place near the fire and sat down. She didn't look up, just stared into the flames, rocking back and forth.

Brenda set about examining each of the men and treating their injuries. There were swollen lips, a few loose teeth, some small cuts, and swollen jaws, but nothing serious.

With bandaids covering their cuts, they, too, sat around the fire, staring quietly into its flames.

A bottle of whiskey was passed around and when it was empty, Clay stood up and stretched. "Laura, anything that happen outside Apache Junction, is the county sheriff's responsibility. Considering everything that's happened, I think we'd better take you to his office come morning. But right now, why don't you go get some sleep. You can sleep in with Brenda. The rest of us will make sure they don't find you."

Laura nodded and followed Brenda into the tent. "I'm sorry for causing so much trouble tonight, Brenda."

"Now you stop that worrying. You're safe here. Nothing will happen to you while you're with these guys."

"What kind of men are they?"

"A very rare kind," Brenda said. "Truly a very rare kind."

Laura closed her eyes and within minutes was enjoying the first sound sleep she had had in weeks.

Brenda tucked the blanket up under Laura's chin and smiled. Closing her eyes, she, too, drifted off.

60

"Chief Blackhorse! Basker here!" The agent shouted into the phone. "Is the meeting still on for this morning?"

Blackhorse grinned at the excitement in his voice. "Sure it is, Charles. When can I expect you guys?"

"Well, it's seven now, give me an hour," Basker replied. "Say, Chief, tell me who might be close friends of Rockford's."

"Well, one I know for sure is the county sheriff, Jack Wilkins. He believes the sun rises and sets on Rockford's ass. Why?"

"I was just wondering who we can trust. What do you think of the sheriff?"

"Can't stand the man myself. I was going to talk to you about it this morning. I don't think we should let him know about the meeting."

"My exact thoughts, Chief."

When Blackhorse hung up the phone, he pushed back and threw his feet up on his desk. Leaning back, he closed his eyes and smiled.

* * *

The DEA agents walked into Blackhorse's office at 8:00am. Chief Blackhorse stood to shake hands.

"Good to see you again, Dennis. Been a while," said Basker. He pointed to the dark-haired stocky built man with him. "I want you to meet my partner, George Long. We've been together now for four years."

Chief Blackhorse shook Long's hand. He felt the hand shake of a sincere man. He would like Long. He led the way to a conference room, where they gathered around a long table.

Basker took the lead. "Now, Chief, where and what are we going to do?"

"There's a big marijuana farm up in the Superstitions. We're going to make plans to raid the place. I think a local rancher named Paul Rockford and the county sheriff are involved up to their eyes." He went right into the whole story about the abduction, as well as the information received from the treasure hunters.

When he finished, Basker whistled. "Damn! It sure sounds good. Think we can find the place? Maybe one of the treasure hunters can show us the way."

"Unfortunately, they're back up on the mountain searching for the Dutchman. I guess we'll just have to follow the directions they gave me. You have to understand that those guys are from the city. They know nothing about these mountains, except the needle. But from what they say, it's not far from it."

"How about a helicopter trip up there today to see if we can spot it?" George Long suggested.

"Can we get one?" asked Blackhorse.

Long stood up. "Got one right outside."

Sunglasses diffused the sun's bright ray as the lawmen scanned the ground below the big gray Blackhawk helicopter. The helicopter had long ago been assigned to the Drug Enforcement Agency in their battle to curtail the national drug flow. It came complete with armament of 7.62-mm guns and air-to-air rockets, loaded and ready to go.

Chief Blackhorse pointed out the window. "That's it!" he yelled, "Weaver's Needle!"

Basker leaned over to look where Blackhorse was pointing. "Beautiful sight from up here, isn't it?"

"Sure is. Not so beautiful down there, though. That's one of the deadliest places in the world."

Long yelled at the pilot, "See anything down there, Justin?"

"Nothing yet. We'll try a little higher and see what we find."

Justin Fletcher had been the pilot for the department for several years. He had flown many missions in Vietnam and with the Agency as it raided marijuana farms all over the world. So far, on this trip, nothing he saw indicated a farm.

Criss-crossing the area on all sides of the Needle failed to turn up the farm. Then pointing toward the ground, Justin said, "Have a look at that!"

Far below, they could make out two large tents and a big green Huey helicopter positioned on a long plateau.

"That's probably the treasure hunters down there. Want to drop in on 'em?"

"I don't think it's a good idea at this time," said Basker. "If it's not them, but someone involved, then we've blown it. They burn the field. That's happened before." He looked down at the camp. "Why don't we look around a little more. If we don't find it, we'll come back tomorrow."

"Good idea," Blackhorse said, "At least we know where they are."

The helicopter moved away and the search continued.

61

The rhythmic chopping above brought Clay from the hard floor of the tent to his feet. He looked at his watch. It was nine-thirty. They had gotten to bed late and slept in. He listened for a minute. The helicopter was close and sounded larger than Rockford's.

Easing the tent flap open, he peeked out. The dull blue gray helicopter was much larger and newer that Rockford's. It hovered in the air some distance away as though it was watching them.

Virgil stepped up behind him and leaned over his shoulder to see the chopper. "That's a Blackhawk. One expensive bird, Clay. Not a rancher's, for sure. Look at the guns still mounted on it. Even got rockets. That's the Federal boys. No one else can afford one of those babies! Want to wave 'em down?"

"No. Just stay right here. No need to let them see us."

By now everyone was awake. They huddled inside the tents, straining to see the helicopter as it finally moved away.

"Think that was the law after us for tearing up Big Alice's place last night?" Rob asked.

"It won't be the law after you for that, Rob. It'll be those two overgrown Mexican bodyguards of hers," Clay said. "No, that's someone new. We'll just have to be careful."

"Hey!" Brenda called from the other tent. "Is it safe to come out yet?"

Clay checked his gun and threw back the flap, then stepped out. "Yeah. Come on out. Let's have some coffee."

Virgil checked his watch. "Damn, you realize it's nine-thirty in the morning?"

"Slept like a log," Ken remarked. "Must have been tired."

"I wonder why?" Brenda said, remembering the fight. "I still don't see how you guys got out of there without losing your hide."

"That was old hat to some of us, Brenda," Brian said. "We grew up in the city, fighting in bar rooms, so a saloon fight was right up our alley,"

"That's right," Rob added. "Hit fast and hit hard."

"Then run like hell," Virgil said, laughing. "That's how you get by without getting hurt too badly. Knowing when to run is very important in any good brawl."

"Yeah, but that big bastard with the machete was getting a little nasty," Clay said. "I think he meant to kill you, Rob."

"So do I," Rob laughed, "It was like Virgil said, just a matter of knowing when to run. When that machete came out, I knew it was time!"

Virgil walked out to the helicopter and climbed in. He was completing his usual check before take off.

Clay looked up at Virgil. He was ready to go. "I think he's ready to head for the sheriff's office, Laura. You ready to go?"

"Ready as I'll ever be, I reckon," she replied and stood up. "Will you guys stay with me while I talk to the sheriff? I don't want to be alone for a while."

"Sure thing. We'll be right there with you," Clay answered.

They loaded into the chopper and the big Huey's engine burst to life.

Twenty minutes later, Virgil was setting the helicopter down in the parking lot of the Pinal County Sheriff's Department, in Florence,

Arizona. They jumped out and headed into the red brick and white stone building.

Sheriff Wilkins was waiting for them when they walked through the door. "Well, what brings the great treasure hunters to town so early?" he asked sarcastically.

Clay couldn't stand this man, but knew he was the legal authority in some parts of the mountains. They would have to talk to him.

"Sheriff," he said, "this lady was kidnapped in Apache Junction several weeks ago and has been held prisoner by Big Alice ever since. Last night we grabbed her from a locked room where she was kept."

Sheriff Wilkins looked at the girl. So that's what Rockford threw everything away for. Maybe she didn't recognize Rockford. He grinned. "Well, now, that's something we can handle. We'll catch the bastard and hang him. Do you know who kidnapped you, young lady? Uh, what's your name anyway?"

"It's Laura Pratt," Laura answered. "It was a man named Rockford that kidnapped me." Remembering the kidnapping, she dropped her head as tears filled her eyes. "He and his two bodyguards took me out to his ranch house. Rockford beat me and forced himself on me. Afterwards, he blindfolded me and took me in a helicopter up to Big Alice's saloon. He told her to turn me into a whore."

Sheriff Wilkins was surprised. This girl was going to be an excellent witness against Rockford. "Paul Rockford? Those are serious charges to make against a very influential man in these parts, girl. You must be mistaken about him. It was probably someone else, wasn't it?"

"No! It was Paul Rockford," Laura deliberately mouthed each word. "And he was going to kill me."

"If you're wrong, young lady, there'll be hell to pay," Sheriff Wilkins said. "You folks wait right here." He got up and walked into the next office.

Clay eased over to the door and peeked in. Wilkins was dialing the phone. He listened.

"Paul? This is Jack Wilkins. I've got that girl you kidnapped and raped here in my office."

Rockford screamed, "You got what?"

"That's right. Those greenhorns you had all that trouble with just brought her in. They helped her escape from Big Alice. She's here right now," Sheriff Wilkins said, reaching down to a lower drawer in his desk and fumbling for a cigar.

Clay narrowed his eyes as he listened. This man was deliberately giving Rockford the information so he could run. Or worse, come back and get her again. He had to think of something quickly. He stepped into the room.

Wilkins stopped talking and looked up at him. "Yeah? What is it?"

"Say, Sheriff, I hate to interrupt you, but where're your restrooms? We've been in the helicopter too long, if you know what I mean."

Sheriff Wilkins pointed down a hallway, glad to get a chance to talk to Rockford a little more privately. "Down there two doors," he said, and went back to his phone call.

Clay turned to his friends and put his finger to his lips. "Shhhhhh," he whispered. He motioned for them to follow him. Slipping out the door, he led the four men and two women toward the restroom.

When Clay reached the door Wilkins had described, he opened it and slammed it shut. He motioned for them to follow him. There had to be another way out. Sneaking down the hallways, they found themselves back in the front lobby. Clay could see Wilkins was still on the phone and headed out the main doors.

Once outside, he ran for the helicopter with the others close behind.

Within seconds they were in the air. Looking down, they saw Wilkins run out of the building, shaking a fist at them.

Virgil leaned over. "What was that all about, Clay?"

Clay looked back at Laura. "Sheriff Wilkins was talking to Rockford on the phone. He was telling the man that Laura was in his office. I figured we had better get the hell out while we could. No telling what they were cooking up."

Laura huddled in the back with Brenda. "What's going on? Why are we leaving?"

Brenda put her arm around Laura. "That sheriff's in cahoots with Rockford. Looks like we're going back to camp to sort this mess out."

Clay leaned over the back of his seat. "Don't worry, Laura. We'll get the bastards if we have to go all the way to the FBI!"

* * *

Minutes later they were high over the mountains, getting ready to drop down onto the plateau.

Virgil looked out the side window. He spotted a blue helicopter coming toward them at a fast clip. "Clay! Have a look over here," he shouted. "That's Rockford's helicopter! Looks like he's coming after us!"

Clay twisted around in his seat to see out the opposite window.

The blue chopper was getting very close.

Clay didn't know if the big Huey could out run the LOH. "Kick it in the ass, Virge! I don't like the looks of this!"

"Clay! The door just opened!" Rob yelled. "There's a man with a gun leaning out. Better get the hell out of here!"

The words were hardly out of Rob's mouth when the sound of gunfire echoed above the roar of the motors.

Virgil jammed the throttle of the big Huey with his left hand, and at the same time, used his right to work the cyclic control.

The helicopter sprang forward and off to the left.

"Hang on, back there!" he yelled. "Looks like we're in for a ride!"

A bullet ripped through the fuselage. Everyone ducked. The sound of automatic fire faded as the Huey gained speed.

Clay pulled his pistol, opened the little window by his seat, and waited to get a shot at the craft.

Virgil had recognized the helicopter as a Hughes 500. He knew it had greater speed. He just hoped the pilot didn't have the experience he had. He swung low over their camp, then took the chopper straight up, using some of the maneuvers he had used in the battles over Vietnam.

The LOH hung on but was slowly falling back in the distance.

Virgil, using both hands and feet, took the Huey through the canyons. First very low, skimming the ground at a slower speed, then, when the LOH got close, he would haul it straight up. He swung close around cliffs, then cut straight away across the valleys.

Wiscoff, thinking they were trying to hide behind the cliffs, would cut around only to find out too late that they were out over the center of the valley. He had to slow his helicopter a little each time he made a corner.

Virgil was playing with the little chopper. It was now obvious that the pilot of the other craft was not nearly as experienced a flyer.

The chase continued through valley after valley, high over peaks, low over the desert floor, and back up above the mountains.

Puffs of smoke could be seen coming from the doorway of the small craft each time it got close.

Though Virgil had been taken back in time as he put the ship through her paces, he decided to end the chase. He fed more fuel to the engine and felt it surge under him with renewed power.

Soon the old gunship was traveling at nearly 150 miles per hour. He looked back.

The blue one had disappeared.

Virgil looked at the fuel gauge. It showed empty. He tapped the gauge to make sure the needle wasn't hung up. It still showed empty. He looked around for an auxiliary tank switch.

Once he located it, he flipped the toggle switch. The engine almost instantly coughed and sputtered.

"Damn!" he said, quickly switching back. The reserve tank was already empty. The engine caught and smoothed out. Virgil knew there were only a few gallons of fuel left. He had to get to an airport right away or they would be walking out of the mountains again.

Clay turned to see why the motor sputtered. "What happened?"

"We've got to get some fuel," Virgil replied. "We're getting low. With all the trouble we've had, I've forgotten to refuel."

"How low?" Clay asked quickly.

"Oh, we've got enough, but we'd better top it off," Virgil lied. He could see the apprehension mounting in Clay's face. "Nothing to worry about."

Virgil began searching the landscape to see if he could see a town or airport. If his senses served him correctly, they were about fifty miles out of Apache Junction, and he knew there was an airport with fuel there. He would like to head for Phoenix and the FBI there, but that was another thirty miles away. They definitely didn't have the fuel to make it there. They might not even make Apache Junction.

62

$\mathbb{B}$ig Alice was angry as she gave Padro and Gonzales instructions. "I want you two to go up there and kill those bastards who tore my place up and stole my girl! Get her back!"

She stood amid the debris that had once been her saloon. "It'll cost me a fortune just to have the saloon repaired," she yelled, "and worse yet, if we don't get that girl back, we'll all end up in jail. Padro, you know what to do. Make it look like an accident. I don't care how you do it, just do it!"

"Sì, Señorìta! We would like very much to do something bad to those gringos for what they did to us," Padro answered, rubbing his swollen face where Rob had planted several hard blows with his huge fists. "It will be a pleasure to do it for you, Señorìta," Gonzales said.

Grabbing their guns and machetes, the two men hurried from the saloon.

It was noon when Padro put the last of their arsenal in the saddlebags. It was dynamite. They mounted their horses and headed out. Padro rode silently as he put together his plan of action.

63

The helicopter coughed and sputtered. It was out of fuel. Virgil expertly eased the chopper down at the little airport in Apache Junction. The engine died. He let out a sigh of relief. "Made it."

Clay looked at him. "I think you cut that one a little too close, Virge." He turned to Laura. "We have to get some fuel here. I want everybody to stay in the helicopter and keep a sharp watch out for Rockford's helicopter."

Virgil jumped out to help the attendant fuel the tanks.

Clay and Rob stood guard.

A police car turned onto the airfield and headed their way. When it was close enough, Clay could see it was Chief Blackhorse. He was alone. Clay watched it pull to a stop.

Blackhorse got out. "I saw your helicopter coming in. I need to talk to you."

"What about, Chief?"

"That marijuana farm you fellas saw up there. We went looking for it and couldn't find it."

"Was that you guys up there in the gray chopper this morning?"

"That was us. Federal Drug Enforcement Agency and me."

Clay looked the Chief over closely. He would really like to trust this man. "Why didn't you get the Sheriff to go with you? He knows that area very well."

"Between you and me, I don't trust that man. Even the DEA wanted to leave him out."

Clay nodded. He had always considered himself to be a good judge of character. He hoped he judged the Chief right. "Chief, the helicopter is ready to go. I have something to tell you. But I want you to know if you give me the wrong answer, we're leaving whether you like it or not."

He pointed to the doorway of the helicopter. Rob, Brian, and Ken stood with their guns showing, but not drawn. "They're trying to kill us, and we're not taking chances with anyone."

"Let's hear what you have to say, Clay," Blackhorse said. "Those guns aren't necessary. In fact, they're against the law, as you stand here. But I'll overlook that if you level with me."

"I guess we have to trust someone."

"You remember the last time we talked, I told you I was going to make a few phone calls?" Blackhorse asked.

"I remember," Clay replied.

"Well, I did. I called the Federal Department of Drug Enforcement over in Phoenix and got them involved. That farm you found is a big operation. They jumped on it. Maybe with them involved, I'll be able to find out something about Laura Pratt."

Clay cleared his throat and looked at Virgil.

Virgil nodded.

"Chief, we found that girl last night."

Blackhorse's mouth dropped open.

"She's in the helicopter right now. We found her up at Big Alice's. She was being held prisoner. She says Rockford snatched her himself."

Chief Blackhorse stepped back truly in shock. "You're shitting me!"

Clay shook his head, "No, it's true. Alice was supposed to turn her out as a whore, but the girl resisted. We went there for a party and she managed to get to us."

"Damn near got our throats cut in the battle trying to get her out," Virgil said. "Busted up Alice's place pretty damn good."

Blackhorse noticed their faces for the first time. He grinned. "It shows."

"We managed to get her out of there," Clay said. "This morning we took her to Sheriff Wilkins. That lousy bastard called Rockford while we were standing right there in the office. Wilkins told him he had the girl he kidnapped in his office."

"What happened?" Blackhorse asked.

"He didn't have her, we did. We ran."

Virgil pointed back toward the mountains. "Wilkins must have told Rockford we had left in the helicopter, because Rockford got after us in his own chopper. Chased us all over those damn mountains shooting at us."

"You see why we don't trust anyone," Clay said.

"You say Laura's in the helicopter, now?"

"Yes," Clay replied.

Chief Blackhorse motioned toward the chopper. "There's no need for them to suffer in that heat. Let's go to my office. You guys are safe with me."

They stood looking at him and thinking it over.

"Boys, you gonna have to trust someone!" Blackhorse said. "Might just as well be me. Wilkins may run the county but I run this city. He'll have no say in anything. In fact, she is totally my case."

Clay waved his arm and the others climbed down, placing Laura in a protective circle, they walked over to them.

Chief Blackhorse stood looking at the girl. He felt a lump growing in his throat. He had never expected to find her alive. As many times as he had sat staring at her photograph these past three weeks, he felt like he had known her for years. He felt so good to see her alive, he had to struggle to control his emotions. "Laura Pratt! My God, it is you. Laura Pratt! And you're alive!"

"Yes, Chief," said Clay. "That's Laura Pratt, your missing girl."

Blackhorse walked over to her and put his arms around her as she started crying again. "Laura Pratt," he said, his voice breaking up. "You go right ahead and cry. You've earned that right by staying alive for us. Your Uncle Gus and I have been worried sick about you. Thank god, you're safe."

Blackhorse walked with her to his car. He leaned inside and called for another squad. When it arrived, they went to his office.

In his crowded office, Chief Blackhorse picked up the phone and dialed. "I want Officer Jane Hollis in here with a tape recorder right away." He hung up and dialed again. "Gus? Chief Blackhorse here. Get over to my office right away!"

He hung up as the door opened and a female police officer walked in. "Sergeant Hollis," Blackhorse said, "this girl has been through an awful lot the last few weeks. I want you to take statements from her and these men," he said, pointing to a side door. "Use that office."

When they had left room, Blackhorse looked at the greenhorns. "What are you guys going to do about your gear up there?"

They looked at each other and then back at the Chief.

"Hell, Chief," said Virgil, "we left all our supplies up there. Besides, we're still having an adventure. We're going back up there to find us that gold mine."

"That's right," echoed Rob. "And nobody is going to run us out."

"We're going back tonight," said Clay. "If you want us to show you where the farm is, we'll come back tomorrow and take you up with us."

Blackhorse had already been embarrassed by not being able to locate it before. He didn't want to chance something happening to them and him not learning the location. "Better yet," he said, "can you take me up this afternoon? We still have a couple of hours of daylight left."

"We can do that," Clay said.

"I'll arrange with the DEA to make a raid on the farm as soon as possible. Might be a day or so before they can get ready." He glanced toward the door where Laura was giving her statement. He slammed his fist down on his desk. "I want that bastard!"

"We'll do all we can to help, Chief," said Clay.

"You've already done plenty," said Blackhorse. "You guys just watch your ass up there. Until Rockford is behind bars, you're in danger."

"You're telling us?" Brian said, laughing. "We've been in danger ever since the first time we stepped out of that helicopter three weeks ago."

The door opened and Gus hesitantly stepped in. He was shaking. He didn't know what to expect. He looked around the crowded room.

Blackhorse stood up. "Come on in Gus. We've been waiting for you."

"What's going on, Chief? Is she...is she...?"

A shiver swept through Blackhorse. The same shiver that had always swept through him when he had to tell the family either good or bad news. It was always the same. He managed a smile. "No, she isn't. She is right over there in that room. She'll be out in a few minutes."

Gus felt his heart jump. "You mean she's really alive?"

Blackhorse nodded. "These boys brought her in just a few minutes ago. Found her up in the mountains."

Tears flooded Gus' eyes. He couldn't see, but he stuck out his hand. "What can I say...?"

"No need to say anything, Gus," Clay replied. "Nothing at all."

Everyone shook Gus' hand.

"Thanks, fellas. Thank you a second time."

Laura Pratt, now set on exacting justice on Rockford and all his people, gave Officer Hollis step by step recorded details of what had happened to her since the night she left Gus' Saloon. She gave her each person's name and what they had done to her, including those of Sanchez and Gonzales, as well as Big Alice.

When she was finished, she and Hollis both sat staring at the slowly turning reel on the recorder.

Hollis shook her head. "What an incredible story. You are a very lucky woman just to be alive today."

Hollis stood and patted Laura's shoulder. "Now let's go get you to a hospital for a through examination."

Gus was still thanking the greenhorns when the side door opened and Laura stepped into the room. He stared at her through a mist of tears. *It really is her. She's really alive.*

Laura ran to him and threw her arms around him. "Oh, Uncle Gus! I'm so glad to see you again. It's been so awful!"

All Gus could do was hold her tightly as they cried.

Clay found it hard to hold back tears himself. He was saved when Sergeant Hollis motioned for him to follow her into the side office.

An hour later, all the statements had been taken. Officer Hollis put her reports on Blackhorse's desk. She turned to Laura. "Let's head on over to Lutheran Hospital. Gus, you ride with us."

The all said their good-byes and watched Laura leave.

After a minute, Blackhorse fumbled around in his desk and pulled out a camera. He stood and picked up his hat. "We might as well head on up to the mountain, fellas."

The five greenhorns and Brenda boarded the helicopter with Chief Blackhorse.

Clay gave up his co-pilot's seat to the Chief. He took a seat next to Brenda. They were engrossed in conversation as the helicopter lifted off and headed for the mountains.

As Virgil circled the helicopter low over the marijuana farm, he pointed out the window. "They know something's up, Chief. Looks like they've been busy harvesting green crops. That field has had more than half of it cut since the day when we were here."

Blackhorse readied his camera and motioned for Virgil to drop lower over the building.

"We'd best not do that," Virgil advised. "They don't take kindly to it."

"I need a closer look," Blackhorse replied.

Virgil eased the chopper downward.

Immediately, the door of the building below burst open and four men ran out with guns and started shooting at the helicopter.

Virgil banked the craft up and away as Blackhorse snapped his pictures. "See what I mean?" He headed the Huey back toward Apache Junction.

Far below, the smoke coming from their guns was very clear to Chief Blackhorse. "Holy shit! Those guys mean business, don't they?"

After dropping Chief Blackhorse off, the treasure hunters returned to their camp. Bailing out of the helicopter, they all hurried to the boulder they had rolled over the bags of gold. It looked undisturbed.

"Think we should dig it out and check it, just in case?" Rob asked.

Brian and Virgil were already rolling the stone aside. The gold was still where they had placed it.

When they searched each tent for signs of prowlers, and found nothing out of place, they relaxed a little. Soon, there was a large fire going and coffee brewing.

"What do you think we should do now, Clay?" asked Virgil.

"Like what?"

"Like keep on searching for the Dutchman, or take what we have and split for home."

Clay tossed a piece of wood on the fire and watched it catch, while he pondered on what Virgil said. "You know the odds are going to catch up with us if we're not careful," he said. "How many times can we get shot at without being hit?"

"You may have something there, Clay," Brian interrupted, "but the Dutchman is still out there. We haven't found it yet."

"I don't look for anything else to happen now that the law is on to those guys," Ken said. "Maybe we should stay on."

Clay glanced over at him. *Boy, has he changed. Three weeks in the mountains has made a real man of him.* Clay felt good that he had been a part of it. He looked over at Rob. "What about you, Rob?"

"Let's see a show of hands," Rob replied.

Ken's hand was the first one up. Then came Brian's and Rob's. Virgil grinned. "No need for us to vote, Clay; the stays have it - again."

64

Chief Blackhorse sat inside the largest hangar at the tiny airport in Apache Junction, listening to DEA Agent Basker give instructions to the large group of lawmen assembled in the room. There were lawmen from the DEA, Arizona State Police, and Apache Junction. Pinal County Sheriff's Department was not represented. A major task force had been thrown together over the past twenty-four hours. With search and arrest warrants in hand, it was about to see it's first action.

Basker spoke loud enough for everyone to hear. "Just so's there's no misunderstanding later, I want all of you to know that the DEA is heading up this task force. That's not to say we are taking it from the rest of you. But we have jurisdiction all over the United States and then some. The farm is also on federal land."

He stopped to look around at the officers. He had worked with many of them in the past and they were excellent officers. He also knew that for many years there had been animosity between local police and federal agents, because many times in the past some overzealous federal agents had taken all the credit for solving cases that had actually been handled by the locals. He had been working to correct that problem. "I want all of you local and state officers to know that we couldn't operate without your assistance. So don't feel left out. We need you a hell of a lot more than you need us." He stopped to look around at all the different departments involved. "We have to be extremely careful who we talk to about this mission. We have information some police officers might be involved with the bad guys."

Several men muttered among themselves.

"I'm happy to announce, however, that it's none of you in this room. Each one of you was hand picked because of your dedication and integrity. Now, with that out of the way, let's get on with the details."

He pointed to Long. "Agent Long will lead one section of this task force to hit the Rockford ranch with an arrest warrant as well as a search warrant. At the same time, I'll lead the raid on a marijuana farm up in the mountains. We'll execute a search warrant there, even though it's not necessary since that's federal land and they're squatters. That's how the Attorney General wants it." He pointed toward the door. "We'll go up there in the three helicopters standing by outside."

He paused for a minute. "After Agent Long has secured Rockford's ranch, he will take some State Policemen and hit Big Alice's Saloon. My team will go to Florence and arrest Sheriff Jack Wilkins, if he's there." He looked around the room. "Gentlemen, we have to hit fast and carefully - don't we, Chief Blackhorse?"

Chief Blackhorse nodded. "That's right," he said. "Those farmers up there shoot first and ask questions later."

"Chief Blackhorse was up there yesterday and was shot at with automatic weapons. That's why we have the DEA swat team with us," he said, pointing to several men dressed in black, their faces painted to match.

"You're thinking that was yesterday, why didn't we hit it then? First we had to get all the warrants and then pick the team. That took a little time but now we're ready. So let's go get 'em!"

Three helicopters lifted off the ground, as several police cars roared out onto the highway leading to Rockford's place, with red lights flashing.

Chief Blackhorse looked out the window. "It should be right over that next ridge."

Basker nodded and tapped the pilot, Justin Fletcher, on the shoulder. He pointed to the ridge. "Just ahead."

The pilot nodded.

The last ridge disappeared beneath them and the open field loomed before him. It was barren. The marijuana had all been cut. The buildings appeared to be vacant. There was no sign of activity around, but there was a huge, double-rotor helicopter near the building.

Justin Fletcher looked it over. "Chief, looks like they were in the process of loading the dope into that big Chinook down there. It could hold a large portion of the crop. Probably close to ten tons."

"Well, don't let the fact that you don't see anyone fool you," Blackhorse said. "They'll be in that long building by the helicopter."

As he said the words, six men ran out with guns, firing toward the helicopters.

Basker yelled into the PA system. "We're Federal Agents. Put down your weapons and lay down on the ground and no harm will come to you."

The men continued to shoot at them.

The lawmen inside the helicopters could hear the plunk of the bullets hitting the aircraft.

"Christ! We're being hit!" Blackhorse exclaimed.

"Don't worry, Chief," said Basker. "You're safe. The armor on this craft can take anything up to a 23 mm cannon shot."

Basker leaned over to the pilot. "Let's get out of range a minute while you give 'em one of our greeting cards," he said. "Right out in front of 'em, into the ground, so they can see it good."

The pilot pulled up his gunsight and peered through it. He pressed a button and the craft rocked slightly as an air-to-air rocket was launched. It left a slight trail of smoke as it plunged toward the men and struck the ground a few yards in front of them. Rocks and dirt exploded into the air and when the dust cleared, there was a huge crater in the ground.

Terrified, the men threw their weapons down and plopped onto the ground.

"God, I love those rockets," Basker said proudly. "They get 'em every time." He nudged the pilot and motioned for him to take the craft down.

Before the helicopters touched the ground, the swat team was out and running toward the men, yelling at them to lie still. Two men restrained them while the rest surrounded the building in a matter of seconds. Their leader looked to Basker for a signal.

Basker nodded.

Without delay, the leader shouted orders, and they crashed through the doors, screaming and yelling. Seconds later, the leader walked to the door and motioned.

Basker waved his hand and they all went inside.

The huge building was nearly empty, except for a small stack of bailed marijuana at one end.

Entering the office, Basker could see by the scattered papers on the floor and the empty floor safe that someone had known they were coming. "God dammit! Just when I thought we had the bastards, they flee."

"Hey, Basker!" the leader of the swat team called out from outside the office.

Basker walked out. "You're in luck. That flying warehouse out there is full of marijuana. Looks like a maximum load - maybe ten tons."

Basker let out a sigh of relief, "We didn't miss after all. Looks like they didn't have time to haul it out."

He snapped orders. "Men! Process the whole damn farm for prints and any other evidence that might have the dealers names on them!"

The men scurried about. Basker turned to the swat team leader. "When you're all finished in here, photograph everything, then burn the marijuana. The buildings...we'll blow up! Let 'em know we care!"

"Blow the helicopter, too, Chief?"

Basker chuckled. "Now let's don't get carried away. That Chinook CH-47A is worth a bundle of money and it's now the confiscated property of the federal government."

* * *

Half a dozen squad cars raced down the road and whipped into the drive leading to Rockford's house. The cars surrounded Rockford's ranch house and barns.

Agent George Long and several state police officers bailed out.

Immediately, Long saw that the helicopter was gone. "Damn!" he said. "I was hoping that helicopter was here. We're going to confiscate it when we find it. It was used in the commission of a forcible felony." Long hoped one of Rockford's flunkies had the helicopter out somewhere and that Rockford was home. His hopes faded fast when he saw Margarita walk out onto the porch, wiping her hands on her apron.

"Ma'am," Long called out, "we have an arrest warrant for Mr. Rockford. Is he here?"

"No, Señor, he leave this morning in the helicopter with Danny."

"Do you happen to know where he was headed?"

"He say something about Mexico City, Señor. A vacation, maybe?"

Long kicked the dirt under his feet. "Damn!" He stood in thought for a minute. "Ma'am, we have a search warrant for the house. These men are going to search it, and I want you to do what they tell you. You are in no trouble yourself, understand?"

"Sì, Señor. I shall do what they say."

Long turned to a state police detective. "After we execute the search warrant, why don't your men secure the property?"

The detective nodded, "Sounds good."

The warrant was executed. Lawmen found papers that tied Rockford with the marijuana farm and tied Sheriff Wilkins in as well. They also laid claim to more than a million dollars stashed in the hidden wall safe.

"Secure the whole ranch and make sure nothing leaves here," Long told the detective. "We're going on up to Big Alice's saloon. You call us if Rockford is located."

Agent Long and five Arizona state policemen hurried to their cars and headed toward Alice's place, thirty miles up in the mountains.

* * *

Agent Basker and Chief Blackhorse stood watching the long building burn. The swat team set charges, and the smaller building exploded in flames that soared high into the air. There was nothing left but burning debris... and the water tower.

Basker assigned one of the swat team pilots to fly the Chinook back to headquarters. When he was satisfied that everything had been taken care of, he headed for the chopper. "Let's go get Sheriff Wilkins."

When the three federal helicopters and the big Chinook were airborne, Basker yelled at the pilot. "Justin, line up on that water tower and give it a rocket."

"Yes, sir!" Justin replied, grinning.

All eyes were on the tower as the rocket struck. It exploded into tiny pieces. The water seemed to hang in mid air for a second, then plummeted to the ground. There was nothing left.

"Move out!" said Basker.

With his prisoners from the farm secured inside the helicopter, Basker's three-chopper team landed at the Pinal County Jail. They rushed out to find Deputy Richmond waiting in front of the building.

He shook his head. "Sheriff Wilkins has already flown the coop, boys," he said. "He'll probably be meeting up with Rockford down in Mexico somewhere. I've been appointed sheriff temporarily - at least until the next election."

Basker hated crooked cops. But according to Blackhorse, Deputy Richmond was an excellent officer and would make a good replacement for the people. He told Richmond what had been happening and that a warrant had been issued for Wilkins.

"Rest assured, Agent Basker, that I will personally put the cuffs on him if we locate him," Richmond said. "I never cared for the man, myself."

"Good. We'll get 'im sooner or later. He can't stay hidden. Not even in Mexico."

They headed back for the helicopters.

"Let's go see if the boys up at Alice's saloon need any help," said Basker.

65

Clay woke to the sound of helicopters in the distance. He jumped out of bed and hurried outside in time to see a fleet of three blue-gray choppers going over the top ridge toward the farm.

Virgil joined him.

"They went up toward the farm, Virge," Clay said, staring off toward the top of the mountain.

"Yeah, they're pulling the raid right about now," Virgil said.

"Maybe that'll end all our problems and we can relax a little."

"It would be nice to have a little peace while we're here," said Clay. He poured water into the coffeepot and put it on the fire to brew.

The rest of the boys were just rolling out of their tent, rubbing sleep from their eyes, when Brenda came out. "How's the coffee and what the hell was all that noise?" she asked.

"Coffee's good, and that was your tax dollars at work. The feds are raiding the farm up there," Clay answered.

"I hope they get every last one of the bastards and hang 'em from the nearest tree for what they did to Laura," Brenda said angrily. "That includes that damn Big Alice, too. She was only nice to me because I could help her and her girls."

"Oh, I'm sure they'll have no trouble getting her. From what I hear, she's always on that porch of hers watching the mountain for searchers," Clay said, patting her shoulder to reassure her.

"Think they'll get Rockford, too?" Brenda asked.

"Sure, they will. He's the big cheese in this mess," Virgil answered.

Rob grabbed a cup of hot coffee. "They'll get him. The DEA is very thorough. They leave no stone unturned as the saying goes."

Brenda stared down into the burning fire. "Rockford will head for Mexico if he gets a chance. He spent a year down there before he bought the ranch he has now."

"DEA has fingers down in Mexico, too. They'll get him," Rob said.

Clay walked off toward the bluffs rising above the camp. "Maybe we could get in a little time with the long-range detector. There's got to be another Spanish cave up there - somewhere." Clay turned back toward the fire. He grinned.

Brian already had the detector out and was hurrying toward him. "How's that for service?" asked Brian. "Now go find us a cave, Clay. We could use some more of those gold nuggets."

After coffee, satisfied their troubles were over, the treasure hunters set out once more, in search of the Lost Dutchman's gold mine.

66

Big Alice sat fanning herself as she watched the parade of cars zipping into her parking lot. Even though deep down she had been expecting it since Laura had escaped, her heart sank. The dread of prison crept over her very soul. She watched the cars surround the saloon and several men jump out with guns drawn. Big Alice knew these weren't Sheriff Wilkins' men. Men she might be able to reason with or buy off. These were state policemen. She could see the Arizona State patch on their shirts. No telling who the ones in plain clothes are, she thought, as she waited for them to make the first move.

Agent Long walked up the steps and approached the big woman. "You Alice Hatfield, nick-named Big Alice?" he asked.

Big Alice looked the man over. If she figured this one right, he was a federal man. "That's me, Mister," she answered. "Now what can I do for you?"

"Alice Hatfield, I am Federal Agent George Long. I have a federal warrant for your arrest for the kidnapping of one Laura Pratt."

She nodded. "I figured as much. But I didn't kidnap nobody. I been right here all along."

"I have another federal warrant charging you with conspiracy to commit kidnapping and unlawful restraint for keeping Laura locked up for weeks in a back room here in the saloon."

Again Big Alice nodded. "Well, I reckon she was here, but it was of her own free will."

"We'll see about that later," said Long. "I also have a search warrant and confiscation order for your business and property. You can consider it closed from this moment forth."

Long slapped copies of the warrants into her lap. He turned to an officer. "See that she doesn't leave that seat until we're finished inside." He turned back to Big Alice. "By the way, where are your two hired men, Padro Sanchez and Manuel Gonzales?"

"They's up on the mountain somewhere," she said, pointing up toward the mountain. "Probably hiding if they saw your cars."

Long motioned for the officers to go inside. He pulled his pistol. He'd heard all about those big machetes, and he was taking no chances.

"Don't you be shooting none of my people. You hear me, lawman?" Big Alice called after him.

Long ignored her as he and the other officers prepared to enter the building. At the door, Long yelled out a warning. "FEDERAL AGENTS! Padro Sanchez! Manuel Gonzales! We have warrants for your arrests. Why don't you just come on out? Don't make a mistake that could cost you your lives."

There was no answer.

Long gave the signal and the door was nearly ripped from its hinges as the lawmen slammed through it and rushed into the saloon.

Big Alice's girls sat in the saloon, waiting.

A search of the place found all the bedrooms empty. Padro Sanchez and Manuel Gonzales were not there.

Long stood at the door to the room where Laura had been kept. He stared at the lone piece of furniture - the bed. He wondered how the girl held out for three whole weeks in this dirty dark hole. He turned to the state crime scene technicians. "I want this room processed from top to bottom for finger prints. I want to put Laura

Pratt's prints in here so they can't deny it later in court. Just one print and we'll really have these bastards nailed down good."

While the crime scene technicians started processing the room, Long's team began conducting interviews of the girls and employees at the saloon.

From the girls, they learned that Laura had been the only one ever held against her will. Even though the others had stayed with Big Alice willingly, they were still willing to testify against her. They wanted it clear to the law that they had nothing to do with the kidnapping or the holding of Laura. They would also testify against Paul Rockford and his two men, Davis and Wiscoff, as well as Sanchez and Gonzales.

Big Alice watched three helicopters land outside her saloon and several men, dressed in all black, jump out. Their faces were even black. She smiled. She had once seen a swat team in action during a news program on television. *This is just like that news. A swat team? Do they think I'm that dangerous?* She watched the men in black run to surround the building.

Agent Basker and Chief William walked toward the porch.

Blackhorse leaned over to Basker. "I'm going to stay with her every minute," he whispered. "Maybe she'll say something we can use."

On the porch, they didn't have to ask who Big Alice was. They walked right to her.

"Alice Hatfield, I'm Federal Agent Charles Basker and this is Apache Junction Chief of Police Dennis Blackhorse."

"I've already spoke to a federal man. He said for me to sit right here. That's what I'm doing."

"I'll just sit here with you," said Blackhorse.

Basker went inside to find Long.

Big Alice looked off toward the mountains and didn't talk.

It was late afternoon when all the statements had been taken. The girls were allowed to leave after giving their statements.

Big Alice watched her working girls, carrying what possessions they had, get into state police cars that would take them to Apache Junction where they would scatter to parts unknown. Some would head for Phoenix while others would cross over into Mexico where their families were. Financially them would be okay as well. Each girl, over the months or years she had been there, had her own little stash of money squirreled away.

When the dust of the departing cars settled, Big Alice turned her attention back to the problems at hand as several lawmen settled back on the porch to wait for Sanchez and Gonzales to come down from the mountain.

67

Clay slowly swept the detector across the rocky surface ahead of him. "There's got to be another Spanish cave around here somewhere," he said. "The one we found is not the big one."

Hours went by with Clay constantly sweeping back and forth. His arm ached worse by the minute, but he kept up the pace.

Several times the antenna hesitated, but would not lock on. Each time, Clay would retrace the same pattern, but the lock was not there. Perhaps a minor mineral deposit, but not enough to worry about.

As sunset approached, Clay lowered the machine and pushed in the antenna. Disgusted, he turned to the others who were close behind, carrying tools and guarding their backsides. "That's it for now," he said. "It'll be dark by the time we get back to camp."

Brian and Brenda prepared supper while the rest sat around the campfire exchanging stories.

Without refrigeration, the selection of food suitable to preserve in the extreme heat of the desert was limited. Canned meats were the order of the day, and this time it was fried spam sandwiches.

As they sat eating, Ken looked out toward the darkness at the edge of the camp. "I can't believe we went a whole day without something happening to us," he said. "I think it's a damn record."

"Don't talk too soon, Ken. It's still a long time 'til midnight," Brian warned.

Rob reached for a beer and popped the top on it, holding it away from him as it foamed over and spilled upon the ground.

"Damned hot beer!" he exclaimed,

"That's the way they drink it in Germany, Rob." Ken said.

"Well, we're not in Germany," Rob replied.

Brian walked over and took one of the beers. "Too bad we don't have a little ice. There's a whole case of beer sitting here. We could have a party."

Virgil stood up and stretched. He strolled over to the helicopter and crawled inside. A minute later he jumped back out, carrying a fire extinguisher. "Grab that big tin can oven Brenda made and put that beer in it," he said.

Brian and Rob piled in the beer.

"Now what, Vigil?" Brian asked.

"Just stand back," Virgil warned, "A little trick I learned in Vietnam." He aimed the fire extinguisher nozzle at the beer in the can and squeezed the handle. White powdery foam burst from the nozzle with a loud swish.

A surprised look appeared on the faces of those that watched.

Within seconds, frost appeared on the outside of the cans.

Virgil gave them one more burst. "Grab a beer," he said, "But be careful. It'll freeze your fingers and lips."

Rob popped a can and brushed off the mouth opening. He took a swig and held the can up to stare at it. "Well, I'll just be damned," he said. "It's ice cold."

Cans popped all around the camp as the group of treasure hunters enjoyed an evening of relaxation and peace around a glowing campfire.

*   *   *

A few yards away, Padro watched through his binoculars as the treasure hunters drank their beer. A good cold beer would certainly help his thirst right now. He and Gonzales had ridden ten miles through the heat of the afternoon to get here, only to be tortured by watching them drink cold beer.

"Manuel," Padro whispered loudly, "I think it's dark enough. We will do it."

The two Mexicans slipped through the bushes to the very edge of the camp light. The helicopter was only a few feet from them.

Padro tapped Gonzales on the shoulder, pointing to the helicopter. "There!" he whispered. "We'll set it there!"

Crawling on his hands and knees, Padro led the way through the small ground bushes to the helicopter. Easing up to it, he slipped his hand into his shirt and came out with a bundle of dynamite sticks. He made the sign of a cross on his face and eased over to the helicopter. Choosing a place under the belly of the craft to conceal the dynamite, Sanchez pulled out a coil of fuse and a blasting cap from his shirt. He stuck the fuse in the primer and crimped it between his teeth to make it stay. Cautiously, he stuck the primer into the middle stick of dynamite and silently slid backward uncoiling the fuse as he went.

Suddenly his feet tangled in Virgil's alarm rope. Cans clattered in the night. Padro's heart jumped to his throat. He flattened on the ground.

Every man in the tents ran out, guns in hand.

Rob yelled, "There's someone near the helicopter." He fired a round toward the dark form he saw drop to the ground.

Everyone began blazing away at the dark figure as it ran through the bushes.

A sudden yelp of pain brought a round of renewed firepower at the bushes. Only when all their gun slides had locked back indicating empty clips, did they cease firing.

"Did you guys hear that?" Brian cried out. "We hit a something out there."

Virgil wasn't as optimistic. "I heard something yell," he said. "Maybe it was one of them wild burros."

"No, it sounded human, " Brian said.

"Those son-of-a-bitches," Rob exclaimed angrily. "Who in the hell can it be this time?"

"Guess you were right back there about saying it's too soon, weren't you, Rob?" asked Kenneth.

"I guess," Rob replied, "but I think one of the bastards has a slug in him. Let's get the lights and go see if we can find him."

When they had secured the flashlights, bright beams of light flashed in all directions as they made a search of the area.

Clay spotted a sombrero with bright green markings, lying in the weeds. "Aha!" he exclaimed. "It's none other than your old friend, Rob."

"What old friend are you talking about?"

"That big Mexican that almost killed your ass in the saloon fight. He wore the only green sombrero in the place that night. Look at the size of that thing! Must be a nine or maybe even a ten!" He walked over to Rob, brushing the dust off the sombrero. "Here!" he said, handing the hat to Rob. "Have a souvenir from Big Alice's Saloon."

"Think we should follow whoever it was?" asked Virgil. "Looks like they headed down the south trail."

"No," said Clay, motioning for the others to head back to camp. "Too damn dark to find them out here without making ourselves a clear target." He stared off into the darkness. He placed his hand on Virgil's shoulder. "Besides, I don't really want to kill anyone, do you, Virge?"

"No, not unless I really have to."

"Anyway," Clay said, as they headed back to the helicopter to see what the man was doing. "You can rest assured that whoever they were, they're long gone now."

"You can bet the bastards were up to no good," Brian said. His light fell on the rope and tin can alarm. He gave a thumbs up to Virgil. "Bastard got tangled up in your rope, Virgil."

Clay examined the helicopter doors and found they were still closed. There appeared to be no damage to the fuselage. He looked around. "You fellas get some sleep. I'm going to get in the helicopter and watch the area from there."

"Good idea, Clay. I'll relieve you in two hours," Virgil said.

When Clay was seated in the helicopter, he could see the whole camp. The boys had already gone into the tents, but he could see Brenda standing just outside her tent. She stood there for a while, then slowly walked toward the helicopter. Clay turned to look at her as she climbed in and took a place in the co-pilot's seat. She didn't look at Clay, but sat looking out the window at the darkness of the night around the camp. "Thought I would keep you company for a little while," she said. "That is, if you don't mind."

"Not at all. Glad to have your company. In fact, it'll help keep me awake just in case they come back."

There was an awkward silence as they watched the camp outside.

68

"Manuel!" Padro whispered loudly. "Manuel! I'm shot!"

Manuel hurried to him and saw the blood flowing freely down his front. He was sure Padro was dying.

Padro took out his matches and handed them to Gonzales. "You will have to go light the fuse, Manuel. It is but right there," Padro pointed to a spot some three or four yards away, "Crawl out there and light the fuse. Then we must get the hell out of here before I bleed to death."

Now it was Gonzales' turn to make the sign of the cross over his chest. He held the matches in one hand, and though trembling with fear, crawled along the ground until he found the fuse. Using his sombrero to conceal the flame, he lit the fuse and scrambled back to Padro.

Both men lay in the dark and watched the orange glow of the burning fuse creep slowly toward the helicopter until it disappeared.

Gonzales ripped off Padro's shirt and used it as a bandage to stop the flow of blood. "Come on Padro! Let's ride!" Gonzales whispered.

69

Brenda turned to look at Clay. She studied his profile. He had a pleasant look about him - one that she could look upon for hours.

He glanced at her steady gaze, then feeling a sudden rush of heat racing through his body, quickly turned back to his window. He stole another glance. She was still staring at him. Now he was getting nervous. He jerked his head back to the window.

"Clay," Brenda said softly, "I know you're married and I'll understand if you tell me to get out, but I need to tell you something."

"What's that, Brenda?" Clay asked, keeping his eyes glued outside.

"I've become very attracted to you, Clay. I can't seem to get my mind off you since you pulled me out of that stream." She stared down at her hands as she picked at her nails. "I feel like I have to be close to you. I know it's not right. I know I should just forget it and go away, but I can't help my feelings."

Clay turned in his seat to face her. He felt that same rush of heat surge through him again. Being alone with her was quite different than being with her while others were there. There is a certain intimacy about being alone with any woman, especially one as desirable as Brenda was. He turned away to look down at the tents.

He was afraid to say anything - afraid his resistance would crumble like a dry cracker.

Suddenly, he felt the brush of her hand against his arm. He didn't move. *Why in the hell is my face so hot? I have to be very careful here. Maybe I've been out in this wilderness too long.* It had been a month since he had made love with his wife, a long month in which he had used hard work and excitement to ward off sexual desires. He was vulnerable now and may not be able to resist his urges.

Brenda turned sideways in her seat and leaned over to him. "Clay, I can't help myself. I've grown to care a great deal for you. Don't you know you're the reason I've stayed up here? You're the most exciting thing that has ever happened to me, Clay."

"Brenda. . ., I, I'm married," Clay said, his voice shaky.

"I know, I know. That's what bothers me so much. I've never allowed myself to fall for a married man."

"I. . .I can't. . . Brenda."

She was so close to him that he could smell the delicious scent of her body. He had to close his eyes to keep his senses. "Br-Br-Brenda, I don't think we should do this," he stuttered.

Brenda slipped her arm around his neck, pulling him close.

He resisted, but only slightly. He struggled with thoughts of the wedding vows he had made long ago and the overpowering aching of his male harmones.

Brenda leaned in and brushed her lips against his.

A firestorm roared though his body. His inner struggle was over. He had lost. He reached his arm around her, crushed her against his chest, and kissed her long and hard, tasting the sweetness of her lips.

"WHHOOOOOO! WHHOOOOOO! WHHOOOOOO!"

Clay and Brenda both jumped. They looked out the window.

The owl was perched on a cactus not twenty feet away.

"Look there!" Clay pointed to the owl. "It's the Owl! Something's wrong."

"It's just an owl, Clay."

"WHHOOOOOO! WHHOOOOOO! WHHOOOOOO!"

The old owl was now moving from one foot to the other.

Clay struggled to see past Brenda's hair to the camp. "When that owl appears, there is usually something wrong." He saw nothing.

He turned back to the owl. It was gone. The Indian stood beside the cactus. He was pointing toward the tents almost as though he was trying to tell them something. "Something is wrong! Something bad!"

Jumping from his seat, Clay spilled Brenda onto the floor before grabbing her arm and pulling her toward the door.

"Aw, come on, Clay. You don't have to try to scare me to get me away from you," Brenda snapped.

"Something's wrong, Brenda. Let's get back to the others."

Out of the chopper now, he ran, dragging Brenda along.

Suddenly, an enormous explosion rocked the camp, blasting everything in its way.

Clay felt something hit him hard in the back, then felt himself lifted into the air. Excruciating pain shot through his left shoulder, then he slammed into the ground. Everything went black.

Brenda was blown though the air to be dumped in a heap among the debris. Dust, rock, and metal rained down on them for what seemed like an eternity.

Finally, everything was deathly quiet.

Clay lay listening for a minute before he opened his eyes. He knew he wasn't dead because of the pain in his shoulder. He opened his eyes. He could hardly see. Dust hung in the air like a heavy fog. Easing himself into a sitting position, he felt his shoulder. His hand came away with blood on it. He felt again. Something was sticking out the back of his shoulder. It felt like a piece of metal.

Clay checked all his major parts. None were missing and nothing seemed to be broken, unless it was the shoulder. He looked around camp. The helicopter was gone, replaced by a huge hole in the ground. The tents were gone, and so were his friends. Jumping up, he screamed their names, "BRENDA! VIRGIL! ROB! BRIAN! WHERE ARE YOU GUYS?"

A single cough was heard.

Clay saw Ken getting to his feet. A few feet away, he saw Rob struggling to pick himself off a rock. He let out a sigh of relief when he saw they were not seriously hurt. His relief was short lived when he spotted Brenda lying in a heap a distance away. She was very still and completely black. Her clothes hung on her like rags. Running to her, Clay dropped to his knees and began examining her for injuries. It appeared there were no bones broken, but she was unconscious. He eased her head up onto his bent legs and held her face in his hands.

Rob hurried over with a canteen of water he had dug from the debris. Pouring some in his hand, he gently wiped her face.

Brenda opened her eyes. She lay still, trying to get her bearings. She stared up at Clay for a long time. "Your wife," she said weakly, "she doesn't by chance practice black magic, does she?"

Clay got a puzzled look on his face. He shrugged. "I don't know, I've never asked her."

Brenda laughed despite her pain. "Well, just in case she does, tell her she has nothing to worry about. I ain't going through that again, not even for you."

"What does she mean by that, Clay?" Rob asked.

"Nothing, Rob. Nothing at all."

Suddenly, it dawned on them that someone was missing.

"Brian! Virgil!" Clay called out. "Virgil! Where the hell are you?"

Clay, still bleeding from the shoulder injury, began searching for his friends. He spotted a large section of the helicopter fuselage lying on top of a collapsed tent. He knew Virgil had been in bed when the explosion happened. He rushed to it and dropped to his knees, feeling around in the darkness. He felt an arm under the tent. "Get over here quick!"

Rob, Ken, and Brenda hurried to him. Ken was carrying a flashlight.

"I think I've found one of them," Clay said, struggling to get the canvas clear of the body. Rob and Ken grabbed the debris and lifted it off the tent. Clay rolled back the canvas and, as the light fell upon the arm, he could see it was Virgil. He was unconscious. Blood gushed from a deep cut on his head. His arm was at a strange angle.

Brenda felt for his pulse. She nodded. His heart was beating. She examined his body. The right arm was broken, but there did not seem to be any more broken bones. "He's alive, Clay, but badly injured. His arm is broken and his head has a terrible cut. He may have a fractured skull." She slapped her hand over the cut and pressed hard. "Find my medical bag. It was inside the tent. Get me anything to use for a bandage."

Ken rushed to where the tent had been. In a panic, he began throwing things aside, searching for the bag. The leather handle caught his eye. He grabbed it and tugged hard. It came free. It was the bag and he examined it as he ran back to Brenda. "It's still in one piece."

Brenda flung it open and grabbed a large pressure bandage. Ripping the paper from it with her teeth, she applied it to the cut. The bleeding slowed. "Rob, grab the gauze and wrap it around his head several times. That'll hold the bandage in place."

When she ripped the end of the gauze down the center and tied it around his head, it was secure. "Let's roll him over."

Carefully, they eased Virgil onto his back.

Brenda placed his broken arm across his chest. "We'll make a sling for his arm for now and set it later," she said, busying herself unrolling gauze to make the sling.

Ken got to his feet and looked around. "Anyone seen Brian?" Immediately, Ken, Clay, and Rob began a search of the camp.

A low moan was heard coming from near the edge of the plateau. Making a search in that direction, they came to the edge of the plateau without finding him.

Another moan was heard. This time they leaned over the edge and shined the flashlight. There was Brian lying, on a ledge about ten feet down. A foot or so away, the ledge ended in a two hundred foot drop - straight down.

"Hang on, Brian!" Rob yelled. "We'll get you up! Just don't move an inch!"

Clay and Ken ran to get more lights. They found two ropes still intact. They hurried back.

With a rope tied to his waist, Clay went over the side and tied the second rope around Brian. "I think his right leg is broken."

"Get me down there! Quick!" Brenda said.

Rob and Ken lowered her over the side onto the ledge.

"Boy, when you do it, you really do it right," said Brenda. "It's a compound fracture."

Working on the narrow ledge, Clay cut Brian's pant leg to his thigh.

Brenda looked at the injury. "We'll have to set it before you can be moved. You're also gonna need stitches, Brian."

"Ken!" Clay shouted. "Find something for splints!"

Two dead tree limbs were lowered over the side.

Brenda put them along each side of Brian's leg, then turned to Clay. "This ledge is too narrow. I can't set the leg from my position. You'll have to do it from there."

"I don't know, Brenda," Clay said, his stomach churning. "I've never done anything like this before!"

"You just do what I tell you to do. Now listen up! Grab the leg with both hands below the break. I'll hold it above the break."

Clay reluctantly did her bidding and squatted with both hands ready.

"Now we try to pull the broken end down and back into place, by pulling in opposite directions." Brenda said.

Brian was in pain. He bit his lip, but couldn't keep a groan from escaping his lips.

"I'm sorry, Brian. I know it hurts, but it'll feel much better after it's set," Brenda said, sympathetically.

Brian started to groan louder.

"Jerk hard! Now!" Brenda shouted.

Clay yanked as hard as he could and felt the bones snap into place.

The scream that gushed from Brian's lips probably scared every wild thing within miles of the camp. When it was over, he lay breathing hard and moaning loudly.

Brenda applied bandages to the torn flesh. "We'll have to stitch it later."

With the leg secured, they hauled Brian up to their demolished camp.

Clay hurried to where Virgil was lying. He had not moved. He was breathing, but his eyes were closed. He would not respond at all.

"He has a severe concussion, Clay. There's nothing I can do but watch over him. He needs to be in a hospital."

"Is he going to make it, Brenda? Is he going to live?"

"I don't know, Clay. We'll just have to wait and see. Something this serious - I just don't know." She looked for the first time at Clay's bloody shirt. "Clay, you're hurt! Let me look at that."

Clay turned so she could examine the shoulder. Now that everything had settled down a little, it hurt like hell.

"You've got a piece of metal imbedded in your shoulder back here. It has to come out." She motioned for Rob to come.

"Rob, find me a pair of pliers. There must have been a tool box in the helicopter."

Rob searched through the debris until he found the toolbox. It had been blasted open and the tools scattered, but it didn't take long to find the pliers.

With pliers in hand, Brenda patted Clay on his good shoulder. "Clay, this is going to hurt like hell. Get a good grip on something and hang on. Rob, you hold his shoulder and arm."

Clay looked around for something to grab, but saw nothing. He closed his eyes, set his mind to reject pain and waited.

He didn't have to wait long. Brenda gripped the piece of metal with the pliers and, using both hands, jerked hard.

The intense pain that shot through Clay's body brought a slight moan from his lips. His face was hot and sweating. His head swirled and he felt like he was going to pass out.

Finally, the metal piece came out, blood shot everywhere and Brenda fell backward. Regaining her position, she quickly slapped a pressure bandage on the injury. "There, that ought to take care of it," she said, placing tape over the gauze bandage.

When the pain subsided, Clay sat with his head down, thinking about what had happened, what they were going to do, and how they were going to do it. He looked over at Virgil, lying so still on the ground. He had to get him to a hospital, and soon, or he was going to die.

After a few minutes, Clay got to his feet and looked around the camp. "Now we know what the Mexicans were up to," Clay said, looking at the huge hole in the ground where the helicopter once stood. The fuselage was in twisted, tangled pieces lying everywhere.

Rob found another huge hole in the ground. He turned to Clay. "Look over here, Clay. That was one hell of a charge they set. It even blew up the dynamite I had buried. Those bastards meant to kill us all."

"We're leaving as soon as the sun rises. Right now, let's see what we can salvage from this mess."

Rummaging around the campsite looking for supplies, they managed to find three pistols, including Virgil's big .44 caliber revolver. To make sure they still worked, Clay fired a few rounds through each one. Satisfied, he handed them out.

They found a couple of blankets and a large piece of canvas. These were placed over Virgil and Brian to keep them warm.

"That's about it," Clay said, surveying the ruins, "unless we find more, come daylight. We'll stand guard two at a time."

Brenda dug through her medical bag and gave Brian a painkiller for his leg.

Rob stood up. "Ken, let's you and me go get the gold."

Clay nodded. "Good idea. I'll go with you. Trying to kill us might mean they know where the gold is hidden. Maybe they watched us bury it the other day."

"I told you that you wouldn't have to worry about Big Alice until you found the gold," said Brenda. "Well, now you have and she's trying to kill you."

"I think you're right, Brenda," said Clay.

As Rob and Ken moved the boulder and began digging up the gold, Clay pulled his pistol and watched the darkness for any sign of movement.

They eased back to the fire. The bags of gold were placed on each side of Brian.

"You just yell if anyone gets too close to these," said Rob.

Brian managed a weak grin. He nodded.

70

A full moon created long shadows around Big Alice's saloon. There were still several police cars around it, and one helicopter. Agent Basker had sent the swat team and the other helicopter ahead with their prisoners. All except Big Alice. She sat with Basker and Chief Blackhorse at a table inside the now empty saloon. Big Alice would not talk to them about anything, so they sat waiting for Sanchez and Gonzales, and watching her.

* * *

Padro and Gonzales slowly approached the rear of the saloon. Padro was shirtless and in pain. Just back of the building they stopped. They could see the police cars parked around it.

"Padro, there are lawmen everywhere. We cannot go in," said Gonzales.

"But I am in such pain, Manuel. Perhaps they are here for another reason. Maybe they are not after us. I must get to a doctor."

Gonzales looked at Padro. It was obvious he needed help right away. He slid off his horse and helped Padro down.

They eased toward the saloon, with Gonzales half-carrying Padro. They had gone only a few feet when they were spotted.

"Hold it right there!" called a state officer.

Padro and Manuel ducked down into the brush.

"Padro Sanchez and Manuel Gonzales! You are wanted on warrants for kidnapping and unlawful restraint. Come out of those bushes nice and easy. We don't want to kill you."

Tired and injured, Sanchez and Gonzales rose from the ground and stepped into the open where they could be seen. They wanted no part of a shoot out.

"What happened to you, Sanchez?" asked an Arizona State Policeman.

Padro reached up and held his shoulder, his face grimacing in pain. "I have a little hunting accident, Señor. My shoulder, it has a bullet in it. I think I need to see a doctor very soon."

Agent Long had heard the officer's commands and came out of the building. He walked over to where they stood. "We'll see to that later, Padro," he said. "Right now, you and Gonzales there are under arrest for the kidnapping and unlawful restraint of Laura Pratt."

Long turned to an Arizona State Policeman. "Handcuff those two and read 'em their rights. Be careful, they don't look like much now, but, from what I hear, they'll kill you without batting an eye." He pointed to Padro. "That one cut a man's head off just three days ago. Right, Padro?"

Padro dropped his head, "Awe, Señor, she make me do it," he said, as he was being guided toward a squad car. "But it is okay, Señor, he was already dead."

When the two were safely tucked away in separate squad cars, Long went inside to make sure everything had been completed. He particularly wanted to make sure they had processed the room where Laura Pratt had been kept hostage.

Long walked over to the table where Basker and Blackhorse sat with Big Alice. "Charles, we just nabbed Sanchez and Gonzales outside. Want to keep them separated until they can be questioned?"

Basker nodded. "You and the state boys take them on in to the federal building. We'll be along later."

"We'll have to stop by the hospital. Sanchez caught a bullet in the shoulder somewhere up on the mountain. He said it was a hunting accident."

Blackhorse grinned. "Five dollars says they tangled with those greenhorns up there."

"That would be my guess," Basker replied. He turned to Long. "Leave a couple of men and cars to secure the property. On the way in, see what you can get out of Sanchez and Gonzales."

Inside the helicopter, Blackhorse sat across from Big Alice. He turned so he could watch her. The flight to Phoenix would be short but it might give him enough time to convince her it would be in her best interest to cooperate. "Alice, the officer has already read you the Miranda warning of your rights," said Blackhorse. "Would you talk to me about Laura Pratt? She did say you were nice to her after a while. Even saved her life."

Big Alice continued gazing out the window. Finally she answered. "I got nothing to say to you without my lawyer."

"Suit yourself, Alice," Blackhorse said. He knew he couldn't go further now that she had told him she wouldn't talk without her lawyer. Anything she said wouldn't be allowed in court. The great Miranda Decision by the US. Supreme Court had seen to that. Many a guilty person had walked free since that blow against law enforcement was enacted. The only hope Blackhorse had now was a voluntary statement. He waited, listening for any word from her that could be used. Although he pretended to ignore her, he was mentally locked in on every move she made.

While the miles slipped past, Alice continued to look out the window into the darkness. She wondered if this would be the last time she would ever see the mountain. She hated the thought of that. She had grown to love this place. "That little girl was a nice kid," she said, without turning her head. "Rockford had no business doing what he did to her, then dumping her off on me. He's got some kind of sex hang up. He likes to rape nice wholesome women. Won't have nothing to do with whores. Sometimes I think he's crazy."

Blackhorse turned quickly in his seat to see if Basker had heard what she said.

Basker gave him a thumbs up sign.

Blackhorse had what he needed. But yet he waited.

Big Alice continued to stare out the side window. "I don't know why I let it happen," she said. "Reckon I was afraid he'd tell his partner, that old Sheriff Wilkins a bunch of lies and I'd go to prison. They is partners, you know?"

"We found that out, Alice," Blackhorse replied. "I'm just glad you stood between Rockford and Laura. Shows you've got more spunk in your little finger than he has in his whole body."

Big Alice turned to face Blackhorse. "He's a killer, Mister Blackhorse. Don't ever think he ain't. Won't do it himself. Sends his men to do it - like Tom Davis."

"What about Tom Davis?" Blackhorse asked.

"Rockford sent him out to kill Laura a couple nights back. He had a knife against Laura's throat and was in the process of raping her when Padro separated him from the hand holding that knife. Bastard was on the floor with his arm squirting blood all over, when he pulled a gun and was trying to shoot Padro. I blasted his ass with my shotgun. It was self-defense, you know."

"What happened to Davis' body?"

"Padro drug it off up the mountain a ways and left it without a head, so's they'd think it was the crazy mountain man that got him."

Blackhorse didn't say anything more, but kept eye contact with her. She was on a roll and he didn't want to do anything to cause her to clam up again.

Big Alice continued. "Anyways, I guess I'm just as guilty as they are. Sho, I kept her here against her will, but Rockford wanted to kill her. Let me tell you, Mister Blackhorse, there wasn't gonna be nobody kill that girl. Not while I was alive."

"I can believe that, Alice," Blackhorse said.

"I want you to know, Mister Blackhorse, that I was good to her. Wouldn't let nobody touch her. I tried to get her to eat right and all. Gave her some good clothes to wear. I wasn't all bad."

"That was good of you, Alice," Blackhorse replied. "She told us that in her statement. She said if it hadn't been for you, she would be dead. That even though you held her prisoner, you saved her life more than once. That'll set well with any judge or jury."

She turned back to looking out the window. "It looks like I'm gonna need someone's help."

Blackhorse sat looking at the back of the big woman's head. *I almost feel sorry for the old gal. Maybe she could have been a good person. Maybe led a decent life if it hadn't been for the lure of the Dutchman's Gold. But then again.... maybe not.*

He reached over and patted the big woman's arm. "I'm sure the judge will take all that into consideration at your trial. Probably cut a lot of time off whatever sentence you get." He turned and settled back in his seat. He stared out his window, a smile on his face. He had just gotten his voluntary statement. Now he could hardly wait to get Alice locked away so he could get on with the search for Rockford before he snatched someone else.

71

Rockford licked the salt from his hand, tossed down a shot of tequila, and bit into a bitter lemon. He and Dan Wiscoff were enjoying the company of two local girls in a saloon in Sonora, Mexico, a far cry from Mexico City where authorities were searching for them. Rockford was fidgety. "It's been a week now. Maybe the law has given up and left. I have a lot of money stashed at the ranch. I need to sneak in and grab it. Maybe make some quick arrangements to sell the ranch and head back here. Start anew."

"I don't know, Boss. Those federal boys never give up. They're probably still staking your ranch out."

"Maybe Sheriff Wilkins could help. He could at least tell us what the hell is going on."

"Your helicopter is too well known to be flying around up there. Every lawman in the county knows it," Wiscoff said.

"That's true." Rockford answered. He sat staring into the tequila glass. He looked up at Wiscoff. "We'll get the bastard painted!"

"That might work. They'd be looking for a blue one."

"We'll paint it bright red and white."

"That's a good color. Might work. At least we could get Tom Davis and bring him down here. Bet he's scared shitless."

"Tom knows to head on down this way," said Rockford. "He's got plenty of money. He should have been here days ago. Maybe he screwed up and let Big Alice catch him." Rockford downed his drink and stood up. "Well?"

"Well what?"

"Let's go get that paint job and head for Arizona."

72

$\mathbb{C}$lay's eyelids grew heavy as the first light of dawn become visible. He stood up, stretched, and nearly screamed from pain that shot through his shoulder. He had forgotten about it. As the pain eased up, he looked around. He saw no movement. Satisfied they were alone, he walked over to check on Virgil. He was still unconscious. Clay shook his head. They had waited too late to get off the mountain. Now, one of them was dying. He managed to control his emotions and hold back the tears. He walked over to Brian. "How's the leg, Brian?"

Brian eased into a sitting position. It was apparent he was in deep pain. "It'll be okay, Clay. I'll make it."

Clay patted him on the shoulder. "Good."

"Time to rise and shine, folks. We have a long walk ahead of us today."

Stiff, slow, and grumpy, Brenda, Rob, and Ken crawled from under torn blankets and ripped canvas covers. Beds of stone had not helped their aching muscles.

With his arms crossed and a defiant look on his sleepy face, Ken announced, "I'm going nowhere without my morning coffee!"

"Finding some coffee will be tricky," Clay said and started searching through the debris for the coffee can.

Rob built a fire. By the time it was burning good, Clay handed him a large tin of coffee. "This is all there is left," he said.

Soon the aroma of coffee filled the air.

"How about some bacon and eggs to go with that coffee, Ken," Rob teased.

Ken grinned, "Make 'em over easy."

Rob chuckled. "They'll be ready in two minutes. Get up and wash your dirty hands."

Brenda was busy checking Brian's leg. She cleaned the wound and put on a new bandage. "How'd you sleep last night?"

"Same as anyone with a bone gouging hell out of them, I guess," Brian said, grimacing when he tried to move the broken leg.

Clay and Rob walked around the campsite to survey the damage in daylight. The two huge explosions had destroyed everything.

Clay was tense. They had to get out of there and right away. He knew whoever had set the dynamite would be back. He searched around for anything he could salvage. "I know we need to get moving. We have to get Virgil and Brian to a hospital, but we also have to try to find some supplies to take with us or we'll die out there in that damned desert."

"I'll go fetch the others," Rob said.

Everyone spread out searching for anything they could salvage. They managed to salvage a few canned goods and a couple canteens of water.

Rob, searching under the tents, came up with a large coil of undamaged rope. He smiled. As Clay had said earlier, you never know when rope will come in handy.

Clay walked around the campsite for the last time. He picked up a piece of the helicopter that looked like part of the radio transmitter, but it was shattered. Clay stood staring at it, an idea forming. *Where's the automatic transmitter for a downed aircraft? I wished Virgil were conscious. He'd know where it is, or if there even was one on this Huey.*

Clay set the transmitter down on a rock and studied it for a minute. He looked around for some tools. From the scattered debris, he pulled a screwdriver and pliers. "Rob, see if you can find the helicopter battery."

"I just found it. It's beyond use - blown apart."

"Okay. See if you can find my metal detectors. They'll have batteries in 'em."

Rob found the detectors and carried them to Clay.

By now Clay had the transmitter apart and was cutting away wires. Grabbing the conventional detector, he pulled out a tray containing seven 9-volt batteries. He set these aside and grabbed the detector. From it he stripped the batteries and antennae.

"That's your new expensive detector you're tearing up there, Clay!" Rob said.

"It cost a hell of a lot less than that chopper we borrowed."

"That's for sure," Rob replied, watching Clay work. "Just what is it you're trying to make?"

"I'm going to make us a transmitter that will hopefully send out a distress signal far enough to reach an airport somewhere. Maybe someone will hear it and come searching for us."

Rob raised his eyebrows in approval. Clay being an engineer, maybe he *could* rig something up that would work.

Clay carefully cut several pieces of wire from parts of the helicopter. He stripped the insulation from some of it and wrapped the bare wire around each battery post until he had tied all the batteries together as one. He connected them to the transmitter. With a bare wire, he made the last bridge between the antenna and the transmitter. He stood back to admire his work. "Well, now," he said. "If my memory serves me correctly, this damn thing should send out a signal of distress. Rescuers will be on the way before you know it."

"Sure would beat carrying these fellas out on foot," Ken replied. "But even if it doesn't work, you've impressed the hell out of me."

Clay pulled the antenna out as far as it would go. He then fingered the toggle switch. Closing his eyes, he prayed he had done everything right. His finger flipped the switch.

A red light began blinking.

"It work, Clay?"

Clay opened his eyes and saw the red light. "Maybe it works."

"What now?"

"We wait. There's no way for us to know if it's getting out. We just have to pray it is."

Six hours later, all eyes searched the sky for planes. There hadn't been any sign so far, and it didn't look like any were coming.

Clay stood up and looked around at the others. He walked over to Virgil. "How's he doing, Brenda?"

"No change, except he feels like he's running a fever. So does Brian. We need to get them to a hospital, Clay."

Clay looked skyward. He saw nothing that even resembled a search plane. He shook his head. "Okay, get him ready to travel." He turned to the others. "Our signal must not have worked. We have to get Brian to the hospital. We walk out - again."

"Nothing new to us, huh Rob?" Ken remarked. "I think I remember doing this once before."

"Yeah, we ain't greenhorns when it comes to walking."

"Rob," said Clay, "let's see if we can put together something to carry these guys on.

Everyone started searching for pieces of the helicopter that could be used.

Clay, Ken, and Rob fashioned two travois of sorts from pieces of the helicopter's superstructure. They were light and strong. They stretched canvas from the shredded tents around the frameworks and tied them firmly in place. The two travois would be rigged with two harnesses from the canvas that one man could slip over his shoulders. When they were finished, they stepped back to look them over.

"They don't look like much, but they'll have to do," said Clay. "Let's get them loaded and get the hell out of here."

Brian and Virgil were secured to the travois with pieces of rope. Brian's leg was tied down so it could not move.

Clay slipped the harness over his shoulders and arranged it so it didn't bother his injury. He tested the pull. It was going to be hell, but there was nothing else he could do.

With Rob pulling Brian, the small troop headed out along the narrow trail leading to the desert floor. Brenda carried what little water and food they had, and Ken carried the heavy bags of gold. They were on constant lookout for the blue helicopter, Big Alice's men, or any other lurking enemy. They knew they could trust no one.

Clay and Rob's muscles strained under their load, and the sun was unmerciful. Soaked with sweat, they trudged on through the weeds, grimacing at the sharp raking of thorns across their flesh. Small rocks they stepped on hurt their feet through their boot soles. Never had Clay labored under such a strain. His shoulders were already rubbed raw and ached from the harness.

Rob toiled along behind Clay pulling his load with the same effects. Neither man complained. There was nothing to say. It was this way or their friends would die.

Clay had to call frequent breaks. His eyes were in constant search of the sky for airplanes or helicopters. As he wiped the salty sweat from his eyes, he searched for a place to get out of the sun for just a few minutes.

At every break, Brenda passed around a canteen of water and examined her injured patients, especially making sure the bleeding of Virgil's head injury had not started up again. She also knew that with an unattended compound fracture such as Brian's, it was not uncommon for a person to bleed to death.

Clay took the canteen from Brenda as she held it out to him. "How much water do we have left?" he asked.

"Not very much."

Clay only wet his lips. He wanted the water saved for the injured men.

Clay looked at Brenda. She was really holding up better than he had expected, but he knew she had to be hurting from the concussion of the explosion and the long, hot trek down the mountain. She hadn't complained one time. Not a word since the explosion. Not since they had been in the helicopter. *Damn! What should I do? What can I do? I need to say something.*

Finally, he got the nerve. "Brenda, about last night,..."

Brenda stepped up to him and put her finger to his lips. "Shhh. There's nothing to say, Clay. It shouldn't have happened, but it did. We just have to make sure it doesn't happen again."

He pulled her to his chest and held her tightly. "Maybe in another time...maybe...maybe.."

They stood holding each other and rocking slightly side to side. Both knew whatever had almost happened was over, but they also knew there would always be something special between them, including an everlasting friendship.

The scorching sun showed them no mercy as it beat down upon them. What little wind there was, brushed hot against their bare skin.

Ken dropped the heavy gold and slumped to the ground to rest in the shade of a tall Saguaro cactus. He wiped the sweat from his forehead as he watched Clay and Rob ease the travois down in patches of shade from stubby pinion pine trees.

"They shoot a horse that breaks its leg, Brian," Rob said nonchalantly, winking at Brenda who had dropped into the shade beside him.

Brian pulled his pistol and placed it across his broken leg. "Any takers?" he asked gruffly. When no one spoke, he grinned and went on. "We'll hear no more of that talk, or someone will be carrying your ass from here on."

Ken tossed a canteen of water to Brian. "You're uglier than a horse anyway. No one could stand to shoot such a pitiful looking critter."

Clay put his finger to his lips. "Shhhhh!" he said, pointing in the direction he was looking.

All eyes followed and came to rest upon a wild burro standing in a small clearing a few yards away.

Clay tried to move slowly as he hastened to get the rope Rob had been carrying.

"Where you going?" asked Rob.

"I'm going to catch one of those burros and load old Brian here and the gold on it."

"Those are wild burros, Clay," Ken whispered. "Not trained pack animals. You can't catch one, let alone break it to carry a load."

"You can do anything if you set your mind to it," Clay said, uncoiling his rope. "Now you just hide and watch." Bending at the waist, Clay stepped into the brush and inched closer to the burro.

The others watched and shook their heads in wonder. Every time he got near one of the skittish animals, it walked off a little and stood looking back at him. This game of cat and mouse went on for well over a half-hour.

Finally, Rob stood up. "I think I'll give him a hand. Who knows, maybe he's got something there."

Ken struggled to his feet and followed.

They walked slowly so as to not frighten the animals into a run. By spreading their arms and making slight motions, they were able to move a few of the burros between them and the rock wall. With no place to go, the animals stopped and watched them.

Clay eased in, speaking softly to the burros. When he was within a few feet of a big black one, his arm shot out like a lightning bolt and the rope snaked around the surprised burro's neck.

The burro stood still for an instant.

Clay gently pulled on the rope.

The burro exploded into orbit, leaping, rolling, kicking, and running, all the while braying loudly.

All Clay could do was hang on. The burro was dragging him along as if he were weightless.

Rob ran after him, grabbing the rope and setting his heels in the sand.

It slowed the burro's movements, but, even with both men on the rope, it managed to drag them around, fighting every step of the way.

Loud braying echoed through the canyon walls and the dust rose high as the burro struggled with its captors.

Clay glanced at Ken through the dust as he and Rob were dragged past. "Grab the damned rope and help us!"

With three men pulling, they were able to get the rope wrapped around a strong stubby pinion pine tree and slowly draw the burro tightly up against it. This prevented him from jumping, but his hind legs were pistons in constant motion.

"Best stay clear of those little hooves," Clay gasped, trying to catch his breath. "They'll cut you to pieces."

When the burro was secure, Rob looked at Clay, "What now, cowboy?"

"How 'bout catching another one?" Ken replied.

Clay stared out into the sagebrush. "The others are long gone. One will have to do."

Rob looked at him. "Now you're going to ride him, right?"

"Bullshit!" Clay whispered through labored breathing. "I'm not riding that damn thing."

"Well, somebody's gonna have to ride it," Rob said.

"Well, it doesn't have to be me," Clay said, stubbornly crossing his arms over his chest. He looked at Ken and Brenda.

Brenda threw up both hands. "Don't look at me. I do nursing, not wild horses."

"It ain't a damned horse, Brenda." Clay looked again at Rob.

Rob shook his head. "Sorry, pal. Big as I am, I'd break that little thing's back."

"I get the message loud and clear. You're all yellow, clear through."

Ken stood up, hiked up his jeans, rolled up his sleeves, pretended to spit tobacco juice, and said in his best John Wayne, "Gimme your spurs, Pilgrim. I reckon this here's a job for a man."

Rob looked at Clay with surprise and shrugged.

They watched Ken edge nearer to the burro. Its eyes rolled back watching his every move.

"No spurs, Ken," Rob said. "Lost them on our last trip through the desert."

"That figures."

Ken reached out to touch the animal.

The burro sprang straight up and began its desperate struggle all over again.

Ken jumped back and waited for the beast to stop. "Give him a little more rope. Let him get away from the bush," Ken said.

Rob and Clay played out a few feet of rope and the burro pulled away. It stood clear.

Ken eased up beside the beast without touching it. He stood for a moment, made the sign of a cross over his chest and flung himself astride the burro. Grabbing what mane it had, he locked his long legs around its middle just as it dropped its head low and erupted into action.

Jumping, bucking, twisting, and braying, the terrified burro ploughed into every sagebrush and cactus it could find trying to scrape Ken off its back.

Rob was trying hard to maintain his hold on the rope as it gradually slipped from his grasp.

"Ride 'em, cowboy!" Brenda yelled from the sideline.

Ken did an excellent job for about the length of time it would take for the whistle to blow in a professional rodeo, then he flew through the air.

All eyes were on him as he made a perfect arc and landed in a batch of spiny cactus. He yelped like a wild coyote caught in a steel trap.

Rob ran to help him while Clay grabbed the rope and brought the burro under control.

Ken had a backside full of cactus spines. He wrenched in pain as Brenda bent him over a large rock and started plucking the needles from his rear end.

Clay handed the end of the rope to Rob and walked toward the burro. It was his turn, and he figured he might just as well get it over with. Cautiously, he approached the animal.

Its eyes rolled wildly as it watched him.

Extending his arm out as far as it would go, he inched forward until he stood beside the burro. Closing his eyes, he jumped, landing belly down on the burro's back just as it jumped.

Clay flung his arms around its neck and held on tightly as it reared, bucked, and fishtailed in the air, then he felt himself slipping. He clenched his eyes shut and held on tighter. He slid off the burro's back and found himself hanging under its neck. He maintained his death grip as the burro twisted and flopped him around like a sack of potatoes - narrowly missing Clay's feet each time he planted his front hooves.

The very sight of Clay and the burro was so comical that even Ken, still rubbing his own aching rear, was laughing.

"Let go, Clay!" Rob yelled. "Let go!"

While Clay was giving the advice a lot of thought, the burro reached the end of the rope and was jerked around. It ran the opposite direction, and Clay took Rob's advice. He let go.

The burro was running full steam ahead as it stampeded over Clay like a speeding locomotive, each hoof coming down hard on different parts of his body. He screamed when a hoof caught him between the legs, then gurgled when the last hoof slammed down squarely on his chest, knocking the wind from him.

Ken and Brenda ran to him.

His eyes were extremely wide. His mouth agape. He tried to suck in air. Strange noises emitted from his mouth.

Just when they thought he was going to pass out, he gasped loudly and sucked in a long breath of air. Slowly, he regained his normal breathing rhythm and lay there staring up at their smiling faces.

They helped him to his feet

Clay looked around for the burro. It stood with all four legs spread apart, its head drooped almost to the ground and its tongue hanging out. He pointed to it. "Get a pack on it," he said hoarsely. "I think we're both broke."

"WHHOOOOOO! WHHOOOOOO! WHHOOOOOO!"

All eyes went to a tall saguaro, and there perched the old owl. It sounded like he was laughing.

"Thanks a lot, pal," Clay said, rubbing his aching crotch.

Rob tied off his end of the rope and grabbed a roll of canvas.

Clay hurried to where Brian lay on the travois. He grabbed the harness and pulled it toward the burro. "Hurry, Ken, let's get this travois tied on him while he's worn down, maybe he'll accept it." Moving slowly and with gentle talk, Rob slipped the canvas straps over the burro's head and tied them securely around his neck and through his front legs with more strips of canvas. The metal braces on the travois were pulled up on either side of the burro and secured to the harness.

Weakly, the burro tried to raise its head. It kicked one leg in resistance, then stood still.

Rob and Ken tied the bags of gold together with rope and slid them over its back, three on each side.

The burro didn't move.

Reaching down, Clay patted him on the hindquarters. "That's not so bad, is it, old boy?" He walked to the burro's head and softly rubbed it between the ears. "We only need your help for a day, or so," he whispered. "Then I'll turn you loose again. How's that? You help us get out of this hellhole you call home, and we'll let you go," said Clay, rubbing his sore crotch again. "And if you don't, I'll personally shoot you right between the eyes and sell your mangy hide to the glue factory."

The burro rolled up its eyes at Clay's words, but stood still.

Clay looked at Brian. "You ready to give it a go? "

"Just don't let him kick me to death with those hind feet," said Brian.

Ken took charge of the lead rope on the burro. "I'll handle him while you two take turns with Virgil." Ken tugged on the lead rope.

The burro moved its feet around slightly but didn't buck.

Hooking himself up to the harness on Virgil's travois, Clay motioned for them to head out.

"You guys just take it easy. If this jackass runs away with me tied to it, it'll drag me to death," Brian said.

"I'll be right here all the time," Ken promised, getting a good grip on the lead rope.

Clay, Rob, and Ken shook each other's hands. They had accomplished another difficult task in the wilderness.

"Great idea, Clay," said Rob.

As they headed on down the trail, Clay looked back to see if the owl was still on its perch. It was gone.

73

Chief Dennis Blackhorse was just preparing to leave the office for the day when the phone rang. "Chief Blackhorse here."

"Chief, this is dispatch. The airport called and said they've been receiving some sort of distress signal since early morning. Maybe from a downed aircraft, but they have none missing. Got any ideas?"

"Where're the signals coming from?"

"From the area of Superstition Mountain, they think."

Blackhorse thought for a minute. "That's got to be those treasure hunters up there. Keep me posted if anything else happens."

The chief hung up and quickly dialed a number. "Agent Basker, please. This is Chief Dennis Blackhorse over in Apache Junction." he waited for the connection. "Charles. Dennis Blackhorse here."

"You're calling to tell me you have Rockford locked up!"

"Not that lucky. But there is something going on up in the mountains. Phoenix Airport has been getting some kind of distress signal all morning from up on Superstition Mountain, but they have nothing missing. I think it's our boys who have either crashed or are in some type of trouble."

"Couldn't be lucky enough for it to be Rockford who crashed," said Basker.

"Think you can get the helicopter again and see if we can trace that signal?"

"We can't get it until tomorrow. How about nine o'clock at your airfield? Who knows, we might get lucky."

"Have you guys had any word from Mexico?" asked Blackhorse.

"Got word from our people down there that he was spotted in Sonora with his helicopter and pilot, but he disappeared before the authorities could get him."

"That's a long way from Mexico City."

"Yeah, and it was just yesterday," said Basker.

"Think he might be coming back here? Sonora is near the border."

"Who knows about a guy like that," said Basker. "He's smart, but if he's like the ones in the past, he's got a few screws loose that cause him to do things irrationally. That's been the downfall of many a criminal."

"I'd like to get that bastard so we can wind up this case, but mostly before he can kidnap another girl," Blackhorse said.

"See you tomorrow."

74

Blistering heat engulfed the treasure hunters as they moved slowly along the narrow path, etched into the mountainside by the travels of wild animals and years of erosion.

Clay, now leading the way, mopped his brow with one hand and wielded a long stick with the other as he moved brush aside, ever watchful for snakes.

"Whhoooooo! Whhoooooo! Whhoooooo!"

Clay froze at the sound. Just ahead of him, in the middle of the path, perched the owl. The hair on the back of his neck stood up as a sense of fear came over him. The owl was blocking his way. It didn't move. Something was wrong. He held up his hand for the others to stop.

They saw the owl. Drawing their guns, they searched for the danger he was warning them of.

Rob eased Virgil's travois from his shoulders and slipped out of the harness. Brenda knelt beside it as Rob drew his pistol and went to help Clay.

Clay turned his head slowly, his eyes darting from one bush to another and on to the boulders scattered about. He searched for any sign of danger. Frustrated, he looked back at the owl. He was still there. "Damn! What do we do?" he said. "I know you're trying to tell us something, but what?"

The owl flew up and over the top of a huge boulder beside the trail.

Clay's eyes darted to it. *That's where the trouble is. Someone is behind that big rock. Danger of some kind is behind that rock.* He hesitated for a time. Taking off his dynamite tattered hat, he slipped it on the end of the stick and eased it out ahead of him at an upward angle. The hat jiggled under his trembling guidance as he stepped slowly forward. The hat was at the center of the boulder.

Without warning, a huge steel blade swung through the air and neatly cut the thick stick off just below the hat.

Clay yelled and dropped to the ground, drawing his pistol as a barrage of shots rang out from behind him, and slugs bounced off the rock in all directions.

Clay held up his hand. The shooting stopped.

When the sound of the shots faded, they could hear crashing of dead brush as someone ran away from the boulder. A loud, hideous laugh echoed through the canyon.

The men listened spellbound until it faded away in the distance.

Clay wiped his sweaty face, shaking uncontrollably. That stick could very well have been his neck, but for the owl. He looked around for him, but saw only the owl perched on a nearby cactus.

Rob came to stand over him, his pistol drawn and eyes searching everywhere. "You alright, Clay?"

"I think so," Clay said, slowly getting to his feet and staring at the spot where the owl had been. "Son-of-a-bitch! Why does it do that?"

"Do what, Clay?"

"Show up, and then just up and disappear!"

Rob shrugged. "Maybe it really is a spirit," he said, still searching the rocks and brush for the crazy man with the big blade.

"I'll bet whoever that bastard was, he's the one that got old Crazy Norman," Clay said, as he picked up his now shorter stick and examined it. "Let's get the hell out of here before there's more trouble."

Each man, gun in hand, eased along the trail with their loads, eyes scanning every bush, rock, cactus, and pine tree for signs of movement. They gave wide berth to large boulders, for fear the crazy man might be lurking behind them.

Just as the sun disappeared behind a mountaintop to the west, Clay stopped. "We'll rest here for the night."

They were exhausted beyond belief. While Rob eased his load to the ground, Ken and Clay pulled the travois from the burro. Once they had Brian laid out on the ground, they pulled the heavy sacks of gold from the burro's back.

Free of the load, the little burro shook itself and rolled in the sand.

Brenda passed around a canteen of water.

Clay took a long drink then poured water into his hat and let the burro drink. He patted its oversized head. "You did good, old boy. Just another day or so and you'll be free again."

Ken dug through the makeshift pack and came up with a canned ham. He cut it into equal shares and passed it around. There was no bread. "We have some beans if anyone wants them." He got no takers.

Clay looked at Brenda. She was exhausted, but had not complained at all. He knew she was stretching her limits. "You doing okay, Brenda?" he asked.

"Having a ball." She managed a smile. "One thing about being with you guys, there's never a dull moment."

"You got that right," Clay answered. "At least on this trip."

"We call it an adventure," Ken said. "We're having us an adventure. Right Clay?"

Clay gave Ken a scornful look, but didn't answer.

Brenda passed the canteen around for the second time.

As each man took his turn at watch during the night, a chorus of howling coyotes in the distance kept them company.

75

There was barely enough light from the coming dawn over Nogales, Mexico to see as Wiscoff stood back and admired the new red paint job on his helicopter. "Not bad," he said. "Not bad at all."

Rockford stood nearby haggling with the painter. "Seems a little high for a lousy paint job," Rockford said.

"The charge, Señor, is high because you wake me in the middle of the night and want it painted right away," the painter explained. "Where else can you get that done so quickly? I must charge you for keeping me and my people awake all night. Si?"

"Si! Si! Yeah, yeah, yeah. Just give me my change and I'm on my way."

"No tip, Señor?"

"Hell, no, no tip!" Rockford snarled. He turned to Wiscoff. "Dan, bring your piece over here and talk to this man. He's giving me a hard time."

Wiscoff pulled the automatic pistol from his shoulder holster and walked toward them.

Now the Mexican couldn't count out the change fast enough. "Here, Señor. All your change. Take it and go. Please!"

Rockford laughed as he walked toward the helicopter. Wiscoff followed, putting away his gun as he climbed in. "Where to, Boss?"

"My ranch first. I hope there's nobody there. I really need to get that money."

Rockford sat thinking while Wiscoff cranked up the engine and lifted the helicopter off the ground. His mind always jumped to the greenhorns up on the mountain. If they had not shown up, he would have had none of this trouble. They had ruined him.

"Maybe we'll even go up and see what happened to the farm," Rockford said, as the chopper leveled off. "Maybe even pay those greenhorns a visit!"

At five thousand feet, Wiscoff pushed the helicopter to cruising speed and headed north across the border toward Apache Junction.

76

$\mathbb{C}$lay blew into his cupped hands and rubbed them together, trying to keep them warm. It had gotten cold during the night, and he found himself actually looking forward to seeing the sun despite its miserable heat. He kept his eyes on the eastern sky. When he could see the outlines of the tall saguaro cacti, he decided it was time to move on. "Time to get up," he yelled. "The sun will be blazing hot in a little while. Maybe we can cover some ground while it's cool for a change."

Grumbling to themselves, they slowly got to their feet and loaded the burro.

Brenda checked Brian's leg and gave it the okay. She then checked Virgil.

Clay walked over and stood beside her. "How's he doing, Brenda?"

"Well, he still hasn't regain consciousness, but all his vital signs are good. He must have really taken a blow."

Clay knelt beside his friend. "Look here, old boy. You better snap out of it or we'll be back in town and you'll miss all this fun we're having."

Clay rose to his feet and started getting things ready to move out. With any luck, they would make the desert floor by dark. Then it was only a hop, skip, and jump to town.

Their progress was slow, but the hours passed. They were easing along the base of a steep cliff, and now and then a loose rock would give way above and come crashing down at the sweaty group. Each time, they would dive for the ground and cover their heads.

All except Brian and Virgil, who were tied on the travois. They could only close their eyes and wait for the rocks to land.

When it was safe, they continued on their way.

77

Chief Blackhorse had come in earlier than usual. He had been unable to sleep, anxious to get in the air. He read the daily reports and drank his morning coffee. When he flipped the last report onto the stack, he glanced at his watch. It was five after nine. He told Basker he would meet them at the airport at nine. "Shit! I'm late." He grabbed his hat and rushed out.

Flipping on his red light, he made the trip in record time. At the airport, he pulled his car out onto the field and drove directly to the waiting helicopter. Beside it stood Basker and Long, both pointing to their watches.

"I know! I know!" Blackhorse apologized, bailing out of his car on the run. "I'm running late."

The three lawmen scrambled into the helicopter, and the pilot, Justin Fletcher, lifted it off.

"Nice bunch of guys, those treasure hunters," Basker said. "Rescuing that girl like that took a lot of spunk."

"Makes you feel good knowing we got one back alive," said Blackhorse.

"Sure does. She was lucky alright. A hundred others out there won't be coming home," Basker paused. "Lots of disappearances are the result of drugs, " he continued. "That's why I get satisfaction from my job every time I snatch a dealer off the street."

Long stared out the window. "Those treasure hunters have sure got a lot of guts to go back up there after all that's happened to them," he said.

"They've sure changed my mind about city folks," Blackhorse replied. He looked out the window, then at his watch. "It's about a 15 minute run to Weaver's needle."

78

$\mathbb{F}$lying high over his ranch, Rockford could see that there was a state police car parked in his driveway. The two officers leaning against it were shading their eyes as they looked up at the red helicopter. "Get the hell out of here before they get a look at us through binoculars," Rockford shouted at Wiscoff.

Quickly Wiscoff banked away.

"Head straight for Big Alice's saloon. At least we can see if Davis did his job right."

Bringing the helicopter around, Wiscoff headed it in the direction of the saloon. Both men searched the ground below for anything unusual - roadblocks or a large gathering of police cars.

Fifteen minutes later, they hovered high above Big Alice's saloon. Rockford looked down on the deserted-looking building. He couldn't see any cars. He motioned for Wiscoff to take the chopper down.

They glided lower. Suddenly, Rockford saw the tops of two cars hidden behind the building. Rockford picked up his binoculars and stared at the cars. "Police cars!" he said. "Son-of-a-bitch! They're everywhere. Get out of here! Quick!"

Wiscoff lifted the chopper straight up and headed for the mountaintop. "I told you the DEA don't give up easy. Them bastards hang onto a case like leeches."

Visibly shaken, Rockford knew he had no place to go. The law was everywhere. He knew there was no need to try for the money now. They would have already found his safe at the ranch. Damn! If those bastards found my money, they've got me for nearly a million dollars cash. All he had to his name was the money he took from the farm safe and a few thousand in the bank down in Mexico. Bastards will probably find that too. Grabbing his mobile telephone, he called the Pinal County Sheriff's Office. "Let me speak to the Sheriff!" he demanded.

"Hello. This is the Sheriff. Who's speaking, please?" Jesse Richmond said on the other end.

Rockford held out the phone and stared at it. Finally he spoke, "Where's Sheriff Wilkins?"

"This is Sheriff Jesse Richmond. Wilkins is no longer sheriff here. Who am I speaking with?"

Rockford hung up the phone. "Dammit to hell, they've even got the sheriff!"

He sat thinking for a minute then threw the phone down. "Dammit all!" he screamed, pounding his fists on the dash. "Fly over the farm. Maybe they didn't get to it. Maybe some of the guys are still there."

Wiscoff headed for the farm.

Minutes later, they were hovering overhead. There was nothing left. The buildings had been blown up, and even the debris from them had been burned.

Rockford motioned for Wiscoff to fly away. He sank back in his seat and stared out the window. He was defeated.

Minutes went by, then suddenly he slapped Wiscoff on the shoulder. "Look down there!" he pointed to all the rubble in the treasure hunters' camp.

"They crashed their helicopter!" he laughed crazily. "At least something good has been happening."

"I don't see any bodies down there, Boss."

"Search along that trail. I want to find those bastards."

Searching the ground below them as they flew, it wasn't long before Rockford motioned toward the ground. "Down there! Get down there! I want to see if that's those damn greenhorns!"

The red helicopter swept low over the treasure hunters.

"That's them!" Rockford shouted, his eyes wide with excitement. "Take her back around and let's get rid of those bastards once and for all! They've cost me everything I own! Now it's time I made them pay."

Wiscoff was reluctant. "Boss, don't you think we ought to be heading on back to Mexico?"

"Head for Mexico? What the hell are you talking about? Those bastards down there ruined me, and you want to head for Mexico? Run away? Hell, no! Now do as I say, or I'll -I'll..." Rockford pulled a pistol from his belt and pointed it at Wiscoff. "I'll blow your damned head off where you sit!"

Wiscoff could see Rockford was losing it. "Okay! Okay! Don't get excited, Boss. I was just trying to help."

"Don't help. Just do as you're told!"

A tired Clay, with the harness of Virgil's travois over his shoulders, stopped to watch the red helicopter closely as it banked around and headed back for them. He knew something was wrong. The helicopter was the same shape as Rockford's, just a different color. He could have painted it.

"It's Rockford!" he yelled. "Head for cover!" He pulled hard against the harness to make cover behind some large boulders before the helicopter got there. He had only a minute or two.

Rob pulled on the halter of the burro to get it moving faster as he hurried after Clay.

The chopper was getting closer.

Clay dropped Virgil behind a boulder and out of view under a palo verde tree. He ran back to Brian, quickly untied his leg and pulled him from the travois and behind a boulder. "Stay down."

Rob, Brenda, and Ken had already hit the dirt, crawling for anything they could hide behind.

In the helicopter, Rockford grabbed an AR-15 assault rifle and leaned out the door, as they approached the group.

Hanging halfway out the door, he fired a spray of bullets at the men below.

Dirt, rocks, and brush flew into the air as the bullets struck the ground around the treasure hunters.

Rockford managed a second burst as they banked away.

Everyone hid behind a rock, a tree, or a thick bush. They drew their pistols and waited as they watched the helicopter make a wide circle and head back toward them.

"I know we don't want to kill anybody," Clay said, "but we're going to get killed if we don't do something. And do it quick." He pointed to the helicopter. "I say we fight that bastard to the end."

"We'd better make our mind up soon," Virgil yelled. They're coming back."

Dumbstruck, Clay jerked his head around. That was Virgil's voice. He quickly crawled toward the boulder he was behind. Brenda was already there.

Pausing on all fours, Clay stared at his friend. The burden on his heart lifted. He grinned. "Good to have you back among us, Virgil. How are you feeling, anyway?"

"I guess I'm okay, except for this broken arm. Just sit me up and hand me my pistol."

Now Clay was excited and scared at the same time. "Brenda, give him a hand, while I go see if I can stop that helicopter."

"Let's do it!" Rob shouted from behind a boulder.

The helicopter was upon them. In desperation, they opened fire. Bullets struck the hull a number of times.

Rockford had second thoughts. "Get back out of range. They'll knock us down if you don't."

Wiscoff banked the chopper away, circling out over the valley.

Jumping to his feet, Clay yelled, "Let's get moving! We have about two or three minutes to find another place to hide. We can't stay out here in the open." He backed away watching the helicopter. "Head for the cliff's edge. Maybe that'll keep them at bay for a while."

When he got to Virgil, he helped him to his feet and they struggled toward the cliff.

Brenda followed, carrying everything she could.

Rob grabbed Brian around the waist and literally carried him as he ran. "Can't leave you out here alone, old boy."

Ken caught up, and, with one of Brian's arms over each of their shoulders, they dragged him down a slope.

Clay eased Virgil down and ran along the wall looking for a place to stand off their attackers. He heard the noise of the chopper grow louder. He looked up to see the helicopter appear above the slope. "Down! Down! Down!" he shouted, diving for the sandy trail.

Rockford once again let loose a barrage of fire that sent bullets slamming into the rocks, pinning the men down. He laughed as he watched the men below huddle behind rocks and bushes. His gun locked open. It was empty. He grabbed another clip and jammed it into the gun. He could see the men below jump to their feet and return fire. A bullet slammed through the front glass.

Wiscoff quickly banked the helicopter out of range.

"Whhoooooo! Whhoooooo! Whhoooooo!"

Clay heard the hooting and raised up from his cover. He searched for the owl. Instead, he saw the Indian standing against the cliff a few yards away. Clay's brows drew together. What was the old man trying to tell them now? The danger from the helicopter was obvious, so it had to be something else.

Clay looked to the sky. He saw the helicopter bank around and head back toward them. He turned back just in time to see the buckskin back of the Indian disappear into the side of the cliff.

Grabbing Virgil up, Clay half dragged him toward the rock, frantically searching the wall. He shouted to the others. "Follow me!"

Through the brush, he spotted what the Indian had been trying to show him - an opening in the wall. It was just a large crack in the cliff face, narrow at the top and wide at the bottom. There was just enough room for one man at a time to squeeze through. There was no time to be cautious. He had to get them to safety. "It's a cave!" he shouted. "Get in the cave!"

He quickly lowered Virgil to the ground and stood over him as he crawled inside the cave.

The others were close on his heels.

Clay bailed through the opening just as a hail of bullets struck all around the entrance.

"How the hell did you know this was here?" Virgil yelled, as he tried to catch his breath.

"The Indian, bless his soul, showed me the way," Clay replied, as he charged back to the entrance and opened fire at the helicopter.

"I'm not about to dispute your word now. Something pointed you in the right direction."

Rockford shouted at Wiscoff, "I'll teach these city bastards to cause me grief." He laughed and threw another burst with the AR-15 as the helicopter slid past the flat surface of the cave entrance.

Bullets bounced around the mouth to the cave. One found its way inside the cave and bounced off the walls, causing everyone to dive face first into the sandy floor.

Clay glanced around the cave. "Looks like a big bubble with only one way out. I guess we're stuck here for a while."

"At least we're out of their sight," Virgil said.

Clay sat thinking. They were safe if a stray bullet didn't get to them. He had to do something. He looked at the others. His eyes settled Virgil's big pistol.

He crawled over to him. "Give me that big gun of yours, Virge. Didn't the outfitter say it would kill your ass a mile away?"

"That he did," Virgil replied. "Why?"

"They are keeping that helicopter just out of range of our pistols. Maybe with that high-powered thing you have, I can get a shot at the pilot. I hate to hurt anyone, but it's the only way we're going to get out of here alive."

"Why you?"

"Just give me the gun, Virgil."

Virgil stared at him for a second. Clay never called him Virgil unless he was dead serious. Virgil knew not to argue. He handed Clay the 44 caliber. "Kicks like hell, Clay. Be prepared for it or it'll jump right out of your hand."

Clay took the gun and headed for the cave opening. He waited until the helicopter made another pass. When it banked away, he ran out and dove behind a boulder. He didn't think he had been seen. From this position, if they weren't shooting at him, he might be able to take better aim and hit the pilot when they got in close.

Breathlessly, he waited as he watched the red chopper approach. He shook to his very soul as he took careful aim at the pilot. *God, I hate to do this! I don't want to hurt anyone. If they'd just leave us alone...*

Bullets ricocheted off the rock wall around the opening.

That helped him make up his mind. Squinting along the sights, he squeezed the trigger. A large spider webbed hole appeared in the front windshield, but he had missed the pilot.

Glass flew through the cockpit and all over Wiscoff. "Holy shit!" he shouted. "They've got a rifle! Let's back this baby out of range."

Rockford was laughing, completely oblivious to what Wiscoff was saying. He had a wild look in his eyes. He was slipping over the deep end. Throwing all caution to the wind, his only mission now was to kill the greenhorns.

Banking the helicopter away, Wiscoff hovered just out of range as Rockford sprayed the area with bullets.

Rockford spotted the puff of smoke from Clay's pistol as he fired another shot. He giggled insanely and emptied an entire clip at the rock.

Clay buried his head in the sand and waited for the inevitable. There was nothing to do except lay low and pray.

79

T he huge gray Blackhawk helicopter buzzed the farm. There was no sign of life around. Nothing had been disturbed.

Agent Basker called out to the pilot. "Let's pay a visit to the treasure hunters' camp."

Fletcher dropped the helicopter down through the valleys and canyons, narrowly missing overhanging ridges, until they hovered above the campsite of the treasure hunters. There was nothing but debris strewn about.

"Damn, Chief!" Agent Long said. "Looks like we're too late. They've had an accident down there for sure." He pointed downward. "Those're pieces of their helicopter lying around down there. Looks like they crashed."

Blackhorse' eyes scanned the area, "I don't see any bodies, or, for that matter, any survivors."

"Set it down, Justin," said Basker. "Let's see what we can find."

A quick search was made. No bodies.

Blackhorse and Basker stood looking down at the transmitter. "Crude, but by God it worked."

Agent Long walked from the boulders. "This wasn't a crash! That chopper was blown up! Looks like someone set the charge and strung a fuse off in that direction. It burned along the ground to the helicopter and exploded. Found some blood back there a ways - somebody's injured." Long pointed down the trail. "Looks like several people headed off down that path on foot," he said. "Looks like they may be dragging something. Could be a litter from the looks of it."

They boarded the helicopter.

"Justin," Basker called to the pilot. "Let's follow that trail. Maybe we can find them."

The pilot eased the big bird up and slowly followed the path.

80

W iscoff made another pass at the cave with Rockford firing the AR-15 constantly. He looked at Rockford. He could see something had snapped in Rockford's mind. He wanted to fly away from the men below, but he was afraid to. He knew Rockford would kill him - maybe even while he was in the air. Rockford looked crazy and suicidal to him.

Rockford laughed wildly, as he dumped the empty clip and rammed another home.

Rockford wasn't satisfied with his AR-15. He tossed it in back.

"I think I have something that will end this real quick." He reached over the seat and pulled out a Laws Rocket.

He began preparing it to fire. "Swing around so I can get a clear shot at the cave. This rocket will blow it to hell and gone. Even get the one outside!"

When the helicopter was in position, Rockford took careful aim through the sights. He glanced back to make sure the back blast would miss the helicopter. He pulled the trigger. The helicopter jerked with the force of the rocket roaring away.

Rockford let out an evil chuckle as he watched the rocket explode against the face of the cliff. "Missed!" He tossed the used rocket out of the helicopter and watched it fall to the ground. He reached for another. "Good thing I brought a spare."

Below, Clay had seen the rocket blast away from the helicopter and had burrowed under the rock as far as he could. When the rocket exploded into the cliff, he was peppered with small rocks raining down. When it stopped, he looked toward the cave. He saw Virgil waving. They were okay. He turned back to Rockford.

* * *

Fletcher guided the Blackhawk helicopter around a bluff and shouted, "Chief! Down there. Have a look."

Off in the distance, they could see a red helicopter hovering above the ground and puffs of smoke coming from behind a large boulder.

"Someone on the ground is shooting at that helicopter," Basker said.

A large burst of fire and smoke came from the helicopter. A second later, the cliff face exploded.

"Damn! That was a Law's Rocket!" yelled Fletcher.

"Stop that bastard, Fletcher," Basker yelled.

Fletcher headed the chopper toward the red one as it began another run at the cliff. As he pulled up the gun sights, Fletcher's right index finger hovered over a bright red button on the end of the control stick.

Rockford swung his head to stare at the big Blackhawk.

Wiscoff was scared. "Let's go, Boss!" He was begging now. "Let's get out of here before they shoot us down!"

"Relax, Danny boy. They won't shoot!" Rockford yelled.

He glanced down at the cave. "Head this bird back for those punks. I want them to pay for what they did to me."

"To hell with you, Rockford. I don't want to die. I think you've finally cracked up!" Wiscoff said.

Rockford jerked the rocket around and placed it under Wiscoff's chin. "Do it, Wiscoff, or I'll blow you damn head off right where your sitting and we'll both die!"

Wiscoff knew it was crazy, but he had no choice. He nodded and turned the chopper to face the cliff again. He placed it into a hover mode and waited for Rockford to fire the rocket.

Fletcher placed his helicopter into hover mode watching the red helicopter. He could see it was turning to face the cliff again. Rockford was trying to get the rocket out the door. Fletcher knew he had to do something, and quick. "That bastard's pointing another Law's at those guys, Chief."

"Order them to land."

Fletcher radioed Rockford. "We are Federal Agents. Land your craft immediately!"

Down on the ground, Clay could see Rockford working on another rocket. He knew they would not survive a second rocket hit. He put the long barrel of the .44 caliber pistol on the rock to steady it. He took careful aim. The helicopter was still out of range. He looked around for the owl. "Come on, my friend," he said. "Help me just one more time."

As the helicopter got closer, it went into a hover. Clay took that opportunity to take careful aim. He could see Rockford trying to get the rocket out the door. He only had a second or two left. He remembered what Liege told them. *Relax, aim, take a deep breath, let it out, and squeeze the trigger.* Doing exactly that, Clay squeezed the trigger. A blast of smoke and fire erupted from the gun barrel and the big pistol bucked in Clay's hand. He kept his eye on Rockford. He saw Rockford jerk hard as the bullet hit him in the shoulder.

Rockford felt the bullet slam his body back against the seat. His finger jerked on the trigger. Terror seized him as the Law's Rocket fired, and the red helicopter disappeared in a huge fireball. Pieces of the helicopter flew hundreds of feet in all directions.

Basker and his crew watched in silence. They had seen the small puff of smoke from Clay's gun, then the huge fireball as the helicopter exploded and rained parts to the ground.

Basker let out a sigh of relief. "You can relax, Fletcher. Whoever's behind that boulder just caused Rockford to blow himself up. Saved us the trouble."

Blackhorse sat with his mouth open in disbelief. He had been a policeman for years and had been involved in some shootings, but never had he seen anything like this. It was over in a second. All he could say was, "By God, boys! By God, boys!"

"Someone on the ground saved us a lot of paper work, Chief," said Basker. He turned to the pilot. "Set down near those people."

Clay slowly rose to his feet. He couldn't believe what he was seeing. He looked down at the gun in his hand. "You do pack a wallop."

The others from the cave joined him. They watched in silence as the remains of the helicopter on the ground, exploded again in a fireball that changed to a mushroom shape, turned red and black, and roared upward.

"Yeeehaaa!" Rob shouted. "Clay! You did it! Man, you did it! I saw it all. You shot Rockford, and he shot down his own helicopter!"

They watched the big Blackhawk coming their way.

"That's the federal boys," said Clay, pointing to the gray helicopter. "Bet they came looking for us."

No one answered. They were all watching the fire of Rockford's helicopter die down.

The military craft set down in a small clearing near the treasure hunters.

Clay and his friends remained close to their hiding places. Just in case.

The door opened and Blackhorse jumped out.

They all gave a big sigh of relief.

"Federal agents, boys," Basker yelled. "Let's keep the hardware down range, okay?"

Clay handed Virgil back his gun. "Hell of a gun, Virge." He turned to Basker. "Sure glad to see you guys show up when you did," he said. "No telling what might have happened."

"You should thank whoever fired the last shot that hit Rockford. That's who saved the day," said Blackhorse.

Everyone pointed at Clay.

"Who put that transmitter together that got us up here?" Agent Long asked. "It sure looked like hell, but it did the job."

Everyone pointed at Clay again.

"Clay, do you know who those people were?" Basker asked, pointing out at the burning craft.

"Yeah. That was Paul Rockford and his pilot," Clay said. "We got a good look at them. He just painted his helicopter. That's the son-of-a-bitch that has been trying to kill us."

"It's no wonder," Basker said. "You boys managed to screw up his smooth-flowing drug business. He not only lost everything he owned, but was going to jail." Basker looked out at the smoking parts of Rockford's helicopter. "Unfortunately, it looks like he's headed somewhere else right now."

Clay dropped his head and kicked the ground. "Shooting back at him was the only thing we could do."

"You did just fine, Morgan," said Basker. "Just fine."

Agent Long looked over the group. "Okay," he said, "you and you," he pointed at Brian and Virgil, "and you," his finger pointing at Brenda. "The three of you will fly out on the first trip. We'll come back for the rest."

Blackhorse walked over to the treasure hunters and stuck out his hand. "Thanks for everything you fellas have done," he said.

Everyone shook hands with him.

"From all the tales I've heard from Laura, I'm proud to have met you."

"From Laura?" Ken asked.

"Yeah, from Laura," Blackhorse replied. "You guys sure left your mark on her. She thinks you're her knights in shining armor. She couldn't say enough good about you."

Ken nodded his head. "She's right, you know."

They laughed.

"How's she doing, Chief?" Ken asked. "You know, how's she handling the rape and all?"

"Very well, I reckon. Saw her just yesterday. She was with her Uncle Gus. He says she's doing as well as can be expected."

Basker motioned. "Okay folks, let's load up. Sooner we get you to the hospital, the sooner we get back for the others."

He turned to Clay and pointed his finger. "Don't leave this spot, you hear me? I don't want to have to search these mountains for you again."

Clay sat down on a rock. "I'll be right here when you get back."

Basker headed for the chopper. "We'll be about two hours."

The wind from the rotors whipped up sand and debris and blasted the faces of Clay, Ken, and Rob as they watched the craft take off and fade in the distance.

"Did you put that gold on board, Rob?" Clay asked.

Rob glanced over him and grinned. "You kidding? I kept it with us so we could protect it." He chuckled. "Never know what the lure of gold will do, even to a federal agent!"

Clay got up and walked around a bit. Heading for the cave entrance, he pulled his flashlight out and pointed it ahead of him as he walked into the cave. He called to the others. "You guys come on in here."

Rob tied the burro up, grabbed his light, and followed Ken inside.

"What is it, Clay?" Ken asked.

"I can see something in back of the cave that wasn't here when we first ran inside. Let's have a look."

"Hold it, Clay. It might be another big cat," Rob said, pulling out his pistol.

"No, it was another opening. A very small one, but an opening just the same," Clay said. "The rocket blast must have caused it."

Clay walked over and peeked into a small opening in the wall of the cave. He couldn't see anything. He started to crawl inside.

"You sure you want to do that, Clay?" asked Ken. "Maybe we should leave well enough alone."

Clay didn't answer. He crawled into the opening.

Ken and Rob looked at each other. They shrugged and followed.

Once inside, their light beams danced off the walls and ceiling as they looked around.

Clay held his light steady. "Hey! Look over here, you guys."

"I'll be damned!" Rob exclaimed.

There were arrows, a bow, a lance, a painted shield, and several other things lying around the body of an Indian.

Rob whistled eerily. "The man's been dead for years, but his body looks as alive as yours or mine. His clothes even look fresh."

"It's him!" Clay said, staring at his face. "My God, it's him!" He looked around. "And this is his burial tomb. He was sealed inside when he died and the blast musta shook the rocks loose."

Clay touched the Indian's brightly colored beaded chest plate. "Shines like new money. Tell me he isn't the same Indian I've been seeing."

Rob stared down at the body. "Well, Clay," he said, "it looks like the one you've been describing to us. If you remember, we've never seen him, only the owl. But then all these Indian Chiefs look alike to me."

After a few minutes, he headed for the opening. "Let's go."

When they were out of the inner cave, Clay started piling rocks in the opening. "We'll seal it back up. Least we can do for a man who has done so much for us."

Ken and Rob were quick to help.

"I don't believe it," Rob said, looking at the now sealed opening. "I'm a reasonable, sane man. This can't be happening."

"Why not?" Clay asked. "The Indians believed in the spirit life. And I can honestly say I've seen that man walking around, can't I? So why can't it be happening?"

Neither Ken nor Rob had an answer.

They silently walked out of the cave to wait for the helicopter.

The helicopter returned and, while it was landing, Clay walked over to the burro that was still standing nearby. Taking off the travois and bags of gold, he laid them on the ground and removed the animal's rope halter. He patted it on the head. "Thanks pal, for all your help. Now just like I promised, you're free to go."

It didn't move.

He waited. "Okay, Mr. Burro, back to your mares. Shoo!" he said.

The burro just stood looking at him.

This time Clay yelled and waved his arms.

Finally, the burro walked off a few steps, stopped, and looked back, then kicked up its rear legs and shook its head. It brayed loudly and trotted back up the trail, head held high, sniffing the wind.

Clay smiled, feeling proud of himself. He carefully rolled up the rope and halter to take home with him as a momento, and headed for the waiting helicopter.

It was late afternoon when the helicopter set down at Lutheran's Hospital in Apache Junction.

In minutes, the three men were in the emergency room checking on Virgil. They found he had already had butterfly stitches on his forehead and a cast on his broken arm.

Brian was in surgery getting his leg repaired.

Brenda hurried to Clay and started unbuttoning his shirt. "You get in there and have that shoulder looked at. It's a mess."

Clay had just about forgotten about the piece of metal that had ripped into his flesh. He took a seat in an examination room and a nurse began cleaning the injury.

Brian was back from surgery and had a new cast on his leg. Clay had been bandaged, and they waited for transportation to the Holiday Inn.

Basker joined them, looking at his watch. "Folks, it's been a long day and I know you're tired, so we're not going to take statements from you tonight. Go to the motel and get some sleep. We'll see you at

Chief Blackhorse's office for statements tomorrow morning. How's that sound?"

"Well it's a long walk to our motel," Clay said.

"I've already made arrangement for you fellas a ride," Blackhorse answered.

Basker shook hands with everyone and left.

Three Arizona State police cars were waiting at the door when they walked out. It was a quiet ride back to the motel.

As they got out of the cars at the motel, they each shook hands with Chief Blackhorse again.

"Thanks, Chief," said Clay. "I know it was you who got things moving on the signal."

Chief Blackhorse nodded, then said, "I don't want you guys to think that all lawmen are like Sheriff Wilkins, who, by the way, we found down in Mexico City. He is now a guest in the federal lockup in Phoenix and he's telling all."

"That's great," Clay replied. "Ever find that other fella, or rather his body?"

"If you mean Tom Davis - yes. Padro told us where he hid his body. Sheriff Richmond sent up a search party and got him a day or so ago," Blackhorse said. Giving the boys a final wave, he got into his car and left.

Brenda made one more check on Brian, Virgil, and Clay and found the treatment given them by the hospital personnel met with her approval. Patting Brian on his leg, she said, "You're going to be fit as a fiddle in no time. Now, I'm going home and soak in a hot tub, crawl into bed and never wake up." She started for the door, then stopped, "I'll see you all tomorrow, won't I?"

"You can bank on it," Clay shouted, as he watched her walk out. "What a gal!" he said to no one in particular.

Hot showers, shaves, and clean clothes made the boys feel like new men. Falling into their beds, they slept the night through.

81

Virgil walked out of the police department shading his eyes from the late afternoon sun. "Can you believe that? All day to give statements."

"Yeah, it sure was a hell of a mess," Clay said. "First the federal boys, then the Apache Junction Police, then the Pinal County boys, and finally, thank God, the Arizona State boys."

Brian hobbled out. "Let's go get the gold and take it to the assay office. Maybe we'll be able to see how much it's worth."

"Good idea," Clay said, "but where the hell do we find an assay office in this town?"

Brenda laughed. "Right down the street from your motel, boys. The outfitter shop has been the federal assay office for years and years."

"You mean Liege is also the assay man?"

"Yeah, and a good, honest one at that," Brenda answered.

"Let's get there!" Rob said excitedly.

Liege Blackhorse leaned against the counter, his elbows resting on top, as he studied the gold nuggets through his eyepiece. He would glance up at the boys from time to time. Finally, he placed one in a metal tray and poured some acid on it. It smoked and sputtered. After it settled down, Liege picked it up to study it again.

Five treasure hunters and a nurse stood breathlessly waiting for an answer. There was total silence in the store while the man worked.

Liege picked through the bags and randomly selected nuggets to test.

The treasure hunters tried to read his face, but a better poker face never sat at a card table. He showed no emotions at all.

Finally, Liege cleared his throat.

Everyone jumped and rushed to the counter. They stood staring at him.

Liege shook his big burly head, cleared his throat again and grinned. "Boys, you've just brought in the highest grade gold I've ever seen."

"Really?" Clay exclaimed.

Liege grinned. "Really," he said. "This is real gold. I've haven't seen anything but pyrite come out of there for years."

"Pyrite?" Rob parroted. "You mean fools' gold?"

"Yeah, fool's gold," Liege replied. "But what you have here is real gold. Assays out at about 95 percent pure."

"What's it worth?" Clay asked.

"Well, let's just see." He checked the scales. "Looks like 80 pounds even." He got out a calculator. "At today's market price for gold bullion, I'd put it at roughly...," he stared at the calculator, "just under half a million dollars." Liege looked at their smiling faces. "Where'd you find it?"

Clay chuckled. "Now Liege. What a foolish question to ask."

Liege grinned. He knew they wouldn't tell anyone where they found the gold.

"Come on down to Gus' saloon and let's celebrate," Clay invited. "Your brother, Chief Blackhorse, will be there, too. We're buying."

"I think I will," said Liege, pulling off his apron. "But first let me get you a voucher for that gold."

"Whiskey!" yelled Clay to the bartender. "And give all my friends some, too. Lots of it!"

The bartender was Gus. He grinned. He was happy to see them. "You're money's no good here, gentlemen."

"But Gus, we just struck it rich," said Brian, his leg propped up on an extra chair.

"Maybe so, but money can't buy what you did for me. Having Laura back safely means more to me than all the gold in the world." He set full bottles of whiskey on their tables. "Besides, I'm going to join your celebration."

Liege, Will Barnett, Gus, the Chief of Police, the five treasure hunters, and one little nurse got rip roaring drunk that night.

82

The small Apache Junction airport buzzed with activity. The greenhorns were leaving for Los Angeles.

Will Barnett, Liege Blackhorse, Chief Dennis Blackhorse, and Brenda Carpenter had come to see them off. Behind them, a twin engine passenger plane roared to life as the pilot pushed buttons and made his usual checks.

Clay looked at them. These people had befriended them, helped them when they could, and gave them tons of advice. It had all been welcomed. He knew it was a friendship that would be lasting.

Handshakes were exchanged all around, though Virgil had to use his left hand and Brian had to lean on his new crutches to do it.

"Boys, it has really been a true pleasure to know you," Will Barnett said. "Maybe some day we'll meet again."

"And that's a promise," Brian said. "I get to missing your cooking, I'll be back for sure."

"You guys' credit is always good at my store," Liege laughed. "Just bring your credit cards."

Virgil winked at him. "Thanks for all your advice, Liege. We'd have been in real trouble without your help."

Chief Blackhorse approached the men as they gathered around the plane. "What about the helicopter? I understand you guys had borrowed it. That's gonna eat into your profits."

Virgil grinned. "I called the owner this morning. The helicopter was fully insured. We won't be out a dime."

Blackhorse smiled. "If you ever want to come back and try for the Dutchman's Gold again, give me a call. I might just go with you."

"We'll be back, Chief. But right now we need a long rest," Clay said.

"Yeah, we'll be back before the dust can settle up there," Ken said. "We still have to find the Dutchman."

Clay had already turned his attention to Brenda. She was going from one to the other, giving each man a hug, a kiss, and a handshake. He stepped up in line and waited.

She grabbed him and drew him close. "Clay Morgan!" she said, looking him right in the eyes. "I won't ever forget you. Please, stay in touch and if that wife of yours ever kicks your butt out, you know where I'll be. Come see me."

Clay, his arms already around her, drew her up tightly and gave her a kiss. "After all that's been happening to me lately, that might not be out of the question," he replied. "I'll keep your offer in mind."

He reached into his pocket and drew out a large gold nugget. He put it in her hand and closed her fingers over it. "Keep this one for luck. As soon as we get the voucher cashed in, we'll send you an equal share. You earned it."

Tears welled in her eyes. "Oh, if it was just another time - another - oh, never mind."

A car came screaming out on the field and skidded to stop near the plane. The door opened. Gus and Laura jumped out. They hurried to the plane.

"Thought we'd missed you," Laura said, looking from one to the other. "I had to come. Brenda called me and told me you guys were going back to Los Angeles today. I wanted to thank you again and tell you that I'm moving to L.A. next month. I'll need someone to show me around that big beautiful city."

Ken's face lit up. "Look no further, young lady. I shall be at your complete disposal."

Brian hobbled around in front of him. "My services will also be at your command, Laura Pratt. You need a real man to show you around L.A."

"I'm a real man, Brian," said Ken. "And I've got the lion claw marks to prove it."

Rob laughed and started to board the plane. In doing so, he dropped a bag. When the bag hit the ground, several papers spilled out. Bold headlines read: THE GREAT LOST DUTCHMAN ADVENTURE - BY ROB CLARK.

Grinning sheepishly, Rob dropped down and started scooping them up. "Do you realize the market for a story like this? Why, as a book, it'll be a best seller. And as a movie, it'll fill the seats for years. It'll be a classic." He looked at Clay. "Of course, you guys will get your fair share."

They all laughed as Rob finished gathering the papers.

Each man took a last look around.

Hidden from sight, Clay pulled the pill bottle from his pocket and shook one into his palm. He stared at it for several seconds, then flipped it back into the bottle and tossed it all into a nearby trash can. "It just dawned on me," he said aloud. "I haven't been taking them for the last few flights and I've done just fine. Besides, who needs brave pills after what we been through."

Virgil had been watching. Clapping his hands he said, "Atta boy, Clay. I knew you could do it."

"Whhoooooo! Whhoooooo! Whhoooooo!"

Everyone stared at the huge owl that flew overhead and landed on the peak of a nearby hangar.

"I don't believe this is happening, " Clay said.

Chief Blackhorse looked up at the owl. "Forget it, Clay. That's just an old barn owl. Not the one from your tales that transforms into the old Indian man."

"Indian Chief!" Clay corrected him.

Blackhorse threw up both arms. "Okay, Indian Chief. You guys said you saw him several times, and that's understandable; but it was just your nerves. You fellas being from the big city and coming cold turkey out into a wilderness area was just too much. Your imaginations ran wild. Just a typical bunch of greenhorns."

Clay looked at Virgil and winked. "Sure, Chief. That must have been what it was. Nerves and imagination!" He looked back at the Chief. "Greenhorns, though? After what we've been through, you'd still call us greenhorns?" Clay asked, shaking his head.

Behind him, Virgil, Rob, Brian, Ken, and even Brenda and Laura, were shaking their heads as well.

"Yeah, reckon I'd have to agree with you there, Clay," Blackhorse said. "Consider it a slip of the tongue. City folk maybe, but greenhorns no more."

With a last wave to their friends, they boarded the plane laughing.

The plane taxied to the end of the runway, turned around and headed back.

Chief Blackhorse stood with Brenda and Laura. They were all waving as the plane passed and lifted off.

Clay patted Virgil on the shoulder and pointed out the window. He yelled at the pilot, "Circle over the airport one more time, pilot."

The pilot made a low slow circle.

All five men waved. The Indian Chief stood where the owl had been on the very peak of the hangar. He was waving back. A big smile on his face.

"Holy shit, Clay. You were right. The owl is an Indian," Rob exclaimed.

Ken and Virgil were speechless, until they spotted Chief Blackhorse staring upward, but not at the plane. He was staring up at the Indian Chief on top of the hangar. His mouth dropped open even wider when the Indian changed into an owl and flew off toward the mountains.

As the plane soared into the sky, Clay looked over in calm satisfaction at his friend beside him. "It was one hell of an adventure, wouldn't you say, Virge?"

"Nothing like it in my lifetime," Virgil replied, scratching at the itch under his new arm cast. "How soon before we come back?"

"How soon can we get another helicopter?"